PRESSURE & PAIN: A DIRTY SOUTH LOVE STORY

By,
Dream

SYNOPSIS

Brothers, Pain, Pressure, and their best friend Allen are three of America's Most Wanted. Not by the law but by all the women they run across. The trio's got it all. Good looks, money, personality, and hella swag. Living the street life in a world full of lust and opportunity, they find it hard to commit to just one woman.

When tragedy strikes the family, they end up on an all-out manhunt for their baby sister, Passion, who has been kidnapped by an obsessed leader of a sex trafficking organization. Now they are forced to reflect on the women in their lives and the way they handle them.

Pressure is smart, charming, handsome, and fine as hell. He is a true sex symbol. With the choice of any woman he wants, he has still managed to stay single. That is until he meets a beautiful, fun, sexy, badass chick named Zoey. Will she be able to break down the wall that he has built and find a way into his heart?

Pain and his longtime lover, Candice, who is also the mother of his two-year-old daughter are on rocky grounds. The breaking up and making up is getting old. When Pain meets Zoey's twin sister Chloe, she grabs his full attention. Will his heart come along with that? Or will Candice fight to keep the love of her life?

Allen is on an emotional rollercoaster. For the last eight years, he has managed to have two super bad ass chicks and keep them both happy. They know nothing about each other. However, his nice quiet world is about to be turned upside down. When lies, deceit, secrets, and obsessions all come back and shake things up, his life becomes a shit show full of drama.

Pressure and Pain is a MUST READ with jaw-dropping experiences! There is never a dull moment!

ACKNOWLEDGEMENTS:

I would like to first of all give honor and thanks to my Lord and Savior Jesus Christ. I am nothing without You. Thank You for saving my life and keeping me covered in Your blood.

- To my guardian angels: LaShonda and Glenda. It took me a minute to get it right, but I got it. I'm working harder and harder at becoming a better person. I have turned from my life of sin, and now I'm doing my best to live a life that is more pleasing to God. You can rest in peace now. I will see you again one day.
- To my four children: Jasmine, Kadeidra, Canard, and JaHrod, I hope I have made you proud. Don't ever give up on your dreams. It's never too late to get it right. I go so hard for you, and I take pride in being your mother.
- To my publisher: Sanaa'a "Karma Monae" Smith, all I needed was a chance and you gave me that. Thank you for giving me the opportunity to show the world that I am who I say I am.
- I would like to give a special thanks to my daughter Jasmine Walker and her wife Kuene Walker for believing in me and going the extra mile by giving me all the tools I needed to prepare this book. Including a quiet place to focus and get away from all distractions. Your love and support were the motivation I needed. Never would have made it without you.
- To Beverly Robinson, I called you in distress when my back was against the wall, and you did not hesitate to help me. That was the most important move in my life, and it was the beginning of my career and a promising future. I can't thank you enough.
- To Denetra Jacobs: My Partna, my road dog, my friend. You traveled all the way from Orlando,

Florida to Texas just to help me type and self-edit this book prior to submission. The passion, hours and dedication that you put into helping me speaks volumes of your loyalty and love to me as a friend. When I ball, you ball. PERIOD!!!

- To Jimarra Fox: Thank you for your unconditional love and support. Your loyalty and dedication to helping me be all I can be is amazing. I will always and forever have your back.

- To Tangela Davis: Your inspiration, your motivation, your energy, your heart, your smile. Everything about you makes it such a blessing for you to be in my life. Thank you for being a true supporter and an awesome friend. We got soul ties!

- To my Dirty Badju (Reggie) over in the Bahamas: You stayed on the phone for hours and hours listening to me read this book from the beginning to the end. That takes time and dedication. I know for a fact you want to see me win. Thank you so much, friend.

- Sheila Inman and Paulette Brown: Y'all were not there when I was popping bottles, blowing money and living life in the fast lane but you were right there when I fell and needed you the most with no questions asked. You showed me the meaning of true friends.

- To Julie Ferguson: You made my time in prison so much easier. Thank you for motivating me to keep writing. You made me believe that this was possible. You encouraged me and now my dreams are reality. We got out and did just what we said we were going to do.

- To JayOne Clark: You were down for me from day one. From the streets to behind the Prison walls, you were right there. You motivated and encouraged me from the beginning to the end and I will always and forever have your back.

- To Book: You know my DC number and that alone says a lot. There has never been a time I needed you, and you were not there. Thank you for being my friend.
- To Andre McCay: What's understood ain't gotta be explained. Through the good, the bad, and the ugly, you were there.
- To my Fiancé Terry Smith: I do, and I will!!!

For everyone else that believed in me and wanted to see me win, it's my winning season, and everything attached to me wins!!!!

CHAPTER ONE

Flying first class was nothing new to Pain and Pressure. If they did nothing else, they always took the time out to enjoy the fruits of their labor. This weekend they were going to Detroit to hang out with Allen, their best friend and business partner. Allen had gotten them V.I.P. tickets to the Rod Wave concert featuring Lil Baby, Kodak Black, Kevin Gates, and other local artists that was being held at a popular strip club in town. They both looked forward to hanging out, relaxing, and fucking on some bad bitches. They also had to discuss business, which they never did over the phone. They ran a small, smooth, low-key, drug ring for the last eight years. Allen was the plug, who sent all the drugs first class through the post office.

Mrs. Paulette was the head supervisor at the Miami Dade Post Office, who was also Pain and Pressure's mother. She would retrieve the packages and deliver them to her boys'. Then Pain and Pressure would distribute them throughout the streets of Miami. They had traps that ran twenty-four hours daily in Liberty City, Carol City, North Miami, and Scott projects. They were a very close-knit family, and together, they were quietly running the streets of Miami.

As soon as they got off the plane, they requested an uber to Allen's house. Allen had planned on picking them up, but they were pulling up before he even made it out the door. They were ready to do what little shopping they had to do and get to the rooms they had previously booked.

Allen was married and didn't hang out very often. He was

really laid back, and even though he had throwback money, he wasn't flashy or arrogant. His only issue was that he was in love with two totally different women.

Shantae was his high school sweetheart. When Allen dropped out of school, Shantae dropped out along with him. He ended up moving in with her and her dope addict mother, who welcomed him with open arms because he was the dope man. Allen taught Shantae everything she knew about the streets, and in no time, she was hustling just as hard as he did. From the outside looking in, you would think they had the perfect hood love story. They were both getting money and complimented each other well. All the local bitches wanted Allen. All the dope boys wanted a sexy down ass chick like Shantae.

By age 16, Allen was paying all of Shantae's bills. When she started getting her own money, he would always tell her to save her money while he still paid all the bills. In his mind, if he ever decided to leave her, she would at least be good financially. That was over ten years ago, and they were still going strong. Allen was still the man she fell in love with all those years ago. He was caring and took great care of her; the sex was amazing every time, and he got sexier and sexier as he became a grown man. His swag was sick, and his demeanor was that of a boss at all times. She adored the ground he walked on.

Allen met Taylor at the gym and could not keep his eyes off her. Taylor was drop dead gorgeous. He fell in love with her at first sight. She was working and going to college at the same time. In no time, her and Allen were inseparable and madly in love. A few months later, she was pregnant. Therefore, Allen moved to Detroit with her because she was in college. After getting pregnant with their second son, they got married. That was six years ago. Taylor was the perfect model wife. To her knowledge, he was a cross-country truck driver. She knew that their lifestyle exceeded a trucker's income, but she never questioned him. He was an excellent father and husband. He relocated to Detroit so that they could be together without interfering with her schooling. He was kind, caring, and Lord, was he blessed in the bedroom.

Allen and the boys were her entire world. This wasn't the life she thought she planned on living, but she wouldn't trade it for the world. She was happy and in love. Allen and the kids had changed her entire perspective on life and love. She now had the perfect family.

Shantae and Taylor were under the impression that Allen drove trucks. That explained why he was only home for three weeks and then away for three weeks. Because of this, he has managed to keep both of them happy for the last eight years.

Allen took Pain and Pressure to do a little shopping and then dropped them off at their rooms. Pain relaxed for a minute but he was ready to hit the streets. He took a shower and got dressed. After taking a couple shots and smoking some good Kush alone, Pain was feeling way too good. He decided to make his way to Pressure's room. Pressure was kicked back relaxing. Just as he was about to get in the shower, Pain knocked on the door.

"Nigga, you over here zoned all out and ain't even washed your ass yet. It's time to turn up," Pain said as he entered Pressure's room.

"You need to turn down. You are gonna be smashed before you get there," Pressure responded.

"Turn down for what?" Pain asked.

Pressure went to jump in the shower while Pain rolled them a joint and fixed drinks for them. "I'm trying to have fun tonight, not babysit. Don't overdo it, bruh."

"I'm looking too good to overdo it, nigga," Pain replied.

They continued to talk while Pressure got dressed.

"Did you holla at Mama before we left?" Pain asked.

"Yea, she is still talking about retiring and getting married to this Steven dude," he answered.

"I'll body that fuck nigga," Pain snapped.

"You are a straight bug, bruh. As long as she's happy, that's all that matters." Pressure shook his head.

"Pops will kill himself if Mama marries anyone else," Pain said. "Shit, *probably try to kill her then kill himself*," he said, reciting lyrics from J.T. Money's *'Ho Problems'*.

They both burst into laughter. They knew that their dad, Vincent, was still madly in love with their mama. They always teased him about the situation and joked about Steven taking his girl. Pain would also tease his dad about Mrs. Paulette and Steven getting married. Pops would always say, *"Your mama belongs to me 'til death do us part. She knows who her real husband is. And your Mama ain't crazy. I bet you won't ever see that nigga laid up over there."*

Pops was right though. They had met her boyfriend but never saw him or anybody else laying up in Mrs. Paulette's house. They always thought it was because of her respect for them, but Pops made it clear that it was really because of the respect she had for him.

"Call Allen with his slow-moving ass," Pain said.

"You ain't doing shit, nigga. You call him," Pressure refuted, so Pain hit Allen up.

"Y'all can come down. I was just about to call," Allen answered.

Pressure checked himself out in the mirror one last time. "Nigga, that shit on point. Let's go," Pain urged.

Allen pulled up jamming *'Emotionally Scarred'* by Lil Baby. That just set the mood. Pain and Pressure jumped in, and their night began. The concert was sold out. All of Detroit was out and looking their best. Allen whipped up in valet parking. They jumped out looking better than the niggas that was performing.

Pain was 5' 10" and 180 pounds of nothing but muscle, with a caramel complexion. He rocked a Rick Ross beard with a low cut. His bottom grill made with wall-to-wall Internally Flawless Diamonds, which is a class higher than VVS diamonds. Whatever he wore matched from head to toe. From his fitted cap, to his under clothes all the way down to his sneakers. His swag was sick, his skin was so smooth, and his personality was lit. He was fun, handsome, and romantic. Pain was a Bonafide hustler and often considered to be a hothead. Ready for whatever and would pop off at the drop of a dime. He didn't play games about his bitches or his money.

Pressure, on the other hand, was a smooth, milk chocolate, dark-skinned, amazing piece of work. His swag was precise. He was a little bit taller than his younger brother, standing at 5' 11" and 185 pounds with a slightly muscular physique. His dress code was very simple but expensive. Other than his 5-carat Diamond earring and 10-carat Diamond pinky ring, he wasn't flashy at all, but truth be told, none of it was needed. He was fine as-is. It was hard to even put in words. If I didn't know any better, I would say the nigga was perfect. He wasn't arrogant, which made him even more attractive. He knew what he wanted out of life and was not willing to settle. He was laid back but firm. His no meant no, and his yes was a definite yes. There was no compromising with him...no in-between. He was book smart and street smart. He was the type that would sit back and take it all in before ever speaking a word. He was very business oriented and totally irresistible. To top it all off, he's kind and generous.

Allen was the shit as well. He was 5' 8", 170 pounds, and muscular, more so than Pain and Pressure. He worked out regularly, so his body was cut up decently. He had dreads and a goatee. He was always wearing some nice jeans with some raw ass Timberland boots. He killed that New York swag. On this particular night, he was wearing a matching jean jacket with a Ratatouille Cuban Link chain. He was handsome as hell. Even though he appeared super mean, he was actually a lover. He took care of home. He was one of those niggas you just knew not to play with though.

Pain, Pressure, and Allen were all superfly. One nigga slapped the shit out of his chick because she was staring way too hard. They just laughed and kept it moving. The line was wrapped around the building, and the club was already jam packed. The chicks were far from shy. When they saw money, they were after it. They sent drinks to their tables, and the girls that were in V.I.P. walked straight up to them.

One of the dancers caught Pressure's eye. As she was coming down the pole, she looked at him so seductively it made his dick jump. Pressure just looked at her. No facial expression, just direct eye contact as he sipped on his drink. After her performance, she made her way around the club. Pressure watched her as she made her way to him.

"Hi, I'm Jamea," she said.

"What's up, Jamea? Are you coming with me tonight?" Pressure asked.

"Why can't you come with me?" She replied.

"Because I'mma man, shawty. Chicks don't pick me up; I dictate my moves," he said with authority.

Jamea loved his aggressiveness. She looked at him and smiled as she walked off with every intention of doubling back when her shift was over. The club was lit. Rod Wave came out first, turnt all the way up followed by Lil Baby.

Pain had two females entertaining him while Allen had a bad bitch dancing for him. He handed her five hundred one-dollar bills but barely paid her any attention. He had the same drink in his hand he poured when he first got there. Pain and Pressure were on their feet, poppin' bottle after bottle. They all were vibing and having a good time. The DJ was lit and kept the vibe going by playing all the right songs.

Out of nowhere, a set of twins walked up to Pain and Pressure and introduced themselves.

"Hi, I'm Zoey, and this is my sister Chloe."

Pressure was intrigued, which immediately converted his interest from Jamea to the twins. "I'm Pressure, and this are my brother, Pain and my homeboy, Allen."

"Pain and Pressure? Love the names. Pain and Pressure go together like Chloe and Zoey," Zoey said flirtatiously.

"Pain and Pressure...that's what we have to offer." Pressure advertised. "What's up with y'all? We in town for the weekend, just trying to have a little fun and enjoy the company of some beautiful, sexy, but nasty young ladies."

"So, you want a nasty bitch that carries herself like a lady, huh?" She said with a sexy grin and an inquisitive look.

"Well interpreted," he confirmed.

Zoey and Chloe stepped aside and chatted for a minute, "Them niggas fine as fuck! And they swaggin' harder than a bitch," Zoey said.

"Bitch, I'm down." Was all Chloe had to say as they both laughed.

Allen laughed as Pain and Pressure went back and forth, trying to decide their lucky winners. "Bruh, I got two bad bitches tonight. I'm not passing that up for just one bitch. I don't give a damn how sexy that one is," Pain said, referring to one of the twins.

"This is still two bad bitches, bruh," Pressure explained. "We finna hit both of them too. The only difference is these are TWINS. We've fucked two bad bitches a hundred times, but we have never had twins…Bad ass twins, at that. We ain't gotta choose; we can have them both."

Pain looked over at the twins. Zoey was sucking on a lollipop, and Chloe was chewing on a Twizzler. They were undoubtedly two of the baddest bitches in the club. With the cutest faces, fat asses, and flat stomachs and model-sized waistlines.

Zoey's hair was in a short, curly cut, and Chloe's was long and curly. They wore cut up Dior jeans that hugged their every curve. Chloe was rocking a red shirt with white Dior stamps and red, white and blue Jordans, while Zoey's shirt was white with red Dior stamps, but she was rocking her fit with red bottom heels. They were the same but so different. They both resembled Ella Mai, and the fact that it was two of them made them so much hotter. The thought of not having to choose was sexy as hell and hard to resist.

"You got it, bruh. Let me dismiss these chicks and we can bounce," Pain said, finally giving in.

Pain did just that and got rid of the two chicks he had been entertaining all night. Allen also dismissed his dancer and the five of them prepared to leave. Pain and Pressure were very impressed at how disciplined Allen was. With two bad bitches already in his life, he had no interest in any other chicks. He turned down more pussy in one night than they had turned down all year. He was fully content with what he already had going on.

Pressure hoped he never fell in love. He had never been in a serious relationship. To him, females always wanted more than what he had to offer. Besides, they start out nice and sweet, then end up bossy and demanding. It never stays fun like it was in the beginning. After Allen dropped Pain and Pressure off, the girls followed in their own car.

Pressure liked Zoey's feistiness. He had already made up his mind that she was going to his room with him first. Chloe and Pain obviously were left to entertain each other in his room. As soon as Pressure and Zoey hit the room, they undressed and got busy.

As they made their way to the shower, Zoey sat at the edge of the tub playing in her wetness. She grabbed his joystick and put all nine and a half inches in her mouth. He grabbed the back of her head and fucked her mouth nice and slow, seeing just how deep her throat really was. That turned Zoey on even more than the fact that this nigga was fine as fuck. Nothing but muscles outlined his stomach. Fuck a six pack; he was blessed with a twelve pack. His smooth chocolate skin looked even sexier with the steam from the hot water beaming off his body as the water ran down. Perfect white teeth. He rocked a low cut with waves that made you seasick. Sexy was an understatement. This nigga was beautiful. A GOD in her eyes.

He sped up the pace 'til he was now literally fucking her face. She relaxed her throat muscles, letting him beat the back of her throat. His dick was getting harder and harder, and the head and veins looked like they wanted to explode. Before he could catch himself, he released himself into her mouth. And without a second thought, she sucked down every drop.

Zoey had honestly given him the best head he ever had. He picked her up and carried her to the bed, sliding on a Magnum and digging deep into her soul. She moaned softly but sensually as the headboard banged against the wall. She had back-to-back orgasms, and soon after, they changed positions. She was now riding him like the true stallion he was. He enjoyed every minute as he spread her ass cheeks and went even deeper. He flipped her over and got an even better view as her sexy soft ass bounced off of his steel frame. Finally, the feeling was just too good, and they both gave in. When he came, she came. They both collapsed on the bed, equally defeated.

"I don't like that shit," Pressure said.

"What don't you like?" Zoey asked, a little confused by the remark.

"You just gave me a run for my money," he responded.

"That wasn't even my best. It gets a whole lot better. And what money, nigga? This one was on the house," she said jokingly with a chuckle. "But seriously tho', I almost tapped out. Very few have lasted that long. Especially once they get it from the back," Zoey admitted.

"Oh, so you're bragging?" Pressure asked. "Well, I ain't your average nigga." He rolled over and retrieved another magnum from his wallet.

"Ok, Ok. I was just playing," she said, quickly recanting her comment.

"Ohhh. So, your mouth is writing checks that your ass can't cash?" Pressure said as he slid the condom on. It was too late to take her comment back.

Before she could respond, he tackled her down, pinning her legs back to her shoulders and slid deep into her once again. Round two was electrifying. After torturing each other with pleasure, they both tapped out. They showered and ordered room service. They then ate breakfast and crashed.

Pain and Chloe, on the other hand, got to know each other.

They both enjoyed reading books which was a very unexpected, yet impressive, interest to Chloe coming from a hood nigga. They talked about all the books they had read, things they liked, as well as the things they didn't like. Finally, they decided to go downstairs to the bar for food and drinks. They sat at the bar and ordered shrimp and wings while flirting and getting acquainted. Afterwards, they made their way back to the room, overly intoxicated and ready to get it in.

Pain kissed Chloe's neck and removed her shirt. She was hot and ready. Before he could take her shirt off, she had already removed her bra and unbuttoned her pants. He slid her pants off and removed her panties, slid on a condom, and slowly worked his way inside her. He stroked her gently while sucking on her titties passionately. As his pace increased, so did her moans.

Pain pinned her legs behind her head, and she threw it back like a pro as he took full control of the situation. He was gentle but also aggressive, and she loved every minute of it. All she could do was take the painful pleasure he was delivering. After what seemed like forever, they both had an amazing orgasm. His body stiffened while her body trembled as they both tried to catch their breath. They both were exhausted and satisfied.

The following morning Chloe and Zoey's alarm went off at the same time, noon, waking them both out of a deep sleep. They never slept past twelve. Their motto was always 'Nothing comes to a sleeper but a dream'. They got up and got dressed, planning to go home, shower up, and come back to show Pain and Pressure the city of Detroit. The girls decided to take them to a place called Coney Island. They sold the best chili dogs, corn beef sandwiches, salads, and soups in all of Detroit.

Pressure and Pain gave them their props; the food was bangin'. After lunch, they went on a tour from city to city, from the hood to the upscale parts of town, ending up at the Fairlane Mall. Neither Pain nor Pressure were cheap, so they allowed the girls to shop freely. Feeling like they were being tested, both girls were very conservative. Once they left the mall, they went to their connect and got some top-of-the-line Kush and two bottles of Hennessy Privilege. It was now time to go back to the room and relax—this time with a new partner. The four of them had a great time together. Both pairs thought that it was awesome to not have to choose. This was what you called having your cake and eating it too.

Before heading back to Miami, Pain and Pressure spent time with Allen and his family. After dinner, they sat on the patio and discussed new business ideas. Being that Mrs. Paulette was seriously thinking of retiring, it was urgent that they figure out a new way of importing their product.

"So, what y'all got in mind?" Allen asked Pain and Pressure.

"I was thinking maybe we can talk Pops into letting us move the work through his truck drivers," Pain suggested.

"Man, Pops ain't going for that. Why would he give up the game just to let another person traffic their drugs through his legal business?" Pressure pointed out. "That would be dumb as fuck don't you think? Maybe we should look into getting our own truck and driver."

"Now that's good thinking," Allen agreed. "I'll look into that. In the meantime, My homeboy that owns the club we went to keeps reiterating to me that he's paying top dollars for hoes from Miami. He talked about relocating them from Miami to Detroit."

"What is he paying top dollar for? Better yet, what is top dollar?" Pain asked.

"Fifty bands, at least, per head," Allen responded.

"Shit, for fifty thousand, he plans on owning the bitches," Pain stated.

"Pretty much," Allen replied.

"What do you mean, pretty much? That's human trafficking, bruh," Pain said in disapproval.

"Selling dope is called drug trafficking, but that is how we make a living. What's your point?" Allen said.

"That is my point. I sell dope, not people," Pain said.

"It's not really considered human trafficking if the girls go willingly," Allen explained. "This is a game of finessing. I'm not suggesting that y'all kidnap bitches. I was thinking more along the lines of y'all getting' some of ya lil' female friends to do the recruiting. That would probably be a lot easier anyhow. Hoes ain't good for just pussy, my nigga. But I'm not suggesting that y'all do it at all. Especially if it can't be done by just finessing. I'm only running it by you."

"You're right about that, bruh," Pressure said, agreeing

to the statement that females are good for more than just sex. Pain also agreed. Both of them instantly thought about the twins.

"Right, now you niggas thinking," Allen said as if he could read their minds. "I'm willing to bet that those chicks already know the game."

"We will most definitely find out what they are into before we leave. In the meantime, we will look into getting a truck, and you deal with getting the driver," Pressure ordered.

Allen laughed at the fact that he knew his friends the way he did. He knew they were thinking about Chloe and Zoey.

"Whatever driver you choose gotta be solid and aware of the risk. With the right driver, this shit could run real smooth. And we can pick up a few jobs along the way. That way it's a legit business, and it all pays for itself," Pressure further explained.

"Sounds good to me. Let's get this shit in motion," Pain said.

They talked a little while longer. Allen told Pain and Pressure that he had slipped up and got Shantae pregnant, but he made her get an abortion. He told them he had dodged a bullet this time and vowed to never hit Shantae raw again. She wasn't speaking to him at this time, and that was cool with him. He had love for Shantae but made vows to Taylor. A baby outside of his marriage was way too disrespectful. Real niggas didn't move like that. For some reason, he thought Shantae could not get pregnant. He had been dealing with her his whole life, and she never once got pregnant.

Pain and Pressure was surprised to hear Allen say his perfect world was falling apart. That nigga had two of the baddest bitches on the planet, and up until now, they all seemed to be happy. He vented to them about the situation but stood on his decision, knowing that it had broken Shantae's heart. He missed her dearly and prayed that one day she would forgive him. In his mind, Shante was a lot stronger than Taylor. Pain and Pressure just listened, making a mental note never to get caught up in the same situation.

Later on, they invited the twins over. This time the four of them hung out and got to know each other. And just like they thought, human trafficking was nothing new to the twins. They once worked as recruiters for some cliques out of Texas and Detroit. To Pain and Pressure's surprise, this was a common hustle in the northern states. In Florida, they sold drugs, guns, and pussy...but not people. They told stories about different chicks they had come across and how they had two cliques about to beef over this bad bitch they had. They ended up getting eighty bands for her.

Zoey ordered food for the four of them using one of the many fraudulent card numbers that her sister kept on deck. They made plans to keep in contact with each other. They promised to send for the girls to visit Miami. This time to show them a good time in their city. Of course, they couldn't leave without waxing their asses one more time. Pain and Chloe decided they wanted a little alone time, which was perfect for Pressure and Zoey. They spent the night getting to know each other even better. The following morning the girls dropped Pain and Pressure off at the airport. This was not goodbye...It was until next time.

CHAPTER TWO

Rays of sunlight were seeping through the curtains and beautifully illuminating Zoey and Chloe's dining room table where they were sitting and talking.

"So, I'm assuming you like Pain?" Zoey asked.

"I do," Chloe responded. "Pressure has the right name. That nigga applies straight pressure in the bedroom, but honestly, I'm feeling Pain more. We have so much in common. He's funny, and I like his swag."

"I'm glad you said that because I'm feeling Pressure more," Zoey said. "He so fucking sexy. Bitch, my pussy starts throbbing when he is in my presence. We kick it like we've known each other forever. I think we really connect, and the sex is phenomenal. He has that take charge demeanor that I love."

"Hoe, you sound like you sprung," Chloe teased.

"I'm far from sprung, but I am looking forward to going to Miami," Zoey replied.

"I can't lie, I'm excited about that too," Chloe added.

"We gotta hustle hard this week so that when we do go to Miami, we will have our own money and transportation. I can see us making some real paper with these niggas and having a lot of fun. All we gotta do is keep our feelings on ice," Zoey coached.

"And we are going to keep it a hundred as long as them

niggas keep it a thousand," Chloe added.

"Right. The sex is good and all, but it's just sex. Because they made it clear that they were only looking to have a good time. And technically, so are we, so it's all good," Zoey said.

"But that's what they all say," Chloe said. "People also say don't mix business with pleasure, but here we are doing just that. But why wouldn't we? It's no fun getting money with sexy ass niggas that we can't fuck. Niggas only say that shit because they know pussy got power. We gotta be trendsetters and reverse all these lil' dumbass myths."

"You're right about that, sis. But don't forget, that dick ain't nothing to be fucked with either. It's just as powerful," Zoey reminded her. They both laughed as they prepared to start their day. They had a great weekend. Now it was time to get to the bag.

The twins danced at a club on the outskirts of Detroit, performing many acts together on stage. The fact that they were twins and super bad made dancing easy money. Not to mention all the green ass niggas they hustled off the clock. They hustled hard and took good care of each other. They had a cute two-bedroom apartment that was nice and cozy, a 2021 Lexus that they shared since they did everything together.
After their father divorced their mother when they were only 12, she really went into depression and just gave up becoming an alcoholic. Between the medication and the alcohol, she was a lost cause, leaving them to basically raise themselves.

So six years ago, when they turned seventeen, they left home and never looked back. They got a job at Stingers, which was a topless gentlemen club. They lied and told the owners that they were nineteen. Quickly, they became a big hit. Now, at age twenty-three, the two of them were a hot commodity and getting paid top dollar.

Their mom eventually drank herself to death, and their father remarried, started a new family, and they never heard from him again. All they had was each other; at the end of the day, that was all they needed. They vowed to always keep it that way.

Back in Miami, Pain and Pressure rented a nice little cottage right off of A1A. It was a two bedroom with a private entrance and a pool. They were not sure how long the twins would be in town once they arrived. Knowing that they would more than likely be spending a lot of time there, they made it as comfortable as possible. It was overflowing with food and everything else they could think of that the girls or themselves might need. It was already nicely furnished and in a nice area within minutes of a busy shopping plaza.

The cottage was close to one of their busiest traps, which was ran by two crazy ass Haitians that were natives to Miami. Shantae and her clique ran North Lauderdale, two young wild niggas from Opalocka ran their spot in Liberty City, and Allen's cousin ran the spot in Carol City. With all four spots running smoothly and effortlessly, they could focus on seeing how things worked out with Chloe and Zoey in the human trafficking industry. An extra three to four hundred thousand right now on top of what they were already making meant they could retire early.

Pressure never planned on being in the game past age thirty. That was the one thing different about the two of them. Pressure's plan was to get out of the game completely and go legit once he had a million dollars saved up. Then, maybe in his late 30s or early 40s, he would settle down and start having kids. But that was a big maybe.

Pain, on the other hand, never spoke of getting out of the game. He had been in an on-and-off relationship with Candice for almost ten years and they had a two-year-old daughter named Treasure. He loved the fast life but also wanted the family life. And for some reason, he didn't feel like he had to choose between the two lifestyles, which is something he and Candice always fought about.

They would break up and get back together. He cheated on her and broke her heart, but she paid his ass right back. Neither of them would allow the other to be happy with anyone else. They fucked then fought, fought then fucked. Pain spoiled both Treasure and Candice royally. He did truly love them, but as the man, he called the shots, and that was just that. He paid the bills and did all the things a man should do. And because of that, he felt that Candice should be more appreciative and less bitchy. It was a circus. But it was their circus, nevertheless. Nobody got involved because everyone knew, at the end of the day, those two loved each other.

Not only did he pay all the bills, but he also paid her college tuition. Candice loved him for that because that was important to her. He always wanted the best for her and took great care of her and their daughter. However, Candice was getting older. She wanted him home at night...every night. Pain knew that was not going to happen, so he never lied to her about the situation or made promises that he couldn't keep. She was number one and always would be. No one came before her and Treasure. That was the only promise he made, and he stood on that.

After situating the cottage that they rented for Zoey and Chloe and checking on the traps, Pain left to go spend time with his daughter, and Pressure went to go check on his mother, Mrs. Paulette. When he arrived, she was outside watering the grass looking like Mrs. Parker from the movie 'Friday'. She was still fine as hell, but dressed very conservatively, wearing her Gucci shades and a big straw hat. She smiled as Pressure pulled in the driveway.

"Well, hello there, son. How was your trip?" She asked as Pressure approached, greeting her with a warm hug and a kiss. "And where is your other half?" She added, referring to Pain.

"He went to spend time with Treasure," he answered.

"Treasure or Candice?" Mrs. Paulette teased.

"Both, but you already know that." Pressure responded.

"And how's Allen?" She asked.

"He's doing well," he replied. "The concert was lit. He showed us a really good time. We discussed a couple of new business ideas. Met a few people."

"Met a few people? Since when you got so friendly?" She asked. "And I know damn well y'all ain't trying to do business with new people. You can't trust nobody these days."

"We are gonna have to do something before you retire," he reminded her. "And at some point, we are gonna have to do business with somebody new, Mama."

"I hate putting y'all in that position, son," she admitted. "But it's time for me to live my life. See the world. That is why I worked so hard for the last twenty-five years…To retire, to live and blow money like y'all bosses do. I hope y'all have been saving and looking into investing in something so y'all can do the same someday. Because that's what real bosses do."

"We are looking into getting a big rig and a driver like Pops," Pressure said.

"That's not looking for a way out. That's looking for a new way to get your dope. Don't play with me, boy. Your mama wasn't born yesterday," she responded.

Pressure lowered his head and laughed. You couldn't pull anything over Mrs. Paulette's head. For her not to be in the streets, she definitely knew the game. "So, you are really ready to retire, huh?" He asked.

"Yes, baby. I've been looking into starting my own business. A laundromat, right in the hood, that's open 24/7. All I would need to do is hire two laundry attendants to work 12-hour shifts," she explained. "Collect my money at the end of the day, twice a week. I was even thinking about only charging the customers to wash but allowing the dryers to be free-of-charge."

"That sound like a good plan, Mama. I like it," Pressure approved.

"Mm hmm. I can travel all over the world and still be making money around the clock," she added. "Seriously though, son. You need to be thinking of you an escape plan too. Everybody that stays in the game too long, ends up spending all their money on either lawyer fees or commissary. You see your daddy got out, and that nigga still got plenty money. He ain't no fool. He wasn't giving his money back to the streets."

"So, you really plan on getting married and breaking Pop's heart?" Pressure asked.

"Your daddy is the only man I will ever love, but he made his bed, so he got to lay in it. I'm getting too old to be laying up with a man with no benefits or security. So yes, I plan on getting married for real," she confirmed. "Steven owns over a hundred acres of land in Georgia. Plus, he's been on his job for over 30 years. If he dies, I will own that land, get spousal support, and a hundred thousand dollars in life insurance. He doesn't have any kids, so everything would be mine. How I feel about him shouldn't even be important after saying all that. You should want me to marry him right now. It's about security, son. And at my age, that's what I need, sweetie."

"I can't lie, Ma. That sounds like gold-digging to me,"

Pressure said with a one-sided grin.

"Call it what you like, hunny. When you fall in love, you're going to do all you can to make sure she feels secure with you. Then you'll understand," she said.

"How am I supposed to know the difference between the one that is really for me from the ones that are just looking for security?" He asked.

"Even if a woman is in love with you, son, she is still going to look for security in her man. You'll know if she is the one. Ain't no guidebook when it comes to life or love. Some things you are just going to have to figure out on your own," she educated.

Pressure sat on the porch with his mother talking for a while. Afterwards, he decided to go home, get some good rest and just relax for the rest of the day. He knew that Pain wouldn't be home tonight. In fact, he might be gone for days. It really all depended on how long he and Candice got along.

ΔΔΔ

Treasure jumped up and ran to her father as he came through the door. Candice couldn't help but smile as well. She had missed him just as much as his daughter did. Candice was madly in love with Pain. She was just over his bullshit. She had outgrown that 'If he can do it, then so can I' attitude. She spent a lot of time alone, trying to convince herself that she wasn't waiting for Pain. She still considered him her man. Everyone knew that she was tough. Candice was going to school full time for nursing and other than that nothing else was important but her family.

She still believed in the power of love. She had a little less than a year left before graduating. If Pain was not ready to settle down by then, she was going to seriously move on. She also wanted another baby before Treasure got too old. She was hoping that he got it together because she dreamed of them getting married with two girls and a boy. Having another man in her life was never a part of that plan.

Across the street from the Broward Mall was a small fair with lots of kiddy rides. Pain had passed it on his way to Candice's place and decided that they would check it out tonight. He told them to get dressed and went into the room to smoke a joint while they did. They went to the mall and did some shopping, then to the fair to let Treasure run wild. Once she had gotten on almost every ride, they left and went to Five Guys for dinner.

By the time they got back home, Treasure was exhausted. Candice bathed her and put her in her bed. After getting Treasure settled, she took a shower herself. By the time she got out, Pain was sound asleep. She got in bed and put the TV on the hit series 'Power.' She caught up on the two episodes that she had missed, then called it a night.

As soon as she got into a deep sleep, she felt Pain's hard dick pressing against her butt cheeks. This was the moment she had been waiting for. He kissed her neck gently as he made his way down her back. He kissed her ass so softly; her love button was already swelling. She rolled over and the festivities began. First, he made love to her with his tongue. Candice was the only woman he'd ever put his mouth on. He knew her body so well. He made her cum before penetration every time. Then again during and sometimes after. There was never a dull moment. They made love for hours and then went back to sleep, this time in each other's arms.

Treasure woke them up way too early. Both of them were

completely fucked out and exhausted. Candice rolled out of bed, took a shower, and got dressed. Treasure had gotten in bed with her daddy by the time she was fully dressed.

"Mommy, I wanna stay home with Daddy," Treasure whined.

"If I can't skip school, you not skipping school," Candice fussed.

"You can skip school too, Mommy," Treasure said as if she was giving her permission.

"I got her, baby," Pain said, stepping in to rescue his baby girl as he always did.

Treasure laid on his chest knowing that would seal the deal. Candice knew she wouldn't win this fight, so she didn't even try. She kissed both of them and started her day a little earlier than usual. Since she no longer had to take Treasure to school, she planned on stopping to get breakfast this morning. Pain wanted to ask her to stay home so badly, but that was something he never did, no matter how bad he wanted to. So he got up and got dressed, then dressed Treasure, and they headed to Mrs. Paulette's house. She could run around with her grandma while he got some much-needed rest there.

Mrs. Paulette cooked breakfast for the three of them. Pain ate, went into the guest room, and went straight to sleep. Treasure and Mrs. Paulette watered the grass and cleaned the house. When Pain woke up, Mrs. Paulette and Treasure were just about to head out to catch a matinee movie. Pain decided he would tag along and treat them to lunch afterwards. This way he got to spend time with his queens at the same time. Mrs. Paulette informed him that she was off the next day and wanted to keep Treasure for the night. She would take her to school the following morning, which was perfect because he would get to please all three of his girls in one day. Now he could take tonight to wine and dine Candice. It had been a minute since they had a candlelight dinner, just the two of them.

After lunch, he rushed home to start dinner for Candice, cleaned the house, and lit candles. He decided to cook filet mignon, lobster tails, garlic mashed potatoes, a wilted baby spinach salad, and asparagus. He planned on running her a bubble bath when she arrived. So, he laid across the bed after he was satisfied with the setup, and before he knew it, he had dozed off.

Candice woke him up with some nice slow head. She took her time and took in every inch of him. Pain had missed that shit. You could feel the love she had for him by the way she made love to his dick. There was never a question when it came to her love for him. And like always, Pain nutted in no time. She knew just how he liked everything; his dick sucked, his clothes cleaned, and his food cooked. She even knew how to roll his joint, and she didn't even smoke. He wasn't crazy enough to ignore the fact that chicks like her came once in a lifetime. He tried to always make her feel special because he knew she deserved it.

"Thanks for cooking, it smells delicious. Where is Treasure?" Candice asked.

"She's with Mama," he answered. Before he could get up to make her bath water, she was already preparing to get in the shower.

"Chill out, baby, and allow me to cater to you today. You done already came in here and raped a nigga," Pain joked.

"I couldn't help myself. I owed you that after your Grammy-winning performance," she said, referring to how he laid it down in the bedroom the night before. He just laughed, knowing that he had put it down properly.

He made her bath water hot and full of bubbles. She hadn't realized just how much she needed that moment of relaxation. She submerged her body into the warmth of the water while listening to the sultry sounds of H.E.R. coming from the speakers and embraced the moment. Pain went downstairs to prepare their dinner. She was used to him cooking over-the-top meals. He was an over-the-top kind of guy.

They sat and ate dinner and then caught up on the rest of 'Power' before they started watching 'Ghost.' It was times like this that kept Candice holding on. They laughed and talked for hours. It was days like these when Treasure would be right there with them on her tablet watching 'Mickey Mouse Clubhouse,' that she loved the most. She loved her family and was ready to take bigger steps forward in their relationship.

As the two of them enjoyed each other's company, Pain's phone rang. It was Pressure, letting Pain know that Chloe and Zoey had surprised them with a pop-up visit, and they were at a hotel down on Miami Beach. He was about to go slide up on them.

"Come get me, dawg. That could be a setup," Pain said.

"Man, them chicks ain't trying to set a nigga up. How can they do that when they don't know shit about us?" Pressure replied.

"You're right. Still come grab me, bruh," Pain ordered.

When Candice heard that, all hell broke loose. She spazzed the fuck out. And just like that, happy days were over...again.

"If you leave me here, Pain, I bet I won't be here alone when you decide to come back this time. So there's no need to even bother coming back," she said.

"All that tells me is that you just like the rest of these hoes," Pain said.

"Who the fuck you calling a hoe?!?" Candice snapped.

"You been fucked good and catered to for three days straight, but if I leave, you won't be here alone when I get back??? What that make you? I didn't call you a hoe, but if the shoe fits... 'Cause you sho' talking like one," Pain explained.

"I rather be a hoe than a fucking fool!" She shot back.

"Well, do you, Shawty! Just make sure that nigga keep your stupid ass and make sure he pay these fucking bills too 'cause I bet I won't be paying bills for the next nigga to come fuck you!" He added.

Candice made a slick remark about another nigga raising Treasure, and before he knew it, he had grabbed her without even thinking about it. The lights from Pressure's car shined through the living room window at the perfect time. He pushed her down on the couch then pointed a stern finger in her face, "Bitch, you better move out town if you think you gon' have another nigga around my daughter. Because if you don't, you gon' end up on a t-shirt playing with me!" He threatened right before mushing her nose.

As he walked out, Candice cursed and fussed. Pain was livid. He couldn't believe she had the audacity to say something like that out her mouth. In his eyes, there was just no pleasing a bitch. Although he was leaving her to go entertain the next bitch, she didn't know that. Nor could she prove that. For all she knew, that could have been a million-dollar phone call. Was he not supposed to go just because she was in her feelings? She was his lady, not his mother. He jumped in the car with Pressure talking mad shit.

"This bitch had the nerve to tell me if I leave she gon' call somebody else over here," Pain explained to Pressure, who laughed. "That shit ain't funny, bruh!" Pain exclaimed. "That hoe need a bitch ass nigga that sit around the house. And I ain't never gonna be that."

"Man, you know damn well she just runnin' her mouth," Pressure said, trying to diffuse the situation.

"I don't know shit! A mad, emotional bitch will do anything when she in her feelings," Pain stated. Pressure let him vent. In no time they were at the hotel. Pressure listened to Pain get it all off his chest.

"Why are we just sitting here, bruh?" Pain asked, noticing that they had not gotten out of the car yet.

"I'm waiting for you to get that shit off your chest because I'mma need you to change your energy before we get out," Pressure lectured.

"I'm good, bruh. She going to fuck around and make me stunt on her ass with Chloe. Sometimes you gotta show a bitch you will move on without they ass," Pain vented as he rolled a blunt. After smoking and talking for almost an hour, the vibe had changed. In no time, they were talking about something totally different.

"I thought they were coming tomorrow?" Pain asked.

"This is their way of showing us they are getting their own money and not looking for us to take care of them," Pressure said as they got out and made their way to the room.

Chloe opened the door and Pain stepped up to her, "Damn, I almost forgot how beautiful you are," he complimented.

"How could you forget that?" She asked arrogantly as he grabbed her and hugged her.

"Damn, can I get to my shawty?" Pressure said. Pressure eased by them and approached Zoey with the most beautiful smile and a hug. Pain noticed his smile as well and had every intention of teasing his big bruh about that later. Pressure grabbed Zoey's hand and headed for the front door.

"Hold up, where y'all going?" Chloe asked.

"Why? You scared to be alone with me?" Pain questioned.

"Why would I be scared? I just wasn't aware she was going anywhere," Chloe replied.

"I'm sorry, Chloe," Pressure said. "Do I have your permission to take your sister for a tour of my city?"

Zoey laughed at Pressure's sarcasm. "I'll be back, sis. Pain got you," she said as he took Pressure's hand and they left.

Pain and Chloe kicked it for a minute, then he grabbed her keys. "Let's go," he said. Chloe didn't ask any questions. She grabbed the room key and they hit the town as well.

"What if they come back and can't get in the room?" She asked.

"They are not coming back, lil mama. Relax," Pain insisted.

Chloe relaxed, quickly realizing that she was acting like a little girl. It wasn't like they were on a lick or like they didn't know Pain and Pressure. They were the reason that they were there in the first place.

Pressure and Zoey went to Benihana's for dinner, and then they went to 'King of Diamonds.' They threw money and got a few lap dances. Next, they went to the casino and gambled for a while. Zoey won seven hundred dollars, and Pressure won fourteen hundred because he doubled whatever bet Zoey made. In the end, he gave her all the winnings. He then took her to the cottage, and they fucked like animals for the rest of the night.

Pain knew his brother well enough to know he would head

south, so he decided to go in a different direction. He and Chloe went to Club Vegas and then Las Olas for dinner. They walked the strip for a while and then decided to go to the beach. There were all kinds of clubs and smoke shops along the shore. So they stopped and had ice cream before calling it a night. Pain was all in his feelings about the argument he had with Candice earlier and feeling way too good. He was about to use Chloe in so many ways. She was clueless about what he had in store for her, but she would soon find out.

He needed to feel in control and feel appreciated. He needed to get his mind off Candice and prove to himself that he could and would move on as well. With all this already on his mind, the night became filled with passionate lovemaking instead of the normal, emotionless fuck that he usually provided to other women. Candice said that she was going to do her, and he hoped that she meant that shit because he was damn sure about to do him.

ΔΔΔ

Like clockwork Chloe's alarm went off at noon the following day. She and Pain both took showers and got dressed. They went to breakfast and then went to the cottage to meet up with Pressure and Zoey. By the time they made it there, it was almost 1:30 in the afternoon. They entered using Pain's key and noticed they were still sleeping. Chloe beat on the bedroom door.

"Bitch, I know you are not still sleeping!" Chloe yelled to her sister through the unopened door.

"What time y'all gotta be there?" Pressure said sarcastically, insinuating that they must have somewhere to be.

"Be where?" Chloe replied in confusion.

"My point exactly," he said, being a smart ass.

"I'm coming, sis," Zoey said while still kissing all over Pressure.

"If you're going, you better stop that before I have you in here face down and ass up again," Pressure suggested. So she stood up, threw on her housecoat and went into the living room with Pain and Chloe. A few minutes later, Pressure joined them.

"Nice house coat," Chloe teased. "You over here like a real housewife."

Pressure looked at Zoey and winked, making everybody laugh.

"Don't worry; you got one too," Pain educated Chloe. "Let me show you our room."

"Our room?" Chloe said, blushing like a schoolgirl as Pain showed her around the place. "This is so cute. Y'all got this for us?" She asked a bit flattered.

"We gotta make sure that y'all are comfortable and want for nothing while in our presence. It's a Door Dash card on the refrigerator if you don't feel like cooking. It's soda, liquor, juice, and milk in the fridge and games in the closet, along with all kinds of cosmetics," Pain informed.

"I can't lie, I'm impressed," Chloe said. "This is such a nice place. Thank y'all so much."

"Show me how much you like it…get on that stove," Pain ordered.

"You ain't said nothing but a word. I love to cook," Chloe said as she went to work with ease. Thirty minutes later, she had prepared Orange Chicken, jasmine rice, and cheesy broccoli. The four of them talked shit and had lunch.

"Now let's talk business," Chloe said, trying hard to stay focused on the business aspect.

"Just my kinda girl," Pain said.

Zoey looked at Pressure, and they both smiled at one another. They were practically eye fucking each other right there at the table.

"That's right, sis. Let's get down to business," Zoey said, trying to stay focused as well. But Lord knows, these niggas were making it hard as hell.

CHAPTER THREE

Mrs. Paulette and Treasure were at the movies when she received a call from Passion to be picked up from the airport. She had come home from college for a visit and had surprised everybody by coming a few days early. Mrs. Paulette called Pressure to see if he could pick his baby sister up. Pressure agreed without thinking twice, but then he realized that he wouldn't be able to drop Zoey and Chloe off and still make it to the airport before Passion's plane arrived. He would either have to take the girls along with him or send a Lyft for Passion, which he was not about to do. He knew she would be expecting a family member after being gone for such a long time. It had only been six months, but it felt like forever.

Passion was spoiled rotten, but she deserved it. She had gotten a four-year paid scholarship to Harvard University, which was among the most prestigious Ivy League colleges in the United States. It was far from home, but this would be an opportunity of a lifetime that most people never have. She would get the chance to spread her wings, travel and live a little bit. As well as get one of the best educations known to Man. Away from her overprotective mother, overprotective father, and definitely her overprotective brothers. She had been missed dearly while she was gone. Mrs. Paulette didn't know what to do with herself with her baby girl so far from home for the first time. She realized that it was time for her to live her own life. These were the moments that all hard-working parents looked forward to—retiring, vacationing, and gardening. She had raised all three of her kids well. They were now grown and living their best life. And now, she deserved to do the same.

Pressure had never brought any females around his mother. Candice was the only female that Pain had ever brought around. Being that they barely knew the twins, Pressure was uncomfortable picking Passion up with them in the car, but at this point, he didn't have a choice. He and Pain discussed the situation as if they were alone in the car.

Zoey looked at Pressure, "We are in the car. Would you like for us to get out at the airport and take a Lyft? I understand that you don't really know us, but I would think that by now, you would be able to feel good energy and detect that we have no ill intentions. I feel safe with you, and I want you to feel the same. But I do understand, so it's not a big deal."

Pressure could see by the look on her face that she was offended. That definitely wasn't his intention. "I'm not trying to offend you, lil mama," he said. "Rules are set in place for a reason. If I break my own rules, how can I expect somebody else to follow them?"

"I feel you...I just thought the rules were set for outsiders," she stated. "Not tryna move too fast, but I thought we were a part of the team now and would be helping to enforce those rules, not still included with the outsiders."

Pain and Chloe didn't say a word as they watched the two of them respectfully go back and forth. Minutes later, they were pulling into the airport. Passion was all smiles as soon as she saw her brothers pull up. She stood there looking like a Diamond Princess. Both Pain and Pressure jumped out and hugged her for what seemed like forever. Pain spun her around like she was a little girl. They missed her so much. They grabbed her bags and loaded them in the car. When Pain opened the front passenger door for Passion to get in, she instantly noticed that they were not alone. Pain jumped in the back with the girls.

"Ok. Bruh, I guess y'all got good taste. They are cute," Passion complimented.

"These are our friends. This is Chloe and that's Zoey," Pressure introduced.

"Hi, I'm Passion. Nice to meet you," she said. "So, since these are just your friends, that means I can shoot my shot?" She questioned her brothers.

"Girl, if you don't sit yo' ass down somewea'...Shoot yo' shot??? What's that supposed to mean, you gay now???" Pain asked.

"I was going to tell y'all later, but they are too cute not to at least try to get one of them now," Passion responded. "Yes, I'm gay. I like girls. Please don't judge me because I'm still the same person...your baby sister." Pain and Pressure was quiet as hell. This was a total shocker. Passion then turned around and asked Zoey, "Will you go with me to the movies tonight?"

"Damn! Can you let me absorb this new information I just received before you start putting your mac game down on my friends?" Pressure interrupted. "Besides, we got grown up plans tonight, lil girl."

Everybody was quiet.

"You really gay, sis?" Pain asked.

Passion burst out laughing. "This nigga over here sweating thinking I was going to take his girl," she said while pointing at Pressure. "Hell no, I ain't gay, bruh. I just miss getting on y'all last nerves. I love y'all niggas." Everybody in the car laughed and were all equally relieved that she was only joking.

"I don't even know why I miss your big head ass," Pressure teased.

"Because who else is there to get on your nerves?"

Passion asked rhetorically.

"So, how's college life been treating you, Passion?" Chloe asked.

"It's okay; I'm adjusting. I'm happy to be home for a few days. I miss my family and friends," she responded.

"Have you looked into any sororities?" Zoey questioned.

"I have, but I haven't joined one yet. I'm trying out for cheerleading when I get back," Passion answered. "Tryouts start next week. That is why I came home a little earlier than I previously planned to."

"I cheered all of my life. I gave it up in high school because I started working," Zoey said. Pain and Pressure just sat quietly as the three girls conversed.

"Oh yea, bruh, before I forget, can you take me to get my hair done tomorrow? I have an appointment at ten in the morning." Passion asked.

"I'm not sitting around all day while you get your hair done, Passion," Pressure said, declining her request.

"But Mama gotta work," she whined. "Will you take me, Pain?"

"Man, you might have to catch a Lyft or something, P," Pain suggested, declining her request as well.

"We can take her," Chloe said. Pain and Pressure just looked at each other.

"Can they take me, Pressure? Please?" Passion begged.

"I would love to get my hair done in Miami. I would get me one of those thirty-inch 'Trina' wigs," Zoey added.

"I like Zoey a lot better than I like Trina...I think you should just be you, shawty," Pressure said. Zoey looked at

Pressure and smiled. It was obvious that these two were feeling each other a lot, and Passion peeped it right away.

Mrs. Paulette's house had been so lonely and quiet while Passion was away. It just wasn't the same without her. When they pulled up, Mrs. Paulette and Treasure were already outside. Treasure jumped up and down when she saw Uncle Pressure's car, but she really jumped for joy when she saw her Auntie P and her daddy get out of the same car. Passion ran to her mother like a lil' girl. Mrs. Paulette had tears running down her face.

"Mama, you're getting soft," Pain teased.

"I missed my baby so much. Shut yo' ass up before I show you soft," Mrs. Paulette snapped. Everyone laughed. Pressure hugged his mother and his niece and then went inside to use the restroom.

"Mama, Pressure and Pain friends' are going to take me to the salon tomorrow," Passion informed her.

"What friends?" Mrs. Paulette asked.

"Zoey and Chloe. They are in the car. They're really nice and cute," Passion answered.

"Well, why did y'all leave them in the car?" Mrs. Paulette inquired.

"Because we were about to bounce," Pain said on his way in the house to get Pressure because he already knew where this was going. By the time they came outside, Passion had gotten Chloe and Zoey out of the car and introduced them to Mrs. Paulette. The four of them were having a full-fledged conversation.

"So, they are taking Passion to her appointment tomorrow?" Mrs. Paulette asked. Pressure nodded his head for confirmation, kissed his mom, then his sister on the way to his car. Pain followed suit, motioning for the girls to follow.

"Nice to meet you, Mrs. Paulette, and don't worry, Passion. We will be here in the morning to pick you up," Chloe said on their way to the car behind Pain.

As soon as they pulled off, Pressure lit the joint. That whole ordeal had stressed him out. He turned the music up and put the joint in rotation. The ride back to the cottage was quiet. Everybody seemed to be deep in thought.

Once inside, they rolled up again, fixed drinks, and talked business. The girls explained to them that back at home, this is a common hustle. They would find girls that were on the streets but not so far gone that they couldn't be cleaned up, then clean them up and let their connections bid for them... The highest bidder won. They took nothing less than forty thousand for each girl.

Normally, pregnant girls sold for way more. However, they personally didn't sell pregnant women. They didn't force anybody; they just basically offered them a better life. The girls would get drugs and food year-round, and they never had to walk the streets again. This was all true. The only thing they didn't tell them was that they didn't have a way out. But truthfully, most of them didn't want a way out.

"And that's it?" Pain asked.

"That's it. The game may have switched up a little, but for the most part, it's that simple," Chloe responded.

"So why didn't y'all deal with pregnant women? More money makes more sense," Pain wondered.

"A baby don't have a choice; the people we chose did. In my mind, the people we chose were really going to a better place. And it was just better on our conscience." Zoey answered.

"So why y'all got out if it's such easy money?" Pain questioned.

"Because there were so many different cliques buying and selling. The prices were getting lower and lower. The old heads started being too messy and greedy. Anybody was up for grabs. Too many women were coming up missing, and because of that, a special task force was put together to crack down on the human trafficking ring. The streets were getting hotter and hotter," Zoey explained. "We felt like we had made enough money to leave that part of the game alone. Besides, we never intended on making a career out of it."

Pressure finally spoke after taking everything in. "If we do this, everyone we deal with must be 100% willing. I personally think that if a chick is on the streets, pregnant and still using drugs, selling her may save the baby's life. She damn sure ain't going to take care of a baby if she is not taking care of herself. So, in my book, we would be helping ourselves, her, and the baby."

"What if the baby gets sold to a pervert that rapes him or her? Or use them for child pornography?" Zoey asked.

"Contrarily, what if the baby gets sold to a rich family that can't have kids, and that family loves the baby, gives them a good life, puts them through college, and that child grows up to become a lawyer or a doctor?" Pressure said hypothetically speaking.

"You both have good points," Pain said. "We will deal with that when the time comes. We need to set an age limit. I say 18 to 30." They all agreed.

"We all split the money four ways. We are partners. No one is greater than the other. If there is a problem or an issue, we sit like adults and talk it out. No matter how much we fuck, the rules for business stay the same. This is some shit I definitely don't plan on staying in for too long. We make two, three hundred bands and get out," Pressure suggested.

"What's understood doesn't have to be explained," Pain said, lifting his glass for a toast. Everybody else lifted their glass up in a friendly toast. "To getting money, elevating and enjoying life at the same time."

"We'll go for a test run tonight and see how it goes," Pressure said. "In the meantime. I'll get a room somewhere for a week. Whoever we recruit will stay there. They don't need to know anything about us."

"I'm rolling with you, bruh," Pain stated.

"Good, we can check the traps while we're out," Pressure agreed. He looked over at Zoey, "You good, baby girl?" He asked.

"I'm good, Daddy," Zoey replied.

"Daddy?!? What the fuck this nigga done did to my sister?" Chloe asked, not actually expecting an answer to the question. Zoey and Chloe laughed.

Pain and Pressure gave each other dap. "I need to tighten up. I want to be called Zaddy," Pain joked.

"I like Papi better," Chloe said.

"Me too when you say it like that," Pain responded. "Let's go, bruh because I gotta get back here asap."

"Please do," Chloe said. "In the meantime, I'm going to prepare dinner."

Pain and Pressure rolled up and then hit the streets shortly after.

"Bitch, I love how he just takes charge. That shit has my insides on fire," Zoey admitted.

"I can't lie, I like you two together," Chloe concluded.

"I like us together too, what's up with you and Pain?" Zoey asked.

"We vibe really good together. I love his energy. He lives in the moment and I like that," Chloe said. "Pressure is a lot more serious, like you. However, something tells me that Pain is still seeing his baby mama. He never talks about them. And he made sure that we didn't meet his daughter."

"Well, I understand that. They don't really know us yet. Would you have a nigga around your child that you've only known maybe a month?" Zoey rationalized.

"No, I wouldn't. I get it. It's just an assumption. I could be wrong," Chloe admitted. "But I'm feeling him for sure, a little too much if you ask me."

"You don't think he is feeling you?" Zoey wondered.

"The way I put down on him, he doesn't have a choice but to feel me," Chloe answered with confidence. They laughed and talked while Chloe cooked. She made fried pork chops, with Spanish rice and corn. Simple but quick and delicious.

A few hours later the guys came back. They ate dinner together, got dressed to hit the streets. There were a few chicks at the gas station on 119th Avenue, but all of them looked old and way too far gone.

"Chicks like those are too far gone," Chloe schooled as they scanned the streets of Miami. As they hit 79th Street, they saw all kinds of tricks out on the streets. Young, old, fat, skinny, trannies and punks: this was a recruiting haven.

"Go to that liquor store over there," Zoey instructed.

"Man, that's punk nation. Real niggas don't go to this liquor store," Pain fussed.

"Real niggas go wherever the money is. We are on a different kinda mission tonight. You don't even gotta get out of the car. We got this," Zoey said.

Pressure loved the way Zoey kept it real about how she felt and the way she viewed things. He took notes as he observed everything about her. So far, he didn't have any complaints. Zoey was fun and playful in bed but when it came to anything else she was a very serious person. He watched as they went into the liquor store, bought a bottle, then posted up outside of the car and fixed them a drink. They drew attention effortlessly; Pretty face, banging body, dressed to kill with lite makeup.

"Y'all too cute to be posted out here," One of the ladies yelled from the bus stop where all the tricks were posted up at.

"Y'all too cute to be sitting at this bus stop," Chloe said as she and her sister walked up to the bus stop and held conversation with the girls standing there.

"This 'Money Corner'," One of the girls said.

"Money Corner???" Zoey said, looking around in confusion. Chloe laughed. One of the girls seemed to get offended. "I'm not trying to offend you but baby ain't no real money on this corner. Real niggas don't won't a street walking hoe," Zoey said, teaching the game. "If you want to get off these streets and make some real money, give us a call. You will never walk again. We provide transportation to our calls, housing, food and drugs. It don't matter what your drug of choice is. We got it."

"This sounds too good to be true," the girl said skeptically.

"Nothing's perfect, you gotta put in work. Sometimes you gotta work when you don't feel like it. But I promise you, the good outweighs the bad," Chloe stressed.

"Just take a couple days to think about it," Zoey said. "We will be in town for a few more days. In the meantime, y'all be safe out here on these streets."

They passed out their number and answered any questions they had as truthfully as possible before walking back to the car. They then slid to the Rolex gentleman club. The dancers there were thick, pretty and all the way live. "This definitely isn't a place to recruit but I want a lap dance," Chloe said.

"My kinda girl," Pain replied as he led her to the area designated for lap dances. They hung out for a few, got a couple of dances and then called it a night.

ΔΔΔ

The following morning the girls were up bright and early ready for their transformation. They arrived a few minutes early to pick up Passion. As soon as they pulled in the driveway another car pulled on the side of them. The chick got out of the car mean mugging them but Passion came running out the house and distracted her.

"Where are you off to in such a rush?" Candice asked.

"I have a hair appointment," Passion answered.

"Who these chicks that you're riding with? I've never seen them before?" Candice questioned.

"Uncle Pressure sent his friends to take me. They have appointments too," Passion explained as she hugged Candice and kept it moving.

By this time, Mrs. Paulette and Treasure were at the door. Treasure ran out and jumped in her mother's arms. They knew for a fact that this click had to be Pain's baby mama. For some reason Chloe was in her feelings. *The bitch cute, but she ain't all that,* she thought to herself. Zoey could see that her sister was in her feelings, but she opted to keep quiet being that Passion was in the car. Mrs. Paulette came out and approached the car. She thanked them and offered to buy them lunch. The girls politely declined. Candice was trying to ear hustle, and everyone could see that, so Mrs. Paulette let them go ahead and go.

"Who are those bitches?" Candice asked Mrs. Paulette.

"Girl calm down, that is Pressure's friend and her sister, and they happen to be some really nice girls."

"Pain and Pressure's friends, you mean?" Candace said, quickly peeping game.

"No, I meant exactly what I said. I don't know anything about them being Pain's friends. They were introduced to me as Pressure's friend and her sister," Mrs. Paulette corrected. "Don't put me in y'all mess, child, standing here with your face all balled up for nothing.

"Me and him aren't talking right now, so if he is seeing somebody else, it's cool. I'm ready to start seeing other people as well. I want a family man. With a nine to five. And a retirement plan," Candice admitted.

"I was just explaining that to Pressure. Maybe I should

have been talking to Pain," Mrs. Paulette said jokingly. They both laughed.

They talked for a little bit over a cup of coffee before Candice gathered Treasure things. The three of them left at the same time. Mrs. Paulette was headed to work and Candice was headed home all in her feelings. There was nothing nobody could tell her. She knew her man, and she knew one of those bitches was for him. She could feel it in her soul.

"I'm finna show this nigga!" She thought to herself.

She had no proof of anything but didn't need any. Her woman's intuition had kicked in, and that was good enough. She went through her phone and went to the name Choncie. Choncie was a handsome, hardworking young man in her class. He was going to school part-time to be a Medical Examiner, and he worked full time at the pharmacy in the hospital. She dialed his number. When he picked up, tears started running down her eyes because once she moved forward, there was no turning back.

"Choncie speaking..."

"Hi, Choncie. This is Candice," she responded.

"Candice," he said, totally surprised. "Wow. This is proof that God does answer prayers." She laughed. This was her escape route. He was the perfect distraction. He was sexy as hell. He would help ease the pain, make sure she's financially secured and hopefully great sex came alone with it. He was a package deal. He had been chasing her for so long. And thanks to Pain, today was his lucky day.

CHAPTER FOUR

Pain, Pressure, Chloe, and Zoey worked very well together. They had recruited six girls that were all willing to relocate to a new state and try something new. Chloe and Zoey had shown them that they were women of their word, by making sure that the girls got high as the sky and ate three good meals every day. So far, the only thing the new recruits needed to focus on was getting plenty of rest until it was time to leave. Knowing that Detroit was such a long way to drive with eight women and the recruits would need to freshen up before the actual drop off; space and electricity was needed. Therefore, Chloe and Zoey decided to return the rental car they were driving and rent an RV instead so that they would all be more comfortable. They were instructed to call Allen in the event that they arrived in Detroit before Pain and Pressure. Now that everything was in place, the girls got on the road.

Pain and Pressure had about nineteen hours to do everything they had to do and get to Detroit. The most important of those things was taking Passion to her doctor's appointment and shopping before leaving to go back to college. Her plane was scheduled to depart tomorrow, 30 minutes before their plane took off. They made sure all the traps were properly supplied and then got some rest. First thing in the morning they would take Passion to the doctor, take her shopping then head to the airport.

The next morning, they picked Passion up and went to breakfast. When they got to the doctor's office, Shantae was there getting a checkup as well. When they saw her coming from the back, they all noticed that her stomach was big as all outdoors. Allen had a rude awakening coming his way if this was his baby. She had to have lied to him about something because he was under the impression there was no baby and there obviously was.

"What's up Shantae, I'm surprised to see you here," Pressure said.

"Shiiiit, I'M surprised to see THAT," Pain said pointing to her stomach.

"And I'm surprised to see both of y'all here...and this is my daughter," she said, rubbing her stomach. "Ya boy thought I was going to kill my baby... WRONG! I'll kill his ass first before I kill my baby. I haven't talked to him in six months but I couldn't care less. Once you find a man to treat you the way you're supposed to be treated, everything else seems so minuscule."

"Minuscule? Wow," Pressure said.

"So, you got a nigga while you pregnant with my dawg baby?" Pain asked.

"Your dawg didn't want this baby. So, what I do, is none of his fucking business," she replied. "And yes, I got somebody to help me get over the pain and take good care of me at the same time. It's not possible for him to really love me if he refuses to have a family with me after all these years," she said as tears filled her eyes.

"There is nothing he can ever say to me. I just hope she's worth it, whoever she is."
Just as her tears began to roll down her smooth cheeks, an older gentleman stuck his head in the door.

"Baby, what's wrong?" He said as he rushed to her aid, wiping her tears away.

"This is Pressure and Pain. These are Allen's friends," she explained. "It seemed as if they knew nothing about the baby, so I was just telling them the whole situation. It's still an emotional subject for me."

"I don't know why. You're not alone, and you don't have anything to worry about anymore. I got you and the baby. And you already know that" he assured.

"I know that baby, but it still hurts," she responded.

"I know, baby," he said right before kissing her on the forehead.

He then turned to Pressure and Pain, "I'm sorry to interrupt. Nice to meet you. I'm Marcus." He went in his wallet, pulled out a business card, and handed it to Pressure. "If either of you ever need a lawyer, I'm the best in town."

Pressure took the card and slid it in his pocket. Marcus grabbed Shantae's hand and they exited the building. Not before she decided to tell them that they were welcome to take over the spot in North Miami. She was no longer in the game and had not been in months, but her customers had still been banging her phone. She could reroute those calls to them if they were interested in the extra clientele. They both thought that was real of her to look out like that, and they respected it, but they still burst into laughter once she and Marcus exited the room. However, they knew that this was no joking matter. Mr. King Ding-a-ling's boat was about to start sinking. His shit was finally starting to catch up to him, and there was nothing he could do to stop it at this point.

"That nigga finna hit the roof when he finds out she ain't get rid of that baby," Pain said.

"He knew better than that, man. I don't know what he was thinking," Pressure said.

"He could not have been thinking at all," Pain said. "I'll kill my bitch. When she get sick of me, she better get a vibrator. Because a new nigga is going to get her and that nigga fucked up. Especially after all these years."

"But you are doing what you want to do?" Pressure asked.

"Well, of course. I pay the cost to be the boss," Pain replied.

"So does he. What the hell does that have to do with anything?" Pressure said.

"I ain't gone lie though, bruh, my bitch will be on the back of a T-shirt, and its gon' be a sad Saturday for her family and friends," Pain joked.

"Oh, so you just like ya daddy, huh?" Pressure teased. *"Probably try to kill her then kill himself,"* he said, again reciting lyrics from J.T. Money's *'Ho Problems'*.

"You got me fucked up, nigga! I said I'll kill DAT nigga, not myself," Pain reiterated.

They laughed and talked shit while waiting on Passion to finish up. Afterwards, they went shopping and then to Mrs. Paulette since it wasn't yet time to catch their flight. Passion told Pain that Candice was there when the twins picked her up, and she was trying to figure out who they were.

"What did you tell her?" Pain asked nervously.

"I told her that Pressure sent them to take me to get my hair done because he didn't want to be sitting around all day dealing with that," Passion answered. "Then I ran and jumped in the car, leaving Mama to deal with that."

Pressure laughed, "My whole crew about to be having hoe problems." This is why he always kept it a hundred with whoever he was fucking. He did not belong to anyone nor did he owe anyone an explanation about anything.

"Hoe problems ain't no problems," Passion said.

"That's a lie. Hoe problems is a big problem," Pain replied. They all laughed because Pain was right. It was becoming a big problem.

Passion would not be coming back home until her 21st birthday party. Everyone was happy her spoiled ass was about to officially be grown. Saying goodbye to her brothers was so hard for her to do. She hated it. As they arrived at the airport, you could see the sadness on her face.

"Why are you looking like you really don't wanna go back?" Pressure questioned. "Because you already know you don't have to. This is your choice, baby girl."

"I know. I just miss y'all so much, and Mama is so lonely now that I'm gone," she admitted. "School is cool; I'll just be glad when it's over. But I'm going back. You know I'm not a quitter. Besides, it would break Mom and Pop's heart if I drop out."

"You're about to be 21. At some point you are going to have to make your own decisions. If you really don't want to go to college, you don't have to. There are a lot of successful businesses with black owners that didn't go to college and still making good money. Some people are smart as hell but don't like school or have no interest in going to college.
If you are doing this for you, I support it. If you are doing it just to make somebody else happy, don't do it. I don't give a damn if it's mom and pop. You've already made this family more than proud. Now is when you start working on yourself and your future...doing what makes you happy," Pressure lectured.

"That's real, P," Pain agreed.

"I'm going back to school. I worked too hard. I can't pass up this good, free education. I'll have plenty of time to have fun. I just hate saying goodbye. Once I get there, I will be okay," Passion concluded.

"As long as that's what you want, I'm all for it. Just know that we are already proud of you though," Pressure added.

"I know that bruh. I love y'all aggravating asses," she said, wiping her tears away. "I was trying not to cry."

"You're soft as hell just like ya mama," Pain teased.
Once they made sure Passion was safely on her plane, they rushed to board their plane. Passion got comfortable and was deep in her thoughts when she was interrupted by a young man. He was handsome as hell, well dressed, and smelling like a real boss.

"Do you mind if I sit next to you?" He asked politely.

"We have assigned seats. If this is your seat, how can I stop you?" She responded.

"Actually, this isn't my seat, but they have me next to someone that's taking up both of our seats," he explained.

Passion smiled right before saying, "I don't own this plane. If you want to sit, go right ahead."

"You're looking like you can use a little cheering up anyways. By the way, my name is Andre, but you can call me Dre," he said as he took a seat.

"Nice to meet you, Dre. I'm Passion. And I'm fine," she replied.

"I can see that, but I'm trying to figure out why the sad look on such a beautiful face," he flirted.

Passion was flattered and wanted to smile, but she couldn't force it.

"You wanna talk about it?" He asked.

"To a complete stranger? No thanks," she said, declining his offer.

"Sometimes a stranger is better. They can't judge you because they don't know you. It's like talking to a therapist," he said.

Passion looked at him and her heart softened. She could tell that he was very sincere and concerned. Before you knew it, she was letting it all out. She explained to him that she was headed back to school and missed her family. It was her first time away from home. She was also kinda tired of school. Dre asked question after question about her and the things she liked to do. Her desire to have kids? Her dream job? Her dream man? The entire flight they talked about her. He was so charming and attentive. He even carried her luggage when they got off the plane. To their surprise, they were parked right next to each other.

"Is this really your car?" He asked.

"Yes, what kinda car did you expect me to drive?" She replied, looking at him like he was crazy.

He laughed. "I just asked because I'm parked right next to you."

"Seriously? Wow! What a coincidence," she said.

"Is it really? I'm feeling like it was meant for us to meet. If I didn't see you on the plane, I still would have seen you once we landed. There was no way around us meeting today. That's way more than a coincidence. It was fate. I feel like this day and this moment was meant to be," he rationalized.

Passion couldn't believe how much she was attracted to him. He gave her butterflies. She wanted to scream, but she kept it together. They exchanged numbers and promised to stay in contact. He waited until she pulled off, then he pulled off in his 2022 Beamer with a glossy, olive-green paint coat and twenty-three-inch chrome Forgi's, which also had olive green colored spokes. Passion could not believe someone that hot seemed to be so interested in her. She was more than sure hoes from all walks of life were at him. Not that she would settle for anything less because she was one of the baddest bitches walking the earth.

But this was no high school crush type shit. He seemed to be on his grown man vibe like her brothers. He even handled her with care the same way they do. She loved it. Her mind was all over the place. They had talked about her so much that she didn't get to ask anything about him. Now she was curious about so many things, like how he was able to afford that hot ass ride. She couldn't wait to tell A'niya about him.

"Smells good," she said as she walked through her dorm room door. Her dorm mate, A'niya was cooking.

"You are right on time. Are you hungry?" A'niya asked.

"Yes Ma'am, I sure am," Passion replied.

A'niya added more meat to make sure it was enough. "Girl, how was your trip, and what's up with those sexy ass brothers of yours?" She asked.

"My brothers...girl, let me tell you about this sexy ass nigga I met on the plane," Passion said with excitement.

"I'm listening," A'niya said.

Passion and A'niya sat down and ate while she went on and on about Dre. A'niya was her best friend. She and Passion would stay up all night talking sometimes. They got along really well. They both were spoiled rotten and in college on a four-year scholarship. They helped each other get through the difficult times. Together they were learning to be young ladies instead of Daddy's little girls.

△△△

Allen was waiting at the airport when Pain and Pressure arrived. This was a business trip, so they had no plans on hanging out. Their presence was needed in Miami, so the plan was to fly back home immediately after handling business. At some point, they had to break the news to him about Shantae. They figured they would handle business first, then rain on his parade. It sucked to be the bearer of bad news, but it had to be done.

Like clockwork, Zoey called and said that they were in town at the truck stop letting the girls freshen themselves up. They agreed to meet the girls there and switch vehicles so that the men could finish the deal and meet back up at Chloe and Zoey's place afterwards. On their way up to Detroit, they managed to pick up two more chicks from a truck stop in Tennessee. All together now, they had eight recruits. Allen had negotiated a deal of $60,000 per female. He would only take $10,000 for each one. That way everybody else would still split the original demanded amount of $50,000 for each girl. Allen hit his peoples up to make sure it was a green light. He was ready and excited. He was hoping to take over the game with these new bitches.

Allen was impressed. "You niggas don't fuck off," he complimented.

"We can't take the credit for this one. These chicks don't play. They cool as fuck and 'bout they money," Pressure admitted.

"With some guuuuuud ass pussy too," Pain added.

"Head even better," Pressure stated.

Allen laughed. "Hot dick ass niggas," he said, shaking his head. When they arrived at the truck stop, the girls put on a fashion show. They had done a great job with the transformation. Everybody was in good spirits and looking good. Now it was time to turn that into money. They pulled up to the address that was given to them. To their surprise, the house was really nice. The nigga had six vicious pit bulls guarding the premises. The gate opened as they pulled up. The dude came out and motioned for the dogs to sit. Simultaneously, each and every one of them sat on their hind legs. Allen exited the car and greeted the dude. They talked for a minute, and then he called Pain and Pressure over.

"I'm Minnesota, but the streets call me Sota. Nice to do business with you," he said.

They shook hands, did a short meet and greet, then got down to business. Pressure called the girls out of the RV. They all got out, not afraid to flaunt what they had. Sota was impressed as well. "I was praying you niggas ain't pull up with no bum ass bitches."

"We wouldn't bring you no bitches that ain't good enough to work for us," Pressure assured.

"That's what I'm talking 'bout. I can fuck wit' y'all boys." Sota said. "Come on, let me show y'all around." The twelve of them went inside. He ordered the eight girls to go to the pool area, where the other girls were already awaiting their arrival. Once the new girls exited the house and headed toward the patio, he continued to show the men around. This nigga had this shit together. He was eating off these hoes.

He schooled them while giving them a tour of the house: "If I spend $60,000 on one hoe and she takes at least one call a day for a thousand dollars, in two months, I've made the money back that I paid for her...The rest of the year is profit. But in actuality, she really sees two to three clients a day. So, I'm actually nearly tripling those same 60 bands in the first three months. This is free game that I'm giving y'all because it's enough money out here for all of us."

He then took them to an office and instructed them to wait there for his return. A few minutes later, he came back with a duffle bag full of cash and counted out $480,000. Pressure took $80,000 of the money and handed it to Allen. They would divide the rest when they got with Chloe and Zoey. Sota walked them to the back by the pool and gave them their choice of any female they wanted free. All three of them declined.

"Boy, y'all must have some super bad bitches at home," Sota said, shocked.

"We just don't mix business with pleasure," Pressure said.

"Hey, you don't have to tell me twice," Sota said, not having a problem with them declining the offer. "Well, I'm always on go, no breaks. You don't even have to call next time... Just pull up," he said as he walked them back to their RV. Just that fast, the deal was done, and they were out.

On their way to meet up with the girls, Pain decided to open the conversation about Shantae. "We saw you baby mama at the doctor's office yesterday," he blurted out. Pressure shook his head. Pain caught him off guard, so he knew it was about to fuck Allen's head all the way up.

There was nothing but silence after Pain's comment. "I'm talking to you Allen," he informed.

"What baby mama?!? Nigga, my baby mama at home," Allen said.

"Yea, not that one. Shantae is about to bust," Pain said. Allen looked at Pressure for confirmation and noticed that he was avoiding eye contact with him. "What is this nigga talking 'bout, Pressure?" He asked.

"Bruh, Shantae did not get rid of that baby. She is seven months pregnant. We saw her at the doctor's office this morning," Pressure confirmed.

"That ain't all," Pain instigated.

"What do you mean that ain't all? Man, just say what you gotta say," Allen said, not having time for the bullshit.

"She was with some old school nigga that she say takin' good care of her and shit," Pain said eagerly ready to gossip. "She was talkin' 'bout how she out the game, and we can take over North Miami. Talkin' 'bout how you broke her heart, but she found a new love in her daughter."

"Daughter??? So, she's having a girl?" Allen asked with a hint of excitement.

"No, nigga, not she...Y'ALL havin' a girl," Pain replied, trying to keep a straight face.

"FUUUUUUCCCKK!!!" Allen screamed as he punched the steering wheel. "Now I have to tell Taylor."

Allen's world was crushed. He wasn't mad at Shantae. How could he be? He respected her even more...But damn! And the fact that it was a girl was really going to crush Taylor because she knew Allen wanted a daughter so bad. He just broke down and admitted that he felt like shit about the way he had handled Shantae. He was so worried about losing Taylor, he never even considered how he made her feel. However, he was happy it was a girl. They listened as he told his story. When they arrived at Chloe and Zoey's crib, the three of them got out and went inside. Pain broke the money down with girls while Allen and Pressure chopped it up.

"Now what? Now that business is done," Chloe asked.

"My boy 'bout to go home, and the four of us 'bout to head back to Florida, but not before we lay up in this cute lil' crib, with these cute lil' ladies and get real ugly for a lil' minute," Pain replied. Chloe grabbed his hand and led him to her room.

Pressure walked Allen to his truck and sincerely wished him the best. When he made his way back inside, the sound of music was coming from the front bedroom, which was Zoey's room. When he stepped inside, he noticed that she was in the shower, so he joined her.

'I can get used to this,' he thought to himself as he caressed her body.

CHAPTER FIVE

The very next morning after Allen received the information about Shantae still being pregnant, Taylor went outside to check the mailbox. There was an envelope addressed to Allen Crawford. It was from the law office of Marcus White.

Law office? She thought to herself.

She wondered what that was all about. For some strange reason, it piqued her curiosity. She put it on the counter and went about her day. When Allen got home, she informed him about the envelope. When he saw 'Law Office,' he knew right then that it was some bullshit. Without thinking, he opened the envelope. It was legal documents asking him to sign over his parental rights to his unborn child. Allen was so upset. Not only was both of them disrespecting him as if he was a deadbeat ass father, but they also sent this bullshit to his house. Now his wife was in his face wanting answers.

"What's going on, Allen?" Taylor asked.

"I fucked up, Taylor. I fucked up real bad. And I need a little time to figure this all out," Allen explained.

He ripped the papers up, threw them in the garbage, and then took the garbage outside to the garbage bin. When he got back inside, he started packing. "I gotta go out of town and look into this situation before I speak on it." Was all he said. He could not look her in the face, and that told her that she had something to worry about.

"How long will you be gone?" She asked.

"I'm not sure, but it shouldn't be long," he answered. He finally looked up at her, and the worry in her eyes broke his heart. He wondered if he would get to see her beautiful smile ever again. There was no fixing this. He just prayed that they had enough love for each other to make it through this. He called an uber, gave her a kiss, and he was left.

As soon as he was out of sight, Taylor went outside and retrieved the letter out of the garbage. She took her time precisely taping the pieces back together. Taylor thought she was going to faint when she saw 'Parental rights of Shantae Murphy's unborn child'. *Who the fuck is Shantae Murphy, and what unborn child were these papers referring to???* She didn't know what to do. There was no way her husband would do something like this to her. As she thought about the look on his face, she realized that it was real. She fell to her knees in tears. Once she pulled herself together, she took a picture of the first page and sent it to his phone.

Allen was at the airport ticket booth about to purchase a boarding pass when his cellphone's text notification rang out. It was from Taylor. Allen's heart sank when he saw the picture of the taped letter and the text message words attached to it that read: *"How can you fix this, Allen? You can't."*

His chin dropped to his chest and his head hung low. His entire body went numb. He couldn't believe he had been stupid enough to throw the papers in the trash right in front of her.

"Good afternoon, sir. How can I help you? Hellooo? SIR?!" Said the attendant waiting to help him at the ticket booth.

The guy in line behind him tapped his shoulder. "My bad, bruh," Allen said as he snapped back to reality.

"Can I help you, sir?" The attendant asked again.

"Naw," he said as he stepped out of line and called an Uber to take him back home. He was a man, and it was time to man up. He went over what he was going to say a thousand times in his head. He walked through that door and saw his wife balled up in a corner crying.

"I'm sorry baby." That was all he could say.

She jumped up and charged at him full speed, swinging with everything in her power. He just held her as she swung until she gave out of energy. "Why, Allen? Why?!?" She sobbed.

"Baby, please stop crying and let me explain," Allen pleaded. He led her to the couch and let it all out as Taylor listened.

"Shantae was my high school sweetheart, my first love. She was with me when I had nothing," he admitted. "Once I met you and fell in love with you, I just married you without ever properly calling it off with Shantae. And before I knew it, we already had kids and had built a life together. I never had the heart to tell Shantae about you or you about her. I didn't want to hurt either of you...especially not you, my wife. Shantae was good to me. She was loyal, and she had never done anything to wrong me. She had been there through thick and thin and the ups and the downs. But somehow, I still found myself falling in love with you. I just couldn't bring myself to break Shantae's heart, so I did just enough to keep her around.

Throughout the twelve years that she and I were together, she had never gotten pregnant. So at this point, neither of us believed that she could even have kids. When I found out she was pregnant, I begged her to have an abortion, and she cut me completely off. We haven't talked in months, and until yesterday, I thought she had gotten rid of the baby. So, I let it be. I thought it was finally over between her and I. I planned on marrying you all over again, just to get a second chance to be the perfect husband to you. We no longer get money together or nothing. Baby, I promise. Pressure and Pain ran into her the other day, and she was big and pregnant. She has decided to keep the baby, and I just found all this."

"So, you were planning on taking your little secret to the grave, but instead, it came back and bit you in the ass?" Taylor said.

"I never meant to hurt you, Taylor. This was a wakeup call for me. I realize how much our family means to me. I don't want to lose you, baby. I fucked up...been fucking up, but I will never ever do anything else to disrespect you or our marriage. This was my one big mistake. I promise you there won't be another. Baby, please believe me," he begged.

"So, are you going to sign the papers?" She asked.

"I'm not signing over my rights to my child, Taylor," Allen explained. "I totally understand if you can't accept her. I felt fucked up for even asking Shantae to kill my baby. My conscience was eating me alive. I've always stood my grounds as a man, but that was some lil' boy shit. It was selfish as fuck. I was thinking only of you. I don't give two fucks about her. She already got a new nigga. He supposed to be a lawyer. This is why she done sent me these fuck ass papers.

She done had that nigga investigating and find out my address and ain't no telling what else. This square ass nigga already doing too much. I thought that I had killed my baby, but she didn't do it. I can't lie. I'm thankful that she didn't do it. I can sleep at night now. But Shantae and I are done. However, we are having a baby, and I plan on being in this baby's life. All I can do is pray that when I get back, you will still be here because I love you and our kids more than words can express."

"Just go, Allen!" She cried.

Allen hated to leave under these circumstances, but this was more important. He called an Uber and headed back to the airport. This time feeling a lot lighter. Everything was out in the open. Now it was time for him and Shantae to deal with whatever issues they had because the bottom line was simple, she was going to have to deal with him for the rest of her life now. As long as she was giving birth to his child, he would be in the picture.

Taylor was overwhelmed. However, at no point was she thinking of leaving her husband. She believed he was remorseful and truthful. She was not about to let another bitch tear her family apart. She poured her a glass of wine and fixed her a bubble bath. She never thought Allen was perfect, but he was so close to it. She never thought he was a hundred percent faithful either, but she knew for a fact that she had his love and his heart belonged to her. And that was more than enough.

But a baby? This was unthinkable. Now she wondered about Shantae. How did she look? Was she in love with Allen? Was Allen in love with her? Was he going to make love to her and apologize for asking her to abort their baby? Her mind was all over the place.

She was being understanding because she too had a past. The same way that he wasn't born with a silver spoon, neither was she. She just made the struggle look good. When she met Allen, she was working as an escort. She dealt with only real boss ass niggas; mainly stars and ball players. But Allen knew nothing about that. She was paying for college and living well, but she sold her soul to do so. When she met Allen, he was different. Kind, charming, generous, and the sex was off the charts. He was her first real date in years. They went out to dinner and went for walks on the beach. They went skating and bowling and took trips to Jamaica and Bermuda. She had never done any of those things before meeting him.

Growing up was a struggle for her. Her mother was a drug addict and died of a drug overdose when she was 15. Her father was a drug kingpin but was indicted when she was 16. After that, she was passed from house to house until she graduated high school. She got a job at a department store during the day, and was an escort at night. In two years, she had saved up enough money for her own place, a new car, and her first year of college. She quit the department store, went to school in the daytime and was now only an escort. When she met Allen, it changed her whole life. He took care of her. He paved the way for her to become who she is today. She was grateful for him, and she loved him. She was ready to fight for what they had built together, for their family, and for their love. But what she was not about to do was play Baby Mama games. This was his last trip to Florida without her. So, he better be handling his fucking business.

ΔΔΔ

Before leaving to go back to Miami, Chloe and Zoey cleaned their apartment really good while Pain and Pressure slept. They trashed any items that were in the refrigerator that could spoil because they did not know how long they would be gone this time around. They paid the neighbor to keep an eye on their place while they were gone. Once Pain and Pressure arose, they all caught an Uber to the airport to fly back to Miami. While at the airport waiting for their flight to depart, Allen called to let them know that he was in Miami. Since they hadn't arrived yet, they informed Allen of the location of the spare key to their house and told him to make himself at home.

Once they arrived in Miami, Zoey rented a car. They did a little shopping then headed back to their little cottage. Chloe made dinner. The four of them ate before Pain and Pressure hit the streets. They checked on all the traps, then ran down on Allen. The three of them chopped it up for a minute before Pain took off to go and see his baby girl.

Pain stopped and bought Treasure some toys and a couple of outfits. He bought a few things for Candice too. When he got there and put his key in the door, it no longer worked. He beat on the door like a mad man. Candice came to the door with an attitude.

> "Can I help you?" Candice asked as she half opened the door.
> "Candice, find you somebody to play with. Where the fuck my baby at?" Pain asked.

"She is sleeping, so you can leave and come back tomorrow. This time please call first," she said.

Pain pushed right past her. He noticed she had on a Publix uniform on. "Publix?" He laughed. "What's up with that?"

"I dropped out of school. I can work and pay my own bills," she said.

"I've spent over eighty thousand dollars for you to go to school, and months before you graduate, you quit to work at Publix?" He asked in disbelief, bursting into laughter. "This that dumb shit I hate about women. When y'all mad, y'all do and say the dumbest shit. Now make that make sense."

"It doesn't have to make sense to you as long as it makes sense to me. I don't have to live like Atlanta's housewives. As long as I can support myself and my daughter," Candice said defensively.

"Your rent is twenty-five hundred dollars a month. How the fuck Publix gon' to pay your bills? If you was smart, you would finish school and get a real fucking job that can really pay your bills," Pain lectured. "In the morning, take them people they uniform back and take your ass back to school. Stop making permanent decisions off of temporary emotions. No matter how mad you get at me, you owe it to yourself and your daughter to at least finish school. You have worked way too hard. If you are that serious about doing you...I'll give you your space. But I didn't spend all that damn money on your education for you to work at a fucking supermarket. You can have your life, shawty, and I'll still pay the bills until you finish school."

"Oh, now I can have my space?" She questioned.

"You did all this to prove a point...your point is proven," he said. "I'm doing what I'm supposed to do for you and our daughter. I can't sit in the house all day and be a bitch-ass house nigga. Every time I walk out of this house, I put at least a thousand dollars in that safe when I get back. You sittin' here worrying about the wrong shit, and all I'm trying to do is set us up for the future." He gave her the combination to the safe.

"That's for you and my Treasure. You can have every dollar if you are serious about me leaving. Just know when I walk out those doors, I'm not coming back. I'm tired of all the back and forth with you. You are the only bitch I love. You are the only bitch I want to have my kids. You are the only bitch I cater to. If you can't see that, I'll leave. You think it's better out there for you... go get it."

"Who were those bitches that took Passion to her hair appointment?" She asked.

"We met them in Detroit. We getting money with them hoes, that's it," Pain said.

"So, you not fucking neither one of them?" She asked.

"Neither of them means anything to me," he answered.

"That's not what the fuck I asked you, Pain," Candice said. "So, its ok for me to fuck a nigga as long as I put a thousand dollars in the safe every time I come in?"

"Do you want me to leave, Candice?" He asked.

"Is it ok for me to fuck as long as I'm getting money? Answer me, and that will determine if you stay or go," she said.

"Fuck No! It's not ok, and if I found out, I would kill you for trying to do the same shit I do all the time. Is that what you wanna hear?" He asked.

"No, I wanted you to say that we are equal, and I have the same rights as you. But you selfish as fuck. You want an in-house bitch while you slang dick wherever you want to. I want a man that's gonna come home to me every fucking night. I'm tired of sharing my man every time a pretty face or a fat ass comes alone. I'm done. I'm not settling anymore, Pain. So, you can go. I'll drop Treasure off to your mama whenever you want to see her," she responded.

He went and gave Treasure a kiss, and he left. His feelings were hurt, but he understood. He would give her what she was requesting. By the time she finished school, he should be ready to settle down. Mentally, financially and emotionally.

The following morning Candice returned her uniform and went back to school. Pain was right. That was dumb as hell. There was one hundred and sixty-five thousand dollars in the safe. She didn't have to worry about bills. Besides, she had been kicking it with Choncie, and he was already spoiling her. They had already gone on their first date, and it was awesome. He was smart and caring. Fun and funny. They laughed all night. After their date, they sat in the car and talked 'til the sun came up. He was everything that Pain wasn't. She had been holding back, but now that it was really over between her and Pain, she was planning on turning things up a bit.

△△△

Pressure woke up and decided to go see Zoey. He was feeling her even though he didn't speak on it. His actions spoke for him. She was down as hell. They kicked it and talked for hours effortlessly. She was sexy and fun. Everything was easy with her. They had a lot of the same interests and the same views on life. Her intentions were not flawed at all. Her disposition was pleasant, her energy was powerful, and her sex was phenomenal. To top it off, she was about her money and took care of business. She made it hard to stay away.

When Pressure returned without Pain, Chloe already knew where he was. She was feeling some type of way. He never told her he would be there every night, but she was getting used to it. They were not together; they were just friends with benefits. So why was she feeling this way? She needed to pull herself together...and fast.

Pressure and Zoey went into the room. When Pressure got in the shower, Zoey decided to go check on Chloe. "Are you okay, sis?" Zoey asked.

"I can't lie, I'm in my feelings. I guess it's something I just gotta get used to," Chloe responded.

"You don't have to get used to anything. You always have a choice. Never fall in love with a man that's already in love," Zoey schooled.

"Who said he's in love? Better yet, who said I'm in love?" Chloe asked.

"I'm just saying, Chloe. Why don't you ask him what's going on with him and his baby mama?" Zoey suggested. "Me and Pressure talk about everything. I ask questions because I don't have time to be guessing."

"We talk about everything except that. That's what worries me," Chloe admitted.

"Well, bring it up," Zoey said. "Understanding comes from communication."

"I'm good, sis. Go enjoy your man," Chloe said.

"That's not my man. That's my friend with benefits," Zoey corrected.

"Oh, that's what I am? Ya lil boy toy?" Pressure interrupted.

"You are way too much of a man to be called a boy," Zoey corrected him as well.

"Good answer," Pressure said. "So, what's the benefit?"

"We getting money, I'm getting some excellent dick, and I've found a really good friend. That's three in one. I say I'm benefiting well from this friendship," Zoey clarified.

"Sounds like a keeper to me,' Chloe said, giving her sister dap.

"Y'all shot out," Pressure said.

"You made the rules; I'm just following them," Zoey said.

"They are my rules. I can change them whenever I feel like it," he said.

"Good night, sis," Zoey said as she followed Pressure to the room. He was wrapped in a towel, looking like a Mr. Goodbar. Before he could say anything, his dick was in her mouth. She got right into action. She sucked him up like she missed it. She put her all into it...every time. She was playing for keeps.

She wanted him all to herself. All she had to do was play her cards right. The chemistry between them was already magical. There was no need to be extra. They went well together. Like Peanut Butter and Jelly. All he had to do was acknowledge the fact that she was indeed the girl for him.

CHAPTER SIX

Passion and Dre had been talking every night. Tonight, they made plans to go on their first date. He planned on taking her out to eat and after that, to the movies. Passion was so excited. A'niya did her hair and makeup. Her makeup had a soft, natural look, and her hair was styled in a messy but sexy bun with a bang. It was simple, but on her, it looked nice and elegant. She was beautiful. She decided to wear a Prada jean dress with heels and a purse to match. She wore her Herringbone necklace and bracelet set. She never took off her rings. She was young, pretty, and innocent but also sheltered and curious about all the things she felt she missed out on during high school. This was her first ever real date. She was nervous. She checked herself in the mirror a thousand times. The closer time came for him to pick her up the more butterflies filled her stomach.

"I can't wait to meet this nigga that got you so intimidated," A'niya said.

"I am not intimidated, I'm just a little bit nervous," Passion admitted. Then, a knock at the door startled them both.

A'niya coached her, "Take a deep breath and relax. You look too good to feel anything but confident. Now let me meet Mr. Cupid."

Passion opened the door to find Dre standing there looking like he should be on the cover of Hot Boy Magazine. He was dressed to kill and smelled good enough to eat. A'niya was in a trance. Passion interrupted by clearing her throat.

"My bad. I'm A'niya, Passion's roommate and best

friend," she said. "Please make sure that she has a great time and that she makes it home the exact way she left. It is nice to meet you."

"Nice to meet you too, I'm Dre. The plan is to bring her back just a little different...smiling even harder than she is right now," he said.

"I see all of your teeth as well," Passion said.

A'niya stepped aside so he could come in. He was smiling so hard as he stepped inside and looked Passion up and down.

"Damn, Shawty, you looking good as fuck," he complimented.

"Thank you," Passion responded, blushing so hard that her cheeks were almost pink. "I know I ain't gotta tell you that you looking good because I'm sure you already know that."

"I try," Dre replied humbly.

"You are doing a damn good job. I gotta give it to you," A'niya said and both Dre and Passion laughed.

"Are you ready?" He asked as he reached for Passion's hand.

"Yes, I am," she said as she accepted his hand and they headed towards the door.

"I meant what I said," A'niya said, now looking dead serious.

"I got you, lil' Mama. Just chill." Dre said as he and Passion walked past her hand in hand, exiting the dorm.

He walked her to the passenger side of the car and opened the door for her. Once she was in the car, he closed the door and jogged to the driver's side. He was just as excited as she was. It was just something about Passion that was intriguing to him. They went to a spot in the hood called 'The Potato Shack.' The line was wrapped around the building, but it moved rather quickly. He ordered a fully loaded seafood stuffed potato for the both of them. It was loaded with hearty chunks of lobster, shrimp, crab, scallops, broccoli, cheese, and a garlic butter sauce with parmesan sprinkle on top. They sat under the umbrellas that were set up for those that wanted to eat outside and enjoyed their dinner. They laughed while making jokes about the people in line like kids.

After eating, they went to Wet Willies on South beach for drinks. She chose a green apple lemonade with a shot of patron. He got the same thing but with a double shot, then headed to the movies. After over an hour at the movies, they opted to leave because the movie was not what they expected. Dre decided that he would take her back to the beach, but this time, instead of getting drinks, they would just get to know each other better. But first, they walked hand in hand through Walmart to find a blanket for them to sit on once they got to the beach.

When they arrived, they sat right by the water and talked about everything. After hours of chilling there, Passion agreed to go with him back to his place. She was feeling herself and him so she was not ready for her night to end. They watched music videos and vibed until they fell asleep in each other's arms. She couldn't have asked for a better ending to a perfect first date. She was all smiles.

ΔΔΔ

Allen pulled up to Shantae's place in a moving truck with everything you could think of. He used his key and walked right in. Shantae was in the kitchen cooking.

"Have you lost your fucking mind?" Shantae asked in utter disbelief. "You can get the fuck out of my house and leave my key. Who the fuck do you think you are?"

"I'm your baby daddy. Ain't this what you wanted? That's who I think I am," he responded. "You already know I ain't going nowhere until you and I come up with some kind of understanding. Because me signing over my rights ain't happening, lil' mama. I came here to make peace between us for our baby. You have every right to feel the way you feel. I don't expect you to ever forgive me, but you will respect my mind as a man and as the father of this baby."

"I'm willing to hear what you gotta say, but don't play with me like I'm a little girl," she said. "Walking in my shit like you're still paying bills. Give me my key now. Then we can talk."

Allen gave her the key because she was right. That was cocky and dead wrong. That was really just his way of saying fuck you and yo' nigga…y'all don't run shit. Shantae knew that, and that's what pissed her off the most.

He pulled out a chair for her to take a seat, and she did. He joined her as he began to speak. "First of all, I want you to know that I mean it when I say I was wrong, and I sincerely apologize. You decided to go against what I asked you to do, and I respect you even more for having your own mind and taking a stand for you and the baby. That also means that you and I have to deal with each other forever now because co-parenting is a major lifelong commitment. I am not signing those fucking papers. As long as there is breath in my body, I'm going to take care of what's mine, and I'm going to be a part of his or her life. No negotiating on that period.

I'm not sure whether or not this bitch ass new nigga you got snooping all in my business told you, but I'm married, Shantae. And I have two sons. So, the fact that this nigga sent anything to my house already got him on my hit list. I don't care nothing about you having a nigga, but he better stay in his lane before his fuck ass disappear or end up walking around with a shit bag. You could not have told the nigga about me for real. Otherwise, he would know better."

"The paternity papers were not to attack you; they were sent to free you," she explained. "You made it clear that you didn't want me or this baby, so why can't someone who does want us to be in his life have full rights to her? That way you and that bitch can live happily ever after."

"Watch your mouth when referring to my wife," he said.

"Nigga, fuck you and fuck your wife! Fuck you mean," he shot back.

"You claim you got you a good nigga now, so what the fuck you so mad for?" He asked. "You already got some old ass nigga shooting worms up in you. It ain't like you sitting around waiting on me."

"Get the fuck out my house, Allen!" She exclaimed. "I will not sit here and allow you to insult me like I ain't shit. I never gave you a reason to step out on me and fall in love with another woman! I did everything you asked of me and you sitting here talking to me like I'm some shit eater? Like I wronged you in some way. Demanding that I respect your wife and shit. Fuck your wife, Allen." At this point, Shantae was overheated.

She was yelling and crying and ready to go toe to toe with him. Now he was quiet and feeling like shit. A woman in tears always broke Allen's toughness. "It took this nigga to tell me that you were married with kids. How could I miss that?"

"You missed it because I still made sure we were good... that you were good. I never changed up on you, Shantae. I never treated you differently," he answered.

"Not until it was time to have a baby with me," she said. "You wanted me to kill my baby...my first baby at that. Just so you can hold on to a bitch. Nigga, she got your last name, but I was there when you had nothing! Where this bitch came from? What did she do for you that I didn't, Allen?! Oh, let me guess, she just gets to have babies and shop and live her best life while I'm down here running the trap making money for Y'ALL! That's how you see me, Allen? After all these years?"

A knock on the door startled the both of them. It was Pain and Pressure. Allen had asked them to help him set up his daughter's room. They had been outside for a minute waiting for Shantae to calm down. You could hear her all the way outside. Figuring Allen probably needed a smoke break really bad, Shantae opened the door. When Allen saw Pain and Pressure, he walked outside. He took two shots of liquor, smoked a joint, and then they started unloading the truck. When Shantae saw them coming with furniture and shit, she jumped up and met them at the door.

"What is this, and where are you going with it?" She asked.

"This is for our daughter's room, Shantae. It's the least I can do," Allen answered.

She moved aside and let them walk by. They unloaded the truck and then began to assemble the furniture. Pain had a bottle and his Bluetooth speaker. The three of them talked shit and had drinks while putting everything together and setting it up. Allen knew the conversation between him and Shantae was far from over. She needed closure. She wanted answers at the least, and she deserved them. He left Pain and Pressure working and slid downstairs to find that Shantae had gone back into the kitchen to pick up where she left off with cooking before he interrupted her when he first arrived unexpectedly. He just stood there and watched her for a minute, realizing that he never let her go because he loves her too.

"You look beautiful pregnant with my baby. You're glowing. I wish I would have been here in the beginning," Allen admitted.

"You chose not to be here," she said without looking at him.

He walked up to her and asked her to sit down as he took over in the kitchen. "Shantae," he said, turning her face to him. "I promise you that I'll always take care of you and be here for you. I feel obligated to do that, not because I have to but because I want to. I've always taken care of you. Hurting you was never my intention. That's why I didn't have the heart to tell you about my wife. I didn't want to tell you because I never wanted it to end between us. I was selfish and inconsiderate to both of you.

You did nothing to deserve this. It's not at all your fault. It's me. I met her at the gym. She was here on vacation. We kept in contact. She came to see me and I went to visit her. The next thing I knew, she was pregnant. Me being excited about having my first child, I spent even more time with her. Finally, I bought a house in Detroit, so I could help with the baby while she finished school. And then she was pregnant again, and I had fallen in love with her. I married her while still desperately trying to hold on to what we had and not wanting to hurt or lose you. I know you and I planned on being together forever. I never thought the day would come where you and I would both be seeing someone else. And I know that there is still so much love between the both of us...too much for us to be enemies. Too much to let somebody else come between the friendship and bond we have built. I hurt my best friend; I regret that more than anything in this world."

Shantae knew Allen meant every word he was saying. It still did nothing to stop the pain. The fact that he was there, begging for her forgiveness, putting their daughter's room together, in her kitchen cooking, had brought back so many memories of him and her together. Just when she was starting to get over him, there he was. Looking good and smelling good. But it definitely didn't feel good. This time he was there to let her go because he had fallen in love with someone else and married them. It hurt so bad, but there was nothing she could do about it. He was being honest. She knew that he loved her, but it was obvious that he loved his wife much more.

"Someday, I will forgive you, Allen. But right now, the pain is far too deep," she admitted. "For my whole life, you have been my everything. Now, I'm trying to learn how to live without you."

"Don't try to live without me," he pleaded. "Let's learn to live together. We have been too strong for too long. Now we gotta raise this baby…together. Anything you or she may need, I'm going to provide." He wiped her tears as they sat and talked out their differences. They agreed to put their issues aside for the sake of their baby. Allen promised that he would be there when she gave birth. Allen finished cooking as they made plans for their baby's arrival.

As Pain and Pressure came down the stairs to let Allen know that they were done and about to leave, someone knocked on the door. It was Marcus. Shantae's new man. She got up and opened the door. Allen moved around in the kitchen as if he was home, letting it be known that he runs shit.

Marcus walked in feeling some type of way. Not only was this nigga in the kitchen cooking, but he had his homeboys with him like this was his house, and Shantae was acting like this was normal. He was so pissed, but he held his composure.

"Marcus, this is Allen. My baby's father. Allen, this is Marcus," Shantae introduced.

"Nice to meet you," Marcus said, holding out his hand to shake Allen's hand.

Allen just looked at him, and without accepting his handshake, he walked upstairs to get his things. When he came back down, he told Shante that he was going to be heading back to Detroit in a day or two but would return before then for the final touches in his baby room. He kissed her on the forehead as if Marcus was not standing there and walked out with Pain and Pressure.

"I'm so sorry about that, baby. I had no idea that he was coming. They were just setting up the baby's room. Are you hungry? I made stew beef," she said.

"You made stew beef? Or did he make stew beef? Because it looked like to me, he was the one cooking," Marcus said with malice.

"Awww, baby, cut it out. You have no reason to be jealous," she said sweetly.

"I'm not jealous, but I do feel disrespected. What was up with the kiss? Or him not wanting to shake my hand," he stated.

"Maybe he's jealous. You do have a really sexy bad bitch that was once his," he pointed out. "I hope that's what it is. I felt like you belonged to him for a minute," he said.

"Baby, stop it. I belong to you and you know that," she said. "We just sat down and aired things out. We agreed to raise the baby together—the four of us. I personally don't have a problem with that. Do you?"

"Not as long as that's all it is. Just don't play me like a fool, Shantae. I have feelings like everybody else," Marcus admitted. "Don't have me working hard to mend your broken heart if you are going to let him break it all over again."

"Baby, you are overthinking the situation. If I tell you that there's nothing between me and him, that's what I mean," Shantae explained. "He has the right to be in his daughter's life if he chooses to. I was not going to beg him, but I am not going to deny him that right either. I understand everything you're saying, and he was disrespectful. But you gotta have faith in me. I'm not going backwards. I'm moving forward...with you. Now give me a kiss and sit down so we can eat dinner." Marcus removed his hat and took a seat. She fixed his plate and then joined him. They sat and ate dinner and talked about his day.

They went upstairs to check out the baby's room. "This is so beautiful," Shantae said with excitement in her tone.
She loved what they had done to the baby's room. It now looked like a fairy princess's room. It was perfect for her little princess to come. Marcus smiled and tried not to show animosity, but inside, he was on fire. This nigga had another thing coming if he thought he was going to walk in and out of Shantae's life as he pleased. She was his bitch now, and he was going to learn to respect that. Or he would end up missing just like his ex-wife.

The next morning Allen came over and finished up the baby's room. They talked about his and Taylor's situation. Allen was honest when he told her that he had no idea what to expect when he got home. He didn't know if his wife would forgive him or if she would be already gone when he returned. He admitted that he was crazy in love with Taylor and would be devastated if she left. This time Shantae sat and listened as a friend. She knew that Allen was stressed out. It was written all over his face. A part of her hoped that Taylor was long gone when he got back home, but did she really want him back on a technicality, knowing that he was really in love with someone else? Her mind was all over the place, but she listened.

"What's up with buddy? You fucking with him for real or just doing something? Does he treat you well?" Allen asked.

"He is good to me. I fucks with him, but it's nothing like what you and I had. I don't think I'll ever love anyone the way I love you," She admitted.

"You ain't supposed to," Allen joked. "I know you put that good pussy on pops already."

"I did not. Who fucks another man other than the baby daddy while pregnant? You already know I don't rock like that. And the pussy ain't too good... you gave it up," she said.

"I'm trying to give it up. I'm thinking about feeding my baby right now. But I'mma try to walk out of here doing the right thing for the first time," Allen said.

"You better. Because when you want it, I'mma give it to you. I care nothing about your wife," she said.

"You are not supposed to," he said, contemplating making love to her just one last time.

They talked for a little while longer, then Allen decided to leave before he complicated the situation any further than it already was. He gave her a friendly goodbye kiss and left feeling proud of himself. He would no longer play games between the two women. He was going to do everything in his power to make things right with Taylor. That means he had to completely let Shantae go. Even that good ass pussy.

ΔΔΔ

When Allen got back home, Taylor was sitting by the pool with a glass of wine. The boys were in the pool having a blast. When they saw Allen, they screamed "Daddy, Daddy!" He took a seat next to Taylor, kissed her and splashed water on the boys, playing with them for a little bit before turning his attention to Taylor.

"For some reason, knowing that you were going to see another woman did something to me. I've barely eaten, barely gotten any sleep. I missed you like crazy. Did you have sex with her this time too, Allen?" Taylor asked slightly afraid of what the answer to that question might be.

"I didn't touch her, baby. I told her the truth. That I love you more than anything in the world and that I was going to do everything in my power to save our marriage. I will not do anything to risk losing you ever again, Taylor," he answered truthfully. She believed him.

"I love you, Allen. I love you so much," she said. "And I made a vow to love you for better or for worse. So that's what I'm going to do. I'm going to try my best to work through this, but there will be no more of you going to Florida alone. From this point on, everything is we. I also had the lawyer draw up documents requesting joint custody. I'm not knowingly sharing my husband with no one. I'm not playing no Baby mama drama. Back and forth with you and this bitch. I'm going to stay in my lane, and she damn sure better stay in hers. As your wife, what's yours is mine. So, WE will be a part of this baby's life together. You and her can get used to me being right in the mix. I'm going to stand by your side, but I'm begging you not to make a bigger fool of me than you already have. I understand that you're not perfect. Neither am I. You loved my flaws away, and I plan on doing the same for you. But there will not be a next time. Next time I'm taking everything you own, and the kids, and you will never see us again. And that's not a threat...that's a promise."

"Baby, I promise you there will not be a next time," Allen assured.

"Good. Can you get the boys ready for dinner and bed? I'm ready to make love to my husband," Taylor requested.

Allen got the boys out of the pool and made them shower up. He put the TV on The Disney Channel and kicked it with them while they waited for dinner to arrive. When the food came, he fixed their plates, and they ate dinner together. After dinner, they washed their hands and crawled into bed. It was barely dark outside, but the kids didn't know the difference. Allen was trying to hurry up so he could get to his Taylor. He had missed her so much, and now that he knew she was not leaving him, he was ready to make the best love to her he had ever made.

When he made his way to their room, Taylor was dressed in a royal blue lingerie with six-inch pumps on. She had let her hair down and applied light makeup. He was a lucky man. She was so beautiful and sexy. She motioned for him to sit in the lazy boy recliner as she danced for him nice and slow. He realized that he had bruised her ego. He had her feeling like she had to do more in order to keep him. Reality sunk in. He had been selfish and inconsiderate, and in the process, he had hurt both of the women he loved.

'Thinking out Loud' by Ed Sheeran serenaded the air. This was one of her favorite songs to dance to as she killed the dance just like the lady in the video. Allen never knew she could dance. Had he been neglecting her? The way she was killing this dance, she had to have practiced it a thousand times. Where was he? How did he miss that? What else had he missed? He felt like such a shitty man and an even more terrible husband. Tears filled his eyes for the first time since his grandma died. Regret filled his heart. He would spend the rest of his life trying to make it up to her.

He changed the song to '*Her Heart*' by Anthony Hamilton and put it on repeat, then grabbed her and pulled her into him. He took his time and made love to her body with his tongue. He went from her putty cat to her asshole. Nice and slowly, he sucked on her ass cheeks softly. She was ready. her clitoris had swollen up as she enjoyed the moment. She screamed in ecstasy while he devoured her body. The cum ran down his fingers as he fingered her while sucking on her toes and every part of her body. She had already cum twice before he slid his girth inside of her wetness. It was like an oven. She was so hot. Her walls gripped his dick like no tomorrow. He couldn't hold back. After a few strokes, he let the first one go. But there was no stopping him after that. He took his time and worked on her slowly, but he couldn't help but speed up the paste. It was too good. He flipped her over and went in even deeper as he beat her from the back.

PAP! PAP! PAP! PAP! Was the sound of his skin slapping against her fat ass. He was about to bite his lip off. It was so good to him. His dick head swelled as her love button hardened. Both of them were completely wrapped in each other's love as they reached another climax at the same time. They were fucking each other with a purpose. They both had something to prove…their love for each other. After that, nothing needed to be said. They were reunited as one, and it felt so good. Together they would stand strong and overcome anything that was meant to break them.

Two weeks later, Shantae received an envelope in mail from the law office of Bill Stoner. It was addressed by Taylor and Allen Crawford. The petition was asking for joint custody of Allen and Shantae's unborn child. Shantae was so furious.

"That nigga just going along with whatever that bitch say! He knows that I'm going to let him see this baby whenever he wants to. That hoe is just mad, but I don't want his dog ass," Shantae went on and on as she read the papers to Marcus on the phone.

"Calm down. You know me. We are going to fight fire with fire," Marcus said, letting the lawyer side of him show. "Let me dig into their lives a little bit more. I'm sure I can dig up some dirt on both of them. I don't want you to worry. It's not healthy for you or the baby. You don't even have to cook dinner tonight. I'll bring home takeout. Just relax until I get there to rub those pretty little feet."

"Okay," she agreed. And she did just that. She took a deep breath, then ran her some bath water. She soaked for a while and then decided to take a nap. Marcus woke her up by ringing the doorbell. He was smiling from ear to ear. "'What the hell are you smiling so hard for?" she asked, not really in the mood.

"Didn't I tell you to let your man handle it?" he said while poorly attempting to hide an envelope behind his back. She eagerly reached for the envelope as he moved it just out of her reach. "Aht, Aht, give me a kiss first," he said then puckered his lips.

"Baby, give me the envelope." She pouted.

He handed it to her, and the contents inside blew her mind. It was pictures of Taylor posing as an escort. Three different ads: One with her wearing all white sucking a lollipop; Another she wore all black with a whip and a trench coat looking like a Dominatrix; The last she had on all red with red bottom six-inch stilettos. She was so fucking beautiful it crushed Shantae's spirit. But this hoe still had nothing on her. At the end of the day, she was a prostitute.

There was no way Allen knew she once sold pussy. He despised that. And there was no way a pussy selling prostitute was getting joint custody of her baby. She grabbed her cellphone, snapped a picture of one of the photos and immediately sent it to Allen with a caption attached that read: *"Did you really think I was going to let a prostitute raise my baby... Ha! Jokes on you."* She hoped that Allen would come running back to her when he found out that for the right price his pretty little wife could be bought.

"Now bring your pretty ass over here and give me a kiss," Marcus demanded.

She gave him a kiss. "I can't wait to give you so much more because you deserve it," she said, smiling from ear to ear. Truthfully, she was not thinking about Marcus at all. She was thinking about all the drama this little envelope was about to cause. She loved how Marcus went hard to make sure she came out on top. He was just as obsessed as she was with making Allen's life a living hell.

'Let the games begin,' she thought to herself as Marcus rubbed her feet with hot oil.

CHAPTER SEVEN

Pain and Chloe had gone out the night before last. They entertained each other and had a great time. Afterwards, they chilled and laid in bed at the cottage smoking on a joint. They sexed each other until the sun came up. It was now noon, and neither of them wanted to move. As Chloe laid there in his arms, she figured this would be a great time to have a heart-to-heart conversation with him. So far, she had been doing a great job of keeping her feelings in check, but it was getting harder and harder by the minute. He was handsome, fun, generous, they got money together, and he was dicking her down properly. They would spend days together, just the two of them. They woke up together every morning and it felt great. But what was it? Convenience? Was she a rebound because he and his baby mama were beefing? Or did she mean something to him? All these thoughts ran through her head at one time. Finally, she just asked the question that she'd been wanting to know for so long.

"What's going on with you and your baby mama?" Chloe asked.

"What you mean?" Pain responded.

"I mean, what's going on with you and her? You talk to me about everything except that," Chloe clarified.

"Why would I want to talk to you about that? When I'm with you, that's the last thing I want to think about or talk about, but what do you wanna know?" Pain questioned.

"I don't know. We spend a lot of time together, and it gets really addictive. Am I going to wake up one day to you telling me that it's over because you're going home? If so, that's cool. I just want to know, so I don't allow myself to fall even deeper for you," she explained.

"I like you a lot...more than a lot. I've kept my feelings at bay as much as possible because I know you have a family, and I don't want to put myself in a situation to be hurt, but you make it really hard for me not to."

"Right now, me and her are not even talking. She says she's moving on and I'm giving her space to do so. Do I want to? No. Of course not, but she's tired of me being in the streets. The streets are all I know. I'm not a lil boy. I'm not moving how she want me to move. I'm a grown ass man. I take care of my home, her, her college tuition, and my daughter, all from the same streets that she hates so much. So, I'm giving her room to find her a house-nigga, if that's what she wants. In the meantime, here we are, doing what we do," he answered.

"Doing what we do?" She repeated, looking at him confused.

"I've been through this many times with my baby mama, and somehow we end up right back together. I don't want her to move on. She don't want me to move on. It's an ongoing emotional rollercoaster. We keep going in circles. I can't promise you that the circles are over or that I won't go back," he admitted. "I love her and my daughter more than anything in the world. I pray that she is still waiting for me when I am ready to be the man she wants me to be.

Until then I am open to whatever becomes of me and you. I'm not running from or fighting the feelings I feel for you. I do care about you...a lot. And I don't want to stop doing what we are doing today. Tomorrow is not even promised."

Chloe was understanding and heartbroken at the same time. She knew better than to try to compete with love. She respected his honesty, and she hoped he would respect hers when it was time for her to move on. She refused to fall in love with someone that was already in love with someone else.

"Now what?" Pain asked, knowing that his response was not what she wanted to hear. He felt like he owed it to her to be truthful. He really liked her and didn't want to hurt her or ruin their friendship.

"Well...I respect that you kept it real," she said. "I'm not really sure how I feel. Maybe I need to explore Miami a little bit more. Explore my options. I'm sure I'll meet someone that doesn't already come with reservations."

Pain smothered her with the pillow. "Wrong answer," he said. "Let's try this again."

They fought playfully in bed, and that led into an intimate moment full of lust because at this point, love was out of the picture. Afterwards they ate lunch. Chloe wasn't mad. She respected his gangsta. She truthfully felt like at the end of the day, she was in the better position. She would not allow herself to fall any deeper. She could still fuck him, just without emotions. When he was spending time with his family, she would go out and mingle. Meet people. They had become regulars at a few of the local clubs. She was not afraid to go alone. Niggas have probably been waiting for the chance to catch her solo. Pain was saving his money and planning to be a better man for the woman he loved. Pressure and Zoey were falling in love. It was only right that she had a man of her own as well.

While Chloe and Pain were out that previous night, they had recruited two new girls, bringing the total to five more new recruits since the last deal. Tonight, they would have to go hard because Passion's twenty-first birthday party was coming up soon. The plan was to make the trip at least a week or two before the party. With only three weeks left, it was time to focus on getting money.

This time the girls were staying in Detroit until further notice. Tonight was ladies' night at G-5, so ladies got in for free and drank free all night. There would be a club full of drunk ass broads. Chloe and Zoey worked one side of the building while Pain and Pressure kept watch from afar. They mingled with the girls all night. Zoey shot niggas down while Chloe collected numbers. Pain knew this was her way of acting out because of the conversation they had earlier. He definitely was not enjoying the night, but he told himself he would take it out on her in bed. Tonight, there would be no lovey dovey. She was getting grudge fucked.

After a few hours there, they decided to go to 'Lady Luck,' which was a well-known trick spot. This was an after-hours joint that opened when all the other clubs closed. The club featured a champagne room that they rented by the hour, so you could get busy right there if you wanted to. Most of the chicks that came there were on coke, pills, molly, flakka, or some type of drug. Niggas came there looking for action. It was the perfect recruit spot. In no time, they had gained four more girls. Ten was the goal, but nine would do.

The following morning, they decided that it was time to turn the recruits into money. Chloe and Pain would ride up to Detroit in the RV along with the girls. Zoey and Pressure planned on flying. They would take the rest of the day to spend time with one another before leaving Miami because they were not sure when they would hook up again once they left Detroit. They all packed up and prepared for the task at hand.

The next morning, Pain, Chloe, and all the girls headed out. Including Chloe, there were ten girls in the RV and Pain. He was like a kid in the candy store. Chloe laughed as half of the girls hit on Pain. They listened to music, smoked weed, and made fun out of their road trip. One of the girls actually caught Chloe's eye. She was thick in all the right places. Smooth dark chocolate skin with hazel eyes and the cutest dimples. She put her in the mind of Gabrielle Union, but she was badder. This chick had no waistline. Her swag was sick. She didn't fit with the other girls. She seemed out of place. As Chloe talked to her and got to know her a little bit, she realized she loved her attitude as well. Chloe just listened as Rein talked and flaunted her confidence.

"I plan to take over that nigga whole empire. In no time I'll be in control of all his girls and cooking breakfast for the boss man naked in stilettos," Rein said. "I know how to take charge and make a nigga see that I'm worth way more than just selling pussy. My pimps always end up falling in love with me and then not wanting me to sell nothing at all."

After being on the road for over ten hours, Pain and Chloe mutually decided to stop at a motel to get rooms and get some rest. They were in no rush. Especially being that it may be a while until they see each other again.
Chloe looked at Pain, "Who's going to be our special guest tonight?" He looked at her like she was crazy. She looked back at him with a serious face.

"Why don't you choose?" Let me see what turns you on," Pain responded.
Chloe looked at Rein, "You're coming with us." Rein jumped out, and the three of them went to the front desk and paid for two rooms. Three of the girls decided to stay in the RV to oversee their belongings. The other five girls went into one room; Pain, Chloe, and Rein went into the other.

Before Pain could undress, Rein was eating away at Chloe… PROPERLY! Chloe loved every minute of it. Pain jumped right into the action. He put on a condom and slid right up into Rein from behind as she continued to feast on Chloe's wetness. After an amazing orgasm, Chloe returned the favor. She gave Rein some of the best head she ever had. As Chloe sucked on Rein, Pain fucked Chloe from the back, and he was enjoying it. Once Rein came, she grabbed her Pocket Rocket vibrator, turned around while lying flat on her back and slid her head beneath Chloe, who was still on all fours, moaning loudly from being hit decently from the back. In the position that she was now in, her titties were directly beneath Chloe's mouth, and Chloe's perky breasts were dangling in her face from above. Her nipples were rock hard.

Rein reached up and placed her toy on Chloe's clitoris softly and let it vibrate while she sucked on her nipples. Pain went deeper and deeper from behind. The feeling was amazing. Chloe had never cum so hard or moaned like that in her life. For the first time ever, she squirted, causing her body to shake uncontrollably. Her and Rein started to tongue kiss, which quickly brought Pain to an explosion. That sight alone was electrifying and super sexy. Not to mention, both these chicks had some good wet ass pussy...he couldn't hold it any longer.

That was just the first of many rounds that night.

Round two, Chloe took all of Pain's hardness into her mouth. She deep throated every inch while Rein gave her the best head she ever had, which in return made her give Pain the best head she had ever given him. He was getting weak in his knees. This shit was just way too good to be true. They switched positions, and now Rein had dick down her throat while Chloe took her to ecstasy. It was a fun turnt up night, and it probably would be the last for Pain and Chloe.

However, it was just the beginning of something new between her and Rein. She liked her... a lot! They had a lot in common, and the head .... the head was a good enough reason alone to keep her. Rein was about to be her bitch, and she would pay for her if she had to.

ΔΔΔ

Pressure and Zoey arrived in Detroit ten hours before Pain and the crew were scheduled to arrive. They took full advantage of their last few hours together before they parted ways. The two of them were exhausted. All the late nights and early mornings, sex 'til the sun came up, plus recruiting had caught up with them. As soon as they arrived at Zoey's place, they ordered food, showered, and headed to bed.

While laying up and watching TV, Pressure looked over at Zoey. "What do you want from me?"

"Why do I have to want something from you, Pressure?" Zoey asked.

"That's just the way life goes. That's not a bad thing unless you have bad intentions," he explained.

"That feels like a trick question," she said. "You have already told me what you have to give. And we agreed on just that. If I want more than what you're willing to give, I would be switching up, and you've expressed to me how much you hate that. So, why don't you tell me what you want from me? I haven't put any limitations on where this could go or my feelings for you."

Her words fucked Pressure's head up. This was a first. A woman that plays by the rules? Most women by now would be already trying to have his baby or move in but not Zoey. She was tough but sensitive and so fucking sexy. A lady in every way. He loved it. He was starting to wonder if he loved her. What he felt for her was unfamiliar. He didn't know how to respond. He felt like he was the one switching up. But fuck it...rules change all the time. As long as he was the one changing them.

"I'm not ready for 'whatever this is we have' to end. I'm feeling you. I enjoy waking up to your scent, your face, and the warmth of your body. I have never let anyone get this close to me. I have never *wanted* anyone this close to me. You make everything so easy."

"That's because it is easy, Pressure. You have a hard time expressing your feelings," she observed.

"That's because I'm not used to having any, baby. This shit new to me. But I ain't trippin'. I kinda like it. I just want to make sure I'm making the right moves. I don't want to ask anything of you if I can't give the same in return," he said.

"Can't give or not willing to give? Those are two different things because you definitely can if you really wanted to," she replied.

"What if I told you that I want you to move to Florida because I can't stay away from you too long?" He asked.

"I would follow you to the moon if you could figure out how to get there. But first, you gotta be 100% sure you want me there. I can't pack up and leave the only life I know if you're not sure. What happens if you get tired of me?" Zoey asked.

"Right now, I can't picture that ever happening. All I can tell you is that if it doesn't work out, the only thing that you'll lose is a lil' time because I can replace everything else. But we'll never win if our focus is on losing," he rationalized.

"I'm all in, Pressure. When you are SURE that you're ready...I'll be waiting. In the meantime, you have nothing to worry about," she assured.

Pressure kissed her intimately, which was something he had never done. He wanted to do things to her that he said he would only do to his wife. He was having feelings that he had never felt. Everything felt so right with them...natural and real. He knew for a fact that he wanted her in his life. In Miami with him. But there was still a part of him holding back. Afraid to give his heart to someone. Afraid of hurting her. Afraid of failing at something.

As he made love to her, so many things went through his head. Was he ready for love and all the drama that came with it? Allen had Taylor. Pain had Candice. Was Zoey his soulmate? Was it time for him to try this love thang? As he made love to her, deep inside, he knew the answer to all those questions. She was absolutely the one, and yes, it was his time for love because he could no longer picture his life without her in it.

After a long night of love making, the two of them slept until morning. The following morning, they went to get breakfast and did a little shopping. With their current predicament still up in the air, they walked hand in hand, enjoying what could be their final moments for a long while because she was not going back to Miami until he figured out wanted to do as far as their relationship was concerned. It actually pissed her off that he had basically asked her to expose her hand when he was not doing the same. She had told him that she was more than willing to move for him, all he had to do was be sure that this was what he really wanted. But it was clear to see that he wasn't because he was still going back to Miami without her. So what was the purpose of their little talk? Just to see how far she would go for him? All the things he said he wanted in a woman were right there in front of him. He just needed to grab them. Instead, he chose to leave them behind.

ΔΔΔ

Pain and the rest of the crew met up with everybody at the truck stop around 2:00 p.m. Allen had already hit up the connect, so that this would be a quick transaction. He was ready. When Chloe got off the RV, Rein was right by her side while all the other girls stayed put. They walked up to Zoey, Pain, and Pressure, who were talking to Allen at the moment.

Chloe politely interrupted, "What's up y'all? This is my girl Rein, and she is staying with me. She was originally going with the rest of the girls, but there has been a change of plans. If anyone has a problem with that, you can deduct $50,000 from my cut. To me, it would be more of an investment than it would be a loss."

"Damn right, baby!" Rein added. "That's a lot of money, but you can rest assured that for you, I will make back every dime and then some. But I just don't want you to throw it up in my face or regret it later."

"Then *make sure* I don't regret it later," Chloe said.

Rein gave her the most seductive kiss. "I promise you will not miss that money because I am money. Nor will you regret this decision because I am a loyal bitch. Your Bitch," she said as she kissed her one more time. All the men were turnt on. That shit was sexy and gangsta. But she was definitely being deducted for it. Business was business, and that was a damn good investment as long as Rein did her part.

"Can I talk to you in private?" Zoey said to Chloe. She was pissed. Rein was a stranger.

Chloe was not about to bring some bitch off the streets into their home.

Before anything else could be said, Pressure stepped in, pulling Zoey to the side. "Baby she has to have a life too. When you're in Miami with me, why should she be all alone? This could be a good thing for her. We both know where Pain is going as soon as we get home. I'm sure she made this decision for a good reason. Besides, we gotta get going, so y'all can discuss this at home. Y'all go to the house and talk about this while we handle business. If you are still totally against it by the time we get back, then we will fly her back to Miami with us."

"She definitely ain't going nowhere with y'all," Zoey said, showing a hint of jealousy, and she was dead ass serious. Pressure laughed. She was sassy and sexy as hell when she was mad. He would enjoy seeing her throw a few fits then fucking a smile back on her face afterwards, he thought to himself as she walked away fire ass hot. He jumped in the RV with Allen, and Zoey jumped in the car with Pain, Chloe and Rein. Pain dropped the two of them off and then headed to the RV rental office, where he would wait to meet and pick up Allen and Pressure once they returned the RV after the deal was completed.

"I love you, sis. I need you to trust me on this and be happy for me. What am I supposed to do while you're in Miami with your man?"

"First of all, that's not my man," Zoey objected. "And second of all, I'm not going to Miami. And if I do, I don't expect for you to be alone, but I never thought you would spend $50,000 dollars on a bitch that you don't even know or bring her into our home without even running the shit by me first. That's crazy as fuck, Chloe!"

"It was a spur of the moment decision that had to be made quickly, sis. I really didn't have time to run it by you. Everything happened so quickly," Chloe said, defending her rash decision.

"That's my point. You don't know her. She could be a fucking serial killer," Zoey said.

"If it works, it works and if it don't, it don't. But I like her, Zoey...a lot. And she's not going anywhere, so can you please stop it? It's mandatory for me that the two of you get along," Chloe pleaded.

"Okay, let me hear your story, Rein," Zoey said, giving her the floor to speak. "I would love to know how you ended up in the RV and somehow into my sister's life. I also would like to know your plans and intentions for my sister."

Rein looked at Chloe as if she was requesting permission to respond. "I don't lie to my sister about anything. You can tell her the truth. I'm grown, and my decision to be with you is final. I just want her blessing," Chloe said.

Zoey looked at Chloe like she was crazy. Chloe gave her a straight stare back.

"Zoey, you are right," Rein began. "I don't know your sister that well. I did not ask her to do this. It was her choice. I haven't even shared my story with her yet. She doesn't even know what a blessing she is to me. We have a connection that neither of us can explain. Your sister don't know that I agreed to come with them to get away from an abusive relationship. I was really afraid for my life. If I had to sell pussy to get away from this nigga, then that's what I was going to do. I felt like nothing could be worse than the situation I was already in. I didn't use my story for sympathy. Me and Chloe just immediately clicked really good. She didn't even know that God was using her to save me because I had no idea what I was going to do. All I knew was no matter where I ended up, I was not about to sell pussy for the rest of my life. I was going to either run away, find a homeless shelter, and rebuild my life or either take over that nigga shit and become the Madam of the operation." Tears filled her eyes as she told her truth.

By the time she was done, they all had tear-filled eyes. Chloe wiped her tears away, and Zoey came over and gave her a hug and a sincere apology. She had judged Rein far too quickly and without even trying to get to know her, and she felt horrible about it.

"I don't want y'all feeling sorry for me," Rein said. "That's why I didn't bring this up before. I didn't want sympathy. I just wanted to be around good people that will treat me the way I'm supposed to be treated and a chance at a fresh start. I will forever be indebted to Chloe. My loyalty to her will never waver. I'm going to stand ten toes down with her and for her to the end. And that's on God."

"Well, I guess the fabulous two just turned into three. Welcome to the family. But, if you hurt or cross my sister, I'm going to kill you myself. And THAT'S on God," Zoey stated.

Chloe hugged her sister so tight. "Thank you, sis. It's not like you're going to be here anyways, but I still want y'all to get along because I have invested in this relationship big time," they all laughed.

"You and Pressure talk like y'all so sure I'm going to be in Miami with him. I told him that I would relocate if he wanted me to. And he still decided to go back without me. Am I the only one who sees something wrong with that picture?" Zoey asked.

"I'm sure he is going to send for you, Zoey. Knowing Pressure like I know him, he's going to get things in order for you first. That's the kind of man he is. And you gotta know that" Chloe assured.

"I hope so because right now I don't like how I'm feeling," Zoey admitted. "I feel abandoned, and I don't even have the right to feel that way. He doesn't owe me shit. I just want him to want this just as bad as I do."

"You got that, sis. Just chill. I promise you everything is going to fall in line. That nigga is fucked up about you. Are you the only one that can't see that?" Chloe questioned.

Zoey was not trying to hear that shit. She wanted to go with him now. She no longer felt right going to sleep or waking up without him next to her. However, she was not going to act like she was desperate. Nor was she about to act like one of his lil' groupies. She was too much of a lady for that. She knew her worth and did not mind waiting until he did too.

ΔΔΔ

Allen and Pressure pulled up on Sota just like last time. They brought the hoes, and he brought the money. In less than thirty minutes, business was done, and they were on their way to drop off the RV and meet Pain. Even though Chloe was willing to pay for Rein, they split the money the same as before. They all respected her decision. Besides, no one wanted to see her alone because everyone knew that Pain was going right back to Candice.

When the five of them all met back up, they gave the girls their share of the pot and said their goodbyes. Pain was missing his daughter and baby mama, and Pressure was ready to find a place for him and Zoey. Playtime was over. And saying goodbye was already hard enough.

Pressure just wanted to get it over with. He kissed Zoey and told her to hold it down until they met again. Pain also said his final goodbyes to Chloe. If he was going to do right from this point on, it was safe to say that he went out with a bang. He couldn't think of a better way to retire. Rein and Chloe had left him feeling like a true King.

Once Pain and Pressure left, Zoey was all alone and in her feelings. She went from worrying about her sister being alone to being the lonely one. Chloe and Rein were now locked up in the room. All you could hear was laughter, and there she was left feeling abandoned.

△△△

With three hours left until their flight departed, Pain and Pressure decided to go with Allen to his house to say goodbye to Taylor and the boys. Taylor was in the kitchen cooking when they all entered the house. She had been pacing the floor patiently waiting for Allen to get home. The look on her face when they walked in the door told all three of them that something was wrong. Pain and Pressure spoke to her and kept it moving on to their nephews who were in the living room watching TV, waiting for dinner to be served. Allen approached her very unbothered by the envelope she held in her hands.

"Another envelope came today. I can't wait to see what this one is all about," Taylor announced.

"Me neither," Allen said with no worry. "I don't have anything else to hide, baby. I've already told you everything." Allen opened the envelope right in front of her.

When he opened the envelope, it felt like a knife had stabbed him in his heart. Taylor's eyes almost popped out of her head seeing the pictures of her posing as an escort. Three different ads; three different websites. She was so embarrassed and afraid of what was about to happen next.

Allen threw the papers in her face. "Out of all the bitches I could marry, I chose an internet whore!" Allen yelled.

Taylor tried to talk to him, but he had no understanding of this shit. Knowing how reckless Allen's mouth was, Pain and Pressure rushed the kids out the back door. Allen went on and on. He told her that he felt like a fucking fool for choosing her over Shantae. "Shantae would never sell her body. She can't be bought!" He yelled while Taylor was crying and trying to make him understand that this was before she met him.

"What was I? A lick, a trick or a meal ticket? What else are you keeping a secret?" he screamed as he made his way to the backyard to get Pain and Pressure.

When the three of them headed for the front door, Taylor tried blocking him. He pushed her so hard that she stumbled and fell. Pressure helped her up and told her to just allow him some time to calm down. There was no use in trying to talk to him right now. She knew that Pressure was right, so she stopped fighting and broke down in his arms.

They jumped in the truck with him and headed straight for the highway. Pain realized that they had passed the airport exit a while ago. He knew that his four-hour plane ride had turned into a fourteen-hour drive. Allen needed the support so he laid back, got comfortable and went to sleep. The ride was quiet. Pressure tried to reason with Allen, but there was no use. All Allen had was the $80,000 he had just made, his credit card, bank card, and the truck he was driving. He didn't know where he was going or if he was ever coming back. He didn't know anything. Not even his wife.

CHAPTER EIGHT

Dre and Passion laid in his bed eating popcorn and watching a movie. They had been seeing each other almost every night. Passion had even invited Dre to her birthday party. This *thing* between them had gotten serious. They were young and in love. She wanted him to meet her family. She wanted her family to meet the man that stole her heart and virginity. A knock at the door interrupted their vibe. It was Marquise, Dre's older brother. Dre had been ignoring his calls for days now because his brother was on some bullshit. He was deep into the streets and assumed that since he raised Dre, that Dre would be just like him, but he wasn't. As a matter of fact, Dre was starting to really despise him. Lately, the two of them had been bumping heads more and more.

"Nigga, why the fuck you ain't answering my phone calls?" Marquise asked.

"I've been busy, bruh. What's up?" Dre responded.

"What are you busy doing? Laid up with a bitch?" Marquise asked.

"Watch your mouth, bruh. That's my lady, not just some random bitch," Dre demanded.

"Your lady? Nigga I keep telling you, you ain't got no old lady. These hoes for everybody," Marquise stated.

"Your hoes be for everybody. Mine is for me only. And let me holla at you outside," Dre said.

"Yeah, let's take this outside, nigga because I don't want your lil' princess to be afraid of me," Marquise said sarcastically. Passion looked at him and laughed. She was not afraid of him. She actually felt sorry for him.

'A *grown man this hateful towards women had to be gay,*' she thought to herself as he and Dre stepped outside.

She had grown up with two big brothers that were so loving and charming, and they loved women. She knew that something was off with Dre's brother, but he didn't put any fear in Passion's heart, which was something that Marquise didn't like.

"Bruh, what the fuck is wrong with you? I don't give a fuck who you are, you don't come up in my shit being disrespectful to my peeps. I already told you that this ain't it and I'm standing on that, bruh. She is off limits," Dre said.

"Ain't no bitch off limits to me, lil' silly ass nigga. You better get ya head in the game instead of stuck up that bitch's ass. And when you see me calling your fucking phone, you pick it up. You never know what the fuck could be going on," Marquise lectured.

Marquise walked off, talking shit to himself. He jumped in his car and sped off. He then called his peoples and put the order in for Passion to be brought to him by any means necessary.

Dre was so aggravated with his brother. He felt as if every chick Dre met was supposed to be delivered to him when Dre was done with them. Dre once worked as his brother's lead recruiter. He had no problem rounding up two to three hoes every day because he was good looking with a hella swag and a nice ride. He was making good money, but he was having trouble sleeping at night because he would see some of the girls months later, and they looked like shit. That didn't sit well with his spirit at all, knowing that he had a part in that. Marquise would get them strung out on drugs and beat the ones that didn't do as he said. He made them work, day and night, selling pussy. Their lives were over once they came across Marquise.

Dre's conscience ate at him. He no longer wanted to do it anymore, and his brother would not accept or respect his mind. As much as Dre hated it, he felt like he would have to stop seeing Passion for a while to protect her. At least until he moved or figured something out. His brother was crazy and didn't care who he hurt to get what he wanted. And he wanted Passion real bad.

"What the fuck is his problem?" Passion asked.

"My brother is really sick in the head. He is dangerous and stupid at the same time," Dre replied.

"My brothers will match his energy and get right on his level. The next time he disrespect me, I will be calling them," she said.

"Baby, this is serious," he said.

"And I'm serious too," she added.

"My brother sells women for a living. He shoots them up with drugs, abuses them, and it ruins them forever. He keeps threatening to kidnap you if I don't cooperate with his demands, and I can't let that happen," he explained.

"Your brother is not going to fuck with me. He may scare you, but he doesn't scare me at all," Passion assured.

"Passion, I'm serious!" His voice was stern. "We are going to have to chill until I figure something out, baby, because I wouldn't be able to live with myself if anything happened to you. Especially if something happens to you because of me," he said.

"Chill? What are you saying, Dre?" She inquired.

"Baby, I don't know what else to do," Dre admitted. "You talking yo' tough girl talk shit, but I've seen him kill for no reason. I know my brother, and he is one of the most heartless people I've ever met. I cannot put you in harm's way, that would be too selfish of me."

"So, we are breaking up because you can't protect me from your deranged brother...is that what you are telling me right now?" She asked.

"Passion, when his mind is set on something, he won't stop 'til he gets what he wants."

"You sounding like a real bitch right now. I just want you to know that" she informed.

"I don't give a fuck about how I sound to you, as long as I know that I'm doing what's best for you. And I never said anything about us breaking up. All I asked you to do was give me a little time to figure this out," he said.

"But Dre, I don't want to stay away from you for no amount of time. This is crazy," she said. "Why did you even bother if you knew this was going to happen?"

"I never cared about any of the other girls. I honestly thought that he would respect my mind when he saw that I really do love you and that I'm actually happy with you," he explained. "Now I see that he has no real love or respect for me, I have to put a stop to this shit. But until I do that, I can't have you around because it's not safe for you. What's more important...us being together or your safety?"

"That's the dumbest question I've ever heard, Dre. And your brother will be hearing from my brothers. Nobody threatens me. He must not know who the fuck I am." She jumped up and gathered all of her things. She was pissed and talking shit with tears in her eyes. But she refused to let them fall.

"Now I gotta explain to my friends that me and my man are not together because he was too pussy to stand up to his big brother that obviously wants to suck my ass."

Dre decided to let her have her fit. Her words cut like a knife, but he took them like a man. She walked out of the door and slammed it as hard as she could. As soon as the door closed, someone grabbed her, covered her mouth and put a gun to her head. "If you scream, I'm going to blow your fucking brains out right here!" the man said as someone else snatched her keys and jumped in her car. Both vehicles pulled off in a matter of seconds. Dre had warned her a little too late.

Passion was scared out of her mind. Dre had just tried to tell her, but she took his words far too lightly. She was panicking, thinking about all the things Dre had told her about his brother. Was he really going to sell her and shoot drugs in her veins? She had no phone to call her brothers. She began to hyperventilate. Her heart was beating a mile a minute. She tried to calm herself down as she prepared to face Marquise. No matter how scared she was, she would not let him see her fear. He was the real definition of a fuck nigga in her eyes, and she would not give him respect that he did not deserve.

As soon as the van stopped and the door came open, the guy reached for her, and she kicked him in the face with all her might. Blood instantly ran from his mouth and nose. It took two of them to pull her out of the van. When she was finally on her feet, Marquise slapped her so hard that she saw stars. She looked at him and spit the blood that instantly accumulated in her mouth, directly in his face. That infuriated Marquise so much that he made the guys that took her out of the van tie her down while he cleaned his face. When he came back, he stripped her naked and raped her for the first time right there in front of everybody.

"The harder you fight me, the harder I'mma fuck you. Until you understand that I run shit. Not you and your pretty little pussy," Marquise said. "You got Dre's nose open wide, but I'm a grown ass man. I'm going to teach you the difference."

He talked to her and humiliated her in front of everybody. They cheered him on as she cried and begged him not to cum inside of her. She and Dre had been very reckless and had stopped using protection. Now her period was late. She hadn't told anyone yet, not even Dre. She was just praying that she lived to make it through this and that she was not pregnant. With everything going on in her life, a baby was the last thing she needed. She decided to calm down and use her head to get out of the situation alive. Finally, she stopped fighting letting him have his way with her. As soon as she submitted to him, he came…deep inside of her.

"That lil' pussy good," he said while pulling up his pants. "I might have to keep you for myself. I see why Dre is holding on to you so tight."

"He's going to come for me too. I hope you know that. If he doesn't, my brothers will. Either way it goes, you are a dead man walking," she threatened.

"So, I might as well enjoy you while I can then," Marquise concluded. "Get dressed, and please don't make this harder for you than it has to be. Truth is, I kinda like you, and I don't want to have to hurt you, but I will if need be. If you try anything stupid, every nigga in this room is going to test that pussy out. Play at your own risk."

He looked over at Tank, the only guy that looked unimpressed by the whole ordeal. "Take her to Room 6 until I'm ready to go. She's going with me." The guy was feeling some type of way because he had met her before. Tank and Dre had been best friends since middle school, and he knew that Dre was crazy in love with Passion. "I hope you don't try to play hero and help ya boy save this bitch. All three of y'all gone end up on a milk carton," Marquise sternly added.

"I got you, Bossman. You already know I'm not going to play with you like that, Big Bruh," Tank responded. He felt like shit walking her to the room. Dre was his partner, his best friend. He only dealt with Marquise because of Dre. He knew that Marquise was trigger happy for real though, and at the moment, he was not about to risk his own life. He needed to talk to Dre first. However, he knew that Marquise was watching his every move, so he played it cool. As soon as he was given the opportunity, he felt obligated to call him. It was the least he could do.

"Please don't leave me locked in this room. Please let me go." She cried and pleaded.

"You just heard what that man said. I can't let you go,

but I will call Dre and tell him that you are here as soon as I get a chance, I promise. Just stop fighting with him and chill," Tank advised.

"Can you please call my brother, please. His number is easy 305-305-3005. Please call him!" She begged. He tried to remember the number, but it was just too much going on in his head. All he could think about was Dre and how he was going to lose it when he found out that his brother had kidnapped Passion and raped her in front of all his boys. He closed the door, double checked to ensure that he locked it, and then joined the rest of the crew. Passion cried herself to sleep.

Hours later, Marquise woke her up. "Let's go!" he commanded. "We are going for a little ride. If you try me or try to run, I'mma kill you. If you act right, I will not hurt you."

Passion followed him to the car quietly. Something deep inside told her that if she just did what he said, he would not hurt her. It was time for her to use the skills she learned in psychology in her real life. Marquise had mental issues, and she was planning on getting inside of that twisted head of his, one way or the other.

They drove for over an hour on the highway. Finally, Passion asked him, "Why were you so insistent on having me? Was it because you saw how happy I made your brother? I think that you are jealous because you have no one to love. Maybe if you weren't such an asshole, somebody could try to love you."

"You sound so young and confused," he said. "Love is just mixed emotions between two fools. I don't need love. I need money, and I need respect. Dre must remember to never bite the hand that feeds him. I'm using you to teach him a lesson."

"He never bit the hand that fed him, and he don't mind sharing his food. Just not off the same plate. Who in their right mind wants to eat his brother's food?" Passion cried.

"This is bigger than you, lil' mama. That nigga done

forgot who raised him. No bitch comes before me," he said.

"Damn, you sound like a jealous boyfriend instead of a big brother," she said, using reverse psychology.

"I like you better with your mouth closed. Unless you want me to put my dick in it," he said rudely.

"Have you ever been in love? Did she break your heart?" She asked, searching for the underlying issue.

"Yea...My mother," he said angrily.

"What happened to your mother?" She questioned.

"I killed her," he said nonchalantly. "Because she wasn't loyal. She put a nigga before her kids. I'm not finna let my lil' brother do the same dumb shit. I'll kill him too, if I have to. Family over everything."

Passion realized that Marquise was really fucked up in the head, and she felt sorry for him. Whatever he had gone through as a child had scarred him deeply. He never knew how to love because he was only taught how to hate. She was in a terrifying situation. She just prayed that he did not kill her just to get his point across to Dre. Now she understood everything Dre was saying. But it was a little too late.

"Well, just so you know, Dre really looks up to you. He talks about you all the time, and he's never shown any malice or disrespect for you. He still must be his own man and live his own life. He's not a puppet, he's your brother," Passion stated.

Nothing else was said the rest of the ride. When they arrived at the house, it was surrounded by a really high gate. He punched in a code, and the gate opened. Passion knew right then she was going to go through hell to get away from this place. All she could recall on the way there were the two signs she saw. One read: 'Tropical Island Drive' and the other one read: 'Interstate 66: 5 miles'. She remembered seeing that sign right before they took Exit 42 to get off the highway. She couldn't remember anything else. The remainder of the ride, they had taken all back roads. This was definitely something he was used to doing. The house was in the middle of nowhere. It was almost impossible for someone to locate them in the middle of the Boondocks. But as long as she had breath in her body, she would not give up or stop believing that someone was coming for her. Until then, she would keep trying to get inside his sick ass mind.

He got out and opened the door for her. When they walked inside, there was a girl sitting at a desk in the front as if it was her office. She introduced herself to Passion as Dominique. She was Dre and Marquise's sister.

"She's a tough one. She thinks that Dre is coming to save her. He don't know nothing about this spot, so I know he ain't coming. If that nigga call you, tell him to call me," Marquise instructed Dominique.

"Why would you put me in the middle of you and Dre's bullshit? That's not fair, and it's too many other bitches in the world for you to be taking his girl. This is some stupid and messy shit. It's bad for business," Dominique said.

"That nigga needs to learn some respect. He is not finna put no bitch before me," Marquise uttered.

"You sound like a control freak," Dominique said. "That boy is grown. He don't have to follow your footsteps, Marquise, and what are you really teaching him by taking the one girl that he loves? It's not like you need her."

"Stop questioning my moves and take her upstairs. No drugs, and don't put her to work just yet. I'm not done with her," he said right before walking back out the door.

Dominique was twenty seven, Marcus was twenty eight and Dre was only twenty one. Dominique and Marquise were always like paper and glue. When she was only thirteen, Marquise came home from school one day and found his mother trying to force Dominique to have sex with a dirty, drunk, old ass white man. When he witnessed his mother slap Dominique to the floor because she wouldn't cooperate, Marquise lost it. He shot his mother and the man. When his father came home, the police were waiting for him. They had both agreed to put the blame on their father, who was the one who got his mother on drugs and into prostitution in the first place.

Marquise hated him for turning his mother into a dope fiend whore, and he hated his mother for not choosing her kids over the drugs. Now they didn't have to worry about either of them. Dre was in school at the time and didn't know any of this happened. He was only six years old, still innocent, and naive. He thought that his parents left to go to the store one day and never came back. This was a secret that Dominique and Marquise promised to take to their graves and never mentioned again.

Dre looked up to Marquise because he was all he had, as far as he knew. However, as he got older, he realized that he hated the way his brother did things, but he never went against him until now. Today he was ready to kill his brother or ready to die to save the love of his life. He no longer was afraid to stand up to the brother that was once his hero. He and Passion had made plans to start their own family someday. And he was going to make sure that happened as long as he had breath in his body.

Dominique was pissed. Dre was her little brother, and she adored him. She wanted more for him. She would never just turn her back on Marquise, but she was not down with helping Marquise destroy her baby brother either. She and Marquise were like Bonnie and Clyde, but Dre was different. She respected that, but for some reason, Marquise couldn't.

She took Passion to a private room with a shower in it and gave her something to put on.
Passion showered for almost an hour, trying to wash Marquise off of her. No matter how long or hard she scrubbed, she would still never be able to wash away what he had put inside her. She broke down and cried her heart out. Dominique could

hear her, and it was something about those cries that bothered her deeply. This was some real bullshit Marquise was doing. The only people he ever had love for was her and Dre. It was because of Marquise that Dre always had whatever he wanted and needed.

Growing up, Marquise would go get food for the three of them, and Dominique would cook it. All Dre had to do was finish school. However, at some point, Marquise noticed that Dre was a ladies' man. So Marquise started forcing him to bring the girls to him when he was done with them, but he also paid Dre for each one of them.

When Dre saw how much money he could make, he was all in. But once he found out what was happening to the girls, he refused to bring any more. That's when Marquise took his car and made him earn his money. It was either bring in the hoes or have nothing. So he continued to bring the girls, but he became wiser.

That same day, Dre had Tank's mother set him up a business account, so he could start saving his own money. He never had plans on staying around long after finishing school. He would get paid $10,000 for each girl. $1,000 went into his regular account, and $9,000 in his business account. He saved up $150,000 in no time. He was bringing chicks back-to-back. That was about four years ago. He bought his own car, his own crib and stayed dressed to kill. Now, no one could take anything from him or tell him what to do because he was a grown ass man and getting his own money. For some reason, Marquise never respected his mind, but that had to stop right here, right now!

ΔΔΔ

Dre woke up and checked his messages. There were none from Passion. She was so upset when she left, so he figured he would give her a little more time to calm down. He didn't know how he was going to make it up to her or what he was going to do about his brother, but he had to be stopped. He had become so attached to Passion that he could no longer see his life without her. The fact that she called him a bitch ass nigga and a fuck nigga bothered him all night. He felt like less of a man. But she was right…it was his place to protect her and make her feel safe.

A'niya had been calling her phone all morning, and it was going straight to voicemail. Passion often stayed at Dre's house, but she never missed school. Today were tryouts for the cheerleading team. They had worked so hard on a routine that they were to perform together. There was no way passion would miss this. After not hearing from her all day, she knew something had to be wrong. A'niya finally hit Dre up. Since she didn't have his phone number, she had to hit him up through his direct message inbox on Instagram.

> **A'niya:** *Where is Passion? We have tryouts today. She hasn't answered me all day.*

Dre hit her back right away.

> **Dre:** *What do you mean? She left here at 4 a.m. after we had a big disagreement. She was pissed, but why would she not go to school or show up for tryouts? Or respond to you at least?*

> **A'niya:***That's what I'm asking you, Andre.*

Dre called Passion back-to-back with his calls going straight to voicemail every time. *They gotta be just fucking with me,* he thought to himself.

He popped up at Passion's house in less than fifteen minutes. When A'niya opened the door, the look on her face told him that this was not a joke.

"You just fucking with me, right?" Dre asked with

concern.

"No, I'm not just fucking with you, Dre," A'niya said as she pulled out her phone and showed him that she had called her over thirty five times, and every time, her phone went to voicemail.

At that moment, Dre knew that this was Marquise's doing. He ran to his car and pulled off, doing the whole dash. He was over the bullshit and sick of this fucked up ass family. He was ready to carry out his and Passion's plans of starting their own. She made him feel normal. She made his life normal. He drove to the spot where they all hung out and kept the girls at. He kicked in all ten doors, but there was no sign of Passion. The girls were now free to run if they wanted to because the doors were hanging off the hinges. He then made his way to the front, where everybody was chilling and talking shit. He punched in the code and entered with his gun drawn.

"WHERE THE FUCK IS MARQUISE?" Dre yelled.
It got so quiet that you could practically hear their hearts pounding. The first nigga that moved, Dre shot him right in the knee cap.

"I'M NOT HERE TO PLAY GAMES WITH NONE OF YOU PUSSY ASS NIGGAS! I WANT TO KNOW WHERE MY GIRL AT AND WHO TOUCHED HER, AND I WANT TO KNOW WHERE THAT BITCH ASS NIGGA AT!" He grabbed his best friend and put the gun to his head. "Everybody in here know how much I love this nigga. I'll blow his fucking brains out to show y'all that I'm not playing wit' you niggas."

"BRUH, IF YOU DON'T GET THIS FUCKING GUN OUT OF MY FACE, IT'S GOING TO BE ME AND YOU!" Tank yelled nervously. "MARQUISE IS THE ONLY ONE THAT TOUCHED THAT GIRL, AND HE LEFT WITH HER HOURS AGO."

"I love you, Tank. I swear to God I do, but don't you fuckin' lie to me. WHERE DID HE TAKE MY GIRL!?" Dre demanded answers.

"I DON'T KNOW, BRUH! But what I do know is that I'm about to make you kill me. I'm the only nigga in this mutha fucka that ride with you no matter what, and you got a fucking gun to my head. THAT'S DISRESPECTFUL AS FUCK!" Tank snapped.

He moved the gun away from Tank's head. Then turned and shot Marquise's right-hand man in both of his knees. "Tell your homeboy I'm going to kill or be killed about mine. Blood or not. Playtime is over," Dre threatened.

Dre then went everywhere he could think of looking for Marquise, but he came up short. Finally, Marquise called him after getting word that the hoes were running wild and two of his people had gotten shot. Dre answered on the first ring.

"Bruh, my whole life I've done everything you have asked me to do. I didn't complain; I didn't ask questions. I just did it. Now I'm asking you for one favor; let my lady go, bruh. I'm going all out about her!" Dre insisted.

"Naw, lil nigga. I hope you through showing your ass or this bitch body gonna be found floating up a river: 'Breaking News.' The next time you bring your ass in my spot acting like you on that, you better be on that," Marquise said on the other end of the phone line with no remorse for what he's done.

"I'M GOING TO FIND YOU AND KILL YOU, MARQUISE! YOU A REAL BITCH ASS NIGGA FOR DOING THIS!" Dre yelled. He hung up and called Tank. Tank picked up still in his feelings about the way Dre handled him.

"I'm sorry, bruh. The gun situation was just to prove a point to the rest of the niggas," Dre apologized.

"What you proved to them is that you got no love or respect for me. That shit was not fucking cool, but I'mma let it slide because I know you going through something right now, so I understand," Tank admitted.

"You gotta help me, dawg. I got her into this; I gotta get her out of it. Her people are gonna be looking for her. As her man, it's my place to protect her. And of all the people who could have taken her, my own fucking brother took her," Dre confided.

"Bruh, I was going to call you. They're all watching me because they know how I rock with you, so I had to move differently," Tank explained. "I told her to relax and stop fighting back because she was giving him hell at first. I assured her that you would come for her. She asked me to call her brother, but I couldn't remember the last four numbers for shit. I don't know where he took her, but she was good when they left. I will keep my eyes and ears open."

Dre went home and tried to get some rest. He couldn't sleep; he couldn't eat; he had to figure something out. He had to be the one to save her or she would never feel safe with him again.

CHAPTER NINE

Zoey was home cooking and cleaning. The sounds of Monica jammed through the speakers. She was in her feelings. Chloe and Rein were always locked up in the room. She went from feeling like the luckiest woman in the world to being lonely and sad, literally overnight. An unexpected knock at the door startled her. When she opened the door, there was a box from FedEx. Sender: Pressure Edwards. She ripped the package open with so much excitement. There was an invitation to Passion's 21st birthday party along with the most elegant dress Zoey had ever seen. It was an all-black, slim-fitting Versace dress with a V-shaped back. The cleavage area was outlined in diamonds. There were also heels to match. Tears ran down her face as she let her emotions run free. Attached was a note that read:

> I'm ready. These few days without you let me know just how much I need you here with me. I miss your scent, your smile, and everything about you. I'm missing a part of me that only you complete.
>
> *Your Man, Pressure*

Zoey was flabbergasted. The package also included a one-way ticket from Detroit to Miami. Leaving on Friday morning at 8:00 a.m. The party was scheduled to be held the following Saturday night. That meant she would get to meet his entire family. Excited was an understatement. She called for Chloe and Rein to come so she could show them the dress, the invitation, and the airline ticket. They were both truly happy for her. They spent the rest of the night helping her pack and reminisce. Zoey would've never in a million years thought that she would move to Miami to be with a man leaving her twin sister behind. However, she could not wait to get to her man. She had no doubt in her mind that this was the man for her, and she would not miss that flight for nothing in the world. She could see herself spending an eternity with him easily.

△△△

Taylor had called Allen a thousand times, but he was not answering the phone. He was a man with pride, and the one thing he took pride in was Taylor. The fact that there was no telling how men had her before he did, enraged him. He had put her on a pedestal so high that even she couldn't reach it. This was not his side piece; she was his fucking wife, and half the world has seen her naked. After realizing that he was not going to pick up, she decided to call Pressure. He listened as she poured his heart out. Pressure saw things totally different from Pain and Allen. He was more mature when it came to passing judgment. That was just something he never did. There could have been a thousand reasons she chose that route. You never know what a person has been through unless you walk in their shoes. Pressure promised her that he would try to talk to Allen, and he did. But it was like talking to a brick wall.

"Bruh, you selfish as fuck," Pressure argued. "You have been unfaithful throughout your entire marriage. She JUST forgave you for having a baby outside of y'all marriage, and you can't even talk to the lady because of some shit that happened before your time. That crazy as fuck."

"You must have been one of her customers, nigga. What the fuck you so mad for?" Allen said.

"Now, you sound like a lil' ass boy," Pressure said. "If I would have fucked your wife, you would've been the best man in our wedding. Believe that."

"Watch your mouth about my wife, bruh," Allen urged.

"Oh, now she yo' wife?" Pressure antagonized. "You need to grow up, man. You can't be real, sometimes...You gotta be real at all times. That lady is good to you, dawg. I just don't want you to lose, bruh. Use your common sense. If the lady was in school, she was trying to change something about her life. You making her feel worthless. Coming from the man she loves, that shit gotta hurt."

"I hear you, bruh. Can we talk about something else now?" Allen asked. "I'll talk to her when I'm ready to talk to her. Even after thinking about everything you just said, I still don't want to talk to her yet."

Pressure finally got up and grabbed his keys, "My bitch smiling from ear to ear. If you don't tighten up, another nigga is gon' be raising yo' jits 'cause yo' bitch gon' be looking for the love and attention that you seem to be incapable of providing to her right now." He walked out of the door and headed to the airport.

Pressure patiently waited at the airport for his woman. As soon as Zoey got off the plane, he hugged and kissed her like it had been months since they last saw each other. She matched his energy like always. He helped her with her belongings as they made their way to the car. He was driving a cute 2020 Lexus Coupe. It was pearl white with chrome rims and white spokes.

"Nice car," Zoey complimented.
"I'm glad you like it 'cause I bought it just for you," he said.

"Stop playing, baby!" She said wide-eyed.

"When have you known me to play?" He asked, tossing her the keys.

When she realized that he was dead serious, she almost dropped her bags. "Oh my God, Pressure, I love it. I don't know what to say. Thank you so much, baby!" She said with sincere gratitude.

"You are more than welcome. I did not bring you here for you to be a doormat. My plan is to elevate you in every way I can, and I believe that you will do the same for me. I'm good all by myself, but I'm counting on you to make me even better and vice versa," Pressure explained.

"I'm going to do my part and more," Zoey assured him. "I'm here because I love you, and I believe everything you just said. I am ready to do whatever we gotta do."

"No more hustling for you. You don't have to anymore. I got you. You can go to school, start your own business, or maybe we will start a business together," he encouraged. "Take your time and figure out what you want to do, and we will make it happen. We ain't finna be on no Bonnie and Clyde type shit…more like Jada and Will. Smart and powerful."

"I like Pressure and Zoey over all the couples in Hollywood or anywhere else. You're the head, and I'm the tail. I will follow your lead," she replied.

"Naw, baby, I'm the head, but you're the neck," he corrected. "The neck controls which way the head turns. I need you to be on point. We are not making any wrong turns. We are equal. We are partners. We are one. It's no more Pressure and Pain or Zoey and Chloe. It's me and you now…Us. We think for us. We move for us. We live for us.

Do you understand what I'm saying, baby? This shit real. I don't waste time on nothing I don't believe in, and I definitely believe in us." His words were perfect. He was everything Zoey dreamed of in a man. She could not stop the tears as they rolled down her face.

"Why are you crying?" He asked.

"Because I'm so happy. You're saying everything I need you to say, without even knowing it," she answered. "I felt it, but to hear you officially say it was all I really needed. Once I stepped off that plane, I left everything else behind me. All I want and need is you. I love the way you make me feel. Safe, beautiful, loved, secure, happy, and blessed beyond measure. I feel so lucky that you chose me. I'm going to love you just the way you deserve to be loved. You chose right. And so did I." She grabbed her Fendi bookbag and passed it to him.

"That's my half for whatever we decide to do. I'm not here for a free ride. I'm following my heart, and my heart is here with you. I trust you, and obviously, you trust me. We are going to put our hearts and minds together and let love guide us."

He pulled into the driveway of a beautiful house and opened the garage with his keys. He looked at her and passed her the keys. She jumped out like a kid in the candy store not ashamed to let him know that she was excited and overwhelmed. The tears rolled down her cheeks once again.

"I'm so freaking emotional. I'm sorry, baby," she apologized. "I don't mean to get all soft on you. This is the best day of my life. Your words meant more to me than the house or the car. Even though I love them both. Today, I truly feel like the luckiest woman in the world."

"I feel the same way, baby. I'm just not doing all that," he said as he pointed to her eyes that were glistening from the tears. "But I get it. And you are not lucky; you deserve this. Don't ever settle for less." Pressure's phone was ringing back-to-back. He was ignoring it until he realized it was his mother. He answered quickly.

"Hey, mama. What's going on?"

"Pressure, Passion has been missing for three days!"

Mrs. Paulette exclaimed.

"What are you talking about, Mama? What do you mean missing?" He asked.

"Her roommate has not seen her in three days. No school, no phone communication, no nothing. She even missed the cheerleading tryouts, and we know how important that was to her. She would never miss that," she said. "A'niya said that the last time she heard from her was when she was headed to her boyfriend's house, but that was normal. He said she left his house at around 4 a.m. and she never made it home. Nobody has heard from her since."

"What fucking boyfriend?" He questioned.

"She told me all about him. She invited him to the party so he could meet everybody at the same time," she said.

"I'mma kill this nigga," Pressure said. "I'm on my way over there."

"Come on, baby. I don't know what the hell is going on, but Passion has been missing for three days," he said to Zoey as they together rushed out the door.

Candice was there when Mrs. Paulette received the call from Passion's roommate about her unknown whereabouts. So she called Pain while Mrs. Paulette called Pressure to inform them of the dire situation. They pulled up at the same time. Pain was surprised to see Zoey, but more than anything he was so glad that Chloe was not with her. Now was not a good time for female drama.

Candice had been avoiding him like the plague. She would drop Treasure off at Mrs. Paulette's, then leave in a haste to ensure that she was long gone before Pain got there to pick her up. But today she would have to face him because she was not leaving Mrs. Paulette alone. She was hysterical crying, pacing the floor, back and forth and back and forth.

For the last month or so, Candice had been dating Choncie. After dealing with a street nigga for most of her life, she was really feeling her little college boyfriend. He was kind, gentle, generous, and he was a cutie. They would stay on the phone all night sometimes. He made her feel alive again, and she had no other women to worry about. Choncie was head over hills in love with her and only her. When Pain arrived, Candice's heart started beating fast and hard. She was nervous. She had butterflies in her stomach, and that pissed her off. After all these years, he still had that effect on her. She was still in love with him. She thought that she was getting over him, but everything she was feeling told her differently.

Treasure ran to him screaming, "Daddy, Daddy" as she jumped in his arms. At the same time, Pressure was coming through the door with Zoey, hand in hand. Allen had beaten both of them there. He was talking to Mrs. Paulette. They all listened as she repeated what A'niya had told her. They called her and asked her everything they could think of asking her. It was mandatory that they talked to Dre and that they tracked her phone. Her mom got on the phone with AT&T. While she handled that, Pressure introduced Zoey to everybody as his lady.

Pain called Candice outside, "A nigga miss the fuck out of you, baby mama. You've been calling yourself dodging me, and I've been letting you have that, but I think it's time we really sat down and had a talk. I know now ain't a good time, but I hope you are going to stay here with Mama until we figure this shit out. I surrender, Candice. I'll change my ways if I have to. I'm incomplete without you and Treasure. I go hard for y'all. Without you, nothing makes sense." Pain was dead serious. He missed her. He had been home alone ever since Chloe left, but he was ok with that. He didn't want to start anything new. He was waiting for Candice to stop acting so tough and hear him out.

Her heart melted when he said those words. She was crazy about this nigga. She had no intentions on leaving Zoey with her mother-in-law. It was mandatory that Zoey knew that Candice was family and not going nowhere. That way she can report that back to her sister. Therefore, she agreed to stay until he returned and to at least hear try him out at that time. He kissed her so passionately that it sent chills up her spine. Then they went back inside to join everyone else.

A'niya had given them Dre's Instagram information. They hit him up. He was already expecting to hear from them. Pressure went in on him, "Listen carefully, I'm coming to see whoever I gotta see 'bout my lil' sister. Your lil' bitch ass better get to her before I do or you just as dead as them. You fucking her and can't protect her? That's two bullets in your head. The more I think about it, the more bullets I put aside for just you. You better get off your ass and get my sister back where the fuck she supposed to be!"

"Listen, Bruh. I'm already stressing and losing my fucking mind. I don't need the added bullshit. I'm going to find her or die trying. I understand your frustration, but I've beaten myself to death already about this shit. So it's nothing no one can say to me that I haven't already said to myself. All that shit is irrelevant right now. I'm going to go just as hard for her as you are. I love her just as much as you do. Like it or not, we are on the same team."

And that was that. Dre was not about to spend his time or energy going back and forth with nobody. He feared nothing except losing Passion. He had already put a plan together. He would follow his brother everywhere he went from now on, until he led him to Passion. He started by renting a small common car that was inconspicuous. He decided on a Honda Accord and then went and got dark tints put on it. He then got war ready. He had a bulletproof vest and guns on top of the guns. He even had grenades. He stayed ready for war. But never in a million years did he think the war would be against his own brother over his woman. At this point, he had no choice.

If he did not save her, he would have niggas gunning for him. Either way, it goes, it was do or die. Everything was on the line. His respect, His girl, and His life.

He figured that he would give them the address to the warehouse, and maybe they would kill Marquise before he did. Or maybe someone there would cooperate more with them than they did with him. He sent Pressure a message:

> 600 Fair hill Ave,
> Cambridge, MA 02138
>
> *Local gang that sells women. I've already been there and shot two niggas but came up with no real info. Maybe y'all can get better results. I truly believe that they are involved. All the niggas in there stay strapped. I personally know these niggas. I used to run with them.*

Mrs. Paulette came up with a different address from 'Where's my iPhone.' They took the two addresses they had and left the house right away. It didn't matter how long the drive was, they were on their way. Pressure ordered Zoey to stay there with Mrs. Paulette.

"Baby why can't-" Zoey started to speak.

Pressure abruptly cut her off. "Because I'm asking you to stay here. This is a good time for all y'all to bond because all y'all are important to this family, so y'all might[WGE1] as well get acquainted and comfortable being around each other. This was not a part of the plan, but sometimes things are not going to go as planned."

"Say less, baby. I'll be here," she submitted with no pushback.

The three of them jumped in the truck and were out. "I'm going to shoot first and ask questions later," Pain said.

"There you go with the bullshit, bruh. How the fuck we going to find Passion if everybody dead?" Pressure asked.

"Y'all niggas better chill out," Allen stepped in and said. "We got a long ride. We might as well make the best of it. Let's talk about something far more interesting, like Pressure and Zoey. And how that nigga kept they shit on the low but wanna Dr. Phil everybody else? This your first girlfriend, nigga. How are you going to tell me anything?" Everybody laughed.

"You got jokes now. You are in no position to tell jokes, nigga," Pressure teased.

"Shit, I'm not worried. Somebody gotta win and somebody gotta lose," Allen stated.

"Yea, bruh, you keeping secrets now? You letting the pussy change you already," Pain added.

"Damn. This is going to be a long ride," Pressure said.

"It damn sho' is, nigga. What's up? Talk to me, bruh. If you are in love, just say that shit," Pain said.

"That's why this nigga so understanding. He done got soft on these hoes. Tender dick ass nigga," Allen teased.

"But for real though, Taylor is a good bitch. I feel like you go way too hard on her," Pain said to Allen.

"I know you ain't talking the way you dun' drug Candice through the mud," Allen replied.

"Yea, but I bet I ain't never hit anybody raw besides her. I would never disrespect my BM like that. We are talking about your wife and the mother of your kids. You foul, nigga," Pain shot back.

"I fucked up. I'm a man. I can admit that," Allen said.

"And she forgave you. That's the only point I was trying to make. Don't be so quick to give up on a bitch that's going to ride for you," Pressure added.

"She's so forgiving because she got her skeletons in the fucking closet. And this conversation ain't about me. Y'all know I don't give a damn how y'all feel about me. I'mma be me.

Now back to you," Allen said, looking at Pressure.

Pressure finally spoke on the subject, "I'm giving it a try. I had to move in silence because this move was for me. I did not want nobody's opinion or thoughts in my head while I was putting this shit together. I'm fucked up about shawty. I told her to come and she came. I had planned on a much more formal introduction at the party on Saturday."

"You already know Candice is going to do the most," Pain said.

"I know, but Zoey can handle herself," Pressure said.

"Candice was happy as fuck when she realized Zoey was with Pressure and I was alone. She probably thinking that I got Chloe somewhere ducked off," Pain joked.

"Bout to make a straight ass out of herself," Allen said. They all laughed knowing Candice good enough to know that she was going to overplay her part.

ΔΔΔ

Zoey was very uncomfortable. She sat quietly in the corner on the couch. "Girl, you might as well come on over here and make yourself at home. Ain't no telling when they will be back with their hard-headed asses," Mrs. Paulette said.

Zoey got up and moved to the table. She sat right across the table from Candice, giving her the same attitude. Zoey was not backing down to nobody, and she knew for a fact that Pressure would not want her too. They all would have to learn how to coexist. So, she was willing to be cordial, but she would also demand her respect.

"Pressure tells me that you moved down here to be with

him. Congratulations. This is Candice. Pain's baby mama," Mrs. Paulette introduced.

"Nice to meet you. I'm Zoey," she said.

Candice just nodded her head. That pissed Zoey off. It was plain to see where this was going.

"Something told me when I first met you that you were the one for Pressure," Mrs. Paulette said. "That's a picky ass young man. I know you must be an awesome person because my baby doesn't settle for less. I didn't think it would be this soon, but love makes things happen that fast. Just keep doing what you are doing. He's happy and definitely in love."

"Thank you so much. I'm happy as well. I need to know his favorite foods and all the pointers you can give me to keep him happy," Zoey requested.

"Is your sister moving here as well?" Candice asked.

Zoey took a deep breath before she responded. "I know Pain already told you about him and my sister. Please don't question me about her or their relationship. I'm not apologizing for her actions or kissing your ass. I'm here for and with Pressure. My only concern is us and what we got going on. But for the record, my sister is not coming, and whatever happened between her and Pain was not serious. Everybody knows that he is madly in love with you.

Let's be grown-ups. I'm sure it would mean a lot to both of them if we were able to all sit down as a family together with no beef. At the end of the day, me or my sister don't owe you anything, and we did nothing to you because we don't know you."

Mrs. Paulette laughed out loud. She couldn't help herself. "I guess she told your ass," Mrs. Paulette teased Candice, still tickled. "You will be just fine. Welcome to the family, Zoey."

"Thank you for having me, Mrs. Paulette. Candice, I hope you don't think I'm being cocky or acting some type of way because I'm not. I just don't want to start this off being fake. However you feel, I have to respect it. I would like for you to get to know me for who I am, not for who I'm related to."

"That's right," Mrs. Paulette agreed, looking at Candice with a straight face.

"You're both right. I apologize. I should not have come at you with the foolishness. That was petty and immature," Candice admitted.

"It's cool, I understand. I'm sure I would feel some type of way too. That's because we are women. We gotta learn to stick together like these niggas do," Zoey said. "My sister is the only friend I have. I'm actually looking forward to hanging out with the women in this family. Girls' night out, creating a real bond; not on no sneak dissing bullshit. But a group of women that can call and count on each other for whatever: The good, the bad, and the ugly."

"You definitely Pressure's kinda woman. I can see that now," Mrs. Paulette said. "Smart, pretty, and strong."

"I guess that would be kinda cool. I don't have any friends either. I come sit with Mrs. Paulette all the time. She's the only friend I have, and that doesn't count because she is more of a mother than anything," Candice said.

"Y'all might as well, because both of y'all gone be around each other way too much for the foolishness," Mrs. Paulette lectured. "Pain and Pressure are super close, and it is going to be mandatory that their women get along. I can tell both of you that now."

They hugged each other and let bygones be bygones.

"So, you mean to tell me you locked Mr. Pressure down?

You got yourself a good one, girl," Candice complimented.

"Girl, I know. I'm excited but nervous at the same time. I have never lived with a man before. This is my first real relationship. I just want everything to be perfect," Zoey admitted.

"Nothing's perfect. But I'm sure y'all will be just fine," Candice said. "You at his mama's house. I know that nigga in love. I've been with Pain for over ten years, and you are the first chick of Pressure's that I ever met."

"Shit, me too and I'm his mother," Mrs. Paulette said.

"So, you and Pain have been together that long?" Zoey asked, realizing that it had to be a lot deeper than what it seemed to be.

"Girl, yes. And he still gives me butterflies to this day. I'm just tired of all the cheating and being lonely with a man. That doesn't make any sense. And as soon as I move on, he is ready to do right. All the back and forth is draining," Candice said.

"That sounds draining," Zoey agreed.

Zoey told them about the car and the place that he had got for them. Mrs. Paulette was proud of her son. He knew how to treat a woman, and she would guide Zoey the best that she could to make sure she kept him happy. A mother knows best what her son likes and needs. They decided to go check out the house. It would be good for all of them to get out for a little bit and get some fresh air anyway. Mrs. Paulette needed it more than any of them. Besides, she loved to decorate and was looking forward to helping Zoey with making their new house feel like a home.

Zoey called Pressure to let him know that she was okay and that they wanted to go see the house. He gave her the address and then hung up. When they got to the house, they came up with all kinds of decorating ideas. Before you knew it, they were on a shopping spree. They took care of all the small things. Her and Pressure would do all the real shopping together. They even planted a garden, went grocery shopping and got all his favorite foods. The next time they looked up, it was dark.

Time had flown so quickly. They decided to call it a night and made their way back to Mrs. Paulette's house. Together they ate dinner and said a prayer for the safe return of the four of them, Passion included. Mrs. Paulette turned it in for the night, and Zoey and Candice sat up all night talking about Pain, Pressure, clothes, and all kinds of girl stuff.

△△△

Taylor was done feeling sorry for herself. She packed her and the boys' clothes, dropped the boys off with their Godmother, and headed to the airport. Allen had her fucked all the way up, and if he was with Shantae, then they were both about to find out that there was a beast behind that pretty face. She had to fight her whole life, mostly just because she was pretty. With that being said, she damn sure was willing and ready to fight for her husband.

CHAPTER TEN

Days had passed while Passion sat in the room alone. Dominique had come and given her clothes that Marquise had bought for her. When Dominique came to bring her food, Passion asked her if she was Marquise's girlfriend? Dominique told her that she was his sister.

"So, you are Dre's sister as well?" Passion asked.

"I am," Dominique admitted.

"So, why would you do this to him? You are no different than your big brother. Of all the women in the world. Why me?" Passion questioned.

"I don't know. I had absolutely nothing to do with this," Dominique said.

"You have everything to do with this. You're the one holding me hostage at this point, not him because he's not even here," Passion snapped.

"It could be worse. He could have fed you drugs or put your lil' pretty ass to work," Dominique explained. She walked out the room aggravated with Passion, even though she knew she was right. Minutes later, Marquise came in and headed straight to the room where Passion was being held. In his hand were shopping bags and food.

"Is this business or pleasure for you? Since when you do all of this for a bitch? What's really going on?" Dominique asked.

"Mind your fucking business," he demanded.

"This is my business because you are making it my business. Take her somewhere else if you don't want me in your fucking business," Dominique shot back.

Marquise kept walking up the stairs. He entered the room as if this was a normal situation for him. "I bought you some clothes and something good to eat. You too pretty to be crying."

Passion looked at him like he was crazy then back out the window, "How can you feel good about yourself?" She said.

"It feels good because you feel good. Didn't it feel good to you?" He asked.

"You are really sick in the head if you could possibly believe that any of this felt good to me," Passion observed.

"I think I can make you feel the same way about me that you feel about Dre, but only if you stop fighting the feeling. I will have you thinking about me instead of him. I promise you that. Now, take them clothes off," he commanded.

"I don't want to have a sexual relationship with my man's brother," she said.

"This ain't about you or what you want. It's all about me and what I want. Now take them clothes off before I rip them off. My plan was to be gentle today and treat you like a lady," he said.

"By locking me up in a room and forcing me to have sex with you. That's how you treat a woman like a lady?" She asked rhetorically before taking her clothes off. "As good as you look, you can't find pussy of your own? You are power struck. What man tries to steal his little brother's girl and then rapes her repeatedly?"

"Lay down, open your legs, and close your mouth," he instructed.

Passion did as he said. He pulled a chair up to the bed and pulled her pussy to his face. He took his fingers and spread her lips apart. He sucked on her clit softly and intimately. He slid one finger inside of her slowly. No matter how hard she tried to block out the feeling, she couldn't. Nothing had ever felt so good to her. Her pussy was dripping wet. He could feel her body reacting to him, and that drove him wild. He sucked her pussy so good. She couldn't hold back her cum. It ran down his fingers as the tears ran down her face. She had just bust the best nut in her life by her boyfriend's brother, her captor. He took his time and made love to her. She was so mad because it felt so good as he made love to her body with his mouth. Passion's body shivered in satisfaction. She tried so hard to control it but she couldn't.

"Why are you crying? Is it because it feels good or is it because you really don't want it?" Marquise asked.

"I don't want it. I really don't!" She cried.

"Yes, you do," he said as his dick entered her body slowly. He even fucked her good. His strokes hit something deep inside of her that she had never felt. He kissed all over her body and caressed her with pure lust in his eyes. She didn't know what was worse, his infatuation with her or her for enjoying every minute of it. She had to get the hell away from him. She didn't throw it back, but she did not have to. Her body couldn't lie; it reacted to what it felt. Once he felt her cum, he came deep inside of her...again.

She ran to the bathroom and showered. Trying to wash away her sins...his sins...their sins. All she could think about was Dre. Poor Dre. Marquise was on a completely different level. He was a grown man for real. Even though she hated him, he fucked her so good. This was the craziest shit ever experienced. The mixed emotions drove her crazy.

When she came out of the bathroom, Marquise was sitting in the chair staring at her. She walked back to the window as he asked, "Are you going to eat?"

"No, I'm not hungry," she responded. "Can I ask you a question?"

"Only if I can ask you one," he replied.

"Has Dre done something to you that bad for you to take someone that belongs to him and turn them into your sex slave for your own personal benefit? Or are you just making it a problem because you want me for yourself? This is not about money or respect at this point. Don't you feel like less than a man?" She asked seriously.

"I would feel less than a man if I did not satisfy you because I know I made you feel good. I feel good. And this started out as business. Now I'm feeling something different. I'm trying to put a baby in you. And if you was my sex slave, I would've had you sucking on this dick the minute I walked in the door. Instead, I'm taking my time to please you. I'm the sex slave, don't you think?" He answered.

"You have really lost your fucking mind," Passion said, realizing that nigga was really psycho as hell.

He laughed, "You will come around in due time. Now, my question. Was that the first time you got your pussy sucked like that? Better yet, did it feel good to you? That's all I really want to know."

"Not only was it the first time, but also, I've never felt something so good in my life. You are far more experienced than Dre is. He is the only person I have ever been with. Now does that make you feel good?" She asked. "Because none of that matters. You are fucking insane. You kidnapped me and forced me to have sex with you, and you think that I'm going to fall in love with you? With someone crazy enough to do some shit like that? Not to mention, how heartless you are. To do your brother this way, I don't think you are even capable of loving a woman."

Marquise got up and headed towards the door. "I'll be here in the morning," he said. "I'm going to wake you up sucking that pussy every morning. Soon, you are going to be up waiting for. Next thing you know, a month will have passed without even a thought of Dre. You'll only be thinking of me. Just me."

He walked out of the room after being in there for two hours. Dominique was waiting, and Marquise was going to give her some type of explanation. For the first time, she was putting her foot down. "What the fuck was you doing up there? This is the first time ever that you are spending hours with a worker. Is she a worker? Or is this personal?"

"I gotta break lil mama in, that's all," he answered.

"Bruh, keep it real with me. What's going on with you and this girl? You had 16-year-old little ass girls in here working, and you never took the time to break them in. What is it, Marquise? Why her?" Dominique inquired.

"I don't know, sis. She so different," he admitted.

"That's why Dre is in love with her. Because she's different. I heard how he went to your spot and shot Poo and Paul. Dre is not a lil' boy anymore, and he is not going to keep allowing you to disrespect him like this. Are you really going to cause all this drama about a bitch?" She questioned.

"Dre will be alright. He will find another girl and forget all about her," Marquise reasoned.

"Why the fuck can't you find another girl? Why he gotta find another girl? You dead ass wrong, and you know it, and when Dre come here, I'm not getting in the middle of y'all shit," she added.

"I don't expect you to get involved. As a matter of fact, I need you to let me handle this. I will deal with Dre," he said.

"Blood thicker than water and money over everything. That's what you taught me. Nothing else makes sense," she reminded him.

Marquise kissed her on the forehead and walked out. There was a look in his eyes that said more than words ever could ever. He was conflicted. He knew he was wrong, but he had no intentions of letting her go. It was like he needed her. He was vulnerable. It was almost like he was in love with her too. Dominique didn't know how to feel or what to do. The only thing she knew for sure was that her brothers were about to go to war, and she was going to be caught in the middle.

ΔΔΔ

Taylor made it to the airport in Miami, and she called all three of the guys, but neither of them answered. Allen had agreed to call her when they returned. They all decided to focus on the task that was at hand. Finding Passion was the only thing they needed to be on their minds at the present time. Finally, she decided to call Mrs. Paulette. She asked for the address so she could catch an Uber, but Mrs. Paulette insisted on sending Candice and Zoey to pick her up instead. She accepted.

Once they made it back to the house, Taylor broke down. She told them about the baby and the fact that he had never been faithful to her since day one. She told them about both envelopes from Shantae's lawyer. She let it all out. Candice and Zoey were in complete shock. Allen was cool, calm, and respectful whenever they were in his presence. It looked like he had the perfect family. She was ready to go to Shantae's house and drag Allen out of there. But first, she had to find out exactly where that was. Mrs. Paulette let her know that Allen was not with Shantae, and she knew this because he was with Pain and Pressure searching for Passion. She explained everything that was going on.

"I'm so sorry, Mrs. Paulette. I didn't even ask how you were doing. I just came in here laying all my problems out like I'm the only person that has them. Forgive me y'all. I'm just so angry," Taylor said.

"Welcome to the round table. This is where problems get solved," Candice said.

"You and Shantae gotta sit down like grown women and figure this mess out," Mrs. Paulette lectured. "At the end of the day, a baby is on the way, so he is going to be forced to deal with you both. Y'all can act like grown women and work together. Or y'all can be at each other's throats for the next 20 years. Shantae don't know you, and you don't know her. Y'all just happen to be in love with the same man. Both of y'all gotta respect each other's position and stay in your own lanes.

Y'all have made a lifetime commitment to Allen. You are his wife, and your job is to love him and be there for him... through the good and bad. Shantae is about to bear his child. As long as this baby exists, they are going to have some type of relationship. If both of y'all allow him to run back and forth, that's exactly what he's going to do. I know Allen loves you, and I know Allen loves Shantae. This is bigger than you and her though. I'm going to give Shantae a call later and see if she will come by. Not for no bullshit, but so y'all can get this situation aired out and get on the same page."

"You know her?" Taylor asked.

"Shantae and Allen have been together longer than

Candice and Pain. Truthfully, I couldn't believe he actually married someone else. It's like you came out of nowhere, but that was where his heart was. He fell in love with you without thinking, and that's what love does. It comes out of nowhere, and before you know it, your heart doesn't even belong to you anymore," Mrs. Paulette explained.

"This is so crazy. It's like a nightmare. I'm not going back and forth playing baby mama games. It's going to be either me or her. She's going to respect that he is my husband, and I'm not going anywhere," Taylor said.

"I don't talk much about this situation, but when my kids were young, Vincent cheated on me too," Mrs. Paulette admitted. "Passion was only three years old when I found out that he was seeing this other woman and that she was pregnant. I felt like the luckiest woman in the world until that day. I will never forget the pain. It was too real. I filed for a divorce the next day. But he never signed the papers. He is still my husband to this day. However, I made him get his own place. He would be here when the kids came home from school and when they went to sleep, he left. They never knew we were going through it.

Once they were old enough to understand, we talked to them about it and made our separation official. It was so hard. I cried myself to sleep so many nights. I missed him very much, but I did not want to look like a fool. What people thought about the situation mattered more to me than my own happiness. But I was too stubborn to forgive him. I have not found a love that came even close to what we had. I haven't found anyone that makes me feel the way he made me feel. If I could do it all over again, I would have forgiven him. Everybody makes mistakes. I finally forgave him not too long ago. The more I read the bible, the more I understand forgiveness. It's not for the other person. It's for your own heart and peace of mind."

"Wow, Ma. You never told me about this," Candice said.

"So, are y'all going to try it again since you've forgiven him now?" Zoey asked Mrs. Paulette.

"He better be happy I'm still his wife. Steve asked me to marry him last month. He is willing to pay for the divorce process and everything," Mrs. Paulette added.

"Are you going to do it?" Candice asked.

"I don't know," she answered. "The more he shows me love, the more I think about the love that I already have."

"I can't picture myself living without Allen. I love him too much," Taylor admitted.

"Ma, you stubborn as hell. Now I see where Pain gets it from," Candice said.

"Pain has always been more like me. He will lose to win. Pressure doesn't gamble with nothing. It's all or nothing for him," Mrs. Paulette said, comparing the two.

The women sat and talked for hours. All of them confessing their love for the men in each of their lives. All willing to fight for what they believed in. Mrs. Paulette realized that she too should have fought for her relationship. If not for her, at least for the kids. Maybe they would have been something other than drug dealers. Instead, she was a part of their drug ring. She had worked so hard to make it on her own financially that she forgot what it felt like to actually live. She did not want these beautiful young ladies to make the same mistakes that she had made.

"Anything worth having at all is worth working for and waiting for," she told them as she regretted not following her own advice.

CHAPTER ELEVEN

When Allen pulled into the driveway of the first address they went to, they immediately recognized Passion's car. Pain almost jumped out of the truck before it came to a complete stop when he saw Passion's car in the driveway. The car was parked in the driveway as if it belonged there.

"There is no way these niggas that stupid," Pressure said. He knew that there was no way Passion was inside willingly while the whole world was looking for her.

Pressure knocked on the door, and a little boy opened it. Pressure grabbed him and used him as a shield while Pain and Allen came in behind him with their guns drawn. Pain secured the house. He made everybody inside come to the living room and lay face down on the ground. Passion's keys were there, but she was nowhere to be found.

"I'm going to ask this question one time and one time only," Allen said. "Where is the girl who owns the car that's parked outside?"

Pain picked the keys up from the table. Next to the keys was her cell phone. "Bruh, ain't these her keys and shit?" He asked Pressure.

"Man, we don't know where she at," one of the men responded.

BOOM! BOOM! BOOM!

Pain put three in the back of his head.

"Wrong answer, homeboy. Who next?" Allen asked.

"Shit just got real, didn't it?" Pressure joked.

"That car belongs to my little sister who is missing in action, and in a few minutes, everybody in here is about to be just like lil' buddy right next to y'all if somebody don't tell me why the fuck her car parked outside and where the fuck she is!" Pressure said.

The little boy was screaming, "Daddy, Daddy!"

"You ready to watch your jit die?" Pain asked.

"Naw, we're going to kill his jit and let him live with the fact that he's the reason his jit head got blown off." Pressure corrected.

"Please don't hurt my son. This nigga drove that car here last night so it wouldn't be parked at the warehouse where Marquise is holding your sister captive," another dude explained while pointing to another man in the room.

"The last time I saw her she was at the warehouse. I don't think she is still there, but I will take you there. Just please don't hurt my son. I'll do whatever you need me to do."

"You decide if your son lives or dies. Get your fuck ass up," Pain instructed. "This is how we are going to do this. Pressure take the jit. If you think this nigga moving funny, smoke jit. I'm going to ride with this nigga because I'm itching to kill all these fuckboys. Allen, make sure when we go through this gate, you make it in as well. I got this hoe ass nigga; I just need y'all right on my ass."

"You really coaching us right now, nigga?" Allen asked.

"A dead man ain't loyal to nobody," Pressure said as he let off four rounds into the nigga's head that drove Passion's car there. He stayed quiet the entire time. Now he would remain quiet forever.

Pressure put the jit in the truck with him and Allen. Pain got in the Passion's car with the dude whose house it was and forced him to drive the car to the warehouse where the nigga who gave the order to kidnap Passion was supposed to be. Allen tailgated behind them. When they pulled inside the gate, Allen made his way through right on his ass. When they got out and walked inside the building, Pain walked in behind the dude with his gun to the back of his head. Pressure entered right behind them, with the gun pressed against the man's son's head. Allen came in with the AK and secured the building.

It was four dudes just hanging around outside. Allen made all four of them kick their guns in front of them in his direction. He ensured that they kicked the guns with enough force so that they were no longer within their reach. Pressure collected all of them.

"Man, these niggas ain't playing, y'all. Snoop and Tony are already dead," the dude said that brought them there. "They're going to kill my son if they don't find their sister, Please tell them where she is," he begged.

"Who the fuck is their sister?" One of the men asked with much attitude.

Without hesitation, Allen let the AK spit. Blood splattered everywhere before his lifeless body hit the floor.

"I didn't like his attitude," Allen said.

"WHAT THE FUCK, MAN!" One of the dudes screamed.

"You got 'til the count of three to tell me where my sister at! That's what the fuck!" Pain said.

Pressure begin to count. "One… two…"

"All I know is that she is wherever Marquise's sister

is...Her name is Dominique. It's like two hours away from here, but I have never been there. I just overheard them talking about it one day," one of the three remaining dudes started singing like a bird.

"I can tell you how to get there, but I don't know the address," the other dude added.

"Then you are coming with us," Allen ordered as he shot the other two niggas.

"Let this nigga take his jit home," Pressure suggested, looking toward the man that brought them there. "They are just dead weight. I'm sure he know what's going to happen if he do anything stupid."

"We usually don't leave witnesses behind, but it's your lucky day. We done already killed too many niggas in one day, and I'm sure this is just the beginning. Get your jit and don't do nothing to make me regret leaving you alive. As you can see, the rest of your crew dead already. We will come back for the both of you if you do anything stupid. You can have the car. If I were you, I would take my jit, and I would relocate. You are the reason for all these dead bodies in yo' boss' eyes," Pain warned. Dude jumped in the car with his son and burnt rubber as he left. They knew that he would not play any games. That nigga was more spooked than his son.

Allen drove the truck as the next nigga of Marquise's soft ass crew directed him to the house where Dominique was guarding Passion. Pain rode shotgun while Pressure sat in the back with the nigga.

"What's your name, Buddy?" Pressure asked with a gun to his temple.

"Diggy," he replied.

"You a smart man, Diggy," Pressure said.

145

"I'm not finna die 'bout no pussy I ain't even getting. I'm not even finna die 'bout my bitch, and we fuck every night," he admitted.

Pain was quiet. He was praying that Passion was wherever they were going. He was tired of this bullshit and all the killing. This shit was out of control. But it would not stop until Passion was safely back with them.

△△△

Dre was sitting in his living room trying to regroup. He couldn't find Marquise for shit. It was like he just dropped off the face of the earth. He called him so many times. Finally, he decided to call Dominique. Since he had been dating Passion, he hadn't talked to her much. Passion had his full attention. The first time he called, she didn't answer. However, the second time she picked up.

"Long time no hear, lil bruh. What's going on with you? How are you?" Dominique asked.

"I know you know what's going on, Dominique. I respect that you have nothing to do with this, but it's bigger than the fact that I love her. Now her brothers are gunning for me, thinking I got something to do with the shit. And this nigga won't even answer the phone. I'm scared, sis," Dre admitted. He knew how to make Dominique feel like shit. If she had anything to do with this, he knew she would not allow him to get hurt if she could prevent it.

"Are you serious, Dre?" She asked.

"On God, Sis. I wouldn't play with you about no shit like that," he answered.

"I don't know where she at, Dre, but I will find out for you. I'm going to call Marquise right now. Stay safe out there, bruh. I love you," Dominique said.

Dre hung up the phone. He had witnessed just how hard Dominique would go for Marquise. She did whatever he told her to do. He just prayed that her love for him was just as deep and that she was not involved in this.

Dominique was pacing the floor. She had called and texted Marquise a hundred times. But he didn't answer or reply. Dominique couldn't understand why the fuck both of her brothers was willing to go to war about this one lil' girl. When Marquise arrived, she was pissed.

"It's niggas out here trying to murk our lil' brother about this bitch, and you won't even answer his calls!" She snapped. "You better figure out what the fuck you are going to do with her by the time I get back. You been coming here every day laying up with this bitch like she yo' lady or something. I'm not stupid."

"But Dre acting like a bitch," he said.
"No, nigga, you acting like a bitch. When I come back, she is leaving. I don't give a fuck where you take her, but she gotta get the fuck up out of here," she ordered. "You can take her to your house with you since you act like you can't live without her. I just told my lil brother the only lie that I'm going to tell about this bullshit."

She walked out the door and slammed it. She was dead serious. Marquise knew that she was right, so he said nothing. Once she was out of the house, he made his way upstairs to Passion. He didn't know what he was about to do. He wanted to take her home with him. Not as a victim of his selfishness but as a girl that wanted him the same way he wanted her. But he knew that was never going to happen.

Dominique and Tank, Dre's best friend, had been kicking it for almost two years, but nobody knew it. They were all slaves to Marquise, somehow someway. This current situation was making them all feel some type of way. She called him and asked him to meet her at their little honeycomb hideout. He always came whenever she called, no matter what he had going on. He put her first at all times. With them both having different roles in Marquise's operation, they barely had time for each other. But today, she needed him. He was her best friend as well, and he always gave her good advice. He told her that he would be there shortly. He had to run to the warehouse to grab something then he would be right there. It was like an hour long drive to get to her. She took a shower and got pretty while she waited for him to arrive.

When he got to the warehouse, there were three dead bodies and blood everywhere. He got the fuck outta there fast. He knew that this was all about Passion. It had to have been her brothers. Dre had told him to stay away from there because they were coming. Now he saw for himself that they meant business. He called the rest of the crew, but nobody picked up. When he got to Dominique, he was so upset. He told her everything that had taken place from the day that Marquise brought Passion to the warehouse. He told her that he had not seen her since that day. She told him that Passion was there where she was and he flipped the fuck out.

"You know that I have to tell him where she's at, right?" Tank said.

"But I don't want either of my brothers to get hurt," she whined.

"That's out of your control. You are just as responsible as Marquise for holding her hostage," he pointed out. "I don't think you understand. Them niggas over there dead as fuck. It was overkill. You are not getting caught up in the middle of this bullshit. I'm not trying to lose you. If I gotta roll with you, I will. I don't give a fuck about Marquise acting crazy. I'm crazy too when it comes to you. Marquise don' lost his fucking mind."

"I can already see that this is not going to end well," Dominique said.

"That nigga is just savage," Tank said. "He can have any bitch he wants, but almost everyone in our crew is dead because he took the wrong bitch, and he don't give a fuck." Dominique began to cry.

"Baby, please don't do that. You really 'bout to make me snap."

He punched the wall. Dominique already knew that Tank was crazy as hell about her as well as in his everyday life. The only reason she kept their relationship a secret was because she saw how Marquise always fucked shit up for Dre, and she didn't know if he would do the same with her and Tank. She knew that Tank would not back down if it came to it. She loved that no one knew that they were an item. Because of that, they never argued about anything. It was just the two of them in their own little bubble.

Now he was all in the middle because of her and his loyalty to Dre. These three were all she had in this world. She was afraid of losing one of them, but in this case, she could possibly lose all three. He couldn't concentrate on consoling Dominique because at this point he was just fed up with it all. He told her to go home and not to open the door for anyone until the issue was resolved. She felt like she had only made matters worse.

Tank texted Dre with the address to the house where Passion was being held.

Tank: *I'm ready for war with you, bruh. Just say the word, and I'm there.*

Dre instantly jumped up and got en route to the address. He was already ready for war. His heart raced as his foot pressed the gas pedal to the floor. He texted Tank back:

Dre: *You have done more than enough, homie. I got it from here. I can't let another nigga go to war for my lady. It's my job to save her. I got her in this shit. But don't worry, I'm going to get what's mine.*

Tank: *I feel you, Bruh. Just be safe. Everybody at the warehouse is dead. I think her brothers might be there."*

"FUUUUUCK!" Dre screamed. This was his chance to prove to Passion that he was a man and would kill anybody who got in the way of them being together. His brother and hers if he had to. Anybody!

Tank understood because he was also getting strapped to go and protect his lady. She had nothing to do with this and was not about to get caught in the crossfire. It was his place as a man to make sure that she came out of this unharmed.

△△△

Passion was restless. She knew that Marquise would be there early like he said. He had bought her a sexy white panty and bra set. This morning she decided to put it on. It was time for her to step her game up. She did her hair and put on light makeup. She told herself that today she was getting away from him.

He was holding a coffee cup and her breakfast when he walked into the room. Passion was standing in the window. She looked so sexy yet innocent, but was not crying. She looked at him and smiled for the first time ever. Marquise felt like he was finally breaking through to her. For the first time ever, Marquise's actions bothered him. Most bitches deserved what they got, but not Passion. He wanted to let her go so bad, but a part of him couldn't. She had something that he needed. She made him feel alive. It was like she could see past all his flaws and see the lost soul that he really was...like she knew that he had needs too.

"Is that a cappuccino?" she asked with excitement.

"Yea, but it's cold now. I'mma go heat it up for you," he said.

He tested her to see if she would run by leaving the door open while he went to the kitchen to reheat the cappuccino and her food. When he walked back in the room, she was laying across the bed naked.

"Who eating first? Me or you?" She asked with her legs slightly opened.

His dick jumped so hard. There was an instant reaction. He decided to control himself. He wanted her to see that he needed more from her than just sex. "You eat first, while the food is hot," he said.

"Your food is hot too," she said, referring to her kitty cat.

"Stop playing with my top, shawty. You don't want this for real," Marquise warned.

"See for yourself," Passion instructed.

She spread her legs wider, and he slid his finger inside of her. It was soaking wet and extremely warm. He pulled it out and sucked all her juices off of it. Her pussy jumped in anticipation. She couldn't wait to feel his mouth on her pussy, and she did not feel bad about it because she knew this would be the last time.

"I don't want any more of that fast food crap. I wanna go out to eat," she insisted. "Sit down and have a glass of wine with me."

"Wine?" He asked.

"I like the champagne glass that its usual served in and the way it makes me feel. Relaxed and laid back…like I am right now," he explained.

Passion started touching herself while he watched her and undressed. She prayed that her performance was good enough for him to at least take her out to lunch. She was tired of waiting to be saved. Today she was taking action in her own hands.

Once she made it out of the house, she would get free somehow. If she had to jump out at a red light or as soon as she saw a police officer in the area, that's what she would do. She laid back and let him have his way with her. She planned on making sure that she got her satisfaction in the process. If she could not stop it from happening, at least she could enjoy it while it did.

CHAPTER TWELVE

Mrs. Paulette was having a hard time falling asleep. She had reopened a part of her life that she tried to forget. Her love for Vincent. She was seeing someone, but it didn't even come close to what she and Vincent shared. She realized that she compared every man she ever met to him, and they always came up short. He was the last of a dying breed. There just was not many like him left. It dawned on her that she hadn't even bothered to tell him that Passion was missing. There she was, fifteen years later, trying to do everything on her own. When the truth was, life was so much better with him. She grabbed her phone and gave him a call. He picked up on the first ring,

"Good morning, Beautiful. You missing yo' husband?" Vincent answered.

"I am, and I need you here with me," was all she had to say. An hour later, he was knocking on the door. When he saw the cars in the driveway, he knew that something was wrong. Paulette opened the door, walked him to her room, closed the door and immediately broke down in his arms.

"Passion is missing!" she cried.

"Baby, calm down," he said. "What do you mean missing?"

"No one has heard from her in almost a week," she said.

"A week?!" He said in a shocked tone. "And you're just calling me, Paulette? What were you thinking?!"

"I was not thinking at all," she replied. "I guess I'm still stuck on that, 'I can do it on my own' bullshit,' but THIS, I can't do on my own."

"It's okay, baby. I'm here now. Stop crying and get some rest. You said the boys went to figure it out. I need you to trust and believe that they are going to do just that," he comforted her.

He stayed with her until she fell asleep. He then went on the porch to smoke and called Pressure and Pain. He could not believe all this was going on and nobody called him. Pressure answered the phone.

"Pops, we in the middle of something. We got this. Passion's alright. Just make sure Mama is good. Love ya." He hung up before Vincent had the chance to say a word.

Vincent knew that all he could really do was trust them. One thing he knew for sure was that he had raised them to be men and to protect the women in their lives. He was sure that they would do whatever needed to be done to correct this problem. He decided to do something to keep himself busy until Mrs. Paulette woke up. He pulled out the lawnmower and started cutting the grass. He was deep in his thoughts when he saw a car pull up. It was Steve, Mrs. Paulette's supposed boyfriend.

"What's up? Can I help you?" Vincent asked Steve.

"Yea, I'm looking for Paulette," Steve responded.
"She's sleeping. Steve, right? I'll tell her you came by," Vincent said, dismissing him.

"Is everything alright? She has not been picking up?" Steve asked.

"Nothing I can't handle, homie. I will tell her to call you," Vincent assured.

He started back cutting the grass. Steve got back in his car and pulled off. Candice, Taylor, and Zoey laughed as they looked out the window. Mr. Vincent was no joke, just like his boys. They saw where their men got their attitude from.

When Paulette woke up, he had cut the grass and cleaned her car. He used to do that every
Saturday until she met Steve. "Your lil' boy toy came by," Vincent told her.

"You still jealous?" Mrs. Paulette asked.

"Why would I be jealous? I told him that he can holla at you when I ain't here. It's my time now. And like a good boy, he hauled ass," Vincent explained.

"Still jealous," she said, shaking her head. They sat on the porch and talked for a while. He had to check in on his driver and run a few errands. In the meantime, Mrs. Paulette was waiting for Shantae to arrive. She agreed to come over and sit down with Taylor. She hoped that she was doing the right thing. She was a mother to all of them and needed peace in her circle.

Zoey and Candice were in the kitchen cooking, ready for the show. Once Shantae arrived, she and Taylor sat at the round table across from each other. Both of them went the extra mile to look their very best. Mrs. Paulette sat in as the mediator.

"Both of y'all are too grown to not be able to sit at this table and talk like women," Paulette lectured. "This ain't the first time two women have been in love with the same man. It's nothing new. The way you handle it is what matters. Say what you mean and mean what you say. This is the time."

Taylor began, "I guess I will start. Both of us are victims of Allen's lies and deceit. However, I am his wife, and I have decided to stand by my husband. Which means that I will be a part of the baby's life as well. So, your assassination attempt on my character means nothing."

"It was not an assassination attempt. It was a revelation of your past. You are who you are. He has the right to know who he married. I know for a fact he hates women that sell their bodies for money. This was not something he was aware of. One of y'all sent me papers requesting joint custody. I sent back a clear message that I'm not playing games about mine. And I'm ready for court," Shantae said defensively.

"If you know so much about him, then you would know that he is not going to leave me," Taylor said. "He's only going to appreciate me more. Now he sees the changes I have made for him and our kids. You may have been before me, but you will never be me."

Shantae shot back, "Be you?! That's funny. A wife with a broken heart and a broken family," she laughed. "You're sitting here talking like your marriage is solid. I was here before you, during you, and I'll be here long after you're gone. However, this is about the baby, not me and Allen."

"This is about the entire situation, not just the baby. I'm not playing 'baby mama' games with you and Allen. I know for a fact that he loves me. Obviously a lot more than he loves you because I am his wife, and he was overwhelmed about our kids. So, I'm not sure what you're expecting, but I'm not going anywhere," Taylor snapped.

"If he was so happy with you, why did he keep fucking me until we also got a baby? The difference between me and you is, a ring and vows that don't mean shit to him. Otherwise, we would not be sitting here right now. You can get off your high horse because that shit doesn't mean anything to me. You can't make me feel like I'm any less than you because I'm confident, sweetie," Shantae retorted.

"This is not what I had in mind," Mrs. Paulette interrupted. "Y'all are both important to him. Y'all are both going to be his baby mama. Now what? How do we get past the bullshit? THAT, is why we're here."

"I came to talk to her with no malice. Allen and I are not together. I don't settle. I'm not playing seconds to nan bitch. We have not fucked in months, and I don't plan on ever fucking him again. I know how to let go and move on, unlike you. The only reason I'm here is because y'all forcing y'all way into my life. If he would have signed the papers, y'all would have never heard from me again. But since that's not going to happen, here I am," Shantae explained.

"Look, I apologize," Taylor said. "This is not a competition. And if it were, both of us would be losing. I'm not trying to go back and forth with you. Your daughter and my boys are going to be siblings, so we may as well figure out how to coexist."

"I'm not going to sit here being fake and act like I'm not still madly in love with Allen because I am," Shantae admitted. "And it hurts so bad that you came along, out of nowhere and this nigga put a ring on YOUR finger. And to top it all off, he had the audacity to ask me to kill my baby, but y'all got two. You're right; obviously he does love you more. I chose my baby over him, and I'm perfectly ok with my decision. Now he's talking about custody?!?!

I loved Allen more than I loved myself, but I love this baby more than I love Allen or myself, and I'm prepared to take care of her on my own. I have no problem with you and Allen being in her life. I have someone in my life that is going to be there every step of the way. There really is no reason for us to be at war. Me and Allen are done. I deserved better, and God sent me just that."

"I can't help but wonder, if you wouldn't have called it quits with him, what would he be doing? Would he still be back and forth lying to the both of us? I've come to realize that my husband is in love with two women. Nothing hurts more than that. However, there is nothing I can do about it. It's clearly not your fault. And I understand how you can still be in love with him because I can't live without him," Taylor added.

They sat across from each other, face to face. Both women were letting it all out. The hurt, the anger, the love, it all spilled out right there on the table.

Taylor continued, "I even understand why he had such a hard time letting you go. You seem to be an awesome person. A lot stronger than I am. I just want things back the way they used to be. I know that's not going to happen, so I'm willing to do whatever I gotta do to save my marriage and keep my family together. I just don't want to be a bigger fool than I already am."

"If he was my husband, I would do all that I could, to save my marriage and family as well. He is worth it. But I'm not his wife, and I will not fight to hold on to another woman's husband. I always promised myself that I would never sleep with a married man, and here I am, pregnant from one, sitting across from his wife, crying and pouring my heart out... and MY Allen is that married man. This shit is crazy as fuck!" Shantae exclaimed, as she wiped her tears and shook her head in disbelief."

"Tell me about it. I'm sitting here crying my heart out to the other half of my husband's heart, who is about to have his baby. This is some desperate bitch shit," Taylor replied.

Everybody laughed, even her. It was sad but true. All they could do was laugh to keep from crying, because they both were tired of doing that.

"You're not desperate," Shantae stated. "You just love

your husband and I truly respect that. Because you love him so much, I know that my daughter will be loved as well. Allen will always be in my heart; I will always be his friend. If he needs me, I'll come running, no questions asked. But I will not be his mistress. It's all or nothing for me. So, I can assure you that I'm not an issue in your marriage any longer. I just want what's best for my daughter. I've already got what's best for me. I also want to apologize for judging you. I'm sure you are a good wife and a great mother. You must be because...shit, you took MY MAN from ME."

"Naw, that might just mean she got some good ass pussy," Candice teased. They all laughed.

When dinner was done they all ate together. They sat and talked for hours. Each of the women took turns telling their stories. All of them gained a mutual respect for one another. They laughed, cried, and bonded as sisters. Taylor and Shantae agreed to communicate with each other. Shantae really was trying to get over Allen. She had no intentions of sleeping with Allen or being with him. She was no longer hating on Allen and Taylor and looked forward to the four of them spoiling the shit out of her baby girl. Not to mention Zoey and Candice, who were officially aunties, and Mrs. Paulette and Mr. Vincent, who were grandma and grandpa. Her baby was surrounded with love and she was grateful.

ΔΔΔ

Pressure parked, and they waited patiently in the woods directly across the street from the entrance for whoever pulled up. They would be in for a big surprise. Thirty minutes later, a black BMW pulled up. Out of nowhere, Allen and Pain jumped in the back seat, and Pressure got in the front. The girl driving the car was caught totally off guard when she realized that there was a gun pointed at her head. They laid low with all three of their guns aimed at Dominique. Pressure gave her orders.

"Do what you would normally do. If you make one false move, you are going to be stinking just like the rest of your crew," he said.

Dominique did as she was told. She punched the code into the gate, and they drove into the garage. She got out and opened the door. All three of them entered right behind her, guns drawn.

"Please don't kill my brother. He did not hurt her," Dominique cried.

"Ooooh, so you already know why we are here? Good girl. You should be begging for your own life because your brother is already a dead man," Pain threatened while securing the house downstairs.

"Call him," Pressure ordered.

Dominique called and he picked up on the first ring.

"How long are you going to be, sis?" Marquise questioned, wondering when she would return to the house where they held Passion and not knowing that she had already returned.

"Marquise, my man, it's been a long day. I had to kill a lot of people to get to you. I say, you let my sister go, I will let your sister go, and we can all go home. Or we can all die in this bitch today. What you wanna do?" Pressure asked.

Marquise was in the same house that they were in. He was upstairs with Passion and had already sucked her insides out. She had cum twice already, and they were going for the third one when he got the call. He jumped up and ordered her to get dressed, pacing the room back and forth.

"Baby, what's wrong?" Passion asked, still playing the role of a willing participant to the tee.

He grabbed her and put her in front of him as a shield. He was not leaving without her. He figured that they would kill Dominique anyway, so he decided to make a run for it. "You already know that I'm not going to hurt you, but if I let you go, I lose and all of this would be for nothing. I promise I will take care of you. I promise," he said to Passion right before kissing her and ordering her to open the door quietly.

They made their way downstairs. Allen held a gun to Dominique's head while Pain and Pressure's guns were aimed in Marquise's direction. Marquise had already opened the garage remotely. All he had to do was get to the car, and he and Passion would be free.

As he moved closer to the side door, Dominique screamed at him, "SO, YOU'RE REALLY JUST GOING TO LEAVE ME, BRUH? WITH A FUCKING GUN TO MY HEAD? THIS IS YOUR DOING. HOW CAN YOU JUST LEAVE ME TO DIE FOR YOUR BULLSHIT?" Dominique was heartbroken. She realized that he did not give a fuck about her or Dre. Only himself.

Passion cried for brothers to save her. "PLEASE DON'T LET HIM TAKE ME!" She cried.

The only reason that Pain and Pressure didn't body him on sight is because he was using Passion as a human shield. As soon as he opened the side door, Dre put an AK to his head and forced him back inside. "Are you going to shoot me, bruh? About a bitch?" Marquise barked.

"YOU DAMN RIGHT...BOUT MINE, I WILL!" Dre answered sternly.

"This shit like the movies. It looks like we are all here for the same reason. You outnumbered homeboy, and I'm more than sure your sister here," Pain said, tilting his head in Dominique's direction. "ain't fucking with you no more now that she see how you really feel about her. Nobody else has to die today."

"Let her go, bruh," Dre demanded.

"Nigga, you ain't got the heart to kill me?" Marquise said to Dre.

"We got the same blood, bruh. It ain't no bitch in me," Dre reminded him. "Don't test me. If you don't let her go by the time I count to three, you will see today, but won't see tomorrow. One, Two…"
Out of nowhere, a red beam popped up on Marquise's forehead. Then a hole appeared right before he dropped to the ground. Dre grabbed Passion as she cried in his arms. Pressure and Pain searched for the shooter while Allen kept the gun to Dominique's head. Tank slid in through the side door with his hands in the air. He had a gun with the beam and silencer in his hand.

"The bad guy is dead. I just want you to let my lady go. She had nothing to do with this. None of us did. That nigga crossed everybody in this room. I say the problem is solved," Tank pleaded.

"You and Dominique together?" Dre asked.

"Now we are because she ain't gotta worry about this dumb ass nigga," Tank replied.

"What y'all say? I say job well done…mission accomplished?" Tank continued.

"I just wanna go home. I don't want anybody else to die because of me," Passion added.

Passion ran to her brothers. All three of them. Allen decided to let Dominique go, and everybody eased up a little. "Let's go home, sis," Pain said before kissing her on the forehead.

"I can't leave without Dre. I love him, Pain," Passion admitted. Pain wanted to blow Dre's head off. His baby sister was in his face confessing her love for this lil' nigga. Pressure and Allen looked straight at Dre.

"I know this wasn't my business," Tank said. "But I smoked his ass because I don't give a fuck about that nigga, but I know he raised Dre, so I didn't want that on his conscience. My dawg fucked up 'bout shawty. I know for a fact that Dre would've smoked his own brother for your sister. That's real love."

"So, let me get this straight. Passion and Dre are in love. Dre's brother kidnaps Passion. Dre's sister holds her hostage. Passion's brothers kill over ten people, just to find Passion and rescue her and when all is said and done, she is refusing to leave without Dre. Did I get it right?" Allen asked.

"That's what's happening, bruh. You got it right," Pressure said. "Ain't that right, Passion?" Pressure asked her directly.

"Yes, Pressure," Passion responded. "That's right. Thank you for everything, I never once doubted that you would come for me, but I knew that Dre would also because he loves me. He tried to warn me, and he tried to call it off so I would not get caught up in the bullshit, but I didn't listen. Instead, I called him pussy and all kinds of things that I really didn't mean. I'm so sorry, Dre."

"Hey, hey. Stop crying, baby. I don't care about any of that. All I care about is you. Us. And our future together," Dre comforted. He wiped her tears away and kissed her passionately. Everybody watched. Both her and Dre were crying, holding on to one another. Neither of them wanted to ever let go. They were young and in love, and it was plain to see.

"I'll tell you what, when I get home, she better be there," Pressure said to Dre. "And you need to be the one to explain all this dumb ass shit to your mama and daddy," he told Passion.

"Hell naw! She finna get her ass in this truck!" Pain yelled. "We ain't do all this just to leave her here. That's crazy."

"Life is crazy, Pain. We can't force her," Pressure lectured. "She is grown, and she thinks she's in love. She gotta figure it out from here on. We did our part. I'm tired and ready to get back to my lady. Straight up."

Allen agreed.

"I promise you she will be there. I'm young, but I'm a man. Not only am I going to take care of her, but I'm going to protect her too," Dre reassured. "This shit won't ever happen again. She ain't leaving my eyesight."

Pain hugged Passion one more time, and then he, Allen, and Pressure walked out the door. Their next destination was Detroit. Allen needed to talk to his wife. With everything going on, he just wanted to hold her, even if just for one night. Their beef was far from over, but at this very moment, all he wanted to do was love her.

Pain hit Chloe up. He asked to be dropped off with her and Rein. He planned on going back to Miami to be the man Candice longed for, but not before one last night with Chloe and Rein. Chloe met Pain at the Popeye's right off the expressway. Pain jumped out of the truck with the boys and in with the girls. Their first stop was the liquor store. They already had plenty of weed and pills. Rein had run off from her abusive partner with over 5,000 pills. Her and Chloe had been popping them and partying like rockstars ever since Zoey left. Tonight, was about to get crazy... They both needed Pain's services.

When Allen pulled up to his house, he knew for sure that Taylor had left him. Neither the newspapers were picked up from the yard driveway nor had the leaves been swept off the porch. You could see the panic in his face. They got out and went inside. Pressure headed straight to the shower. Afterwards he called his mother and let her know that Passion was safe and would be heading home soon. Five minutes later, Pressure was sound asleep.

Allen took a shower and tried to contact Taylor. Her phone went straight to the voicemail. He tried several more times. He was restless. Where could she be? He noticed that she had packed a suitcase for her and the boys. She was gone. He checked the safe, but all the money was still there. She had no friends; he was her fucking friend. She had no family; he was her fucking family. So where could she be? He called back and this time he left a voicemail.

"Taylor, I don't know where you are with my kids but I'm not asking you...I'm telling you to come home. I love you, and we can get through this. I may have overreacted a little, but I now understand how you feel because just the thought of somebody else between your legs sends me into a rage. But none of that matters. You need to get home. This is where we both belong." He hung up the phone and punched the wall in frustration.

"She will be back, bruh. She is probably somewhere looking for you or just trying to let you see how it would feel without her and the kids. Taylor is not walking away from you that easily," Pressure said, trying to calm him down.

"I don't know. I did and said some fucked up shit," Allen admitted, beating himself up about his harsh words.

"Your good outweighs the bad, Allen. God is going to show you favor. Y'all gon' be alright, and if not, you still gone be alright," Pressure assured him.

"That's real," Allen said.

Pressure and Allen sat up and talked for a while, and then they both decided to call it a night. The following morning, they went to pick up Pain. Chloe was cooking, so she invited Pressure and Allen to join them for breakfast. A hot breakfast sounded like a good idea so they accepted her invitation.

"Pressure, I fucks with you. Please take care of my sister," Chloe said. "She has never lived with or loved a man. She's in love for the first time in her life. Please be good to her. I trust you, and I believe in you, Pressure. Don't let me or her down."

"Man, your sister hit the lottery," Pressure teased. "On a serious note, she is the luckiest person in the world, but so am I. I give you my word. I will love her the way she should be loved."

She gave him a brotherly hug full of love and continued cooking. They all sat, talked shit, and ate breakfast together. Pain and Chloe played around in the kitchen. This was the end of the road for them, and they both were perfectly okay with that. Now that playtime was over, it was time for these men to get their lives in order. They gassed up and hit Interstate 95, heading south.

CHAPTER THIRTEEN

Dre and Passion left out right behind Pain, Pressure and Allen. The ride was quiet. Passion couldn't stop the tears from falling. Dre was completely broken. His family had caused her so much pain. She was so innocent before meeting him. Words could never explain the sympathy he felt for her. Their lives had changed forever in such a short time.

The first stop was to the hotel where Dre had been staying. He had his most valuable possessions there. The next stop was to his apartment to grab his clothes and his collection of Jordan sneakers and fitted caps, along with his jewelry and safe. Life as he knew it in Massachusetts was over. There was no looking back. He had a total of $286,000 and what was left of the girl he loved.

The next stop was Passion's college dorm. She gathered her things and went to find A'niya. There was no way she was leaving without telling her best friend goodbye. When she saw Passion, she screamed so loud. Everybody stopped and looked. When the on-lookers realized it was Passion, they all clapped and surrounded her. She broke down and cried as she held onto A'niya, not ever wanting to let her go. She informed everyone that she would not be returning this semester. They begged her to stay. She promised that she would think it over, knowing deep down inside that she would not return.

She then went to the administration office. They too tried to convince her to stay. They were willing to let her take some time off and return when she was ready to do so. They also offered to extend her scholarship so that it would not expire during her time off. She agreed to consider it, as she walked out of the office.

Dre was right by her side through it all, afraid to let her out of his eyesight. He vowed to never fail to protect her again.

On the ride home, Passion informed Dre that there was a possibility that she could be pregnant. Before this whole incident, her period was already a week late. However, this did happen on occasion. To make matters worse, Marquise also had ejaculated inside of her several times during her time of capture. If she wasn't pregnant before, her chances of being pregnant now have increased drastically.

Dre was distraught. The one thing that he prayed did not happen to her, happened. His worst fears had just been confirmed. She was violated in the worst possible way by his own flesh and blood. He couldn't find the words to say to comfort her. He was sure she was tired of hearing him apologize. And why would this nigga nut in her anyway? What was he really trying to prove? But Dre couldn't punish the nigga anymore; he was already dead. His mind was all over the place.

"FUCK!" Dre screamed as he punched the dashboard with tears rolling down his face.

"I'm ok, Dre. I really am," Passion stated. "I just don't want my family to know about this. If I do happen to be pregnant, I am going to have an abortion."

Dre objected, "You already told me your views on abortion, Passion."

"Yes, Dre, I DID. That was before being with two brothers. One of which violated me continuously!" Passion stated, full of emotion. "My views on EVERYTHING are totally different now."

"I know a part of you has to hate me for all that has happened to you. Do we even stand a chance?" Dre inquired.

"This is hard, but living without you would be even harder," she replied. "Now we are going to see just how deep our love really is. I know this isn't going to be easy for us. Everything with us is happening so fast. I don't know what's wrong or right anymore. But what I do know is, I don't want to go through this alone. I can talk to you about things that I would never discuss with my family. It's like you're the only one that really knows me. A part of me feels like this is all my fault."

"This happened to you because that nigga was power stuck, greedy and jealous. You can blame me as much as you want, but I will NOT allow you to blame yourself," he said.

"I can't blame you for someone else's actions. This was neither of our faults," Passion rationalized. "We survived it, that's why we're still together. So, let's just focus on moving forward to the next chapter of our lives together. What's the plan when we get to Florida?"

"As soon as we get settled, I'm going to get a job," Dre answered. "I have almost $300,000. We gon' be good, bae. Trust me on that."

"$300,000?!?!" She exclaimed. "Where the HELL did you get that much money from?"

"Baby, I've been saving since I was 17 years old; I'm 21 now. I've done it all for the love of money, but I'm done with that life. I've been paying rent, taking care of myself, and doing grown man shit for a long time. But I'm going to go ten times harder for you. I'm willing to work like a slave and do whatever must be done to keep you happy. I need a permanent smile on that beautiful face," he said.

Passion smiled, "From this day on, We focus on our future."

Simultaneously they said, "Together!"

Everything was starting to get real for Passion. She went from being the family's sheltered little girl to being this strong survivor of a very traumatic experience. She was now an independent young lady with a man, and it literally happened overnight.

As they continued heading south along the dark roads, Passion couldn't believe how much her life had changed. "I can't believe I'm headed back home and with a man!"

"Your brothers gon' hate me forever," Dre said with worry.

"You're too much like them for them to hate you," she said. "But Pain is going to hate you if you don't get me a new car because that was his graduation gift to me."

"Ok, well, we need to handle that before we get there," he agreed.

"And a phone," she added feistily.

"Say less, baby girl," he uttered as she looked over at him and smiled. "I don't ever want you to lose that smile again."

"Then make sure I don't," she said as she held the smile. "I'm kinda excited about us living together in our own place. Waking up with you every morning is going to be a breath of fresh air. I used to hate leaving you to go back to the dorm."

"I hated it more when I rolled over to your side of the bed, and it was ice cold because you were no longer there to keep it warm," he admitted.

"Well, we won't have to worry about that anymore. That's one problem solved," Passion concluded.

The two of them continued to talk and make plans during their trip. They drove throughout the night. The sun was beginning to rise. The first open car lot Dre spotted, he whipped in. He jumped out with a duffle bag and ordered Passion to follow.

"Pick the car you want, baby," He said.

"Are you serious, Dre? This could've waited," she said.

"Just pick your car and make sure you love it," he added.

They walked around until she spotted the one she wanted. It was a burnt orange 2021 Nissan Altima with mob tint and already outfitted with rims. It only had 5 miles on the odometer and was priced at $29,999.99. She ended up driving away in her brand-new car at a steal for only $25,000.

She weaved in and out of traffic with Dre closely tailgating behind. As he followed her, Dre's phone begin to ring, startling him. It was Dominique. He quickly answered.

"Are you ok?" Dominique asked with true concern.

"I am," Dre replied.

"I love you bruh. I'm so sorry for the role I played in all of this," Dominique cried.

"I understand your position sis. Stop crying, I'm ok," Dre said.

"Where are you?" She asked.

"I'm headed to Miami with Passion. I don't know what the future holds for us but I do know that I can't live without her. She is convinced that everything is going to be ok and I trust her. Where are you?" He then questioned Dominique.

"I'm at the house with Tank. You don't have to worry about me. You already know that he's going to make sure that I'm good. We only kept our relationship a secret to keep Marquise from destroying it like he always did with any relationship that you attempted to have. I'm so sorry. I should have stepped in and done something to stop this long ago," she sobbed.

"Stop crying sis. All of this is behind us now. We can live our lives freely. I have no ill feelings towards you. As a matter of fact, I thank you and Tank for leading me to Passion. You did the right thing," Dre comforted her.

Dominique broke down. Dre listened as Tank stepped in to comfort her. Finally, Tank took the phone from her and spoke.

"Burh she good and I'mma make sure of that, always. Together we will figure this shit out. Right now, you just focus on taking care of your lady and I'mma take care of mine. When the time is right, we will meet up again. Just keep in touch and stay safe," Tank said.

"Say less," Dre said and hung up the phone. He immediately turned his attention back to Passion.

They were now within the city limits of Miami. Passion was home sweet home, which is now THEIR home. She pulled in at a Days Inn right off of the highway.

Dre got out of the car, "Baby, of all the places we could've gone, you choose a Days Inn?? Your brothers are gon' think I'mma bum!"

"First of all, my brothers aren't coming here," she corrected. "Second of all, we are not spending $200 to $300 on a room when we have no idea how long we will need to be here. We have more important shit to do. We have to get an apartment, furniture, as well as all the necessities. We're not blowing money just to impress my family nor to get their approval. My approval is all you need."

"Yea, talk that big boy shit now," Dre said, knowing that

Passion was just running her mouth. She was tougher and feistier than he had expected. She was pretty and smart with a take charge attitude. A lil' bossy thang...just perfect for him. He loved everything about her. He grabbed their bags and followed her.

To Dre's surprise, the room wasn't bad at all. It was actually bigger than his apartment. They showered and got dressed then headed to her mother's house. Passion decided to drive her new car. She couldn't wait to show it off and her new man.

The closer they got to Mrs. Paulette house, the more nervous Dre became, and the more Passion came alive. When they pulled up, her father was outside smoking a cigarette. Once they pulled into the driveway, Passion told herself that this was no time to play daddy's little girl. She would have to stand strong behind her man.

"We got this," Dre said.

He got out of the car, walked around, and opened her door. When she stepped out of the car, she ran to her dad and broke down crying in his arms, like a little girl lost without her father. Mrs. Paulette came outside, hugging Passion as tears fell. Dre just stood back and observed, wishing his family was half of what hers was. The love was so visual. Not only could he see it, but he could also feel it. It was genuine. His bossy ass chick turned out to be just an innocent daddy's little girl after all.

Once all the hugging came to an end, Passion grabbed Dre's hand, "Dre, this is my mom Paulette and my dad Vincent. Mom, Dad, this is my fiancé, Andre. He's transitioning from Massachusetts to Miami, so we can be together. He's a great guy and I really love him." she explained as she smiled and looked into his eyes.

"We're moving into our own place and once we're

settled, I'll be taking classes at Miami-Dade for a while. Please don't give us too much 'cause we've already been through enough. We are financially situated, and Dre is going to work while I go to school. I really want y'all to trust my judgment and support my decisions." Mrs. Paulette gave him a hug and welcomed him to the family. Mr. Vincent shook his hand firmly.

"We'll talk in a minute," Vincent said.

The four of them went inside, where Passion introduced Dre to everyone else. "This is Zoey, my brother Pressure's girlfriend," Passion started. "I told you," she said to Zoey jokingly as they both burst into laughter. Passion then noticed that both Taylor and Shantae were present.

'What the fuck!' She thought to herself.

"This is Taylor, my brother Allen's wife," as Passion continued the introductions. "This is Shantae, Allen's soon-to-be baby mama. This is my beautiful niece Treasure, my brother Pain's daughter, and her mother Candice." She looked over to the women in her brothers' lives.

"Listen y'all, my brothers are on the way, and I need y'all to please get y'all men in check. 'Cause they are not about to be handling him any kind of way or trying to run our life. Y'all know they are protective of their little sister, but I'm grown. They have their happy relationships, and I'm extremely happy in mine. I don't need anybody's permission, but I really would like everyone's respect and support."

"Y'all ladies go ahead and have dinner. I know everybody is ready to eat because we've been waiting on y'all to get here all day. Me and Dre are going to step outside for a minute," Mr. Vincent instructed. He and Dre stepped outside.

"Are you alright, young man?" Vincent asked.

"I'll be alright," Dre responded.

"I never ask a man about his financial status, but I need to know that you are going to be able to take care of my little girl," Vincent added.

"ABSOLUTELY!" Dre assured with confidence. Whatever she wants and needs, I'll make it happen. I'm also looking to invest in some sort of business for the both of us. Until we figure out exactly what that will be, I'm willing to work two jobs to make sure that she is well taken care of."

"Alright now. I don't want my baby girl struggling with a nigga 'cause he is too proud to ask for help," Vincent spoke sternly.

"She will never struggle with me. I'm not that kind of nigga. And I'm definitely not too proud to ask for help. I come from the sewer. If I wouldn't have asked for help at some point, I would've died a long time ago. We good, sir. We will be looking for a place this week, and like I said, once we get settled, she's going back to school, and I'm clocking in on someone's job," Dre stated.

Mr. Vincent laughed. "Young and in love, y'all got it all figured out. I hope y'all do, son. That's my pride and joy. I just want her to be happy."

"That makes two of us because her happiness is all that matters to me," Dre agreed. "She's the only normalcy I have in my life. She's the only person that has ever made me feel like everything is gonna be alright. And it is."

"You remind me of me back when I met their mom," Vincent admitted. "I knew I was in love, and NO ONE could tell me different. I felt she was the one for me, and that was the one thing that I was right about because I still love her to this day. But I fucked up, son. If you keep your dick in your pants and respect your household, everything else will work itself out. Respect, loyalty, and communication is what builds a solid foundation."

"Mr. Vincent, I can assure you that I am going to love her just as much as you love her," Dre concluded.

Vincent smiled. "Well, if that's the case, son, welcome to the family. Let's go eat."

They went inside to find the ladies eating, talking, and asking Passion a thousand questions. Everyone stopped talking when they realized that the men had re-entered the house.

"You must be starving?" Passion asked Dre.

"I am," he said as they went into the kitchen to fix his plate.

"You're a lucky man, Dre, 'cause they mama don't give a damn whether or not I eat," Vincent teased.

"I remember when you were just as lucky," Paulette defended. "And for the record, I do care. Your plate is in the microwave, nice and hot."

"Y'all two may as well stop lying and get back together," Passion stated. "I would love to see my mom and dad back in the same house again."

"We've been talking about it, and I've been considering it," Paulette said.

"Are you serious, Mom?" Passion said with excitement.

"Yes I am," Paulette answered. "With you going missing, we realized just how short life is. There's still so much love between the both of us. Maybe it's enough to give it another try. They say its better the second time around. Hopefully, he's smart enough not to fuck it up this time."

"Oh, you ain't gotta worry about that, baby girl," Vincent conceded.

"Mr. Vincent don' came over here and put the Mac down on mama," Candice joked. Everyone laughed.

"No comment," Vincent responded as the laughter intensified.

ΔΔΔ

The fellas had been on the road for over fifteen hours straight. Mrs. Paulette had called them to let them know that Passion was home about 6 hours ago. They had three and a half more hours to go before arriving in Miami. The only time they stopped was for gas and food.

Pressure could not wait to get home to Zoey. They had a fresh new start waiting for them. Pain was happy about going home as well. It had been harder than he expected staying away from Candice for so long. And even though he had a blast, he was missing Treasure and the family life. Of course, he missed Candice too, but it was just something about Treasure being in the middle of him that made it that much more special.

Allen wasn't sure what he was going to do. He still hadn't talked to Taylor. He did not know where she was. He had handled her horribly. She had never seen him act that way. He had never called her out of her name before. He had fucked up way more than he realized. He was tired as hell and emotionally drained. All he wanted to do was go home, lay under his wife and listen to his boys run around being hard-headed as hell. At the end of the day, he really was a family man, and he missed the hell out of his family.

Everyone seemed to be deep in their own thoughts when Allen's phone rang…it was Taylor. He answered the phone quickly, "Where the fuck are you with my kids?!?" Allen demanded.

"Whatever you can do, I can do. Remember that!" Taylor snapped. "It doesn't feel good when you're the one being ignored, does it?"

"You gon' make me fuck you up, Taylor!" He warned. "Where the hell you at!"

"I'm on my way to hospital with Shantae; her water just broke. So, you need to get here ASAP!" Taylor informed. "We're headed to Jackson Memorial." She abruptly hung up the phone.

Allen had a smile on his face and a frown at the same time as he filled in his brothers, "Man, Taylor is on her way to the hospital with Shantae. Her water just broke."

"Nigga, it don't get no realer than Taylor," Pressure said. "That's what you call a woman dea'. Yo' fuckass better suck her booty hole or sumthin', whatever you gotta do to make that shit right."

"How the fuck did they end up together?" Pain asked out of curiosity.

"I have no idea. She had the nerve to tell me that she was iggin' me just to show me how it feels to be on the receiving end," Allen said.

"Damn right! 'Cause you was dead ass wrong, nigga," Pressure said, taking Taylor's side.

"Nigga, you sound like a fuckin' cheerleader!" Allen shot back. "Just shut the fuck up and get me to my wife and daughter!"

"I am because I'm tired of seeing yo' tough ass pout like a

bitch!" Pressure antagonized.

Pain was laughing his ass off as Allen and Pressure went back and forth. Pressure had the pedal to the metal, trying to get to the hospital before Shantae had the baby. About two and a half hours later, they arrived at the hospital in the nick of time.

Shante was pushing when he walked through the door. Taylor was holding her hand, coaching her along. Allen pulled Taylor into his arms, hugging and kissing her as if they were the only two in the room. Taylor then removed her gown, put it on her husband, and stepped aside to allow Allen to grab Shantae's hand as she pushed out their 6lb, 6oz baby girl. Allen cut her umbilical cord. He had never seen anything so precious in his life.

"Allani. That's what I'm naming her," Shantae announced.

Allen agreed with Shantae's name choice for their new bundle of joy as Shantae held her baby in her arms for the first time.

Taylor had never felt so conflicted in her life. Here was a beautiful baby girl. Allen and Shantae's baby girl...not hers. Both Allen and Shantae could see the pain in her tears. "I'm sorry, Taylor. Had I known about you and your kids, I would have NEVER. And I mean that from the bottom of my heart," Shantae comforted.

Taylor stepped up to the bed, "I can't hide the sadness, but these are also mixed with tears of joy. We'll get through this together. I'm sure she going to bring all of us lots of joy," she said.

"Can I hold her?" Allen asked.

"Of course," Shantae replied as she passed her baby girl to her father.

He adored her. She was so precious, so tiny, so beautiful, and so wrong. Allen realized just how wrong he was, how much he had hurt his wife, and how awesome she was for still standing by his side through the pain.

Out of nowhere, Marcus came running in with his delivery gear on like *he* was the father. He froze in his tracks. If looks could kill, everyone in the room would be dead.

"OH, SO THIS WHY YOU DIDN'T CALL ME!" He shouted.

"YOU NEED TO CALM YO' ASS DOWN! This is Allen's wife, and she has been here with me. Allen just got here. I was going to call you, but I couldn't do that while I was pushing out a baby."

"That's no excuse! You should've called me long before you started pushing." Marcus was so upset.

Allen looked over at him, "You alright, buddy!? Cause you lookin' like you got a problem. Come running in hea' with yo' delivery suit on like you thought you was finna delivery my baby or sum shit!"

"*Your* baby??" Marcus asked sarcastically.

"Yeah, nigga. *My* baby," Allen repeated. "Unless you know some shit, I don't know."

"Baby, you need to calm down," Taylor urged.

"No, Marcus is the one that needs to calm the fuck down," Shante corrected. "And what was that supposed to mean anyway? Do you know something we don't know? And why would you be upset that my baby's father is here, with his wife? That should tell you that this is not about me and him. It's about my fucking baby!"

Marcus just laughed. "Watch your vocabulary and tone when you're talking to me."

Allen looked at Shantae, "Man, pops gonna be a problem," he

said.

"He's not gonna be a problem. He just feels left out," Shantae said.

Shantae had never seen her man act like that before. She was hoping that she was right and Allen was wrong. She prayed that Marcus was going to accept that Allen is going to be a part of Allani's life.

Allani Charnae Crawford; their little bundle of joy.

CHAPTER FOURTEEN

After sixteen hours on the road and rushing Allen to the hospital, Pain and Pressure had finally made it back to their mom's house. Zoey met Pressure at the door with a beautiful smile and a breathtaking kiss. Treasure nearly fell two or three times, trying to get to her daddy. Passion and Dre sat at the table hand and hand with her parents. Both Paulette and Vincent got up and hugged Pain and Pressure, grateful for the role they played in the safe return of their sister.

"Mom and Dad are getting back together," Passion said, full of excitement.

"What she gon' do about Steve?" Pain said, being funny, knowing that his father would turn up

"FUCK STEVE!" Vincent shouted. "She ain't gon' do shit bout him. Steve gon' respect that this is my wife and sit his ass down somewea'." The room erupted in laughter.

"I'm just fuckin' wit you, Pops. Congratulations. Mama need a real nigga in her life," Pain said with a grin.

"You don't know what I need, boy. I'm too old to be dealing with real niggas. I need a real MAN," Paulette said.

"You got one already," Vincent corrected. "Everything you need is right here."

"Y'all shot out," Pressure said as he grabbed Zoey's hand and headed for the door. "We'll see y'all in a week or two. We got a lot of catching up to do."

He then looked over at Dre, "Don't make me kill you, lil' nigga."

Passion got up and hugged her brother so tight, "Thank you, Pressure. I knew that you would come for me. I never for one second doubted it. I love you so much, bruh."

"I love you too, sis. I gotta get used to someone else being your hero," Pressure replied.

"How you her 'Hero?' What the fuck am I?" Pain interjected.

"I definitely wanna know what that make me?" Mr. Vincent chimed in.

"You sholl got a lot of competition, sweetie," Paulette said to Dre.

"I see," Dre replied.

Pressure gave Dre and all the other men dap, then hugged his mom, Candice and his sister. Zoey said her goodbyes and they were out the door, off to hibernate in their own little bubble.

Candice was helping clean up when Passion joined her. Treasure was picking up her toys from all over the house. "Y'all ain't gotta do this," Mrs. Paulette said. "I got this.

"*We* got this," Mr. Vincent said, reminding her that she didn't have to do anything alone anymore.

"That's right, Pops. Get her mind right," Pain instigated. "All that 'ME' shit is out the window now, Mama. Now it's WE. We, as in, the two of you."

"Yeah, well, we like y'all together too. You, Candice, and Treasure, the three of you. Not just you," Paulette said sarcastically. "Practice what you preach, son."

"I know that's right!" Candice agreed.

Pain grabbed her and kissed her passionately. "Let's go home, baby. It's just us now. Me, you, and our baby. I'm coming home every night, like a real man supposed to. I've cut all ties with all the other females. It's just me and you. I don't expect you to believe me but stay tuned, you'll see that this time I'm for real. So, if you need a minute to tell ya lil' boyfriend it's over, I'm finna go holla at sis while you handle ya business. But make it snappy 'cause I'm ready to go."

He went in the kitchen and pulled Passion aside, "Sis, I get that you're grown and all that bullshit. But you gon' always be my little sister. If you ever need me, hit me up. I care nothing 'bout the fact that you have a nigga. I'm still here for you whenever you need me."

He then turned to Dre, "Lil' nigga, that's precious cargo you got. Please handle with care. Welcome to the bottom." He gave Dre dap and Passion a good, tight hug. Then he grabbed his baby and told his mom and pops goodnight as he walked out the door.

Candice seemed to be having a hard time letting the nigga she was on the phone with down. So, Pain grabbed the phone. " It ain't no easy way for her to tell you this, buddy, but I'm back home. So whatever y'all had, is over. It's really kinda simple." Pain then handed her the phone back and laughed as she disconnected the call.

"I don't know why you even play with niggas feelings like that," he said to Candice as they got in the car and drove away.

"I'm not playing this time, Pain," she said. "And I don't feel good about hurting his feelings. He's a really good guy, and I love the way he loves me."

"Ok, so you wanna call dat nigga back?" Pain questioned. "If you think he's gonna love you better than me, then call the fuck nigga." He busted a U-turn and went back to his mom's house. He got out, but not before grabbing Treasure.

"Go get that nigga if that's what you really want. I'm not finna compete with nan nigga. I got bitches lined up waiting for a chance with me. I'm trying to do right by you, but that don't mean I'm finna kiss yo' ass."

"I'm not kissing your ass either, Pain!" Candice yelled as Pain went inside, and she pulled off burning rubber. They were both equally pissed at one another just that quick.

The following morning, Pain took Treasure to breakfast and then took her home. To his surprise, Candice was not home. His feelings were crushed. He thought for sure last night she was going home like he did. But this bitch really went to this nigga. He sat in the parking lot for a while. Just as he was about to pull off, a black C-Class Benz with Forgiato rims and dark tint whipped in the complex. It was a car he had never seen before. He couldn't make out who was inside, but something deep inside told him that it was Candice and her dream guy.

As the car approached, he looked each other dead in the eyes. Pain quickly blocked the car in and jumped out of his. Before Candice could open her door, he had snatched her out of the car.

Choncie jumped out of the car and stepped between Pain and Candice. "Ain't none of that going down, homie. Not in my presence," Choncie asserted.

Pain immediately hit him with a one two combo and dazed him. Treasure was in the car crying. Candice was screaming to Pain to stop, but he had completely lost it. Dude tried to stand his ground but couldn't hang with Pain. Candice grabbed Treasure from the car. Her cries were the only thing that stopped him. He heard her screaming, "DADDY NOOO!" and instantly stopped. He never wanted her to witness that side of him.

"Put my baby back in my car and continue yo' date, shit eatin' ass bitch," Pain demanded. Candice couldn't believe he spoke to her that way, especially in front of their daughter. "Better yet, give me my baby and help ya nigga up off the floor." He snatched Treasure, jumped in his car, and pulled off. Candice ran to her friend's aid. He had a swollen eye, a bust lip, and a bloody nose. He was so upset.

"I will fight that nigga every day for you, if you're sure you want to be with me," Choncie said. "But if you're just going to just run back to him, anyway, then don't take me through this. Just let me go."

Candice's tears begin to fall. "I've never seen him act like this. I am so, so sorry," she cried.

"To see the woman you love with another man will make you snap like that," Choncie admitted. "If you were mine, I would act the same way, Candice. The question is, ARE you mine? Or do you belong to him? I'm not asking where your mind and body is... What I need to know is, who does your heart belong to?" Choncie questioned.

"I love everything about you," Candice said. "Like right now, even though he just did this to you because of me, you're still so gentle with the way you handle me. But I can't promise you that I won't go back. I almost went back last night, and it felt so right until I thought of you. Truth is, I'm scared to let you go if he hasn't changed."

"Get in the car," he said.

She obeyed. "Where are we going?"

"I'm taking you to get your car. The truth hurts, but I'm man enough to accept it," he replied.

"What are you talking about?" She asked.

"Your heart belongs to him, baby. I can't compete with that," Choncie concluded.

The ride to Candice's car was quiet. She has such little faith in Pain. She knew he held her heart. She knew in the end she would choose Pain. But this time, it felt wrong and stupid. It was hard to let this one go. She had prayed so long for love like this. She asked God to send her a man just like Choncie, and He answered her prayers. And yet, she wasn't ready for him. Because she wasn't ready to give up on the man that she loved so much and for so long.

Now Pain was saying that he was ready. He would never play with her emotions like that. Maybe he was ready for real. He always said that she could never force him to be the man that she wanted him to be. Last night he said, himself, that he was ready to be that man. Her emotions were all over the place. She had crushed Pain's spirit, bruised his ego, and possibly broke his heart. He was angrier than she had ever seen him. Truth is, she would've acted the same way if the shoe was on the other foot and she had caught Pain with another woman.

She didn't had sex with Choncie last night. They only went out to have drinks and then parked at the mountaintop and talked until dawn. After that, they had breakfast. She was coming home to shower and change clothes before they studied for a final exam that was to be taken next month. However, Pain changed all of that.

When they arrived at her car, Candice asked, "Can they at least still be friends and study sometimes at the library?"

"We won't plan to meet there, but if I run into you there, then we certainly can," Choncie replied.

"I'm not mad at you. I rather we end it now than wait until I'm in way too deep to walk away without malice. Today I understand. Tomorrow, I might be mad as hell. So, you better go now," he said in a playful tone. She gave him a goodbye kiss with tears in her eyes.

"You're too pretty to be crying." He got out of the car, went to her side, and opened the door. She got out, and he wiped her tears away. He hugged her until his heart said let go and gave her one last kiss. "If you ever need me, I'm here for you."

With that being said, she couldn't ask for more. She got in her car and went home. Her first thought was to go running to Pain. But she was exhausted from being up all night and emotionally drained. She went home, showered, and got in her bed. Then she cried herself to sleep…alone, once again.

Hours later, Candice was awakened by her phone ringing and a knock at the door. She opened the door to find Treasure standing there holding a bouquet of long stem roses.

"Hey, Mommy. These are for you," Treasure uttered.

"Thank you, Princess. They're beautiful," Candice smiled.

"Daddy said he sowwy," Treasure said. "Right, daddy?"

"That's right, Princess. Daddy is so sorry," Pain confirmed.

"Would you do me a favor, Princess?" Candice asked. "Can you tell daddy that mommy is sorry too?"

Treasure laughed innocently, "He just heard you, mommy."

Candice found a vase, and put the flowers in it with water. She sat them in the middle of the dining room table. "Treasure, why don't you go build something really nice for Mommy and Daddy while we talk?'

"Ok, but no fighting," she ordered while pointing her finger at them.

"No fighting, Princess. Daddy promise," Pain assured.

Treasure took off running to her room. She emptied out all of her blocks and began to build.

Pain sat at the dining room table with Candice. The aroma of the fresh roses lingered in the air. "I didn't mean to react that way towards you or in front of Treasure. Truthfully, if I was strapped, I probably would've smoked both of y'all," Pain confused.

"It was all fine and dandy for me to do me as long as you were doing you, but now that you 'claim' that you're ready to settle, it's a problem. The world don't revolve around you. You don't know how much I sacrificed for US. How many nights I cried myself to sleep when I didn't have to.

I think you forgot that I'm a bad bitch too. My line of niggas can get just as long as your line of hoes, and that new nigga gone cherish me the way you should have. The things about me that you take for granted, someone else is praying for those same characteristics in a woman."

"You think I don't know that, Candice?" He said. "You think I'll keep running over here if I didn't see the beauty in you? You think I'll keep paying your bills and putting you through school if I didn't know your worth? I love you! I know you deserve better and I'm going to give you that now."

"Now, Pain?" Candice retorted. "As soon as I found someone who treats me right? What if you made up your mind a little too late?"

"Then just tell me that and I'll respect it," Pain said. "No matter how much it hurts. If you really feeling that nigga, then I'll step down and let you see how it goes."

"I wanna be with you, Pain, but I'm scared. I'm scared of letting go of someone that is so right for me to chase after someone that is so toxic," she admitted.

"Contrary to what you may think, it's impossible for someone to love you more than me," Pain expressed. "I'm ready, Candice. I have enough money now to give the streets up. From here on out, I promise to put you and Treasure first. All that bullshit with Passion was enough for me to know where I want to be and where I'm supposed to be. That's here, with you and our daughter, working on making her a sibling to play with and coming home at a respectable hour every night. I know what you want, and I'm ready to give you that. When I wasn't ready, I made that clear. Now I'm here, ready and willing. But if you've already given up, I have no choice but to let it go."

"I've already said my goodbyes to him. Because I know that I am still deeply in love with you. I believe that our family is worth fighting for. Besides, how can he protect me if you're gonna keep beating his ass?" Candice said as they both laughed.

"It's not funny, Pain. You really shouldn't have done that."

"No, *you* shouldn't have done that," Pain said as she laid her head on his shoulder. He lifted her head so that he could look into her eyes, "I got you, baby. It's going to be different this time around. I know I have to prove myself; I just need you to have a little faith in me."

"I got too much faith in you, Pain. That's the problem," Candice said.

"That 'was' the problem...Now, that's my motivation," Pain corrected.

Treasure came running out of the room, "Mommy, Daddy, come look at what I made." They both followed her to her room, and as they entered, they noticed a tiny house made of blocks standing in the center of the floor.

"That's beautiful, Princess, but that house is not big enough for all of us," Pain teased.

"Daddy's right, Princess.' Candice added. "But I have a better idea. Let's build a castle." Treasure agreed, and together, the three of them made a big castle out of blocks.

Once Treasure ate dinner and fell asleep, the two of them showered and made love like it was their very first time.

ΔΔΔ

Once Allen and Taylor had left the hospital, they took a Lyft to get Allen's truck. There were still so many unsettled issues between the two of them. Neither of them spoke along the ride.

Once inside Allen's truck, he looked at Taylor, "I know this is not what you thought our lives would be like when we got married, but I promise you that I love you with all my heart and soul. Just as much today as I did on the day I asked you to marry me. Allani is going to be in our life forever, but I can assure you that what Shantae and I had is over. I'll never put my hands or dick on another woman as long as we're together. You are more than enough. You were never the problem; it was me."

Taylor sat quietly with tears blocking her vision. They would not stop falling. The pain was like a stab wound: sharp and deep. Allani was so beautiful. She already has so many of Allen's features. She knew he wanted a daughter, and he got one alright. However, she was not gonna keep crying over the situation. It was something she had chosen to accept. So, from this point forward, she would learn to live with her decision and still find a way to love and trust her husband. She just wanted their life back the way it was when they were happy and deeply in love.

"Shantae is pretty cool. I see why it was so hard for you to walk away from her."

"Baby, after everything I just said to you, that's all you got to say?" Allen questioned. "You're cooler and prettier."

"It's ok, Allen. I'm not comparing myself to her. I'm simply complimenting her. If she was ugly, we probably would be getting a divorce," she joked. She and Allen both laughed. "I love you, Allen."

"I love you too, baby," he responded.

"Allani is beautiful," Taylor complimented. "Now that you finally have your girl, I can get my tubes tied."

"You crazy as hell. If God blesses us with another baby, you gon' have that one and another one and another one," Allen ordered.

"Nigga, please," Taylor objected. "You not finna have me bad bodied with a house full of crying ass babies. Then you leave me for a snatched bitch with no kids and a quiet house."

Allen shook his head, "I would never do no shit like that to you, and I'm definitely not leaving."

Taylor noticed they had pulled into the Four Seasons Resort, "Aww, baby, this is where you proposed to me at."

"I want to remind you what that moment felt like," Allen said. "I need one more chance to make you feel that way again." He jumped out and opened the door for her like he used to do. Then he grabbed her hand and escorted her inside.

After sitting down at a 5-Star restaurant located in the resort to have dinner, he led her to the Penthouse Suite, which he had already reserved for them. He connected the Bluetooth speaker and played the 'Slow Jam Remix' by Usher featuring Monica. This was the first song they danced to at their wedding.

He reached for her hand, "May I please have this dance?" She took his hand, and they swayed to the music. Memories of that moment consumed their hearts. She loved this man so much. Yea, he had fucked up, but so had she. He loves her with her flaws and all. And she planned on doing the same.

The following morning, they went back to the hospital to spend time with Allani before heading back to Detroit. They agreed to meet up again on the 4th of July. Allani would be a month old, and the boys could meet their baby sister. Shantae and Taylor made all the plans, and Allen just agreed. Marcus walked into the room, and this time, his attitude was much more in check. He was very apologetic about the day before. Allen and Taylor took that as their cue to leave to give them some alone time.

They said goodbye to Allani, and Allen handed Shantae a rubber band of cash. "I shouldn't have to tell you to call me if you need me because you already know that, right?" Allen confirmed.

"Right," Shante answered.

Allen and Taylor then walked out of the hospital. They went to say goodbye to Mrs. Paulette and thank her for helping them to sort out their mess. They could not wait to get home and get their family back in order.

They arrived home in Detroit and had a magical night of reliving old memories and making new ones. They both missed the time when their lives were easy and simple. However, giving up was not an option. It was now time to get back to the basics.

CHAPTER FIFTEEN

Passion sat inside her doctor's office, nervous as hell as she waited for the pregnancy test results. Dre was right by her side. Moments later, the nurse came back and congratulated them. She was pregnant indeed. The blood work indicated that she was two weeks pregnant. She had been home for over a week now. The first time Marquise had raped her was a week before her rescue. Prior to her capture, her period was already a week late. Based on her calculations, she felt that it was Dre's baby. But it was a matter of days that could be the difference. She had decided, either way it went, she would keep her baby and love him or her regardless. Dre vowed to do the same. Deep in her heart, she hoped that it was Dre's baby, but she wanted to be sure, so she questioned the nurse.

"How can I find out the paternity of the father immediately?"

"Well, there are many ways, thanks to technology," the nurse answered. "But you would have to be fourteen to twenty weeks to try any of them. The most commonly used method is with an Amniocentesis procedure. That is when amniotic fluid is drawn from the sac that the baby is growing in. Early on in the pregnancy, inserting a needle into the sac can be a very risky procedure, which could result in injury to the developing embryo.

However, in the second trimester, the risk of the procedure slightly decreases because the embryo has developed into a fetus. This makes the baby a little stronger and more likely to withstand the procedure. This also provides more room in the sac as well as more amnio available to draw for the test."

"What's the worst that can happen?" Passion asked.

"Well, very rarely and in extreme cases, the procedure could possibly lead to a miscarriage or a still born," the nurse regretfully informed.

Tears begin to fill passion eyes before falling to her cheeks. Dre quickly wiped them away. "Baby, you said that you wanted to keep this baby no matter who the father is. I'm going to be the best father in the world. I'm even willing to sign legal adoption papers if the baby isn't mine if that'll make you feel better. I'm going to love the both of you unconditionally, regardless. So why does it even matter? But if it is a must that you know, why don't we just wait until after the baby is born? It's a lot simpler and safer that way," Dre pleaded.

Passion looked at the nurse, "I know I've been coming here my entire life and that you're very close to my family, but I would like to keep my business private and confidential."

"That's the law, Passion. And we don't break the law here," the nurse clarified. "Once you turned 18, your medical records became completely confidential unless you say otherwise. Now, do you want to tell me what's going on, Passion, so that I can help you make a wise decision?"

Passion took a deep breath and then revealed that she had been raped several times by her boyfriend's brother while being held captive and that there's a strong possibility that the baby could belong to her captor. She agreed to cooperate to keep him from being violent, but it was still rape because she kept saying no repeatedly.

"Did you contact law enforcement?" The nurse asked with great concern.

"He's dead," Dre replied with no emotion.

"I see," the nurse replied with understanding. "If deep in your heart, you're going to love the baby regardless, then I would say, get the paternity test after the baby is born to keep from always wondering. If your captor ends up being the biological father and you're not sure whether or not you're going to still be capable of loving this child the way a mother should, then I recommend that you set the appointment as soon as possible."

Passion looked at Dre. "You may never fully understand this, but I need to know," she said.

"Set the appointment then," Dre said.

"Alright then. I'll be right back with you next OB/GYN appointment and your appointment for the Amniocentesis procedure," the nurse announced.

When she walked out of the room, Dre was honest with Passion. He admitted that he really didn't want to know, but he understood her need to know. He'd already given the situation to God. Either way, the child had his blood, and he would love it as his own.

A few minutes later, the nurse returned with both appointments. On October 21, 2022, she would determine the paternity and the sex of her unborn child.

ΔΔΔ

Marcus was in valet parking strapping the car seat in, waiting for Shantae and Allani to be brought out of the maternity ward of the hospital. When she came through the automatic doors, she thanked the orderly for bringing her down and placed the baby in the car seat. Marcus opened the passenger door and helped her get comfortably inside. She was still a little sore from the stitches on her episiotomy but other than that, she felt great. Everything seemed to be working out.

Marcus was happier than ever. He seemed more excited than she was about the baby. Shante noticed that he was heading in the opposite direction of her house and questioned where they were going. "It's way too soon for me to be hanging out," she said.

"Baby, just chill. I have a big surprise for you," Marcus said with excitement. He pulled up to a really nice house in a gated community. He scanned a card and the gate opened.

"Wow, this is where you live?!?!" Shantae asked.

"This is where WE live," he replied.

Shantae had never been to Marcus' house. She liked him but not like that. He was a great distraction when she and Allen first separated. He helped her get over Allen. He was a nice guy; she just was not attracted to him sexually. And the fact that he had brought her there without asking, really pissed her off. All she wanted to do was go home and lay in her own bed. But she decided to just go with the flow. He helped her out of the car, unstrapped the baby, and they went inside.

"SURPRIIIIIISE!!!!!!" Everyone shouted. It was a group of people that she had never seen before. She didn't recognize anyone. She did, however, recognize HER furniture. Welcome home balloons and stickers were everywhere. The baby's room was beautiful, but it had none of the stuff that Allen had just bought. Their bedroom was full of all of her stuff. Her bed, her dresser, her bed linen, her clothes, and even her curtains.

"It's such a pleasure to finally meet you," a woman uttered. "I'm Joyce, Marcus' mom. And this is his father, Marcus Sr."

"Nice to meet you," Shantae replied.

"I'm so happy to finally have a granddaughter," Joyce exclaimed.

Granddaughter? Shantae thought to herself.

This nigga is crazy as fuck! He just moved my shit out of my house without even asking me. And how the hell did he even get in my house while I was in the hospital? She was overheated but decided not to embarrass him in front of his people, whom he had obviously lied to by telling them that Allani was his baby.

"I'm happy to finally be a mother, it's a dream come true," Shantae replied to Joyce's comment. Marcus interrupted their conversation when he stepped in without the baby.

"Where the hell is my baby, Marcus?" Shantae said in a panicked tone.

"She's in good hands, baby. No need to worry," Marcus replied.

"There is a need to worry," Shantae retorted. "I don't know anyone here. And I don't want my baby being passed from one stranger to the next."

She stormed out of the room on her way to get her baby. She was beyond furious. When she entered the living room, the woman that he introduced as his secretary was rocking the baby. That angered her off even more. Every lawyer she knew was fucking their secretary, so why would he be any different.

"Excuse me, I would like to lay down with my daughter," Shantae said as she reached for her baby.

The woman passed the baby. "Is everything ok?" the woman asked.

"Everything is fine," Shantae answered. "I'm just tired, and a bit overwhelmed. All of this is way more than I expected."

"Understood," the woman replied.

Shantae went in the room and closed the door. She broke down and cried like a baby. All she wanted to do was go home, but apparently, this was her home now. Marcus came in a few minutes later, and she gave him a piece of her mind. "Have you lost your fucking mind?" She asked with anger. "First of all, how did you get in my fucking house while I was in the hospital?"

"Calm down, baby. I been made a key in case of an emergency," he replied. "What if you would've gone into labor while you were home alone?"

"I would've dialed 9-1-1. That's what you do in the event of an emergency," she said matter-of-factly. "You don't take it upon yourself to move my shit out of my house without my permission. I like being in my own shit and having my own privacy and space. This is inhumane and a total invasion of someone's privacy. And where is all the stuff that Allen bought for Allani?"

"FUCK ALLEN!" He screamed. "And whatever he bought. I'm trying to give you and Allani a better life than what you've had. As long as you're in my house, I don't wanna hear Allen's fucking name."

"*Your house?*" Shantae repeated. "Well nigga, take me back to my mutha fuckin house!"

"This is your house!" Marcus reiterated. "I already did the paperwork terminating your lease."

"Is this why your wife left you?" She said sarcastically. "Did you pretend to be sweet, innocent, and caring and then turn into this monster overnight? Because two can play this game, Marcus. I'm not staying here. I want my shit back in my house or I'm calling the police." She went through her purse, searching for her cellphone, only to realize it wasn't there. She then searched the baby's bag, as well as the car. Her phone was nowhere to be found. Marcus went back to entertain his company while Shantae went crazy looking for her phone. Finally, it dawned on her that he must have the phone.

"When you are done showing your ass, you can lay down and get some rest. Here, you get more with honey than you do with vinegar."

"Give me my fucking phone, Marcus!" She demanded.

"If you make one wrong call, you're going to disappear just like my wife did. The wife that you assume left me. Nobody leaves me!" he threatened.

He threw her the phone. It was already on Do Not Disturb. She had already missed several calls. A part of her was mad at herself because she really didn't have any friends. All she knew was Allen, and at one time in her life, that was enough. Now he had moved on, and she was still alone. She was trying to get over one man by running to another, but he was definitely not the right man for this task. Everything about him was too good to be true. She now realized that her duck was really a vulture.

She desperately wanted to call Allen and Taylor but didn't even know where she was. She had only been a mother for three days, and already Allani was in a house of horror. If she called them, she would seem needy and unfit. And what did he do with his wife??? Was he planning on hurting her too, and raising her baby as his own? She went to the kitchen, got a knife and put it under her pillow. If she had to kill him to protect her and her baby, she would. She laid down with Allani tight in her arms. After everyone had left, he came to bed like everything was fine. He moved her hair out of her face and kissed her softly on her neck.

She pulled out the knife and put it to his throat. "DO NOT FUCKING TOUCH ME!" She warned.

"I'm not as nice as you thought either. I will not hesitate to kill you. I'm willing to do whatever I have to do to protect me and my baby. But I'm willing to play this little game with you for as long as you want me to. One thing I know for sure is that Allen is coming for me and his daughter. Now get the fuck outta my face...and lock the door behind you."
He decided not to test Shantae at that moment. She was way too upset. She just might hurt him for real.

"I'm sorry, baby," he said. "Just know that I love you, and I'm doing what I think is best for you and the baby. I thought you wanted a big house for Allani to run around in and a man who REALLY loves you."

"I don't know who you are right now, and until you show me the man I met, stay away from me and my daughter," she insisted.

She noticed that Marcus had taken her phone again and was heading for the door. "The man I thought I knew would never take my phone and treat me like this," she said.

"And the woman I thought I knew would actually appreciate a man that loves her and her baby. She would accept the fact the nigga she is in love with already has a big house with kids running around. Not to mention, a BEAUTIFUL wife that he loves deeply!" Marcus defended.

Shante was so mad that she couldn't sleep. From that moment on, she started putting together a plan to bring him down. Allen was the first and last nigga to ever hurt her. If this nigga thought that he was going to get away with this shit, he was wrong. She was going to put his punk ass in jail. He was book smart, but she was both book smart with street credibility.

With no real mother around to make her stay in school, she eventually stopped going. She dropped out in the twelfth grade to run the streets behind Allen. Her mother couldn't care less. Allen was taking care of her and Shantae. He paid all the bills and kept her high on dope.

As soon as she turned eighteen, he got her an apartment, her own place. The same one that Marcus took the liberty of moving her out of. She planned on making him wish that he would have left her right where she was.

The next morning, he went to work, taking her phone with him. She had another phone that was disconnected, but at least she could still use it on Wi-Fi. She went through every purse until she found it. To her surprise, there was no Wi-Fi inside the house. She tried to go outside to connect to a neighbor's Wi-Fi, but there were deadbolt locks on all the doors. Shantae was so mad and hurt. Why would he? How could he switch up on her like that? What the fuck was wrong with that desperate ass nigga? She broke down, realizing that she was locked in this house alone. What if something happened to her or the baby? Once she found the phone, she charged it up. She decided, if nothing else, she would use the phone to record their conversations. She didn't want to just be free. She wanted to ruin his career, break his ass down. Because he thought for some reason. he was above the law and everyone else.

CHAPTER SIXTEEN

Mrs. Paulette and Mr. Vincent decided to give their love another try. Mrs. Paulette decided that it was time for her kids to meet their sister. It was because of her that they never got a chance to meet her. She felt that she and Vincent owed all of them a sincere apology, starting with Victoria.

Vincent called Victoria and set a dinner date for the three of them. Victoria agreed. Vincent and Paulette picked her up Saturday night, and the three of them went to Giovanni's and had dinner. To their surprise, Victoria's mother had already told her the story of how she was conceived and why she moved away. Just like Paulette, her mom was heartbroken and angry, and her way of dealing with it was to just cut all ties. And that's what she did. She had lots of regrets later on in life, but she lived with it.

None of that mattered to Victoria. She just wanted to meet her sister and brothers. Growing up as an only child, she was lonely. This was like a dream come true. She just prayed that they accepted her. At the end of the day, this wasn't her fault nor theirs. She had been going through a major transition and could use a sister to talk to and brothers that made her feel protected.

They sat and talked throughout dinner. Mr. Vincent decided that he would get all of them together and introduce her to the rest of her siblings. The following weekend he called all of them together for a family meeting. He stressed that it was mandatory that everyone was present. The way he called, making demands had everyone thinking he was about to die of

DREAM

cancer or something serious.

At seven o'clock on the dot, everyone was present. He had told Victoria to come at 7:30. That gave everyone time to settle in. Once she called and said she arrived, Vincent stood and addressed the family.

"Thank you all for coming. I don't want to waste any more time. The reason I brought you here today is to meet someone very special to me," he began.

At this time Victoria walked up to him looking just like Pain. She gave him a big hug as everyone wondered where he was going with this conversation.

"This is your sister, my daughter, Victoria," Vincent continued. "You all should have met her many years ago, but we are not going to dwell on the past. Your mother was angry because I had a baby outside of our marriage. Her mother was angry because I refused to leave your mother. In the end, I lost them both and also missed being a part of Victoria's life. She's now eighteen and has made her own decision to be a part of this family."

"Nothing good comes from being selfish. I thought only of myself, instead of all the people that my bad decision would hurt. Today I'm asking for forgiveness from all of you. I would like to give all of you a chance to express what you feel, even if it takes all night, because we're leaving here as a family. Victoria, you have already met my wife, Paulette. This is your sister, Passion," he said, introducing the two.

Passion stood up and gave her a hug. "I'm going to try to be as honest as possible without offending anyone. I don't like the fact that I've had a sister all this time as much as I wanted one growing up. Neither do I like the fact that I'm no longer the baby. It's funny how God works. He gives you whatever you ask for but in his own way. I constantly complained about being

204

treated like a baby. Now I'm sure I'm going to miss it. I look forward to spending time with you and talking with you about all kinds of stuff. Welcome to the family," she said.

"Victoria, this is your brother, Pain and his daughter Treasure," Vincent said. Pain stood and gave her a hug as Treasure followed right behind him.

"This is crazy," Pain said. "When I look at you, I see myself." Everyone agreed that they looked a lot alike. "You're definitely one of us is all I can say. Welcome to the family."

Vincent continued the introductions, "This is your brother, Pressure."

Pressure welcomed her with a big hug. "Welcome to the family, shorty," he said. "Whatever happened between your mom, my mom and pops, has nothing to do with us. We're all here for you if you need us. Sorry we missed out on so much time together. I look forward to being your big brother."

"Victoria," Vincent said, giving her the floor.

"This is kinda overwhelming," Victoria said. "Growing up as an only child, I've always wondered what it was like to have a sister or brother. I've known for a long time that you all existed. But fear of being rejected caused me not to reach out. My mom died of cancer two years ago, and I've been so alone since then. If I had never reached out to Pops, I probably would've gone crazy. I'm not looking for sympathy or money, I just want to have a relationship with my family."

"Well, you have family now," Mrs. Paulette said. She gave Victoria a napkin to wipe her tears and then a big hug as she reassured her that everything would be just fine. Passion called for her to come and sit next to her. They ordered food and asked her a thousand questions. She did the same. Everyone was amazed at how much Victoria, Treasure, and Pain resembled one another.

Mr. Vincent then stood once again. "I need your attention one more time please," he said, getting everyone's attention. He grabbed Mrs. Paulette's hand and pulled her close to him. He hugged and kissed her and then got on one knee.

"Paulette, I've loved you and only you since the day I laid eyes on you. I'm not perfect; I have made mistakes in the past that have made me a better man. I am asking you for a second chance to love you all over again. This time I will love you the way you should have been loved the first time. I promise to honor and respect our vows. I just want to spend the rest of my life with you. Literally, until death do us apart," he said as he pulled a box out of his pocket and opened it.

"Will you marry me one more time?" He proposed.

Mrs. Paulette was blown away. She never saw this coming. She loved this man so much. It felt the same way it felt the first time he had asked her to marry him. This time their kids cheered them on. It was beautiful. She cried as he slid the ring on her finger.

"Of course, I will." She accepted his proposal.

Everyone in the restaurant stood and applauded them. The waitress and waiters did their little march and dance as confetti came down. It was so amazing. That moment alone made everyone watching believe in love all over again. Once everyone was back seated, Passion got everybody's attention.

"Well since we are all celebrating, I figured this would be a great time for me to tell everybody that I'm pregnant."

Pressure looked at Dre with straight venom. "Bruh, I got her. Just like you got Zoey," Dre said to Pressure. "I promise you I'm going to take care of your sister, Pressure. I'm no different from Victoria. Y'all all I got, and I'm not here with no ill intentions. I'm infatuated with Passion. I've never seen any one more beautiful. I've never wanted something so bad... She is good with me, bruh. On God."

Pressure knew that Dre meant what he was saying, but it did nothing to change the way he was feeling. He just wanted so much more for his baby sister. He was disappointed and he was not trying to hide it. He did not know how to be fake. He seen so many young girls throw their life away for a nigga that moved on and left them high and dry in the end. He was going to get over it eventually, hopefully sooner than later. But right now, the thought was killing his vibe, so he opted to leave instead of being a party pooper. He whispered in Zoey's ear that he was ready to go. She was not the type to question him; she just started gathering her things. He then announced that they were about to leave but not before he asked Victoria her plans for the future. She informed him that he would be at Mrs. Paulette's house. He got her phone number and promised to keep in contact. Zoey said goodbye to everyone, and they left.

Passion felt pure jealousy. Was Pressure going to replace her with Victoria? He was having a hard time accepting that she was an adult now. Pressure always spoiled her and treated her like a queen. He was so overprotective had she not gone to college, she probably would never ever have a boyfriend or a baby. He was going to have to get over it. There was no going back now. She was determined to prove him wrong. Her life was not over, it was only just beginning.

Starting with the fact that she and Dre had just gotten a two-bedroom, two-bathroom condo in Clover Leaf Condominiums. They both had been working hard to make it nice and cozy. It was right next to the Clover leaf Bowling Alley. She invited everyone over on Sunday. She planned on cooking dinner, playing games, and then ending the night bowling. Everyone agreed. She told Victoria to make sure she told Pressure.

"Passion, I love you, baby, but I'm not eating your

cooking. Since when you know how to cook?" Mrs. Paulette teased.

"Yes you are, mama. My roommate taught me how to cook. Plus, Dre can cook everything. I promise we got this. You are going to be impressed. If not, we will take you all to dinner. Nobody better not bring nothing but my housewarming gift," Passion demanded.

Pain and Candice were in LaLa-land. Treasure sat in between them, going from one plate to another. The mood was right. Love was in the air. Secrets had been revealed. It felt good for the family to be in a good place after all the drama. Not to mention that the King and Queen were back in their rightful place...on the throne together.

ΔΔΔ

The following Sunday everybody showed up to Passion's apartment with all kinds of gifts. She and Dre had woken up early and started cooking. Passion cut up a bag of potatoes and made garlic butter potatoes. Right before they were done, she added steamed carrots and broccoli. She poured her special butter sauce over it and let it simmer for another twenty minutes. Dre had baked four different flavors of chicken. He decided upon lemon pepper, barbeque, and orange-pineapple and plain oven roasted, all cooked to perfection. Cooking was something Dominique had taught him growing up. She taught him everything she learned from working at Lula's Soul Food Restaurant. Once everyone arrived, they put the dinner rolls in the oven and cooked the chicken in the air fryer for the salad they were serving. Homemade lemonade, Iced Tea, Pepsi, and water were the drink choices.

"Mama got us fucked up," Passion said to Dre as they did

their thang in the kitchen.

"She sure does," Dre said, giving her a kiss, then another one and another one. "I love you so much. Thank you for giving me the one thing money couldn't buy."

"And what's that?" Passion asked, knowing exactly what he was referring to.

"Unconditional love and family. And my son that's going to be fly as hell following me around," Dre joked.

"You mean your daughter that's going to be cute as hell, looking just like me, following you around?" Passion challenged.

"Let's make a bet," Dre said.

"What's the bet?" Passion asked.

"If it's a boy, you give me a girl right after that. But if it's a girl, we will wait a while because girls need way too much attention," Dre proposed.

"I know you ain't go there," Passion contested. They talk junk back and forth as they put their finishing touches on dinner. Passion left Dre to finish up as she showed the girls around.

"Oh my God, I love these lamps," Zoey complimented. "They must have cost a fortune."

"Girl, I bargain shop. I found these online at a place called Celebrity's Trash," Passion informed. "They have so much cute stuff that was once owned by stars and all kinds of rich and famous people. The prices are unbelievable. I paid $100.00 for each lamp, and they threw the curtains in for free. If bought brand new, these same lamps are selling for $850.00, and the curtains are $350.00 normally."

"I can't wait to check it out. I still haven't done much to

the place besides breaking in our new bed," Zoey admitted.

"Oh Lord. Grandbaby number three will be coming soon," Paulette said.

"Maybe four because me and Pain are definitely trying for another one," Candice added.

"Yea, this week y'all are. Next week y'all will be trying to kill each other," Mrs. Paulette said, knowing them way too well.

"Lately everything has been great. I think he's really ready this time. He's been home every night, helping 'round the house. We haven't argued since he has been back," Candice said.

"Do you want kids?" Passion asked Zoey.

"Right now, we are both too selfish for kids. Maybe in a few years. We are planning to start a business and travel a little bit though," Zoey answered.

"Yea, because everything has to be perfectly planned out with him," Passion said.

"I like that about him. I'm the same way. He's a male version of me. We think a lot alike. We are perfect for one another," Zoey replied.

The girls talked about all kinds of stuff while Dre entertained the fellas. They all talked shit about playing basketball like who could beat who and so on. By the time the girls reunited with them, Dre was coming out of the room with three pairs of gym shorts and one pair sneakers for Mr. Vincent.

"Put your money where your mouth at," Dre said as he passed out the shorts.

Pain and Pressure accepted the challenge. It would be Dre and Mr. Vincent against Pain and Pressure. They headed to the basketball court. Both Pops and Dre felt like them niggas talked too much shit. They had something to prove. Dre's mission was to prove that he was just as good as they were at everything. Pops just wanted to show them he still had it.

While the men were outside playing basketball, Candice told the girls all about how Pain beat Choncie up. She told them how nice he was to her, yet and still, she broke his heart and chose to work things out with Pain instead. Everyone agreed that Pain needed that wake-up call. Mrs. Paulette listened and caught all the tea while fixing plates in the kitchen. Passion had made it very simple. She had put out paper plates, plasticware, plastic cups, and to-go containers so that they could take the leftovers. She was not planning on being left with a bunch of food that they were never going to eat.

Victoria and Treasure looked like twins. Treasure followed her everywhere she went, and Victoria loved it, so did Candice. It felt good for Treasure to give her a break by aggravating somebody else. This newfound freedom was everything.

Finally, the ladies made their way to the court to cheer their men on. The score was now 21-23. Pain and Pressure were winning. However, Dre started showing out the minute he saw Passion. He hit a three-pointer giving him and Vincent a one-point lead. They fought hard to keep the lead. The score was up and down, but eventually they tied the game. Finally, Dre hit another three-pointer to win the game. Pain and Pressure with 48, Dre and Pops with 51 was the final score.

"We let you niggas win because we couldn't break Mama and sis heart," Pain argued.

"Take the ass whooping like a man, son. You win some, you lose some, but you live to fight another day," Mr. Vincent said imitating Pops on Friday. Everyone laughed.

Once they made their way back inside, it was showtime. Mrs. Paulette passed out the plates, and they dug in. Passion and Dre watched as they all demolished the food. Even Mrs. Paulette admitted that everything was delicious. Next was Family Feud. Victoria decided to be the host. That way Dre and Passion could play as well. After debating, they decided the girls would play against the guys.

"It's my house, so I get to make the rules," Passion said. "First rule: If you get the buzzer sound, you take a shot...Period. Second rule: You have 60 seconds to give an answer instead of thirty because half of y'all weeds heads and need more time to think. I cannot drink, so Dre will be taking my shots. And that's it. Let's get it."

"Let the games begin," Victoria announced, like a real game show host. "Representing the ladies is Mama Paulette and for the men Papa Vincent. Question #1. On a scale of one to ten, how would your spouse rate you in bed?"

Mrs. Paulette hit the button first. "He would say I'm a 10," she replied.

"Do we have the number 10?" Victoria repeated. DING. "10 was the number one answer. The ladies will start off with a 42-point lead. Do you want to play or pass?"

"We will play!" The ladies screamed.

"Zoey, on a scale of one to ten, how would your spouse rate you in bed?" Victoria asked.

"He would say I'm a 10, but it's already up there, so I guess I'll say a 9," she responded.

"Is there a 9 on the board?" DING. "9 was the number two answer for 28 points," Victoria continued. "Candice, on a scale of one to ten, how would your man rate you?"

"He would say I'm off the scale. This thang is on a whole nother level," Candice answered.
"Is 'off the scale' on the board?"

The buzzer sounded.

"The ladies now have their first X on the board. Someone pour the beautiful 'off the scale' Candice a shot please," Victoria announced. She was doing a great job at hosting, as Pain argued that Candice shouldn't have to take a shot because she was telling the truth. The game went on for hours before the women finally won. Together they all had a blast.

"Before the night ends, we would like to give the men a chance to redeem themselves over a game of bowling. We have already reserved two lanes at the bowling alley next door. This time the couples will compete as a team. We already know that the men will never win without the women," Passion stated. All the men protested. "It's a proven fact that we make y'all better and stronger."

"I guess I gotta find me a man," Victoria said.

"Well, until then, why don't you entertain your niece instead?" Pressure suggested.

"Great idea, bruh," Pain chimed in.

"Welcome to the family, girl. I had to move outta town to get a man. Good luck with that," Passion said, looking directly at Pain.

"And she will not be following your footsteps," Pressure added.

"I happen to like my steps," Passion shot back. "Let's kick their ass, baby, and show them that together we are the perfect dream team."

"Let's do it, baby," Dre replied.

They all headed out to the bowling alley. They all decided to walk because it was right next door. Something about the fact that they walked together as a group made it so much more fun. Everyone was feeling good. The shots they took while playing Family Feud had kicked in and they were ready to battle and talk shit. Once inside, they got right to it. After about ten rounds, Pain and Candice were up by over 50 points. It was safe to say that they were the power couple of the night. They walked back to Passion's crib and finished the rest of the food. Right before calling it a night, Pressure called everyone together for a toast. He knew how much his approval meant to Passion, so he gave it to her. Truthfully, she deserved it.

"I would like to propose a toast to Passion and Dre. You two have done a great job at being responsible adults. Dre, I see you standing your ground as a man, and I respect it," Pressure praised. "The place is nice, she got a new car outside, y'all got a baby on the way; but more than anything, she's happy. Keep it that way, and together I want to see y'all rise above the statistics and stereotypes and elevate as a young black couple. I can see y'all do big things together. I'm here to help in any way I can. Congratulations."

Everyone held their glass up and made the toast. "Thank you so much, Pressure. You don't know how much that meant to me," Dre said with sincerity.

"I do," Pressure said as he wiped Passion's tears of joy.

After everyone was gone, they cleaned up and took showers. Dre had a few drinks while Passion sipped on a glass of wine. It had been a long day but a great one. They both were celebrating their new life together. Dre was happy. Things couldn't be better for him. God had shown him favor in so many ways. He pulled Passion's feet across his lap and began to massage them.

"Thank you for choosing me," Dre said. "You could have any man you wanted, but somehow, you chose me."

"You chose me as well, baby," Passion added.

"God chose you for me. You define the phrase 'Sent from Heaven'." They began to kiss then Dre pulled back.

"Why do you keep pulling back from me? Ever since I have been home, we haven't had sex once. Do I turn you off now? Is the fact that now your brother has had me as well? What is it, Dre?" She questioned, feeling like less of a woman.

"Baby, of course not. My dick gets hard every time you walk by me. I know you've been through a lot. I was just trying not to be insensitive. I did not want to move too fast. But you can get it if you want it, baby girl."

"Have you ever had oral sex?" Passion asked him out of nowhere.

"What do you mean? Have I done it or received it?" Dre asked.

"Have you done it?" she replied.

"I've tried it," Dre admitted.

"Did you like it?" Passion questioned.

"She liked it. That's the goal to make sure the person you're doing it to likes it. Where is this coming from, Passion? Do you want me to eat your pussy?" Dre asked, trying to get to the point of her question.

"I do," she answered truthfully.

"Did he do that to you? Did he eat your pussy?" Dre asked with pain in his eyes.

"NO, Baby! I hear the girls talking about it all the time," she lied.

"Is that right?" Dre said, being sarcastic.

"I'm trying to find out if what they're saying is right,"

Passion responded.

Dre removed her housecoat and spread her legs. She had been thinking about getting some head constantly. Marquise had sucked on her so good, she craved it now. He made her body tremble and feel so good. How could she admit that to Dre? There was no need to. He was about to add it to their sex life. Now instead of imagining it was Dre, it really was Dre. A part of her felt so guilty. The other part anticipated this moment.

There was something about the way Passion was moving her hips that told Dre that this wasn't new to Passion. Something deep inside told him that his sick-in-the-head ass brother had taken his time and made love to his girl. But he had to push those thoughts out of his head in order to properly give his lady what she wanted. After she came, they both laid in silence. The unsaid words hurt more than anything.

Passion started crying. As Dre wiped the tears away, she began to speak, "I lied to you, baby, and I've never lied to you about anything. I will not do it again."

"I already know, baby," Dre said. "We do not have to talk about it because my heart can't take it. I'm not mad at you. None of this is your fault, baby. I'm going to love the hurt and the pain away. I promise. However you want me to do it, I will." He went down and ate her pussy again. This time felt way better than the first time. He was competing with a dead man. A dead man that obviously introduced his girl to the world of oral sex. And she loved it.

CHAPTER SEVENTEEN

Over the next couple of months, Shantae recorded conversation after conversation of Marcus using her freedom as a bargaining tool. He had forced her to have sex with him repeatedly. At this point, her determination was directed more towards making him pay for his actions than it was on getting away from him.

Whenever she finally did get away from him, she had nowhere to go. He had terminated her apartment's lease, and she had no idea what he had done with her car. She had no choice but to contact Allen and Taylor. She sat in the den everyday waiting to see the neighbors in their backyard. Finally, she saw a little old lady watering her grass. She banged on the window so hard it almost broke. Tears filled her eyes. This was her moment... she had to get the lady's attention. She went and got a piece of paper and wrote a note on it. The lady looked several times, but she would not come to the window. The lady realized that something had to be wrong, so she went and got her husband. Her husband stepped a little closer. Shantae put the note in the window. He couldn't figure out what the note said so he stepped closer.

> *PLEASE HELP ME. THIS MAN IS HOLDING ME HOSTAGE WITH MY 2-MONTH-OLD DAUGHTER. I'M AFRAID THAT HE WILL HURT US. PLEASE HELP US.*

She urged the man to come to the window. Finally, he and his wife came. Shantae told them everything and begged them not to play hero because she did not want to tick this man off. She felt he was capable of killing her and her baby. She explained that he was a high-powered lawyer that was very smart, manipulative, and dangerous. Marcus' neighbors could not believe that something such as this was going on right next door to them. They agreed to check on her every day at noon. If she did not come to the window by noon, they were to call the police. However, if his car was home, they knew she would not come to the window. She could not risk him knowing that she had made contact with anyone. She had found a screwdriver and unlocked the den window. It now was able to slide up and down. She passed them a letter and the phone containing the recordings and begged them to send it to Taylor.

> Taylor,
> I don't know who else to turn to. Marcus has me and Allani locked in his house, and he has taken my phone. He is the one responding to any calls or messages that you may have placed. We are not in major danger other than the fact that he forces me to have sex with him constantly. Allani is fine. She has a doctor's appointment on August 5th. This is the only place we are allowed to go. Please be there to rescue us. The address is 2380 Sunrise Blvd. Lauderhill, Florida 33311, Suite 103.
> This phone has recordings of him threatening to kill me and forcing me to have sex. I want the police to hear this. I want him to pay for the shit he's doing. Please do not allow Allen to take the law into his own hands. I could have done that a long time ago. I don't want Allen to end up in jail. I want him to see Allen's face on his way to jail. Because I'm so tired of him throwing Allen up in my face. I pray to God that you are there. If not, I'm going to kill this fuck nigga, and Allani is going to need y'all.
> -Shantae

The neighbors sat down and listened to the recordings before sending it off with the letter Shantae wrote. They were outraged at how he used her freedom as if she was a child given privileges if she did as she was told. The threats, the manipulation; the nerve of this psycho. They wanted to call the police so badly, but they gave their word that they would not unless they felt Shantae or Allani were in real danger.

After listening to the recordings, they rushed to the post office and mailed off the letter and phone using the quickest shipping method available...Overnight Express Mail. They added a phone number for themselves so that Taylor could confirm that she had received the package. Now all Shantae had to do was make it until Allani's doctor's appointment and pray that Allen and Taylor would be there.

Nadene and her husband George owned Grandpa's Bakery. They were well respected in their community. They had retired and left their two daughters to take over the bakery business. They wanted to make sure that the people whom Shantae was putting her trust in would actually come through for her. So, just in case Taylor and whomever else Shantae expected to rescue her did not show up, Nadene arranged for a police officer to be present at the doctor's office as well on August 5th, along with herself and her husband. Just to be on the safe side.

Shantae was nervous. She prayed that Marcus' neighbors had done what she asked them to do and nothing extra. That phone was her only proof of what was going on in that house and she had put it in the hands of strangers. However, at 12 o'clock, she looked out the window and Mrs. Nadene was standing outside waving. When she gave Shantae a thumbs up, she knew that meant that Mrs. Nadene had done exactly what she asked her to do. Shantae jumped for joy. Mrs. Nadene came close enough to show her the receipt from the post office. Shantae knew from that moment on that it was just a matter of time. This nigga was going to pay for what he had done to her.

When Marcus came home, Shantae had music playing. She had cooked dinner and cleaned the house. Allani was vibing in the swing. She put on a sexy dress and threw her hair in a messy bun. In her mind, she was celebrating her victory in advance. Now she wanted to build his trust and make him feel like he was winning.

"What's going on here?" Marcus asked.

"I don't know. I just feel good. I have been praying and talking to God. He told me that everything is going to be alright, and I believe Him," Shantae answered truthfully. "How was work?"

"It was ok," he responded. "I got two new clients. Both claiming to be innocent even though all the evidence proves that they're guilty as fuck."

"So, why would you take the case?" Shantae asked, totally confused.

"They're paying me $40,000. I give the judge $15,000, and he gives them a slap on the wrist this time," he said nonchalantly as if that shit was cool.

"Are you serious, Marcus? That's crazy as hell," she scolded.

"That's politics, baby. This ain't nothing new," Marcus admitted.

"What did they do?" Shantae asked.

"One is being accused of statutory rape as well as lewd and lascivious acts on a minor. The other, home invasion, assault, and battery with a deadly weapon," he answered with no shame.

"Marcus!" Shantae said in shock. "You mean to tell me that you are going to let someone who messes with kids just walk free?"

"I'm not letting him go free, Shantae...the judge is," he corrected.

Shantae was so mad that this conversation was not being recorded. Why hadn't she thought of this before? His demeanor spruced up when she showed interest in his job. It made him feel powerful. She could clearly see it. She instantly began to strategize. She was going to have to get the neighbors to get her a tape recorder so that she could plant it in a place that would capture all of their conversations at all times unbeknownst to him. She would get him to incriminate himself without the slightest idea or clue of him doing so.

The next day at noon, Mrs. Nadene was outside. She told Shantae that she had spoken to Allen and Taylor, and they both agreed that they would be there, no questions asked. She told her that Allen was very angry and talking about sending his boys to get her and Allani. They were able to calm him down, but it wasn't easy. He felt that it was his fault that you ran to some other guy in the first place. He also wanted you to know that he loves you and Allani very much.

"I wish I could hug you right now, Mrs. Nadene. Thank you so much. I hate to even ask you this, but I need one more favor," Shantae said.

"What's that, darling?" She asked.

"Would you happen to have a tape recorder or anything that can record our conversations? I'm going to make sure he pays for everything he's done wrong. Not just to me but to everyone," Shantae promised.

"I do. Hold on a second," Mrs. Nadene said as she ran into the house to retrieve it. She came back with an old school tape recorder that held up to 72 hours. Shantae had three days to get all the dirt on him that she could. She placed the recorder under the wine rack in the kitchen. He always sat in the same spot at the table and talked to her as she cooked dinner or anytime made his food. It was in a perfect spot.

The following evening Shantae pushed the start button on the recorder as soon as she saw Marcus' car pull in the driveway. It was sho
w time. Lately, they have been chilling and talking after he came from work. Today she planned on pressing extra hard. He fed right into it, giving up all the specifics about different judges and cases that they had fucked over for the love of money. She couldn't wait to see the look on his face when his own words came back to kick him in his ass.

Taylor and Allen could not believe that Marcus was this insane. He had been texting back all kinds of bullshit. Allen assumed that Shantae and Marcus were being assholes and just shutting them out of Allani's life. He should have known that Shantae would never do that. She had always been solid and a woman of her word. Taylor always felt that something wasn't right. The responses to her text were extra as hell. It just did not seem like the shit Shantae would say. However, she didn't know her well enough to say what she would or would not say. Neither of them expected that she was going through what she was going through.

"Where will she be staying when she leaves him?" Taylor inquired.

"I have no idea," Allen responded.

"What do you think about letting her move in with us for a while?" Taylor suggested.

"Hell no, baby. We can get her a place if she wants to come up here. But we are not finna be dealing with all that," Allen replied, looking at Taylor as if she had lost her mind.

"Dealing with what? Two women that love you or two

women that you love? Both your baby mamas are getting along. What's wrong with that?" Taylor confronted Allen.

"Taylor, stop the madness. We both would be uncomfortable," Allen explained.

"Speak for yourself," Taylor snapped.

Allen looked at Taylor like she was crazy. Knowing him and Shantae's history, why would Taylor even suggest some shit like that? It was a trap that he was not going to fall for.

"Are you afraid that you might fuck her or feel something that you don't want to feel?" Taylor asked.

"Yea, I am. I'm afraid of all that," he admitted. "I am trying to fix our marriage. I don't want any more problems. I just wanna be happy. I want our lives back the way it was."

"She has always been a part of our life. That's all I'm saying," she said.

"Taylor, what do you want from me? There is no way you can possibly think her moving in with us is best for us. We can find her a place. Help her get on her feet, so she doesn't have to depend on anybody," Allen advised.

"We can do that too," Taylor said.

"We are going to help her get on her feet. That's all, that's it," Allen said as he walked out, leaving more room for discussion on the matter.

For some reason that whole conversation pissed him off. It was like Taylor was not understanding just how hard it was for him to try to sever ties with Shantae. He loved her. He hurt her. He missed her. His body responded to her naturally. His dick knew every part of her body. He had cheated throughout their entire marriage…with her. He did not want to do any of that anymore. But what was Taylor's goal? Was she trying to invite

Shantae into their house or into their bed? The thought turned him on and scared the shit out of him at the same time. He needed a better understanding of where Taylor was going with this.

"If we invite her in our home, we might as well invite her into our bed, Taylor. I honestly can't see one happening without the other," Allen admitted as he re-entered the room.

"I just feel like she is so broken, and you're the reason why, Allen. Maybe if she still had a part of you, she would be able to heal and in due time, be whole again," Taylor suggested.

"And you are willing to share a part of me with her?" Allen questioned.

"I've always shared you with her. Remember?" Taylor answered.

"And let me guess, you are going to just sit back and watch?" Allen pried deeper.

Taylor looked at him with a straight face "No, I'm going to participate," she said.

Allen laughed. "Are you serious, Taylor?"

"I'm dead ass serious. If my only competition is right here with me, who can I lose to? I won't have to worry about her ever again. There is no way that the both of us can't keep you satisfied," Taylor said

"Baby, you don't have to worry about her or any other woman. My mind, my heart, my soul, my money, my dick, this mouth...It's all yours. You satisfy me to the utmost. Shantae and I had emotional ties. Ties that I have put behind me for us. You don't have to compete with anyone, not even her. I don't want nobody but you. I'm in love with you, Taylor," Allen said in a pleading tone.

"What if I told you that I envy her? At the same time, I think she's beautiful and sexy. I often wonder what she looks like naked and how she is in bed. I feel like together we will make you a happy man," she said.

"I'm happy with just you, baby," he replied.

"How can you say that like you are so sure, Allen? It was never just me and you." Taylor said.

Allen was silent. She was right and he was all out of rebuttals. "Would you feel some type of way if I developed a sexual relationship with her?" Taylor asked.

"I'm starting to feel like you are the one that's not satisfied. Obviously, this has nothing to do with me not being satisfied because I'm telling you in every way that I can tell you that I'm satisfied. So what's really up, Taylor?" He said.

"I can't explain it, baby. When I saw her, I wanted to fight her. Once I got to know her a little bit, I wanted to fuck her. I pictured the three of us together and everyone was happy," Taylor admitted.

Taylor started doing laundry as she continued to go on and on about her infatuation with Shantae. The thought had turned Allen on. Taylor may have wanted to fuck Shantae, but he was more than sure she wouldn't want to watch him fuck Shantae. When he and Shantae fucked, it got down and dirty. Nobody knew his body better than Shantae. Nobody sucked his dick like Shantae. At this point, he was confused as to how Taylor had actually stolen all of his attention away from her, to begin with. He had not one complaint when it came to Shantae, but yet and still, here he was married to Taylor. And he loved her dearly. He put her first. She was his wife. And he took his vows to her seriously even though he had cheated. Their family was first and most important. It was not a good idea to bring Shantae into their bed. In no way would that help her or their marriage.

"Baby, our goal is to help Shantae. I'm not putting my dick in nobody but you. We cannot help her by giving her false hope. Besides, I have never known Shantae to be down with having sex with a woman, nor being involved in a threesome. She probably would be offended. You need to get focused. You got me feeling like I ain't sucking that pussy good enough," Allen said, getting tired of talking about Shantae.

He picked her up and put her on the washing machine. He threw her legs over his shoulders and went in on her pussy, sucking it like he had something to prove. When she reached her peak and began to cum, it ran out like water. Taylor screamed in complete ecstasy.

"You think Shantae is going suck that pussy like that?" Allen asked arrogantly.

"I don't know, but I will find out," Taylor replied.

Allen just shook his head. He was done protesting. If Taylor convinced Shantae to come move in with them, cool. But he would not allow her to play victim if shit did not go the way she thought it would. He had damn near begged her not to do this. If that is what she really wanted… by all means, he would stand in the paint. He had enough for both of them. At the same damn time.

△△△

Shantae had stacked up substantial evidence on Marcus. He talked about how Judge Bailey pissed him off asking for a 50/50 instead of the usual 60/40 to free some guy that hired someone to kill his wife. The guy who actually committed the murder went to prison, but he walked. He bragged on case after case of them just letting real criminals walk free. Rapists, murders, and all sorts of violent people, but slammed all the drug dealers. She questioned him about his wife repeatedly. He would always say, 'Just don't do what she did, and you won't have anything to worry about.' She could not wait until the world heard just how corrupt he and our judicial system really was.

Over the next few weeks, she tried to remember all she could. She had three days left 'til Allani's doctor's appointment. This journey was finally coming to an end. In the meantime, she continued to play her role.

"After Allani's appointment, can we go out to eat or something?" She asked. "I'm so tired of being in this house. I wanna dress Allani up like a princess, which means her mama gotta look like a queen and papa gotta look like a king," Shantae said.

"You have been good to me. Your cooking is good, but that pussy tastes even better," Marcus said, kissing her on the neck.

"You used to take me out all the time, Marcus. What happened? Why did you change?" Shantae asked seriously.

"You were going to go back to him. I could see it in your eyes. I couldn't let you do that," he admitted. "That nigga left your heart broken into tiny pieces. I put it back together. I will not allow you to let that happen again. I'm your man. I'm Allani's father. We made plans to raise her as a family, and that's what we are going to do."

Shantae questioned him further, "So this is how you love? Your way of loving me better is locking me in a house and threatening to hurt me. The Marcus I fell in love with would never do this to me. The Marcus I met would never hurt any woman, especially not me."

"Well, you better do what you gotta do to keep the Marcus you met." He kissed her again. "Let's not kill the vibe," he said.

"I'm not trying to kill the vibe, baby. I'm simply trying to make all of this make sense. That's all," she replied.

"Everything else in my life makes sense. My love for you doesn't. I can live with that," Marcus said.

I hope you can because soon you will have to, she thought to herself as she changed the subject.

She did not want to change his vibe; he was feeling good and powerful. He felt like he was on top of the world, and she wanted to allow him to stay there as long as he could because he was about to take a long hard fall, all the way to the bottom.

CHAPTER EIGHTEEN

Passion and Dre were nervous as they waited for the Amniocentesis to be performed. The doctor came in along with the nurse and got right to it. Dre stood right by Passion's side, holding her hand.

"This will only take about five minutes," the nurse said. "You may feel a bit uncomfortable. Just please try not to jump or move. First, we are going to do an ultrasound so we can see the best place to retrieve the fluid samples without coming in contact with the fetus."

They both got a chance to see their baby and listen to the heartbeat. The young couple was so amazed and excited. They both prayed every night that Dre was the biological father. However, they would indeed love the baby regardless. But a daily reminder of what she had been through would make life so much harder. It was easier said than done.

"Take a deep breath," the nurse instructed, as the doctor stuck a long needle into her abdomen. The doctor retrieved the fluids he needed and just like that the procedure was over with. She then took a sample of Dre's DNA. "I'll be back to check on you in about fifteen minutes. As long as everything is good, you guys can be on your way."

The nurse returned about twenty minutes later, and Passion was feeling good. She told her that it was okay for her to get dressed and wait in the waiting room for the results. As soon as Passion stood up, a clear liquid along with blood came running down her legs. She was hysterical. The nurse rushed to go get the doctor. He instructed Passion to calm down and lay back down.

"Please do something, Doc! Please don't let my baby die!" Passion cried.

"Miss Edwards, you must calm down," the doctor urged. "I promise you that we are going to do everything in our power to correct the situation. But you gotta calm down. The calmer you are, the better it is for your baby. This is not the first time we have seen this happen. Everything is going to be ok. We are going to examine you to see what's going on." The doctor ordered the nurse to start an IV to replace the fluids that she was losing and an ultrasound to see what was going on.

"First, we are going to move you into a private room for the night. Just for observations," the nurse got right on it.

The air was so thick. Passion was having a hard time breathing. She was afraid and broken all over again. The two of them were on an emotional roller coaster. Both of them blamed themselves. Dre walked out the room to clear his head. He was breaking down, and he could not let Passion see him like that. As soon as he walked out the room, Passion called Zoey, not knowing that Dre stepped out to call Pressure. They both needed support at this time. This shit was just starting to be way too much. The shit that happens one out every fifty thousand happened back-to-back for them. They were young and strong but why them?

Dre was searching for some kind of understanding. He sat on the ground in a corner and just broke down. He questioned God...Why? As he went through the motions, he felt a hand grab his hand. Pressure pulled him up and hugged him as he cried.

"Go ahead and let it out, bruh, then pull yourself together. You can't hold her down if you fold," Pressure said.

Dre let it all out and then pulled himself together. He washed his face, then he and Pressure went to the parking garage to Pressure's truck to take a shot and smoke a joint. They talked man to man. Pressure told Dre that he was counting on him to love Passion back together again. However, if he could help Dre strengthen himself, he would be there for him. He liked his ambition and determination. Pressure knew for a fact that Dre was in love with Passion, and because of that, he had love for him. He and Dre sat in the truck for over an hour. When Dre was ready, they went back inside.

Zoey got right in the bed with Passion and held her as she cried her poor little heart out. After about an hour of complete silence, Passion told Zoey the full story leaving nothing out. She even told her the way Marquise made her feel. Zoey told Passion to stop blaming herself and not to blame Dre.

"Marquise was just an evil, nasty, good head having ass nigga," Zoey said and Passion laughed. "When you're beautiful, you go through things that normal people don't go through. Who would have been that obsessed with an ugly bitch?" she joked.

Passion and Zoey went from crying together to talking about decorating the house. Zoey was cool as hell and funny as hell, but she was real. She made Passion feel so much better. She felt like Zoey understood her. It felt so good to have somebody to talk to.

Pressure and Dre walked in high as hell. They had prepared the young couple for what was to happen next: good and bad. They both were rejuvenated and ready for whatever. Together they would overcome any obstacles that came their way.

The doctor came in with all the results at the same time. "I have all of your test results. Would you like to discuss this in private or is it ok to speak in front of your company?" The doctor asked.

"It's ok," Passion said. "Go ahead."

"Well, first, it looks like you're in the process of miscarrying," he regretfully informed. "That was the first thing we explained to you, is that this could happen. Nine times out of ten, this procedure is very successful. But every once in a while, the sac is just not strong enough. The fluids are leaking out of your sac at a rapid pace, and there is nothing we can do about it. There is no way the baby can survive without the proper fluids. Within the next forty-eight hours, the baby will pass." Passion cried as Dre held her tightly.

"Baby, we got forever together. We are going to have a house full of kids. Don't worry about it," Dre said as he comforted her. "You can finish school now like you planned on doing from the start. While we have fun making another baby. It's okay, baby."

"The good news is that Andre was 99.99% the biological father of your unborn child. I'm sorry for your loss, Miss. Edwards," the doctor said as he delivered the news.

They were both so happy about that. At least they knew that they had another chance to make another baby because they made the first one. They was relieved that Marquise was not successful at what he attempted to do. She could finally make him a thing of the past and move forward.
When Passion looked up at Pressure, he had tears in his eyes. This was the first time in her life ever seeing her brother emotional. She didn't know if he was happy or sad. But it did not matter as long as he was there.

"Oh my God, are you crying?" Passion asked Pressure.

"Stop playing with me, lil girl," he said as he made sure that tears didn't fall. "But seriously, I hate to see you doing all this crying and shit. You know a nigga ain't cut for that. So I need you to tighten up. Bruh got you. Y'all going to be alright, and me and my baby are going to make sure of that. We are about to bounce, but if y'all need us, call at any time," Pressure said as he kissed her on the forehead and dapped Dre up on their way out the door.

Passion asked them to inform every one of the miscarriage but nothing more. They promised that their secret was safe with them. Zoey thanked Passion for calling her. She appreciated the fact that Passion looked up to her enough to do so and really considered her family. She gave Passion and Dre a hug, then followed Pressure's lead like always.

Once they were alone, Dre got in bed with Passion and laid right next to her. She put her head on his chest. "Baby, this one just wasn't meant to be. You needed time to heal from everything you have been through already anyway. Next time you'll be my wife and finished with school. And I will already be a successful businessman. You will be able to stay home and let me cater to you and just spoil you rotten. Rub your feet, bathe you, bring you breakfast in bed and all that good shit," Dre went on and on.

Passion had stopped crying and fallen asleep listening to Dre making plans and promises that she knew he would do everything in his power to keep. She was defeated and drained mentally, emotionally, and now physically as well.

Once she was sound asleep, he snuck out and went to the nearest jewelry store. When she woke up, he would ask her to marry him. He needed her to know just how much he really loved her. No matter what they go through, he would always be right by her side. He wanted her to know that he still thought she was beautiful, and that he adored her. He wanted her to understand that he wanted forever with her. No matter how hard things got, together their love could conquer all.

He found a nice 5-carat diamond ring and bought a dozen

roses from a guy standing outside of the hospital. By the time he made it back, the entire family was there. Passion was up, and had a more cheerful disposition. He greeted the family and then gave her the roses and a sincere kiss. He was happy to see her smiling again instead of crying. The worst part was over. Now it was time to rebuild. He wanted her to finish school no matter what. She never had to work a day in her life unless she wanted to. But it was mandatory that she finished school. He knew for a fact that had Passion not met him, she would have already finished school by now. He would not be the reason she did not follow her dreams. He was going to make sure she followed her dreams while making new ones.

The family didn't stay long because the nurse had stressed to her that her body had been through a lot and she really needed to get some rest. The bleeding had slowed, and most of the baby had passed through her birth canal already. She had mentally accepted that it just was not meant right now, and she was okay with that. It was bad timing. She wanted to be way more prepared. She knew that Dre would provide for her and the baby, but it was about way more than money. She wanted to be in a good place mentally and spiritually. With everything that had taken place, that would take some time.

He went and sat right beside her. "Passion, you know that I love you more than anything in this world, right?" Dre asked with a dead serious tone.

"Yes, baby. I know that, and I love you even more," Passion said, just as serious.

"Then that means you are ready to be my wife," Dre said as he went in his pocket and pulled out the ring. "Will you marry me, Passion? I want to spend the rest of my life with you. I want to be your husband. I want to love, protect, and provide for you. Will you let me do that? Will you be my wife?"

Passion was crying all over again. This time tears of joy. "Of course, I'll marry you, Dre!"

He slid the ring on her finger. "It's beautiful, Dre. I love it, and I love you." She kissed him passionately.

"You complete me, Passion McCray," he said.

"I like the sound of that," she said as she kissed him once more.

Passion was super excited. She took a picture of her ring on her finger and started a group text to everybody. 'His purpose to me.' was the caption at the top. 'I said yes' was at the bottom.

Everyone started calling and texting to congratulate her. Dre felt so good watching her glow as she showed off her ring. Her smile was priceless. Although this was one of the worst days of her life, he had managed to turn it into one of the best days of her life. He was ready to do that for the rest of his life with ease.

CHAPTER NINETEEN

Shantae got her and Allani dressed. Today was her big day. Marcus had taken the day off. After Allani's doctor's appointment, they had plans to go shopping and out to eat. Whatever Shantae wanted to do. She had earned a day out on the town. She was nervous as hell and just hoped everything went as planned. As long as Allen was there, she knew everything would be alright. She made sure she had the tape recorder and as much as she could take with her without making him suspicious. This was the last time she would be locked behind these four walls. She had no idea where she was going or what she would do next. None of that matters at the moment. She had to focus on one thing at a time. As they headed out the door, she took one last look around, making sure she didn't leave anything important. She wanted to start over. If it was up to her, she would leave all that shit behind and start over straight out the mud, leaving as many memories as possible of both Allen and Marcus behind.

Taylor and Allen had contacted Detective McCann. Allen knew him from school. He works as a lead detective in the North Miami District. He and Taylor had arrived in Miami two days prior to Allani's appointment to make sure that this matter was being taken seriously. Allen made sure the detectives understood if Marcus was not taken into custody, he was going to disappear permanently.

Luckily, Detective McMann's partner was a woman, named Ms. O'Brien, that hated men like Marcus. The entire situation pissed her off royally. She couldn't wait to take him into custody and expose his ass. Seeing as that he was supposed to be such a hotshot lawyer, his arrest would give their career a big boost. The neighbors had contacted 'Good Morning America,' and they would be there as the story unfolded. By seven o'clock A.M., Channel 7 and Channel 10 were present along with the arresting officers. Allen and Taylor arrived around seven thirty. Everyone was in position.

When Marcus and Shantae pulled up, Marcus saw the news vans and got excited.

"Somebody done fucked up and we right on time. I'm sure somebody needs a lawyer right now. The news ain't here for nothing," Marcus said, unaware that he was the person that was going to need a lawyer.

Shantae was glad that he didn't suspect that any of it had anything to do with her. "Wonder what happened?" she asked, playing her role perfectly.

"Probably some kind of medical malpractice or something like that. It's like four doctor's offices in this building," Marcus replied.

"I hope it ain't at my doctor's office. They ain't touching my baby if they fucking people up," Shantae assured.

"Just make sure you're looking good. Because we don't know where the cameras are going to be," Marcus said arrogantly.

"Nigga, I was born camera ready. I woke up cute. You sleep on a bad bitch," Shantae joked.

"Oh, I ain't sleep. That's why you my bitch," he replied.

"Oh, I'm a bitch now?" She asked.

"You said it, I just followed suit," Marcus said in his defense.

Shantae checked herself one last time in the mirror before she got out of the car. She noticed Allen's truck, so she knew he was there waiting to rescue her. She took a deep breath and got ready. It was showtime.

Marcus grabbed Allani as she sat in her car seat without a care in the world, looking like an angel. When they walked in the doctor's office, Shantae signed Allani in. A guy in a nice two-piece suit approached Marcus. As Marcus looked around, shit got really clear to him. He locked eyes with Allen and Taylor.

"Marcus White?" The detective said as Allen approached him and took his baby out of his hands. "I'm Detective McCann, and this is my partner Detective O'Brien." He pulled out his badge and began to read him his Miranda Rights. Simultaneously, his partner pulled out her handcuffs. "You are under arrest. Anything you say can and will be used against you in a court of law..."

Marcus watched as Taylor consoled Shantae while she let out tears of joy. She had done it. She survived this ordeal and got her and her baby out of there safely. Now it was time for him to pay. She pulled out the tape recorder and let him listen for a few minutes while the camera was rolling.

"This is just the beginning of your downfall. I'm going to make sure you pay for every nut you busted, you psychotic, arrogant ass motherfucker," Shantae said as she passed the tape recorder to Detective McCann.

Marcus laughed, "This is a joke, right?" He said. "How long do you think they are going to keep you around, stupid bitch?"

Allen launched at him. Out of nowhere, Pain and Pressure appeared and began to hold Allen back. They walked in at the perfect time. Allen was ready to go down with him for beating his ass.

"Be smart, bruh. The cameras are rolling. He is trying to trick you off these streets. Let that pussy take this ride alone. Don't give him leverage or ammo on you. He is already a dead man walking," Pain pleaded with Allen.

"You ain't stupid, boy. I wish you would put your hands on me," Marcus said, testing Allen's patience.

The moment he let those foolish words spill from his mouth, Pain and Pressure loosened their grip on Allen, and he dropped Marcus with one only punch. The officers threaten to take all four of them to jail if they didn't defuse the situation right away. Marcus was then cuffed and taken into custody.

Shantae ran to Mrs. Nadene as soon as she saw her. "Thank you so much." She knew that she never would've been freed had they had not helped her. She then hugged Mrs. Nadene's husband as well.

It was an emotional moment, and the cameras caught it all. This story was being aired lived live...Breaking news. The reporter from Channel 7 news approached Shantae, Taylor, and Mrs. Nadene and began to interview them.

"Shantae, how are you feeling right now seeing the neighbor that helped you out of this crazy situation?" The reporter asked.

"It feels great. Once she told me that she had mailed the letter and the phone to Taylor, I knew everything would be okay. It was just a matter of time. Mrs. Nadene and her husband George were a blessing from God. I owe them my life," Shantae answered as she hugged Mrs. Nadene again.

The reporter then turned to Taylor. "Taylor, correct? You are the wife of Allen, who is the father of Shantae's beautiful daughter?"

"I am," Taylor said with no shame. She was a boss

bitch at all times. She could care less about what other people thought of her and Allen's marriage. As long as they understood each other.

"How did you feel about getting a letter asking for help from someone who had been secretly sleeping with your husband?" The reporter asked Taylor, being messy.

Taylor responded like such a lady, "Anyone attached to my husband is attached to me. I jumped into action, doing whatever we had to do to help her out of this situation. I have no ill feelings towards Shantae. We ain't the first and won't to be the last women to be in love with the same man. Now if you will excuse us, we must be on our way." She grabbed Shantae's hand, and they walked away.

"That hoe should've got slapped!" Taylor mumbled as they walked off hand in hand.

Allen was coming out of the building just in time. At this point, they just wanted to get gone. Shantae was overwhelmed and emotional. She took his ass down and proved to herself that she was stronger than even she knew.

As they drove to the hotel, Taylor's phone was blowing up. It rang back-to-back. Taylor looked at the phone, but she would not pick up. It was her kids' Godmother, Janae. Taylor had not mentioned that any of this was going on, and Janae could not believe it when she saw it on the news. She had a thing or two to say to Taylor about the entire situation. Once at the hotel, Taylor answered the phone.

"Hey, Janae. What's going on?" Taylor asked calmly.

"You tell me what the fuck is going on! Allen is an asshole for taking you through this, but you represented like a boss ass chick. You made it look good. But how are you really? Why didn't you tell me, Taylor? I thought we told each other everything. And why were you holding that bitch hand? Don't play with me, Taylor," Janae was pissed.

"I'm okay, Janae. I had to figure this one out on my own," Taylor responded.

"So, what now? Y'all plan on bringing her to Detroit? You think you're just going to be all about this bitch now and just forget all about me?" Janae asked, all in her feelings.

"Cut it out, Janae. This is not the time for you to start tripping. How am I going to forget about you? You're tripping. I'm just playing my part. Nothing more, nothing less," Taylor said.

"I know you, Taylor. Please don't play me like a fool because I wouldn't do it to you. And you know that. Promise me that you will not put your hands or mouth on that bitch," Janae demanded.

"I promise," Taylor said, knowing deep inside, that was a promise she would not keep.

Janae and Taylor had been fucking for the last five years. Janae was head over heels in love with Taylor. Up until now, they were perfect for each other. Janae's husband worked as a trucker and was always on the road. Allen used to be gone as well; supposedly he was a trucker also. Janae and Taylor comforted each other while their men were out doing God knows what. They would have sleepovers with the kids. Once the kids were sleep, they would fuck like animals. And it was enough for them to keep their marriages strong. It was like having the best of both worlds. Janae was not about to let Shantae come take her place. Taylor was her bitch, and that was that. No compromising.

Allen had already gotten two rooms for three days. That was long enough to give Shantae time to figure out her next move was going to be. The boys were at Mrs. Paulette's house. Later they would pick them up. Right now, both of them just wanted to be there for Shantae and Allani.

A bit of jealousy consumed Allen. He needed to hold Shantae. But not for her...for him. It was his job to protect her. He promised her that he would when she first gave herself to him. And up until now he had kept his promise. He had failed her and broke her heart. Now she had been taken advantage of. He would do everything in his power to help her get back on her feet.

Shantae could see the distress in Allen's face. They spoke to each other without saying a word. She knew that he was trying his best to not overstep his boundaries and that was understandable. What she did not understand was how Taylor was so understanding. For some reason, it seemed genuine. But so did Marcus in the beginning. Her judgment was so off with him. Could she be misreading Taylor as well? Her mind was all over the place. As long as Taylor didn't show her any signs of foul play, she would not cross the line. She would respect that Taylor was Allen's wife. She couldn't stop her tears from falling. Here she was bowing down to Allen's wife. Her life was beyond crazy. This shit was completely out of control.

"Baby girl, you gotta stop crying. I can't take much more of that. It's killing me softly," Allen admitted. "I never meant to hurt you and I'm sorry. I handled you wrong, and I will never forgive myself for that. But I need you to forgive me and believe that I'm going to make it up to you without crossing the line. I will never lie to you or my wife again. You have always kept it real with me, and none of this would've happened if I had done the same." He grabbed Allani and her bag, and he walked out the room. He needed air. He was crying inside. A part of him hoped that Taylor would do whatever she had to do in order to make Shantae feel better. He just could not stand seeing his ride or die so broken.

When Allen got to Mrs. Paulette's house, the boys were outside playing with Treasure. Stress was all over his face. Mrs. Paulette hugged him tightly. "Are you okay, son?" She asked, as she reached for Allani.

"I fucked up, ma. I played the game all wrong. Now my main bitch is my side bitch, and she is crying in the arms of my current main bitch. Nobody had to get hurt. All I had to do was keep it real from the start. Now I'm trying not to overplay my part while I watch my wife overplay hers. This shit is crazy," Allen confessed.

"Would you rather they be enemies?" Mrs. Paulette asked.

"If it was up to me, they would have never met. But we past that now. I just don't like the fact that I put her in this situation," Allen admitted.

"Baby Shantae chose Marcus because she believed his lies. That has nothing to do with you. You hurt her badly, but you had nothing to do with her running to another man looking for love. That's her fault," Mrs. Paulette comforted. "These women gotta learn to be independent. How to make it on their own. They are looking for love and stability in all the wrong places, and that's nobody's fault but their own. You did fuck her over, but that happens in life. Learn from your mistakes and move on. You were good to both of them. Somebody had to win. Somebody had to lose."

"You're right about that. That is why I told Taylor I'm going to help Shantae get on her feet and get some kind of legal independence going on. I can't have her fucked up out here nor can I have her running from nigga to nigga with my baby girl. I just gotta keep my hands off of her and do something for her that really matters. Like maybe helping her start a business. Maybe a shoe store or something she loves doing. I gotta show her love in a different way. I think I can do that," Allen said.

Pain pulled up, and he and Allen chopped it up for a while. Then he gathered the boys and made his way back to the hotel. He and Taylor would keep Allani tonight. He wanted Shantae to get some rest before he introduced her to the boys. They were a handful. They were in love with Allani already. She was like a little doll to them. They wanted to hold her and feed her. It was cute but scary as well. Allen stopped and grabbed food for everybody. And then headed back to face reality. Shantae had finally stopped crying. She and Taylor were kicking it like the best of friends.

"I'll go feed the kids while the two of you talk," Taylor said. She noticed that Allen was looking like he was scared to be alone with Shantae. "It's okay, baby. Be yourself. She needs you right now. I understand. I know where I stand in your world, and so does she," she said.

Taylor went next door with the kids. Allen held Shantae for about ten minutes. He needed that hug more than she did.

"I'm going to start out by saying I love you today just as much as I did when I first laid eyes on you. If I would have known that you would go through what you went through, I would have done everything different. I thought that you were strong enough to handle it.

It was not that I loved you less. However, I had to make a choice, and now I gotta live with that choice. Don't ever feel like you did something wrong or that you were not good enough because you were good to me. You deserved a ring on your finger and a house on the hill. Just because I did not give it to you, doesn't mean you did not deserve it," Allen said.

"Allen, I'm okay. I'm learning that all fairy tales don't always come true. It just doesn't seem real. Taylor is making it hard for me to dislike her," Shantae admitted.

"I want to fuck you so bad right now. I wanna just lay

up with you and promise you that everything is going to be alright. However, I know that ain't the answer to our problems. I wanna love your pain away, Shantae. I promise, on all three of my kids, that I'll never hurt you again," he said.

"Allen you can't pull me back in because I never left," she replied. "I don't lie to Taylor. She knows that I'm still very much in love with you. I'm just trying hard to stay in my lane. I don't plan on overstepping my boundaries. I'm going to respect your wife as long as she respects me. I gotta find my own way this time.

"Allani makes me feel like I can do anything because I will do anything to make sure I'm an excellent mother. That's all I'm focused on right now, I gotta build a life for me and my baby. If you wanted me back right now, I would welcome you, but because I see how much love and respect you have for Taylor, I wouldn't subject myself to additional pain. I'm learning to let go. One day at a time."

Allen's mind was telling him to lay her down and dick her down really good. There was no letting go. She had him all fucked up...but that was the old Allen. The new Allen needed her to let go. So, he gave her a kiss on the forehead. Taylor would have to be the one that opened Pandora's box...not him.

"Are you okay, for real?'" Allen asked.

"I'm good now...The look on that nigga face was priceless. He never saw that shit coming. It felt so good to see his fuck ass go down. He constantly reminded me that you had a beautiful wife and a beautiful life and that you did not give a fuck about me or Allani. I had to tell myself that he was wrong. I know you love me, and I don't know where we went wrong, but I know we gotta do better moving forward. I'm going to take time to love myself first. All is forgiven. Besides, everybody is going to be trying to get this pussy. It's good enough to get me kidnapped and held hostage," Shantae joked.

"That pussy is good. I swear to God. It's hard to shake," Allen said.

"It ain't too good. I can't keep a man," Shantae shot back.

"I got a few missing screws. Anybody in their right mind would keep you. I'm starting to feel like something is wrong with me," Allen admitted. "I don't want to give you false hope, but lately, none of this makes sense to me. I don't understand the decisions I made. And it doesn't feel right. It feels wrong. I'm more confused now than ever before. This shit is crazy."

Their conversation was interrupted by Taylor knocking. When Allen opened the door, Taylor had a plate of food that was nice and hot and a Sprite.

"Thank you so much, Taylor. I'm starving," Shantae said.

"You can stay if you want. I'm going next door to chill with the kids," Allen said.

"Ok," Taylor said. "I wanted to talk to her anyway. The sooner we figure out how we're going to get you situated, the sooner we can get back home."

"Do y'all thing, I'll be next door," Allen said before disappearing.

Taylor sat on the bed next to Shantae. "How do you feel about moving to Detroit with us until we find you a place and get you situated?" She asked. "I'm sure we can find you a really nice place and get you a job. And we will all be there to help out with Allani."

"Taylor, the fact that you're willing to bring me and baby into your home speaks volumes about your character. But being under the same roof as y'all would feel crazy to me. I don't want to violate you in any kind of way because you are fucking awesome. I'm still vulnerable and broken, and I don't trust myself alone with Allen," Shantae admitted.

All Taylor could do was respect her honesty. "I already know that," she said. "He doesn't trust himself around you either. See, that's the thing. There is absolutely nothing I can do about the love that you two have for each other. He's trying everything in his power to respect me and our marriage while trying to be there for you as well. My suggestion is that you just come with us. If you're the only bitch that I have to worry about, why not make it easier on everyone and just learn to share the man that we both love?"

"WHAT?!?!" Shantae exclaimed. "That's crazy as hell. You can't be serious."

"I'm dead ass serious," Taylor responded. "And I already talked to Allen about it."

"And I know he didn't agree to no shit like that!" Shantae added.

"That's because he's worried about my feelings as if I can't clearly see the love that y'all still have for each other," Taylor said. "Besides, for some reason, I think that I would enjoy you in our bed. I think you're beautiful and sexy, and I would like to know what it feels like to make love to you."

Shantae laughed. "Taylor, I've been through way too much to be playing games with you right now."

"I'm serious, Shantae," Taylor said. She then closed the space between them, palmed the back of Shantae's head, and kissed her. Shantae's pussy throbbed with the rhythm of her heartbeat. She had never been with a woman before and always wondered what it would be like. But Allen's wife... HELLLL NO. This was way too crazy.

Taylor sat back on the bed waiting for a response. However, Shantae was speechless. She didn't know what to say or do.

When she failed to respond, Taylor took matters into her own hands and pulled Shantae next to her. She slid her panties off and kissed her softly on the stomach while her fingers fondled her body. Shantae knew that she should have stopped her, but she did not. She had never felt a touch so gentle in her life. Taylor laid her down, removed her fingers from her insides, and inserted her tongue. Shantae's body tensed. She let out a soft moan as Taylor continued to suck on her pussy while rubbing her clit. She was being so gentle with her, and it felt SO good. Taylor made her cum faster than any man had even been able to make her climax. Shantae's body shook uncontrollably as she released an extremely intense orgasm. Taylor then slid her fingers back into her, finger fucking every drop of cum while gazing deeply into her eyes.

"I'm willing to share him with you, if you're willing to share yourself with me," Taylor said. She slid her fingers out of Shantae and then kissed her once again. She washed her face and hands and left Shantae to ponder the offer that had just been presented. After what just happened, as well as the thought of still having Allen, she was confident that she would definitely be coming along.

When Taylor left out of the room, Shantae ran herself a hot bubble bath and submerged in it. Her mind was going a hundred miles an hour. She could not believe that Taylor was for real or that she was willing to share Allen. And to top it all off, the bitch had some fye ass head. She would go, no questions asked. All she needed to know was that Allen wanted her there as well. After her bath, she dozed off thinking about the opportunity.

Taylor mentioned to Allen that she had offered Shantae to move to Detroit with them. "If that's what you really want, baby, I'm down," Allen said. "But if shit get crazy, you better figure out how to make it work."

"I think the three of us should sit down and have a talk to set boundaries and come to an understanding," Taylor said.

"Sounds good to me," Allen replied. "Later though. Right now, let's just enjoy this little time away. When we get back home, I need you to focus on finishing that last semester of college 'cause I plan on gettin' out the game soon. I still got to get off the last lil' bit of work I have and figure out our next chapter. It's time to get our life back on track."

"Sounds good to me, baby," Taylor agreed. "Would you like to go to the beach?"

"Let's do it," he said.

They packed up the kids and headed out, leaving Shantae to think and rest. They hung out on the beach until the boys were exhausted. Allani was such a good baby. As long as she was fed and dry, she never cried. By the time they got back to the room, Shantae was awake. Allen figured that it was time that she met the boys. They were way too young to understand what was going on. Once he got the boys settled, he invited Shantae over.

"Wow, you look well rested," Taylor observed.

"Thanks to you," Shantae said with a subtle smirk.

Shantae watched as the boys tried to feed Allani. They were so cute, and she looked just like them. And they looked just like him.

"Jahrod and Jahnod, this are Ms. Shantae, Allani's mother," Allen introduced. "She's a good friend of me and your mom."

"Hi, Ms. Shantae," they said together.

"We're taking care of Allani," Jahnod said.

"She's our baby sister," Jahrod added.

"That's awesome," Shantae responded.

"Is she staying with us?" Jahnod asked.

"Maybe for a little while," Shantae answered.

"YAYYYY!" They both screamed.

Taylor prepared the boys a lite dinner. She sat them at the dining room table while the three adults proceeded to the living room to talk.

"So, Taylor tells me that she invited you to come to Detroit with us?" Allen started.

"Yea, to my surprise, she did," Shantae replied. "And how do you feel about that?"

"I'mma tell you like I told her, that's her call. But if shit get crazy, she better figure out how to make it work because this was her idea," Allen said. "She insisted that you come, and I ain't no punk, so it's whatever. Y'all decide. I can handle it."

That was all Shantae needed to hear. "Well, I guess it's settled then. We're moving to Detroit," she said.

"YAYYYY!" The boys screamed again unaware that the boys were even listening.

"We'll finish this conversation in your room, once we get the boys to bed," Taylor concluded.

"Sounds like a plan. I'll get Allani bathed and put to bed. I'll see you two in a lil' bit," Shantae said to Allen and Taylor. "Goodnight, I'll see you handsome little boys in the morning." She said her goodbyes to Jahrod and Jahnod.

"Awww man, do you have to take Allani?" Jahnod whined.

"Yes, sweetheart, because the two of you are about to get

ready for bed. So, I'm going to get her ready for bed as well. Don't worry, you're going to have lots of time to spend with her," Shantae promised.

About an hour later, Taylor and Allen came over to Shantae's room with a bottle of wine. Because there were only two chairs, Shantae and Taylor sat at the table while Allen laid across the bed.

"First of all, I want to thank you for coming with us," Taylor began. "As I told you previously, I can clearly see the love that you and Allen have for each other. We both love him, and he loves the both of us. And I applaud him for trying to respect our marriage. I was also upfront with him about you being a part of our marriage. I made it very clear to him that I want to fuck you just like he does. So why not do it together? It's a simple solution to a big problem."

"So, what are the rules?" Shantae asked.

"For one, you and Allen are not to have one-on-ones," Taylor said. "Is that a problem?"

"Yes," Both Allen and Shantae said in unison.

"That's going to be a problem," Shantae continued.

"Why is that?" Taylor asked.

"That would be setting us up for failure because there's a great possibility that we will violate that rule, and I'm more than sure that Allen agrees. Sometimes shit just happens," Shantae said. "I don't want to get all the way up there to play games. And besides, if we're sharing him, then we're sharing him. It should be anytime, anyplace with all due respect for the kids. I'm sure you and I will have plenty one-on-ones."

Allen was surprised at Shantae's boldness about the situation. At the end of the day, she was right though.

"I just don't want to lose my position as your wife," Taylor said. "As selfish as this may sound, I want you to always put me first."

"That's not selfish because you are my wife, and you should come first," Allen corrected.

"Shantae, can you seriously respect that?" Taylor asked.

"I can," Shantae reluctantly agreed. "Now I have a question. Let's say I meet someone, and I want to settle down and be faithful to only them. Where does that leave us?"

"Let's get one thing understood. The biggest goal for me is to help you get you back on your feet and to help rebuild the self-esteem and the confidence that I took from you. I don't want you to ever have to depend on a man. When you leave us, you will be able to stand on your own two feet. All this extra shit, I'm going to take advantage of it, of course because I'm a man, and it's being offered. But you are not bound to us in any way. If you meet someone, then you are free to do as you please. Your stability is what really matters to me," Allen clarified.

"Understood," Shantae replied.

"Any other questions, suggestions, or concerns?" Taylor asked. "If so, it all should be addressed now."

"This yo' show, Boss Lady," Allen said.

At that moment Taylor prayed she didn't start some shit she couldn't finish. It was too late to turn back at this point. They drank wine together and told her all about what to expect in Michigan. They talked about apartments, available jobs, places to go, and things to do. The vibe was phenomenal.

Before it got too late, Allen and Taylor said goodnight to Shantae and retreated next door to their room. Everything was final. Neither of them spoke on it, but inside, they both felt victorious. They celebrated by getting one in quietly before the boys woke up.

CHAPTER TWENTY

Shantae contacted her old landlord to find out what happened to all of Allani's things. They informed her that everything was still in her apartment. She then called the investigating officer on her case to see if it was possible for her to retrieve some of her things from Marcus' apartment. She hated to seem petty, but her clothes and shoes were worth more than her furniture. She was not about to just leave everything behind. Taylor rode shotgun with her. While they took care of business, Passion, and Victoria had decided to take all of the kids to the movies.

Dre had invited Allen, Pain, and Pressure over for booze, blunts and business. Allen was glad that he was in town and able to join them while also enjoying this much-needed time away from Taylor, Shantae, and the kids. All the fellas arrived at Dre's house around the same time. He had prepared a platter of different flavored wings and another plate with only rolled blunts. Each of the fellas brought a different bottle of liquor.

First, they had a few drinks and a blunt or too while eating wings. Afterwards, Dre presented his business plan. "As you all know, I've been home for the past couple weeks with Passion. We spent a lot of time cuddling and watching her favorite show, and one in particular caught my attention and got me to thinking." He grabbed the remote and flipped to an episode of Flip This House. "I present to you, 'Four Brothers Reality'." They laughed but were very intrigued.

"The four of us are looking for a way out the game. I say we flip houses, like we flipped dope and hoes."

"Lil nigga, what you know 'bout flippin' dope or hoes?" Pain teased.

"This lil' nigga ain't just jump off da porch. I been doing dis'," Dre shot back. "My family is far from perfect. I came up flippin' hoes. And I know dope boys from a mile away. My intelligence tells me that you niggas flippin' bricks...maybe hoes too. But I do know that houses ain't no different."

As Dre pointed to the episode of 'Flip This House,' that was airing, he narrated, "We buy a run-down house that's affordable, preferably a foreclosure. There are also auctions held daily for houses where the bidding usually starts at $1. For fifty bands, we might fuck 'round and get a whole apartment building or hotel at an auction. That's when we go in and rebuild, remodel, reconstruct, then re-sale. Allen knows Detroit, I know Massachusetts, and y'all know Florida. We can start here and then expand to all three states. This may take a little hard work and a little time away from our families, but it's legal money, and its good money. I know y'all have seen a nigga take a raggedy bitch and show her a lil' love. Feed her good, fuck her good, thicken her up a lil' bit, spend a few dollars on her, now all of a sudden, she da baddest bitch in town.

That's what we wanna do to these run-down properties. We can get a hotel or two, but instead of selling it, put someone in the office to run it. And the same at an apartment building. Whatever makes sense for good business. With the four of us chipping in on the property, we will still have enough for whatever else our women may want to do. The point I'm making is that if we work together, I can see us building a multi-million-dollar business. We can live comfortably and not have to look over our shoulders. This will ensure that we will be around to watch our children grow up and go to college. This da shit we need to get on."

By the time he was done, he had everyone's undivided

attention, and so did the show. But he was starting from scratch and doing big shit with these houses and all for a little bit of cash. They all felt that Dre had got his point across, and it made so much sense. To top it all off, he had already printed a list of foreclosed properties in their area.

"Passion has already started working on getting licensed and bonded, which basically makes the business 100% legit. The ladies can start looking for properties, good deals, auction dates, etcetera. Teamwork makes the dream work."

"I must admit, bruh, I'm very impressed," Pressure said. "You done came up with some shit that I never would've thought of, and it's a great idea. And you right, Real Estate IS where the money at."

"I'm damn sho' wit' it," Pain agreed.

"Just tell me what you need me to do," Allen added.

"I'll have Passion make copies of this list for everyone," Dre said as he raised the paper. "I'll also give you a list of websites so your wives can look for additional prospective properties in their spare time. When we run across something that we feel may be a good investment, take pictures. Have an electrician, a plumber, and a roofer inspect the property because those are the most expensive and important repairs to be made. It must have a solid foundation."

"Shit, we in, bruh," Allen concluded.

Dre raised his glass. "Let's make a toast to a newfound brotherhood that consists of family, gettin' money, and loyalty." The four of them extended their glasses in for a toast. After the toast, they drank, ate wings, and laughed at Allen, who continuously choked from the weed.

Allen then told them about Shantae moving in with him and Taylor in Detroit and about Taylor wanting to have sex with her. Everyone thought that it was some real pimp shit except Pressure. He felt like Allen should take a little more time to get to know his wife. She couldn't be as innocent as he thought if she was down with shit like this. The difference between Taylor and Zoey, was that he already knew his lady came with a past. Therefore, there were no surprises...but that was in the past.

But who was he to be challenging his homeboy's decisions. All he knew was that him and Zoey were not rocking like that. If she felt like he wasn't enough for her, then she could get to steppin' and vice versa. Pain was down with the bullshit because he knew that Candice would NEVER. And Dre knew Passion's feisty ass was not with it either. So, Allen was crowned king pulling off the unthinkable.

△△△

Shantae and Taylor were taking care of business and getting to know each other as well. As they went through Shantae's clothes and shoes, Taylor was playing around, trying on different things. Before you knew it, her face was between Shantae's legs, and she did not resist. She wanted it...badly. There was no turning this down. She couldn't have Allen, and she hated Marcus, but she was gonna take advantage of this. The part that turned her on the most was that this was the bitch that Allen left her for, and she clearly had some sort of infatuation with her. This is something she would have never done if she was Allen's wife because, unfortunately, she was loyal to his fuck ass. They were interrupted by the officer that was waiting outside while she retrieved her things. He had told them to take their time, but they were so caught up in the moment that they had completely forgotten that there was someone waiting for them.

"I'm cumming," Shantae yelled to the officer as Taylor continued to suck and fondle her pussy.

"Literally," Taylor whispered as Shantae reached her climax, causing cum to run down the back of her hand.

They freshened up, gathered the rest of her belongings, and headed out the door.

"Don't you think this is considered cheating?" Shantae inquired. "This makes you no better than him."

"Who said I was any better than him?" Taylor questioned. "Maybe I'm able to understand him because I am just like him. But don't get it twisted, I love my husband. And there isn't one nigga on this earth that can get this pussy other than him. But I'm a sucker for a pretty face and a fat ass. And you're no better than me 'cause you want it just as bad as I do. You didn't stop me."

"And I'm not going to stop you...but I'm not married," Shantae stated. "And if I was, I wouldn't cheat regardless of gender."

"I can see that you're loyal. That makes you even sexier to me," Taylor said. "And it also makes me understand my husband's feelings for you even more. He has good taste."

"You are really off the chain, Taylor," Shantae said. "I never in a million years pictured you to be the way you are."

"And how is that?" Taylor asked.

"Gay as hell, for one," Shantae clarified. They both laughed.

"Well, I never thought you were the way you are either," Taylor said.

"And how is that?" Shantae asked.

"You're cool as fuck. You're honest, strong, and surprisingly tasty," Taylor listed.

"Keep going, there's more," Shantae said arrogantly.

"Seriously though, I'm not doing this to get back at Allen," Taylor said. "I really am enjoying your company and getting to know you. And at any time, if you start to feel uncomfortable with what we're doing, you can tell me, and I'll respect it. It's not like I have a fucked-up sex life. Because he does please me. I'm just enjoying pleasing you. I don't want you to feel like you're obligated to do this. Either way, we're still going to make sure you and Allani are straight."

"We good, Taylor," she said. "I haven't cut any corners with you so far. And I'm not going to start now. The rule is, that there is no rule. So, I'm down. Sometimes I just have to see where your head at, and make sure that you don't have any hidden agendas."

"Well, I guess in due time, you'll see. But I can assure you that I don't play games. My husband and my kids come first in my life. I cook, clean, fuck and go to school. I am happy. And I wouldn't trade my life for anyone else's. I feel like I'm actually the luckiest woman on earth. Even through all the bullshit. Nothing's perfect, but we're not far from it."

Her response surprised Shantae. She made it clear that she was madly in love with her husband. At the end of the day, she was just something Taylor enjoyed doing. Shantae understood her all too well because she felt the same way. For a moment, neither of them said a word as they loaded her stuff in the van. They went to the post office and shipped the boxes filled with her things to Detroit so that they would not be uncomfortable and cramped on the ride back home.

Once all their business was taken care of, they went to say goodbye and thank Mrs. Paulette. They headed back to the hotel to rest up and think things over. This was a big move, and it could be a big mistake, but for the most part, it was worth a try. They both hoped that they were doing what was best for everyone. So far, they got along very well. Hopefully, when Allen was around, everything would remain the same. He had been avoiding them as much as possible, but after tonight that would be impossible.

About two hours later, Passion and Victoria dropped off the kids. This was the first time Shantae had been away from Allani since she was born. And as much as she loved the free time, there was nothing she enjoyed more than being her mother. As soon as she heard the boys in the hallway, she opened the door looking for Allani. She was wide awake, and her face lit up when she saw her mother. That melted Shantae's heart. The boys insisted that she come over. They asked her a thousand questions, and she answered them as best as she could.

Hours had coasted by when Allen came in. He had one joint and one drink too many. He looked around and smiled. "So, this is what it is," he said. "One big happy family. I stressed all these years for nothing; here we are together. I should be the happiest man in the world, but instead I worried and drunk as fuck." He made his way to the bed and was out like a light.

Taylor took his shoes off and tucked him in. The boys were laying across the bed, watching TV. Taylor and Shantae shared a glass of wine, and Shantae called it a night. Taylor took a long hot bath, sipping on wine, listening to Monica, trying to figure out why Allen was so worried. Was he worried about his feelings, Shantae's feelings or hers? She was now thinking, maybe she should be worried too. In the midst of her thoughts, her phone rang. It was Janae.

"Hey, love. I apologize," Taylor answered. "I'm sorry, baby. I've just been so busy. I didn't realize it was gonna be this much work. But how are you?"

"I'm ok," Janae replied. "I'm just checking in because if I didn't, you obviously wasn't."

"Are you really playing the jealousy card?" Taylor asked.

"I'm not playing, Taylor," she responded. "It's been you and I from the start. Now, you got all this new shit going on in your life that doesn't include me, and I'm feeling some type of way."

"Listen, Janae, some things are out of my control," Taylor reasoned. "I didn't plan on my husband cheating on me, and I damn sho' ain't plan on becoming friends with the bitch he cheated on me with. Sometimes you gotta keep your enemies close, but it's no reason for me to hate on her. She didn't even know I existed."

"So, that's your 'best friend' now?" Janae said sarcastically.

"Stop it, Janae," Taylor said. "This is not the time. Besides, you already know where you and I stand. What we have is special and cannot be compared to what's going on with me and her. You have no reason to be insecure."

"I'm not insecure!" Janae snapped. "I just feel like you're going to let this bitch move in and take my place and I'm not about to let that happen. So, you better figure this shit out."

"Did you go by and check on the house?" Taylor quickly changed the subject.

"Yes I did, and everything was fine. I'm missing you, Taylor, so you need to get here," Janae informed

"I will be home tomorrow night, and I will make this up to you," Taylor promised

Janae didn't even say goodbye; she just hung up the phone.

Taylor loved the fact that Janae was head over heels for her. It made her feel just as powerful as a man. She was not used to her acting jealous, but she never had a reason to before now.

ΔΔΔ

The following morning Allen was up bright and early. He got the boys dressed, and they went to have breakfast while the ladies slept. They brought back food and woke them up so that they could eat and then get ready to hit the road.

"Rise and shine, sleeping beauty. Playtime is over," Allen said to Taylor as she arose. "Your breakfast is hot. Get up and get ready. We are outta here in an hour."

He then took Shantae her food and informed her that they would be leaving soon.

"Are you sure you want us to come, Allen?" Shantae asked.

"If you feel like you can handle it, I can handle it. This was her call so we rockin' with it. Get ready because we are leaving soon," Allen answered.

Shantae loved his take charge demeanor. That was an order, not a request. She just smiled and started gathering her things. Her and Taylor had done their thing, but she could not wait to get her hands on his ass. She was going to fuck him like they were the only two in the room. It didn't matter who was watching.

She freshened up Allani and got dressed. Before you know it, Allen was knocking on the door. He grabbed her bags and the two of them headed downstairs. "Do I seem desperate to you?" Shantae asked.

"Truthfully, if I was you, I would go. A lot could go wrong, but not with you," Allen answered. "Because I got you regardless. So, let's ride."

As she followed behind, she thought to herself, *What the fuck! This nigga still gives me butterflies.*

The ride was long but nice. They listened to music, ate good, and vibed. The three of them took turns driving. When they arrived, it was about 3 a.m. Allen took the boys and Allani inside. Taylor and Shantae grabbed the light luggage. Allen then came back for everything else.

"Let me show you around," Taylor said.

Jealousy consumed Shantae. Their house was so big and laid. She realized that she had definitely been playing the side bitch role. However, that was the past. This was a new beginning.

"This is the guest room, which will be your room." Taylor motioned to the beautiful room. "You're welcome in our room whenever, but every woman needs her privacy at some point."

She showed her the boys' room, the dining room, the kitchen, and the rest of the house. As she headed to the master bedroom, out of nowhere she heard Allen yell, 'WHAT THE FUCK!?'

Taylor and Shantae rushed to see what was going on. Janae was laying across the bed in the sexiest lingerie Allen had ever laid eyes. She had on an all-white, completely sheer lace two-piece ensemble, made up of boy shorts that her perfect chocolate ass was eating. Ass was everywhere. Not to mention that pussy was fat and sitting perfectly in that outfit. The top piece was so skimpy that there was barely enough fabric to cover her nipples. It was a tight-fitting, sleeveless top with the bottom half of her breasts exposed. Directly beneath her perky breasts was a thin strip of the same material wrapped around a torso that began the most perfect, flat and femininely toned stomach that he's ever seen. *'Do you want to'* by Xscape, was playing softly through the speakers. Allen was startled and confused. Janae looked at Shantae and rolled her eyes, then focused on Taylor.

"If anyone is going to be in the bed with you and your husband, I think I've earned that right," Janae demanded. She then looked at Shantae. "The guest room is clean and waiting for you."

She directed her focus back to Taylor. "I just knew you were lying when you said you were not going to bring her!"

"Are you serious, Janae! I already told you it's nothing like that! Have you lost your fucking mind?!?" Taylor said.

"Nothing like what?" Allen questioned.

"Are you going to explain or should I?" Janae asked, ready to put it all out there.

"Janae, put on your fuckin' clothes! I'm taking you home now!" Taylor demanded.

"Naw, let Janae explain!" Allen said sarcastically.

"JANAE, PUT ON YOUR FUCKIN' CLOTHES NOW!" Taylor yelled.

"Taylor, shut the fuck up and let Janae say what she came to say!" Allen commanded. "We all wanna hear this."

"And who the fuck is we all?" Janae said.

"Me, my wife, and my baby mama. Cause she apart of us now!" Allen clarified.

"That's just what I thought. You're a fucking liar, Taylor!" Janae said. "I asked you straight the fuck up if this was what was going on, and you lied! So, you was just gonna play with my feelings and make me look like a fool after all these years?"

"I guess she's been playing with my feelings too," Allen said. "Because I'm not understanding what's going on."

"Taylor and I have been sleeping together for the last five years and it's deeper than just sex," Janae explained.

"If you say another word, I'mma slap the shit outta you, Janae!" Taylor snapped. "If you really fuck with me, you will get dressed, and let's go."

"And if *you* say another word, I'mma slap the shit outta YOU!" Allen interjected. "Don't fuckin' play with me, Taylor! 'Cause right now, you got me looking stupid as fuck in front of my peoples, and THAT will get you fucked up with the quickness. So, you may as well sit yo' ass down 'cause you ain't goin' no muthafuckin' wea'."

At this point, Janae was crying like a baby.

"Go ahead, Janae. Say whatever is on your chest," Allen said. "She wasn't thinkin' 'bout yo' feelings when she was about to play you the same way she been playin' me. And when you're done clearing your chest, I'm gon' give you exactly what you came here to get."

"Maybe I should just leave," Janae said.

"Leave for what?" Allen said. "You in my bed, lookin' good as fuck...waiting on me and Taylor to get here. We here, baby girl, get comfortable. Cause it's gon' be a long night. So, let me get this straight...You and my wife been fucking for the past five years and you're in your feelings right now because my baby mama is in the picture, and you feel like if anybody should be in our bed, it should you? To add insult to injury, your best friend and lover, Taylor here," he pointed to Taylor, "is lying to you and telling you that my baby mama is not a factor, knowing that she is. Am I understanding that correctly?"

At this point, Janae was discombobulated. Allen looked over at Taylor, "This is *your* best friend and *your* lover, you gon' just let her cry? It's obvious that she's hurting right now because of your actions."

"She don't give a fuck!" Janae said.

"You out of line, Janae. I would never have done this to you! Friends don't violate each other's trust!" Taylor said.

"WE'RE NOT JUST FRIENDS, TAYLOR!" Janae exclaimed. "You can't just start something with someone else and just think it's no big deal...like we haven't been fucking on each other for the past five years."

"You know what's crazy, Janae?" Allen said with his fingers on his chin. "This was all Taylor's idea. We don't really know this lady, do we? Because she's been cheating on me for five years of our marriage with a woman. How many men are there, Taylor? What's next? If you knew that you and Janae had this love affair going on, why would you insist that Shantae come? Me and Janae together, still wasn't enough to satisfy you? What, you a nympho? I know my pipe game is official."

Taylor was so mad at Janae that, as bad as she wanted to, she couldn't bring herself to console her.

"Have you and Shantae had sex yet?" Allen asked Taylor.

"Allen!" Shantae said, surprised he had asked that question.

"Stay out of this, Shantae. I'm talking to Taylor," Allen said. He then directed his attention back to Taylor. "Answer the question."

"We did. She didn't do anything. I did everything,"

Taylor admitted.

Janae charged at her. "HOW COULD YOU TAYLOR!?" Janae screamed as she swung her fists at her like a madwoman.

As Janae cried and fought, Taylor just held her until she got tired of fighting. "I'm sorry, Janae. Please calm down and stop crying." Taylor could no longer play hard. She never meant to hurt her. Janae was her best friend, her only friend, her kids' Godmother, and she was a damn good lover too. Taylor finally broke down and cried with her. "I was not going to hurt you, Janae. All you had to do was trust me."

"Trust you?!? *Really*?" Janae said. "When you already eating this bitch pussy."

"When everything is going wrong in my marriage, you give me peace," Taylor explained. "I have love for you, and you have love for me. When everything is going good in my marriage, I still have you as my best friend. You would've never had to compete with anyone else. I just didn't want my best friend and true lover sleeping with my husband because I would never sleep with your husband. And when I say, 'true lover', I don't mean above my husband, but I mean above any other woman in my life. Shantae is here because she fills Allen's empty void, and you do the same for me."

"Oh, I'm getting that pussy tonight. Just as sho' as my wife fucked my bitch, I'm fucking hers," Allen said.

"No, you're not, Allen," Shantae said. "You finna let this thirsty bitch go home. I don't know what you and Taylor got goin' on, but I didn't come here to be a part of a freak show."

"If you gon' be fucking my bitch then I'm fucking yo' nigga!" Janae said out of spite.

"I'm fuckin' everybody in this muthafuckin' room 'cause at some point all y'all felt comfortable fuckin' without me,"

Allen said. He started removing his clothes, went in his drawer, got a Magnum condom and slid it on.

Shantae was pissed. She walked out of the room, went into her room, and slammed the door.

"I wanna see what happens when I'm not here. Five whole years of fuckin'? That shit gotta be good," Allen said while stroking his hard dick.

Taylor was now the one crying. "What the fuck you cryin' for?" Allen asked. "You wanna be the only one gettin' all the pussy?"

"Come here, Janae," he demanded and she obliged.

He looked at Taylor. "You gonna watch or join in? You been gettin' this pussy for a long time, and now you cryin' 'cause I'm finna get it?"

He bent Janae over and slid his dick into her gently. As he thought about the fact that she was in love with his wife and had been playing him just as much as Taylor, he began to grudge fuck her. He went in and out of the pussy deep and hard. Janae was loving every minute of it. Taylor was livid.

"Oh, you mad?" He asked Taylor as he continued to beat Janae's pussy roughly. "You want this pussy all to yourself, huh? You in yo' feelings about this chick?" He pulled his dick out, took the condom off, then turned to Taylor, "Go ahead and fuck yo' bitch. I'mma go fuck mine."

He walked out of the room and approached Shantae's room door. It was locked. He ordered her to unlock the door. When he stepped in the room, she tried to knock his head off. "This is why you chose this bitch over me? 'Cause she a freak?" Shantae said angrily. "Don't you fuckin' touch me, Allen 'cause I asked you not to fuck that bitch."

Allen grabbed her hands. "I had to do that, baby. I had to prove my point," he said. "I don't want that bitch. I did it because

Taylor begged her not to do it. I didn't even cum. I pulled out and left them two to fight because it definitely ain't not fuckin' goin' on in there. But you already know. I been waiting to get my hands on you." He grabbed her and kissed her. Just like that, the fight was over. She was ready. It was passionate and intimate. They devoured each other as they made love for old time's sake. They loved each other for real, and it showed whenever they made love.

Taylor and Janae argued. Taylor was pissed, but this was all her fault. After over an hour of arguing and fighting, she finally took Janae home. She dropped her off and made her way back home to face the music. Allen had showed his ass tonight, but she deserved it. Now she had to go home and convince him that he was still the most important thing in her life. Hopefully, he and Shantae were done. She knew that her husband was just acting out of anger. When she got home, Allen was in the shower. She was sitting in the recliner when he stepped out of the bathroom.

"Can we talk?" She asked.

"No, but we can fuck tho'," Allen responded.

"Allen don't talk to me like that," she said.

He laughed. "What, I'm supposed to treat you like a lady? You 'round this bitch suckin' on all the hoes like Pac-Man. Suck on this dick then. Do you even like dick? 'Cause you gettin' way more pussy than I'm gettin','"

"Allen, stop it," she begged.

"No, *you* fuckin' stop it," Allen said. "From now on out, every bitch you fuck, I'm fuckin' 'em too. You already know they gon' get hooked on this dick. You really want them problems?" She was now crying again, and he didn't give two fucks. He was on a roll. "You finna suck on this dick or what? I saved that part for you since you like suckin' on shit."

"Allen, please stop talking to me like that. You already know it's not like that. Janae and I were something that just happened, it wasn't planned. All the lonely nights while you were away with Shantae, she was there to help me get through it. I've always known that there was someone else. I just thought you had more respect for us and our marriage than to actually get someone pregnant. Janae is my best friend and I do love her.

Having sex with her was more so for what she needed from me, but the companionship and love is what I needed from her. You can't blame me for finding a way to balance my life when you're the one that knocked it off balance to begin with. Did you really want me sitting in the house alone and lonely or would you rather me fuck a man?" she said.

Allen was quiet. He took in every word of what she said and couldn't help but blame himself for the way things had turned out. He had left his wife and kids for weeks at a time and she never once complained or bitched about it, knowing that he was being unfaithful. And now he knew why.

"So why bring Shantae into this?" He asked.

"Because you love her, and I know she loves you," she answered. "For some reason it makes more sense to let her stay to keep you happy than to make you choose and be unhappy. I never really had real love growing up. So, any love is better than no love at all. I'd rather share you than lose you." Shantae was now standing in the doorway. They both looked at her and kept talking as if she wasn't there.

"Taylor, I told you that you make me happy. Yes, I still have love for Shantae, but I married you. If you would have given me the chance, I would've proved to you that I can be faithful and happy. But this isn't just about me, is it? Because the moment we made this arrangement, you fucked her before I could."

"I also think that she's beautiful and sexy. I have this crazy attraction to her," Taylor admitted.

"That's understandable. And I'm sorry if I made you feel as if you don't complete me, Taylor because you do," he said.

"*We* complete you, Allen, and I'm ok with that," she said.

"So, what are you gonna do about Janae?" He asked.

"I'm going to fix it. I have to. That's my friend and I love her for real," she said. "I'm supposed to build her up not break her down more than her husband is already doing. But the love I have for her does not compare to the love I have for you. You are a man. Nothing turns me on more than you tight abs and that hard dick. The way you take control and make demands. How you take care of me and love me and our kids. You're all I need and more. No other man in this world can ever get my attention. You gotta know that."

"Did I come here for all this fighting and arguing? I thought this was a big happy family," Shantae interrupted.

"It normally is," Taylor replied, "I'm sorry that I didn't tell you about Janae."

"Yea, 'cause I wanted to slap her ass. Givin' me all that attitude," Shantae said. "I was thinking to myself, 'Bitch, Taylor the one cheated on yo' dumb ass, not me.'" Allen and Taylor both laughed.

"And then she got the nerve to tell me that the guest room is clean for me because that's where I'm sleeping. It took everything in me to not get on her ass," Shantae added. "Y'all have a very dysfunctional relationship. Thank you for making me a part of it. It's my first day in your area code and we are not about to spend it fighting about feelings we can't control."

"We can control them," Allen said. "We just don't want

to."

"Me and you are going to love each other no matter what," Shantae said. "However, you love Taylor a little bit more. That's out of my control. Taylor and Janae are friends and lovers and that is not going to change...that's out of your control. Taylor and I have some kind of crazy, sexy, cool attraction to one another and that's out of control. And Allen is the man in the middle of it all. It is what it is. Either we love each other, or we fight against each other. I personally need all the love I can get. And I have plenty of love to give to the both of you in return."

"Show me, don't tell me," Allen said.

Shantae came in, closed the door and locked it. The three of them got naked and loved on each other with no holding back. No jealousy, just good sucking and fucking until everyone was satisfied.

"This is what I wanted it to be like," Taylor said. "You got enough for the both of us. Plus, we're all blessed to have each other."

"Well, you cheatin' on us 'cause you got two women and a man," Allen said sarcastically.

"I got a best friend, a baby mama and a husband. It's a difference," Taylor clarified.

"I got a baby mama and a baby daddy and together we have three beautiful kids. And we're going to raise them right and be good to one another. No one has to understand what we got going on but us. That's all that matters." Shantae eased out of bed, got dressed and headed to cook breakfast before the kids got up.

Before she was out the door good, Allen was snoring, and Taylor was right under him sleeping like a baby. She looked at them and smiled. Them two had a lot going on and she was caught right in the middle...which wasn't a bad place to be.

CHAPTER TWENTY-ONE

Dre, Pain and Pressure stood in front of the first house they purchased. They bought it for $100,000. Each of them, including Allen, put in $25,000. The grass was past the windows, but the electricity, plumbing and roof was in excellent condition. Someone had already attempted to rebuild this house at some point. Whoever it was made it easy for them. All they had to do was clean up the yard and gut out the insides, replace the old drywall and appliances and then do the floor by replacing the old dingy carpet with shiny new tile.

Zoey had become the first lady of Four Brothers Realty. She took her job very serious, being that she was the only one not in school or working on obtaining a career. She felt the need to do something positive for herself. She turned out to be a great negotiator. She kept track of every detail dealing with the houses' condition and what needed to be done. She Googled prices and compared numbers to determine whether or not it was a smart investment. Passion had given her lots of different websites to look for bargains. She took her time and researched the best bargains overall. So far, everything had been going well.

Pain and Pressure still had the trap houses, and this is where the smokers came in handy. They gathered a crew and put them to work. The leader of the crew cut down tree limbs that had grown over the house and powerlines. One smoker chopped down the grass, another did the weed eating, another one did the edging surrounding the house, while another raked and dragged chopped tree limbs. Lastly they went over the grass with a riding lawnmower and blew everything off neatly. It took about five hours, $200 and seven grams of some good dope to get the job done right. A professional would have charged them $3,500 easily for a job that big. These were the bargains that were going to make flipping houses affordable and lucrative.

The next step was cabinets, sinks and toilets. Chloe was very good when it came to fraud. So, Zoey hit her up and had her order everything, including cabinets, sinks, tubs, toilets, showerheads, cleaning supplies, paint, tile, etcetera. The order came up to almost $13,000. With online discounts and coupons for more than 35% off, it brought the total down to $8,300. In the process, she had also gotten approved for a Home Depot credit card using the identity that she bought. In the end, she paid the $8,300 with the Home Depot credit card and agreed to make monthly payments of $173 towards the card balance and just like that it was done. $13,000 in appliances and household items and all she paid was $50 for a credit card number that came with a person's Social Security Number who had a good credit score. After all of that, she only charged her sister $5,000. She called Zoey to get the name of the person that would be picking up the order. The guy who did the lawn agreed to pick up the order for an additional $250.

Pain and Pressure's uncles, Stevie, Earl and Pete, all did home improvements. These guys were professionals. They were willing to come in and install everything the right way and flip the house for real. They were only charging their nephews $7,500 for everything. When they were finished the value of the house would double and the house would be ready to be sold. In the end, they would spend $13,225 to totally remodel this house with brand new appliances and the whole nine yards.

They then posted the house for sale starting at $250,000 but they would happily accept $213,225...basically a $100,000 profit which doubles the original investment. This process had taken about 2 weeks to complete. Now it was time to sit back and watch the money flip itself.

Zoey was the negotiator for the crew. She had been studying a realtor dictionary and learning the real estate language. She wanted to learn the business inside and out, so she took a realtor class that was held at City Hall every Wednesday for nine weeks. From that point on there was no turning back. Once she became a licensed realtor, her confidence shot through the roof. She was smart, pretty and she knew the game. She used it all to get great prices on buying houses and even better deals when it came to selling them.

Zoey had Pressure's nose wide open. She was learning how to cook his favorite foods and how he liked his laundry done. She and Mrs. Paulette had become very close. That was the only person that could give her advice and pointers on how to keep her man happy. She took it all in and put it to good use. Zoey knew that her sex game was official. However, she had enough sense to know that to keep a man like Pressure satisfied, it took way more than sex. And because of that she went the extra mile to make sure that his focus stayed on her and only her. So far she was doing a damn good job.

ΔΔΔ

Mrs. Paulette had been busy planning her vow renewal ceremony for the last few months. She and Vincent had agreed to sell both of their houses and buy a new one together. They wanted their kids to see that there was power in Love. That together they both were happier, stronger and would gain so much more. Paulette had spent most of her life trying to prove that she could live good and be okay without Vincent and she did just that. But she wasn't happy without him.

Now that he knew she could make it without him, none of that even mattered. In the end she was happier with him. She had grown so much over the last twenty years. The same child that tore them apart, she now loved like her own. The same man that broke her heart had mended it as well. She realized that the time they did spend apart was the same reason they would love each other so much better the second time around. They both needed that time to grow as individuals. Now they both were even better for one another.

Mrs. Paulette had so much unused vacation time. Now she was taking advantage of all of it. Before she was to retire, she had almost four months of vacation time that she planned on taking in the next six months. She had only been to work for two weeks in the last two months, and she was still getting paid. Vincent was the boss of his company, so he was free to travel as he pleased. They had been to Vegas for a week, Africa and New Orleans. They were making up for lost time. Sex was better than before because they were grown and had nothing to prove. It was just good old-fashioned love making. The two of them had throwback money, dope money, 401k money, retirement money and all they both did was save money. They were finally enjoying the money they worked so hard for and living life to the fullest. This is what Mrs. Paulette had been preaching to her kids about: saving and actually getting to enjoy the fruits of your labor.

The wedding would be held on a beautiful yacht that was made for this particular occasion. It was called The Love Boat. It came with a chapel, a dance floor, and a dining area that seated over a hundred people easily. Passion would be the maid of honor and Dre would be the best man. This decision was made because there was no way Vincent could choose between the three boys. Well at least that was what he told everybody. The truth was that Dre had come to Vincent and asked for his blessings to marry Passion. Vincent gave it to him with no hesitation. Dre wanted to surprise Passion and marry her on the same day, when Vincent and Paulette renewed their vows. A double wedding, two different generations, one occasion... LOVE.

Passion had accepted Dre's marriage proposal, but she wanted to wait until they had enough money saved, she had finished school and they at least had a house of their own...the list goes on and on. Dre just wanted her to be his wife and together they would work everything else out. They would have the blessings of family and God as well. How could they go wrong? But after everything that had already happened that was so unplanned, Passion wanted everything to be perfect this time around. Dre understood that nothing would be perfect, and he was okay with that.

Dre was not around when Paulette and Vincent were apart. All he sees is how happy they are together right now. They have a beautiful family with so much love. A mother and a father that love their kids and have raised them well. Unity and unconditional love. He had never had nor even seen families like this except when he was watching "Good Times" Or "The Fresh Prince of Bel Air." He wanted this for him and Passion. He wanted to have kids and see their kids have kids. He wanted to grow old with her forever and ever for real.

Mr. Vincent knew that Dre meant every word he said. And he believed that Dre would deliver on his promises to love Passion with all of his heart and soul. Dre had lost so much but in the end he gained much more. Everything he had, he invested it in this one girl, and he had no regrets, he just needed her to know just how much he really loved her. He wanted the world to know.

ΔΔΔ

Shantae and Taylor had agreed to both walk down the aisle with Allen for the wedding. Just to show off since everybody had something to say about their three-way love affair. Allen had bought himself a pimp Gucci hat and shades with matching shoes. The three of them were destined to steal the show and bring laughter into the atmosphere.

Everything seemed to be going well. However, Shantae wasn't really feeling this, long term. She loved Taylor as a person, and she loved riding her face because the head was amazing. They connected in many ways, but they were still very different. Watching Allen make love to Taylor was like stabbing her in the heart with a butcher knife. It never got easier to accept. She felt the same deep cut and hurt every time. She realized Taylor was cut from a different cloth. She was loving every minute of it. It did not bother her at all to watch her husband make love to a woman, who he was emotionally and sexually attached to.

Shantae felt that at the end of the day she was still settling. She held no weight in his life. His love and loyalty was with Taylor. She was the desperate houseguest. He had chosen Taylor over her, but she was at the point where she could accept that and not feel bitter. It was Allen's loss, not hers. She was definitely the better woman for him. She was loyal and dedicated to him. Taylor needed her, him, and another bitch... All she needed was him. But it was what it was. She knew that Taylor was going to be the one to break his heart. He had invested so much in her, and it still wasn't enough. Taylor was his karma and that was all on him.

Shantae wanted more for her, and her daughter. She would step out on faith and build the life that she wanted for them and she would do it on her own for the first time. Thanks to them, she was ready to take that step. She had made up her mind that after the wedding, she would not return to Detroit with Allen and his family. Starting over would be hard, but playing second for the man she had given her all to was much harder. She felt like he had given the life he promised her to someone else. She no longer wanted a piece of the pie. She wanted her own pie. This time she was okay with walking away without him. Hopefully by the time he realized that she was the one for him, she would be in love with someone who truly respected her values and loyalty. She definitely wanted to be the one to tell him, 'I told you so' when Taylor broke his heart.

In the meantime, she had a token of their love. Memories that could never be replaced. Allani was starting to look more and more like him every day. She was proof of the love that Allen and her once shared and that was more than enough.

Until they parted ways, Shantae planned on getting as much of Allen and Taylor as she could get. The two of them together in bed was a bad ass sex team, and she was not giving either of their ass a break. Once they got to Florida, it would be the end of this emotional rollercoaster ride. The end of this Fairy tale. The end of her and Allen.

△△△

Candice and Pain had been doing great. Pain had done a whole 360. He was home every night; they went out on dates and the sex was better than ever. Candice had no complaints. However, there was a bit of fear in a small part of her heart, that one day he would go back to being the Pain that afflicted so much, of just that...pain. She had waited so long for him to be the man that he was now being, to the point that it just didn't seem real. It was like living in a glass house. One false move, and your whole house is shattered. She was expecting that some bullshit would jump off. But this time, Pain was going to prove her wrong. He felt good about being home and doing right by Candice. He did not want to lose her. So, he was giving her the best of him because she had already endured the worst of him, and she stood in the paint through it all.

Pain had bought her an engagement ring, and on her graduation night, he planned on popping the question. He wasn't in a rush, but he figured it was time. Besides, he was happy with just her, so why not make it official? He had already fucked the baddest bitches on earth, clubbed, and lived his best life. Now it was time for him to get on his grown man shit. He wanted to buy a house then have another son or daughter. This time, he wanted to be around when they took their first steps and said 'dada' for the first time. Running the streets had caused him to miss the little things like that in Treasure's life. He was in and out of town and him and Candice were off and on. Mainly due to him fucking off with other bitches but they had still made it through and overcame the obstacles. He planned on making things even better. There was always room for improvement.

The first step was buying them a house. He called Zoey and asked her to help him find a three-bedroom house with two bathrooms and a big yard in a nice area. He told her that he didn't want Candice to know anything about this. It was all a part of her graduation gift. Zoey took on the job with pleasure. Zoey was good as hell when it came to finding houses and negotiating the buying price. She had become a beast. The classes she had taken really worked out in her favor.

A week later, she sent him pictures of what she felt like was the perfect home for them. It was exactly what he had asked for. It also had a screened-in patio in the backyard. The house had already been remodeled. With less than two months until Candice's graduation, it made sense to buy a house that needed little to no work. Zoey had negotiated buying the house for $188,000. The elderly couple owed $33,000 left on the house. COVID came through, and their business was suffering, causing them to sell at least one of their three homes. This was the smallest of the three and the least used. The couple lived in Wisconsin and hardly ever made it to Florida on vacation. Right now, they were willing to take less for the house over losing it. Pay off the $33,000 and invest half of the remainder into their businesses. Pain didn't hesitate to jump at the opportunity. The house was beautiful, and $188,000 was a Godfather's deal.

Candice didn't think there would be a big celebration for her graduation, but Pain was going all out. Candice was about to become a RN, and Pain was into real estate. With the money they already had saved, they had a bright future ahead of them. It was time to settle down and do things the right way.

△△△

Chloe and Rein had been going strong. They both were true hustlers and worked together well. They ran into Minnesota at the same club where they met Pain and Pressure. After a long night of having sexual fun with him, the conversation turned to business. Chloe had put two and two together and figured out that Minnesota had to be Pain and Pressure's plug. She asked if he knew them, and he confirmed that her speculations were correct. He made them the same proposition...$60,000 a head for each girl they bring. That was all they needed to hear, and they were off to Miami.

The first two trips, they didn't even tell Zoey they were in town. It was strictly business, and she didn't want to hear any lectures. Rein had introduced her to popping pills and she loved it. She had lost about ten to fifteen pounds, but she still looked stunning, and the money was flowing properly. They partied five nights a week. They were young, pretty, with no men, no kids and no worries. So why not party like rockstars? However, she knew Zoey would not approve of the lifestyle she was living, and she was not trying to hear it. For the first time ever, she was doing her. She didn't feel the need to answer to Zoey or anyone else. She loved her sister to death and respected that she was ready to settle down and experience the married life.

She, on the other hand, was not ready for any of that. She was enjoying her life and felt there was no need for change. And she needed Zoey to respect her wishes. However, on the next trip, she was definitely gonna spend some time with her sister. She missed her dearly.

CHAPTER TWENTY-TWO

It was a beautiful sunny day. Everyone was dressed to impress. Vincent stood at the altar in front of the pastor with Dre to his left and Passion to his right. They were the Best man and the Maid of Honor, and they also held the rings. Next was Victoria guiding the kids as they threw rose petals and did a cute little wave to the audience. Pain and Candice both were flawless. Pressure and Zoey complimented each other to the tee. But Allen and his women took the cake. They both wore the same dress, and they both looked good enough to eat. Taylor was on his right arm, and Shantae was on his left arm. Everyone in the crowd applauded them due to the fact that they got along so well despite all the B.S. Most chicks would be at each other's throats, but they chose unity instead. They proudly represented Allen.

Passion scanned the crowd and saw Tank and Domonique sitting on the front row. Her heart skipped a beat as flashbacks of what happened to her filled her memories. Ultimately, Tank had save her life but it was Dominique that lead Tank to her even though initially she had played a role in holding her captive. It was obvious that at the time Dominque was torn between her love for both of her brothers. In the end she did the right thang. At this moment Passion realized that she had forgiven all parties involved. It was a blessing to see them there. That meant a lot to her. She gave them a soft welcoming smile and focused her attention back on the reason they were all gathered there. She had the slightest clue that Dre was about to ask her to marry him as well.

Everyone stood as *"You"* by Jesse Powell filled the air and the bride entered the room. Mrs. Paulette looked young and beautiful. Vincent's eyes locked on her, and they both smiled at one another. It felt like the very first time. As she met him at the altar, everyone took their seats, and the pastor began to speak:

"We are gathered here today in the name of Love. For over a quarter of a century, these two have been joined in marriage, and today they are renewing the vows that they made to each other 25 years ago on this day. Each of them has written their own vows. Ladies first, as always."

"Vincent Edwards, I stand before you today as your wife and your best friend. I thank God for giving us four wonderful kids, and now our kids are having kids. The love I have for you is just as strong today as it was when I married you twenty years ago. You are my rock, my protector, and my sunshine on a rainy day. I look forward to another twenty-five plus twenty-five plus twenty-five years with you right by my side. Loving each other for life. You as my husband and me as your wife."

"Ring please," the pastor requested. Passion stepped forward, handed her the ring and Paulette placed it on Vincent's left ring finger. The pastor then motioned for Vincent to step forward to recite his vows.

"Baby, we are the roots to this family. The foundation in which it was built on. I promise to love you the way you should be loved so that we set the right example to our kids and Grandkids and generations to come. Through sickness and in good health, for richer or for poorer, through the ups and the downs, my love for you will never grow cold. My love for you will never get old. With you is where I want to be. With you is where I belong. Our love will overcome any and all obstacles, and we will withstand the test of time. You are forever my lady, and I am forever your husband. I will love you always."

Dre then stepped up and passed the ring to Vincent and he slid it on Paulette's left ring finger.

"You may now kiss your wife," the pastor said. Vincent and Paulette kissed like newlyweds. Everyone was on their feet in celebration.

The pastor then requested that everyone quiet down and take a seat. Once everyone had returned to their seats, the pastor asked Dre to step forward and handed him the mic. Paulette and Passion looked confused. Vincent just stood tall with a smile on his face, "Go ahead, son," he said to Dre in encouragement.

"Good evening, everybody," Dre began. "Today is a special day. It's filled with love and over twenty-five years of memories. I want to thank Mr. Edwards for giving me his blessing when I told him how much I loved his daughter. I also went on to ask him if we could share this special day. He didn't quite understand, so I explained to him that I wanted to marry your daughter on the same day that you and your wife renew your vows and twenty-five years of Love. I wanna celebrate my 25th anniversary on the same day that you're celebrating your 50th. Because I believe that our love is just as strong, and I know it will last just as long. And he gave me his blessing. So, at this time," Mr. Vincent grabbed Passion's hand and walked her directly in front of Dre. "I would like to ask you, Passion Edwards, to be my wife. Right here, right now."

Passion had cried off all of her makeup, and her mother wiped her tears away. Dre got down on one knee and took a right out of his pocket. "Will you make this day even more special? Will you be my wife?"

"Of course, I will," she said as he slid the ring on her finger. He then stood next to her, and the crowd went wild. Rose petals came falling from the ceiling. It was definitely a special moment and a day to remember.

"Please take your seats as I join this couple in Holy Matrimony," the pastor said. Everyone took their seats and watched as Dre and Passion were joined in unity. After saying their vows, the pastor said, "I now pronounce you, Man and Wife. You may kiss your bride."

No one saw this coming, not even Passion. It was such a pleasant surprise. At the reception, everyone congratulated them as well. And they all celebrated and partied the rest of the night away.

Mr. Vincent had already booked an all-expense paid stay in Cancun, Mexico, which included airfare, rental car, and the honeymoon suite as their wedding gift. As soon as the yacht arrived back to shore, Passion and Dre would go back home to pack and prepare for their honeymoon.

Everything with them always seemed to happen with them so fast. One day they were engaged and trying to figure out when would be a good time to get married. The next day they were married and preparing for their honeymoon. Both of them were young and in love. They had a bright future ahead of them, and because they were doing things the right way, their marriage was sure to be blessed.

They were good together. They motivated each other in the best way. Both of them wanted to see the other winning. Dre insisted that Passion go back to school. He would work from sunup to sundown and pay every bill until she finished school. Everyone loved the way he loved her. He was very persistent in making sure that she was still able to follow her dreams. They couldn't have asked for a better husband for Passion.

Dre came from a very dark place, but thanks to Passion, he now knew that true love existed and that he was also entitled to be loved, just like everyone else. He was not a product of his environment. He had overcome and rose above all that. He grew up in a very dysfunctional family, but God had just given him a new one. He still needed a little guidance, but only because he was young. He was definitely a man. He had a team of great guys around him, and they respected him and his efforts. He was at a place in his life that he never thought he would be at such a young age, and it felt so good.

Passion was the happiest she had even been. Nothing had gone the way she had planned, but it never did. God clearly had His own plans for her life. She would never be able to help others with their struggles if she had not had any of her own. She had survived being kidnapped, raped repeatedly, and a having a miscarriage in one year. And she was only twenty-one years old. She was now back in school studying criminal justice and psychology. She was doubling up on her classes so that she could be finished in two and a half years instead of four. She was also married to a wonderful husband. He was young, sexy as hell, and he loved and supported her in every way. She loved everything about him, and even though they were young, she knew that their love was real. This was the beginning of something that was very special and would last for years to come.

As they packed their bags and prepared to leave, Dre grabbed her hands and looked her in her eyes, "Baby, I know I kinda put you on the spot today. I hope that I'm not pressuring you or moving too fast. This is what you want, right?"

"Dre, I've never been happier in my life," she replied. "I've always felt like weddings and all that money spent is just a show for the people. You know I don't care about putting on a show just to please people. But this was perfect, and I couldn't be happier. We're already married, and it didn't cost us a dime. Now, all we have to do is focus on building our future together."

"Shiiiit, that ring cost way more than a dime," Dre joked. They both giggled as she raised her new ring into the light and admired it. "But you are worth that and much more. So, you don't feel like you missed out on walking down the aisle in a pretty white gown?"

"We got plenty of time for that," she responded. "Maybe for our ten year anniversary, we can actually have a wedding. By then, we will have at least two kids and a successful business of our own. And we will have 100 bands to spend on a wedding. Right now, I just want to love you and build a solid foundation for our kids."

"I just can't wait to start doing what it takes to make those kids," he said.

"Oh, tonight. I'm finna give my husband the bin'ess," she said.

"Naw! Tonight, my wife 'bout to get da business," he corrected.

They were packing bags like they were running away, moving through the house so fast. When they were done, they left the kitchen light on and headed for the airport. Their plane would be departing in less than two hours.

Mrs. Paulette and Vincent planned a simple honeymoon. They rented a cabin in Key West for the week. They both loved to fish, so they hitched his boat to their truck and drove down south. The cabin was in the middle of all the festivities. There was a fishing competition going on with 1st, 2nd and 3rd place prizes. There was a boardwalk with restaurants and bars all within walking distance. The cabin was made for lovers. It had a heart-shaped bed, a heart-shaped jacuzzi, and mirrors everywhere you looked, including on the ceiling. There was an area in the backyard with a gazebo with candles and lights. Surround sound had been installed inside and on the exterior of the house. The sound of Luther Vandross played through all the speakers, setting the perfect mood. Mr. Vincent fixed them a drink and sparked his blunt.

"Pass that shit," Mrs. Paulette said. "For old time's sake."

Mr. Vincent passed her the blunt and she hit it like a champ the first time. But the second time, she almost coughed her lungs up, but she felt it.

"Let's dance," she said as '*Here and Now*' by Luther Vandross played softly. Mr. Vincent was feeling suave as he took her hand, and they swayed to the music. They danced, talked, and laughed the night away. They didn't have to go to Mexico or Hawaii to call it a honeymoon. They only needed each other, doing what they loved to do, wrapped in each other's love was more than enough for them.

Passion and Dre couldn't believe how beautiful the beaches were in Mexico. The first night there, they had a picnic on the beach. They talked and made love until the sun came up. They took pictures of the sun setting in the evening and rising in the morning. The next day they went jet skiing and canoeing. That night there was a glow party at the casino and hotel where they were staying. They partied and took shots back-to-back. Once they made it back to their room, they made love until they both were completely drained. Passion gave Dre head for the first time, and he seemed to have really enjoyed it, which gave her the confidence she needed to do it again. It wasn't as bad as she thought it would be.

To her surprise it turned her on. She felt good pleasing her husband because he damn sho' had been pleasing her. They were so good together. They talked about everything openly. The good, the bad, and the ugly. They made a vow to always be honest with one another, even if the truth hurt If either of them ever got bored with the sex or just tired of being in a relationship, they would be honest and then put in a real effort to change whatever needed to be changed. They promised to always love and respect each other.

Passion had studied Human behavior, and the study showed that 75% of marriages failed because of lack of communication. She was going to make sure that communicating was not a problem in their marriage. Right now, everything was perfect and Passion planned on it staying that way. All they had to do was not change up. What's real, stay put Passion was always told. They would never have to talk about how things used to be if they kept things the way they were right now. Both of them were in love and caught up in each other's raptures. And that was where they belonged.

After the wedding, Shantae, Taylor, and Allen went back to their room and made love. When they were done, Shantae broke the news to them. She told them that she would not be returning to Detroit with them. Neither Taylor nor Allen saw that coming. That was because, at some point, Allen had lost his way. Knowing Shantae, the way he knew her, he should have known that she was not happy and wouldn't stay around too long. There was no way she was comfortable being second in his life. She had done a great job at pretending to be happy, and now she was revealing her true feelings. She wanted Allen in Allani's life everyday like he was with his boys, but this was not the way she thought it would be. Allani was too young to even know what was going on.

"So, when did you decide this?" Allen asked.

"Weeks ago," Shantae admitted.

"Listen, I appreciate both of you. I appreciate your attempt to try to fit me in and make me a part of your family," Shantae explained. "But I'm done being a third wheel. Allen has chosen you to be his wife, and I have to live with that, but this is totally out of my character. I want a man of my own. My own life. I want to be someone's wife. I came here broken and confused, and I blamed myself. I had to realize that it's not my fault that Allen chose you over me. It's not my fault that Marcus was a sociopath. But the decisions I make are my fault. From this day forth, I'm not settling for anything less than what I deserve. I'm nobody's side bitch. It's all or nothing for me. Someone will value my worth and appreciate my loyalty. I'm a bad bitch that just made bad choices when it came to men. Now I'm learning to pour all of that love into myself, and now that I have a daughter who depends on me, it's mandatory that I make better decisions and teach her the proper way to love herself and how she should be loved by a man. How can I do that when I'm settling for less than what I deserve and living a lie? I have to lead by example."

"So, where do you plan on living?" Taylor asked.

"Mrs. Paulette said that I can stay with her for a while. Victoria agreed to watch Allani while I work," Shantae responded.

"Allani can stay with us," Allen snapped.

"If that's what you think is best Allen, I'm ok with that," Shantae said. "Just as long as there will be no issue with me coming to get my baby once I get on my feet."

"Wow! You're really serious," Taylor concluded.

"I'm dead serious, Taylor," Shantae confirmed. "If you were in my shoes, then maybe you would understand, but you're not. I didn't devote my life to a motherfucker to play second to his wife. And I'm not gay either. I love men, and I want one of my own, not bits and pieces of someone else's, and I don't want to be bitter 'bout the situation. Right now, I'm ok with everything, and I trust you and Allen with my life, so why wouldn't I trust you with Allani's? I have to do what I have to do to get my life together because this shit ain't cool. I don't want my baby daddy and his wife taking care of me like I'm some charity case. I lost the man I love…I did not lose my life. Since I was fourteen, I have lived for Allen. Now I want to live for Shantae."

Shantae was letting it all out. She was in her feelings and not afraid to let it show. This was no longer about Allen. She wanted more for herself and her daughter. As she cried and spilled her heart out, Allen realized that this was coming to an end. Shantae was about to walk out of his life forever. He saw the pain and determination in her eyes. He could feel the hurt that she was feeling.

After a moment of silence, Allen finally spoke up, "Can I at least put you in your own place? That's the least I can do for you, Shantae. You already know money ain't a thang," he insisted.

"No, thank you Allen," Shantae said. "I'll be fine with Mrs. Paulette. When I move into my own place, I want to invite whoever I choose to come and spend time with me. I am done waiting and worrying about if Allen is coming. I am trying to free myself and you at the same time. Mrs. Paulette is working on getting me in at the post office. I'm going to work, save my money and take care of myself. It's time. All I ask is that you take care of my baby. Give me a chance to build a home for me and her that's safe …that's mine and mine only. Can you do that, Allen?"

Allen laughed. "So, you got it all figured out?"

"I do. For the first time in my life, I have figured it out on my own," Shantae shot back. "And it feels good. I'm looking forward to starting over from the ground up. And I'm going to do it with pride and respect for myself. I'm not mad at anyone. You made your decision a long time ago, Allen. Now I have made mine. If you don't mind, I would like for you to take me to Mrs. Paulette please."

Allen was in his feelings, and he could not hide it. He grabbed the keys. "I'll take her," he said.

"*We* will take her," Taylor snapped.

She was in her feelings as well but for a totally different reason. She was okay with Shantae leaving if she wanted to leave because she was right. She would never come first. Second was the only open position available. What pissed her off was the fact that she knew Allen was heartbroken. He wanted a chance to be alone with Shantae so he could beg her to stay with them. He did not want to lose her. He loved her... *too* fucking much.

"That's another thing," Shantae said. "The man I fell in love with barely exists. He took charge. He was a boss at all times and in every situation. You are clearly not running shit here. You're losing what turned me on the most. Your power."

Taylor knew that Shantae's comment sent Allen from zero to hundred, but she didn't give two fucks. She was running shit, but she still respected Allen as the man and head of household. He was able to have his cake and eat it too. Why would he complain about anything? Her running the show worked out in his favor until now. The ride to Mrs. Paulette's house was super quiet, bittersweet for everybody.

Once they arrived, Shantae gathered her thighs, then she hugged Taylor and said her goodbyes. She honestly had no problem with Taylor. Her problem was with Allen. Well, it used to be.

Allen felt like he was walking out of heaven, but he did nothing to stop it from happening. He had made his choice, and now he had to live with it, but the shit didn't feel good at all. The boys had gotten attached to her. He had gotten attached to her all over again, and now they were separating all over again. It was truly an emotional rollercoaster.

When Allen and Taylor pulled off, she did not know what to say to him. Seeing him all in his feelings tore her up inside.

"Where are we going?" She finally asked.

"I'm going to get her a car and then we are going home," Allen answered.

"I thought we were leaving tomorrow," Taylor said.

"Well, stop thinking for me," Allen replied.

"Don't give me a fucking attitude. I have done everything in my power to give you what you wanted. You can stay here with her if you are that upset that she is ready to move on," Taylor snapped.

"Taylor don't go there. I'm not in the mood," he responded. "And you did what was best for *you*, not me. Everything you do is for you, so stop playing the innocent housewife. I don't wanna talk about this anymore. Hopefully, we can go back to the way it was before all of this shit took place."

"Hopefully?" Taylor questioned.

"Yea, hopefully," he responded. "Because she's right. I have let you change me. For one, I'm the man and I call the fucking shots. For two, a bitch that want more pussy than me can't be my wife. And third of all, she's a lot more loyal than you ever were, and you're my fucking wife! I fucked up once, and I regretted it and begged for your forgiveness. You been fucking up just as much, but you think it's ok. I didn't sign up for this bullshit."

"Oh, now it's my fault?! That you in love with this bitch and she not in love with you no more?" Taylor inquires.

"She gon' always love me. It's the *we* shit that she tired of," Allen corrected.

"Like I said before, you can stay here with her if you that in love. Because I'm tired of all the bullshit with your ass as well," Taylor responded.

"Shut the fuck up while you still ahead, Taylor," he snapped. "I'm done talking about this situation!"

They pulled into a parking lot that had all kinds of used cars. He selected a 2019 Honda Accord for her. He paid for it with cash, and when the paperwork was all done, he instructed Taylor to follow him to Mrs. Paulette's house. When they pulled up, Allen get out of the car, and Taylor followed.

"Get the kids and get back in the van because we're about to leave," Allen ordered.

When Shantae opened the door, he handed her the paperwork and the keys to the car. He handed Mrs. Paulette $3,000. A thousand for each of the three months that he assumed she would be there. He then informed Shantae that they were about to leave right away. Shantae begged him for just a little bit more time with Allani but Allen was ready to leave, and he was not about to leave without his daughter. Shantae cried as she handed over Allani and her things. All Mrs. Paulette could do was comfort her. It was the hardest thing that Shantae had to do. It was also her greatest motivation.

As Allen drove off, he realized that he was leaving his heart behind. Which was also the hardest thing that *he* ever had to do.

CHAPTER TWENTY-THREE

Candice was in her feelings a little bit. It was her graduation night, and no one called to congratulate her. None of her girls were attending. She supported everyone and was in attendance at all of their graduations. Pain didn't even seem excited. He made plans to take her and Treasure out to dinner after the ceremony. This graduation was such a big deal for her. There were so many times that she felt like she wasn't going to make it to the finish line. It had taken her an extra year, but she did it. She finished…and with a 3.8 GPA. She took a shot of Patron as she got dressed. This was her night, and she was going to celebrate her accomplishment even if no one else did.

Pain and Treasure were already dressed and waiting on her. He was praying that everyone did their part in preparing for her graduation party. He worked so hard to keep this a secret from her. He was so proud of her, but he couldn't show it until after graduation. He could tell she was in her feelings, and he knew why, but it was only temporary. Tonight, would be a game-changer for the both of them.

As they headed to the graduation, Pain told her that he was extremely proud of her, and he never once doubted her from the beginning. So many people dropped out when it got tough, but not Candice. She stood in the paint and tonight was her night to revel in her success.

She looked over at Pain and smiled. "I could never have done this without you. Thank you for believing in me and wanting to see me succeed. Not to leave out sponsoring it."

"That was the least I could do," he said.

"That was the most important thing you could. That meant more to me than the hoes you were fucking. I had to keep the picture painted in my head and because you take such good care of me and my baby, I had no choice but to fight for us," Candice responded.

"Was it worth it?" Pain asked.

"You're worth it," she replied.

"You're really the one worth it," he said. "I really don't deserve you, but you're mine anyway."

She just smiled because he was right. He didn't deserve her, but there was no other place in the world she'd rather be. Her little family was not perfect, but it was hers nevertheless, and she loved it.

Graduation went smoothly. Pain recorded her as she walked across the stage. They took pictures as a family with the photographer that was set up by the exit of the auditorium. When they were done, Candice assumed that they were going to dinner. "Where are we eating at?" Candice asked.

"Somewhere special," Pain answered.

Candice adjusted the music, sat back, and took another shot. As they rode for what seemed like forever, they finally arrived at a house. Candice noticed that everyone's cars were in the driveway.

"We're gonna crash this party for a few before we go eat. I promised them that I would come," Pain explained.

"Whose party is this?" Candice questioned.

"It's Dre's birthday," he advised. "And this is one of the houses we just bought. We decided to throw him a surprise party here." Candice took one more shot. This time pain took one with her. Treasure was wide awake, bopping her head to the music.

"Should I take this cap and gown off?" Candice asked.

Pain leaned over and kissed her. "You look sexy as fuck, baby. Let's go." They marched inside hand-in-hand. Candice was feeling good as hell. Pain was taking it easy 'cause he already could see that he had to be responsible for Candice and Treasure tonight.

When they walked inside everyone screamed... 'SURPRIIIIIIIISE!' And the cameras started flashing. Everyone showered her with gifts. She had never felt so loved. Pain then gave her the keys and the deed to their house with both their names on it.

"This is our house, baby," he explained. "This is your graduation gift from your man."

"Pain, stop playin with me," Candice said in disbelief.

"You already know I don't play. You deserve this," Pain replied.

Zoey stepped in, "As your realtor, I would like to show you around your new home. I selected this property specifically for you."

"Oh My God, this is for real?" Candice asked.

"Yes, baby girl. It's for real," Zoey confirmed. "And I hope you like it. Pain was very clear about what he wanted for you, and when I saw this house, it had your name written all over it. Let me start by showing you the outside."

"No, no, no," Pain interrupted. "Take your time showing her the inside of the house because I need like twenty more minutes."

"Say less," Zoey replied.

He kissed Candice and then disappeared. Since everyone was mingling in the living room, Zoey started Candice's tour of her new home in the den.

"This is your den, cute but simple." Candice pointed to a slightly ajar door, "That is the half bathroom. Perfect for guests or anyone else for that matter to use when chillin' here in the den. It's just a toilet and a sink...nothing major."

The den was cute and simple just as she said. There was a black leather sectional that stretched from corner to corner that was big enough to comfortably seat ten people, give or take. It was decorated with several pillows that alternated in color between black, white and gray. There were four randomly placed pillows that had a marble design containing all three colors with a matching ottoman. The coffee tables were black with silver trimmings. Victorian Lamps sat on the two small tables at each end of the sectional. The smart TV that was mounted on the wall was the biggest of all the TVs in the house. It was a 72'...practically wall-to-wall. There was also a black leather Lazy Boy in the corner. Candice was sure that this piece had to be Pain's idea.

Zoey then led Candice to the kitchen area. "This is your kitchen and dining room area," Zoey stated. "It is fully accessorized with state-of-the-art appliances including a black and silver Samsung voice activated refrigerator that is uniquely programmed for you and Pain's voice only. But we'll set that up later. You have a matching flat surface range and double oven. The cabinets are fully stocked with Ayesha Curry Porcelain Enamel Cookware and the finest crystal glasses and fine China that money could buy. There's also this." Zoey gestured to the stationary Island in the center of the kitchen floor.

"As you can see, this Island is where your sink and dishwasher are installed, and it also provides extra counter space for cooking larger meals. Oh, and I almost forgot to mention, that the counters have been equipped with top-of-the-line black and gray marble."

Candice was amazed at how beautiful and large the kitchen and dining room area was. She noticed an exquisite crystal chandelier hanging directly above the dining room table, which was so big, it looked like it could seat a King and his entire empire. The tile floors were so shiny and clean that you could practically eat off of them. Zoey led her out of the kitchen, and they headed upstairs into a hallway.

"Down the hall to the right is the full guest bathroom which has a full bath and shower with a mounted and a handheld showerhead. And of course, the basics...toilet and sink."

They spent very little time on that part of the house. They continued down the hall as Zoey resumed the tour.

"The first room you see here on the right is your guest room which doubles as an office or secluded workspace when needed." Zoey turned, looked at Candice, and leaned into whisper in her ear, "Don't let Pain turn this room into a Man Cave now." They both laughed.

The room had a nice cozy feel to it. There was a Queen size bed with a thick Serta Memory Foam mattress, outfitted with a beautiful Teal comforter set with hints of brown and beige in the design. Four fluffy, color-coordinated pillows and two small decorative pillows as well. There was an oak dresser with six drawers and two matching nightstands with two drawers each on both sides of the bed. Mounted on the wall at 50' tv for their guests' entertainment. Lastly, there was a black desk in the far corner with a computer, printer, and a small bookshelf to the right. They left the guest room and proceeded a little further down the hall.

"To the right, is your Princess' room," Zoey said as

they entered Treasure's room. Immediately upon entering, the first thing she noticed was the eight huge, glittered, rainbow-colored letters on the wall: T-R-E-A-S-U-R-E. The walls were pink and baby blue. There were pictures on two of the walls of unicorns that complimented the wall color perfectly. On the third wall above the bed, was a big professional photograph of their family... Herself, Pain and Treasure. All dressed in matching outfits. The twin sized bed was small but perfect for Treasure, who at the tinder age of two was growing quite rapidly. The design on the comforter set matched the unicorn photos on the walls and so did the 2 oversized pillows. On the fourth wall, directly across from Treasure's bed was a 50' TV which had Treasure's favorite show airing on it, 'Mickey Mouse Clubhouse'. Up against the right wall was a large bean bag, which Candice was almost certain that Treasure would never sit in, and a treasure chest full of toys with her name painted on it as well.

As they exited Treasure's room, Candice was pleased. "Did you really take the time to do all of this, or did he have one of those bitches to do it?" She joked as they laughed.

"Girl, I don't know what you have done to this man, but his *only* focus is you. I promise you, you ain't got nothing to worry about."

"For now, maybe," Candice responded, showing her skepticism about how long this 'new' Pain would really last. "But what if he's for real this time?" She added.

"*What if*?!? Girl, he is dead ass for real," Zoey assured.

"What makes you so sure?" Candice asked.

"I just know true love when I see it. He's not the same Pain that I met, and I can tell that he has made those changes for you."

As they entered the master bedroom, Candice's face changed

from anticipation to confusion. She looked at Zoey and simultaneously Zoey began to speak.

"I know, I know," she said with a slight smirk. "He insisted on leaving this part of the house for you to personalize how you see fit. After all, this is your comfort zone." Candice's face then changed to understanding, and she giggled, feeling a little ashamed for her original reaction.

The room was furnished, but there was no real sense of style. The king-sized comforter and pillow set was all white. The headboard, footboard and dressers were a beautiful bold cherrywood but with no lamps or anything decorative for that matter. There was a huge 65' TV mounted on one of the plain white walls. However, she definitely appreciated and understood the reasoning behind the lack of decor. There was a closed door in the room that obviously wasn't the bathroom door. When Candice opened that door, she was amazed to see one of the biggest walk-in closets that she ever saw. There was so much space and room that she could use it as a 4th bedroom, but she was definitely up for the challenge of trying to fill it up. She concluded that with her and Pain's love for shopping it wouldn't take long.

She walked out of the closet and to the left was the master bathroom. It was decked out with all chrome faucet fixtures and knobs. There were four beautiful lights with flower-shaped frosted glass coverings along the top of the mirror. The all-glass, no-step, walk-in shower was so big that no doors were needed. There was no regular showerhead, only a handheld version that was mounted on the wall. When not using the handheld shower head, the water would just fall from the ceiling above the drain. There was also a jacuzzi bathtub that Candice adored since she frequently took bubble baths with fragrant candles burning all around her.

As she and Zoey exited the bathroom, she noticed a sliding glass door that led to a balcony. They stepped out on the balcony which was furnished with beautiful earthy-colored patio furniture. She looked over that railing and noticed a sparkling blue, dimly lit swimming pool and everyone looking up at the sky. When she looked up, she noticed a plane circling. It took a minute for her to realize that the lettering read: 'Candice, Will You Marry Me?' When Candice looked down, she noticed Pain down on one knee holding a box with a shiny diamond engagement ring in the air. Candice stood there for a few seconds in disbelief.

The sound of Mrs. Paulette's shouting voice broke her out of her trance, "HE'S WAITING ON AN ANSWER!"

"Candice, will you make me the happiest man alive by taking my hand in marriage and becoming my wife?" Pain reiterated.

"YES, OF COURSE I WILL, PAIN!" She said as her eyes filled with tears of joy.

"Well, brang that ass down here to Daddy then," Pain demanded.

Without hesitation, Candice turned and sprinted full speed to her Fiancé. Caught in the moment, she forgot she was still wearing her long graduation gown and almost rolled down the stairs trying to get to him. Had she fallen, it would not have even mattered because Pain was right there to catch her. Once she finally reached the bottom step, she fell into his arms. Pain slid the ring onto her finger which was a perfect fit. They then kissed for what seemed to be an eternity while everyone cheered them on. Every doubt, every fear, every unsure bone in her body had all vanished. At this very moment, she knew he was for real this time around.

The music came on, and the party began. It was food on top of food, drinks, and the whole nine. All Candice heard was congratulations all night. Pain had really done his thang. He went all out for her, and it felt so good. All she had been through was worth it. She was happier than she had ever been not only due to her successful graduation but also because of Pain. This was all she ever wanted from him. She wished that this moment would last forever.

Pressure was so proud of his lil' brother. Candice loved him so much. When he had nothing at all, she loved him. There was no question at all about her love and loyalty for Pain. He had dragged her through the mud and back, and she never gave up on him. She deserved his all. It was beautiful. Pain was finally turning from his childish and selfish ways, and he felt good about it. He was just as happy as Candice. Pressure walked up to Pain and gave him a hug.

"I'm proud of you, bruh. You are smarter than I thought," Pressure said.

"I play crazy but I'm not. I'm just glad I did not wait until it was too late. I'm fucked up about that Bitch, man. I know she for me," Pain said, staring at Candice with a smile. Once she noticed they were watching her, she smiled back as she made her way to her man.

"Congratulations, Candice, on both your graduation and your engagement. You worked hard for both," Pressure said to her as he gave her a big hug. "I always knew you would be the one, I was just praying this nigga ain't let you get away".

"Thank you, Pressure. You know that Zoey da' one for too, right?" Candice said.

"You think so?" Pressure asked, as he scanned through the crowd and locked eyes on Zoey.

"Stop playing, bruh. You know she da' one. I can see it in the way the two of you look at each other," Candice pointed out.

"You know what? I think you right," Pressure said. He then walked off, heading straight to Zoey, who was all smiles waiting for him as he approached her. "I love you" he said as he kissed her passionately.

"I love you too, baby. This is Candice's night, and I'm so happy for her and Pain, but I still feel like the luckiest woman in the room," Zoey said as she matched his kiss. "Let's go home."

"It's a door right behind you," Pressure said.

"Baby, we got to say goodbye to everyone," Zoey giggled.

"That takes too long. Besides Bruh and Candice watching us, they already know what time it is," Pressure told her right before slapping her on the ass.

When she looked over at Pain and Candice, they were indeed watching them. Zoey waved goodbye and smiled. She grabbed Pressure's hand and out the back door they went. They couldn't wait to get home and make love to one another. They were about to put a fairytale ending to such a beautiful night.

"I think we should do the same thang," Pain said.

"We can't leave all these people in our house. And what about Treasure?" Candice protested.

Pain pulled out his phone and texted Victoria asking her to keep Treasure for the weekend. She immediately responded with, 'My pleasure. Consider it an engagement gift, Have fun.' He let Candice read the message.

"We can stay here all night if you want to; this is your night. We got the entire weekend to ourselves," Pain said.

"One last dance and we can tell everyone that we are leaving afterwards," Candice said.

"What song would you like to dance to? I can have the DJ put it in rotation." Pain asked.

"*Slow Jam,*" Candice replied, referring to a song by Usher featuring Monica.

Pain slid over to the DJ booth and told him to play the song that she requested followed by "*My First Love*" by Keke Wyatts and Avant. Candice started crying as she and Pain danced to the song of his choice. Pain and her both loved that song. Today it was perfectly fitted for the occasion. He sang Avant's lyrics to her, and she sang Keke's lyrics to him. They acted as if they were the only two in the room like they usually were when they were at home.

Everyone watched and cheered them on as they sang to each other. When the song was over, Candice thanked everyone for coming. She then told them that they were welcome to party until the sun came up, but she was about to start her honeymoon early. Everyone laughed and said goodbye to them as they headed out the door.

On the ride home, Candice admitted to Pain something she'd been holding in. "Until tonight, I had very little faith in you, bae. But my faith in you has been restored. I still want to know what made you decide that you were ready to settle down and do right by us?"

"When I saw that your interest was elsewhere," Pain answered honestly. "I re-evaluated me. I had to ask myself was all the little things that I did not want to give up worth losing you? And I realized that nothing was worth losing you. All the shit that I was not ready to give up for you, didn't even compare to you. Being a father to Treasure and a better man to you was far more important. Besides, I want more kids. I want all my kids from the same woman. I can't comprehend how a nigga can decide what days he spend with which kids.

Christmas with this one and Thanksgiving with the other. That shit crazy. I can't deal with two or three baby mamas. I need all mine under one roof. I hate that Victoria missed out on so much love and time with us because of shit like that. I never wanted two, three different families. I'm good with the family I already have. I feel like it's time to expand our family and start preparing to grow old together. You make me happy, Candice, and I'm in love with you, for real. I can't even picture doing any of this with anyone besides you."

Candice just looked at him and smiled. She took a moment to give thanks to God. This man was her everything, and she had endured so much, but in the end, it was worth it. Her prayers had been answered. This was way beyond her. It was the blessings and favor from a much higher power. She couldn't wait to get home and start working on expanding their family as he so elegantly put it.

△△△

It had been almost four weeks. Shantae had started working at the post office and she loved it. Mrs. Paulette was training and preparing her to take over her position as the boss at the post office after her quickly approaching retirement. Mrs. Paulette did not play the radio when it came down to demanding respect on her job. Shantae knew that she would have to follow her lead. Her job was to make sure that everyone else was doing their job. A few of the girls had already attempted to give her attitude. They were hating because they had applied for this same position and did not get it. Someone had spread rumors that she was fucking Pain. Some said it was Pressure she was fucking. But none of that mattered to Shantae. She was the boss, and as long as they did their job, they could say what they wanted to say and feel how they wanted to feel. She was not a blood relative, and she was more than qualified by the resume she had submitted, which had been confirmed for accuracy... supposedly.

Mrs. Paulette made sure that she trained Shantae properly and professionally. Once she trained her by the book, she then showed her all the little shortcuts and who she could and could not trust. She showed her all the messy females and pointed out the ones she could call on when she needed them. She made sure that nothing was left out. She also taught her how to receive the packages that Allen sent in. She knew exactly what she was doing when she hired Shantae...A hustling ass female that would keep the money flowing. She was turning everything over to her, but she still wanted her cut, and everyone was cool with that.

There were a few girls there that had worked hard and deserved the position, but unfortunately for them, sometimes to get ahead in life, it's not what you know but who you know. People in Mrs. Paulette's position usually looked out for their people first, and this time was no different. Shantae needed it. Financially, mentally and spiritually. This job was going to make her a better and stronger person, and Mrs. Paulette felt good passing it on to Shantae. Besides, it would have been too hard deciding which girl to choose.

Allen FaceTimed her daily so that she could see Allani. Her and Taylor hadn't spoken much since she had left and that was fine with both of them. In fact, Allen and Taylor hadn't talked much either, and they lived in the same house. Both of them were trying to get things back on track, but it wasn't easy. Taylor was back in school full time, and so were the boys, which left Allen home alone with Allani most of the day. He didn't mind at all. He did what he had to do. At the end of the day, Allani belonged to him.

However, Allen noticed that there was a big change in Taylor's interaction with her. She would often tell him, 'Your baby is crying,' instead of just checking on her. Whenever she left, she would always take the boys and never take Allani. But when Shantae was there, she always played the role of the 'loving stepmother'. Allen never complained, it just showed him how fake she was.

Shantae had made herself a new Facebook and Instagram page. She was doing so good, and Allen was so proud of her. He would 'Like' all of her pictures, but he never left a comment. Taylor would look at all of the pictures, but she never would 'Like' any of them. Shantae knew that things between Allen and Taylor would never be the same again and didn't care one bit. Once she walked away, she was done. A couple of the guys on the job were hitting on her and buying her lunch. She had given one of them her phone number but was in no rush to start dating or getting to know anyone. This was her me-time. She wasn't going to move too fast this time around. Between Marcus and Allen, she was sick of fake love and her heart was on ice.

ΔΔΔ

Candice and Pain had moved into their new home over the next two weeks. Victoria insisted on moving in with them, which was perfectly ok since she was always with them anyway. She would be starting school for nursing in the spring. And now that Candice had found a job at a private doctor's office, Victoria was able to pick Treasure up from school, which worked out great.

Pain, Pressure, Dre, and Zoey had gotten a small office that they worked from. All of them were hands on. They went out to different properties to make sure that things were being done the way that they wanted it done. The office was basically just a meeting spot for them to discuss business, look at houses online, have appliances shipped, and meet with potential buyers. Four Brothers was doing big things. Allen had started flipping houses in Detroit. Things were looking up. Zoey was the Queen of the business. When she was in the office, she was strictly business, but when they went home, they left all the business in the office. They had all agreed that home was to relax and enjoy your family and work was work. It was important for them to keep the two separate. Neither of them wanted to get so caught up in work that they forgot to live.

Pressure and Zoey had become best friends. They did everything together. Friday night was their date night. They would go out to a nice restaurant and maybe catch a movie or a comedy show. Sometimes they would go clubbing. They met a couple that was looking to buy a house. The prospective buyers invited bowling, and after a fun night of kicking ass, they joined their bowling team, which occupied their Saturday nights. It was nice to have friends outside of family, which was something that neither of them had until now. Sunday was family day. They all got together on that day of the week; the location just rotated. Monday through Thursday, they worked hard and after work stayed in their own little bubble. Making love, eating, talking, laughing, and enjoying each other's company. They had even started discussing starting a family. Zoey was ready, but Pressure was hesitant. He liked the fact that they could just go when they wanted to and do whatever they wanted to do. However, whenever Zoey was ready, he would do whatever it took to make her happy. In the end, he would love to have a mini-him and a mini-her running around. With that being said, he no longer was using protection. Whenever God was ready to bless them with a little one, they would be ready to be good parents.

CHAPTER TWENTY-FOUR

Over the next few months, things had gotten no better between Allen and Taylor. She had made it clear that Allen was 'on his own' when it came to raising Allani. Allen had found some apartment buildings that he was interested in and the bidding was on Saturday at 2 p.m. It was hot, and normally there was nowhere to sit. It was simply just no place for an infant. He never asked her to watch Allani or to do anything for her. The one time that he swallowed his pride and asked her to watch Allani, it caused a big fight. He explained to her that there were three apartment buildings, each of them having ten units...that's thirty units on one property. The owner had lost the buildings to the bank, and the bidding was starting at little to nothing. This could be a very profitable business opportunity. If he rented each unit for $1,000, he could stand to bring in an extra $30,000 a month. He wanted the property badly. If he bought it at the right price, this could be his most lucrative investment. Taylor told him that she and the boys were going to the waterpark with Janae.

"Ok and you can't take Allani with you?" Allen asked.

"My kids are at an age where they can run astound and play," Taylor responded. "I don't wanna spend my day holding a baby. You have to make those types of sacrifices, not me."

"So, you was really just being fake as fuck when Shantae was here? What happened to 'You'll do whatever need to be done'?" Allen argued. "Now you act like you hate to even look at my baby."

"You said it better than I ever could...*your* baby," Taylor retorted.

"If you feelin' some type of way about my baby, then we got a big problem. Because she gon' come before any woman, just like my boys," Allen snapped.

"That's cool, and I understand that she comes before me. But that's exactly why she's going with you and not me. Let's go, boys," she instructed. They grabbed their book bags, which had snacks and swimming gear for their outing, and she grabbed her keys and was out the door before he could say another word.

Allen was sick of it all. Fuck those apartment buildings, fuck this house, and fuck Taylor. He had enough. He packed his and Allani's clothes and all that was important to him. All that could fit inside and on the back of his truck. He strapped Allani in her car seat, and they were out.

Over the last month, he and Shantae had talked often. She had gotten her own place and was doing well. She missed Allani so much. It was so many nights that he just thought about leaving and running back to her, but he assumed that he had fucked that up a long time ago. Shantae was definitely the better woman for him. He loved his boys to death, but he and Taylor's time was up. He missed that homie, lover, friend relationship that he had with Shantae, and Taylor's stuck-up bougie ass was just not cutting it anymore.

He would never put a bitch before his daughter, and her behavior towards Allani let him know what they had was over with. One thing about Shantae, she loved his boys like they were her own. They asked about her every day. There was nothing fake about her. He prayed that it wasn't too late to fix things between them. He had been thinking about leaving for some time now and was finally ready to divorce Taylor. Ever since he met her, he had given her the world and put her first, but it was never good enough. She was never faithful, and neither was he. What he thought was love ended up only being lust and infatuation. It was never real; it was all an illusion. He had real and gave it up for fake. Now he desperately needed that real shit back in his life.

He hated the thought of leaving his boys, but he would have to figure that out later. He never wanted to be the type of nigga that wasn't in the home with his kids. He wanted to be a great father and give them a better childhood than he ever had. He grew up with no father, a drug addict for a mother, and different niggas running in and out of his life. He would do the best he could to make sure that he was always a part of his kids' life.

By the time he arrived in Florida, it was 3 a.m., and he hadn't even called Shantae. She had no idea he was coming. He found himself in her driveway wondering where he went wrong and praying that he could fix it. He got out, unstrapped Allani from her car seat and knocked on the door. After knocking for about five minutes, the porch light came on.

Shantae opened the door to find Allen standing there with Allani sleeping on his shoulder. She reached for Allani with so much excitement. "Why didn't you tell me that you were bringing her?" she asked.

"I didn't know," Allen answered.

"What do you mean you didn't know?" she questioned.

"I just packed my shit and got in my truck and drove. This is where we ended up at," he responded.

"*We*?!?" she inquired with a confused expression.

"Yes. We," he replied. "Are you gonna let us in or not?" She stepped aside, and he walked in. "Before you say anything, let me try to explain. Everything between Taylor and I was good as long as I knew you were still in the picture. Ever since you and I parted the first time, something's been missing. I fucked up, Shantae. No one is better for me than you, and I always knew that deep inside. I don't know what made me think the grass was greener on the other side, but it ain't. So, I'm here. Right back where I started, where I belong. And I'm begging you to give me another chance."

"So, what's going to happen with you and Taylor?" she asked. "Because I'm definitely not with the running back-and-forth."

"I'm filing for a divorce, and we can get joint custody of the boys," he explained.

"A DIVORCE?!" Shantae said in disbelief.

"Yes. A divorce," he reiterated. "Taylor has ill feelings towards our daughter, and that is unacceptable in my world. I realize now that I never needed both of you. You've completed me from the beginning, and nothing feels right without you."

"How do I know that you won't change your mind six months from now?" Shantae wondered.

"Because you know me. The *real* me," he answered.

"There is no changing my mind. I thought long and hard about this move before I made it," he assured.

Shantae's heart was fluttering. She wanted to jump in his arms but was scared. She was just starting to get over him and getting to know herself. And there he was, back again. She loved him way too much to not give it a try though.

"Are you hungry?" she asked.

"Starving," he replied.

She laid Allani in bed then went back to the kitchen to fix him a plate of what she made for dinner that evening. She warmed it up and took a seat at the table with him. She listened as he told his story. Shantae wasn't surprised that his marriage was ending because she always knew that it was impossible for any bitch to just be that forgiving, but Taylor did a damn good job performing. She would be sure to give her a piece of her mind about the way she treated her daughter whenever she called looking for Allen. There was no way she could be a real friend of hers, the way she treated her baby. But for now, none of that was important. Allen needed her, and she was happy to be there for him.

After talking until the sun came up, Shantae got dressed and went to work. Allen went shopping and stacked the house up with groceries. He bought a playpen for Allani to play in while he cooked dinner and cleaned the house. When Shantae got home, Allani was with Mrs. Paulette and Allen had made dinner for just the two of them.

"Don't start nothing that you ain't gonna finish," she said.

"Oh, I'm gonna finish," Allen said.

"I'm not talking about that, Allen," she said. "I'm talking about you being here with me and Allani."

"I came here praying I hadn't lost you," he said. "I'm here to make things right with you. I ain't ever leaving you again baby and that's on God! I had no business leaving in the first place. I never meant to hurt you, Shantae. I would not have come back to you if I wasn't going to love you right. You didn't deserve none of what I put you through. My biggest regret in life was giving my all to someone other than you. Knowing that you were the only one that truly deserved it. I need you to forgive me and give me just one more chance. I promise that I will love you better than I've ever loved you before."

He grabbed her, kissed her, and undressed her at the same time. They didn't even eat dinner or make it to the bedroom. They made love right there on the kitchen floor in the heat of the moment. It reminded Shantae of when they were young and wild. Before she was bold enough to bring him home. When they snuck and had sex anywhere.

She could tell that he really missed her. It surprised her that she hadn't missed him just as much. She was so focused on getting him out of her system that she had suppressed all of the memories...good and bad. But now that he was there, all the pain he caused didn't matter anymore. She just hoped that this time he was there forever.

After making love over and over again, they took a shower and decided to go and pick up Allani. This would be their first night alone together as a family. When they pulled up to Mrs. Paulette's house, Zoey and Pressure was there.

"Oh, that's how you doing it, homie?" Pressure asked Allen, not knowing he was in town.

"Naw, bruh. It ain't like that. It's just so much going on. I was definitely gonna hit you up once I got a moment," Allen corrected. "A nigga got so much making up to do."

"I hear that, bruh," Pressure said. "If you need me, you got my number. And if you back home for real, when the honeymoon is over, ya ass need to be in the office just like everybody else."

"Yes, Sir Boss," Allen replied jokingly.

"I'm not ya boss, bruh. I'm ya Partna, and if you back, we gon' split the work just like we split them checks," Pressure stated.

"I feel ya, bruh. Give me a few days. We just gotta get Allani situated," Allen responded.

"Nigga, you already know Mama got Allani," Pressure added.

"So, I guess I'll be seeing you in the morning," Allen said with a small laugh.

"Now that's what I'm talking about, bruh!" As Pressure dapped him up.

Allen confirmed that Mrs. Paulette would indeed care for Allani while he went to work. She was retired now and didn't mind because she had already rearranged the house a hundred times and was bored out of her mind. After being on the same job for twenty-five years, she was having a hard time getting used to being home all day. Allani would occupy some of her time. Mr. Vincent had started working with Pain and Pressure, not to mention still running his trucking business. There was always something to do and extra money to be made. Whenever he was home, they went out to eat, to the movies, to the casino, fishing or whatever came to mind.

△△△

Taylor didn't even bother to call Allen. She too felt that they needed a break. But what she didn't know was that this was not just a simple break. A week had passed, and she received divorce papers, along with a petition for joint custody of the boys. A month later, they had their day in court. To everyone's surprise, Taylor asked the judge to give Allen full custody of the boys. Even though she was a good mother, none of this was a part of her plans. She never wanted to be a mother or a wife. She just fell in love with Allen, and he was so good to her, one thing led to another. But if she and Allen were not going to be together and he was going to be playing daddy to Allani, then he may as well take the boys too. They agreed with absolutely no problem. They also agreed to sell the house and split the money. He would take the truck and the boat, and she would take the car.

There were no hard feelings on Taylor's behalf. For some odd reason, in her head, what her and Allen had was very special, but it was not meant to be forever. She had grown and become a woman. Allen and the boys had taught her how to love. She had learned self-respect and furthered her education. Their time together had changed her for the better and she thanked him for that. Now it was time for her to find herself...what she really loved doing. Did she really want to be with a woman or be with a man? She had married at such a young age so now she looked forward to her freedom. A part of her felt guilty for feeling this way. She loved Allen, and she loved her kids. But she was now going to be able to enjoy going wherever she wanted to go and do whatever she wanted to do. She even looked forward to being able to screw whoever she wanted to screw.

As she packed the kids' clothes and toys, she was interrupted by a knock at the door. She opened the door to find Allen and Shantae standing there. They had left Allani with Mrs. Paulette and rented a U-Haul.

"You got they stuff ready?" Allen asked.

"I'm not quite done. They're still in school," Taylor explained.

"I know that. I figured that we could load up the truck while they are in school. That way when they get out of school, we can just hit the road," Allen responded.

"And you brought her to do what? Throw it up in my face?" Taylor said sarcastically.

"I came here to get the rest of me and my baby shit and to help you and him however I can," Shantae shot back. "That lil' girl shit you on is for lil' girls. You knew when he left you, he was coming to me. You knew I wouldn't turn him down or around. So, miss me with the theatrics. Now, if you'll excuse me, I'm going to start loading me and my baby's things. Y'all can go back and forth, I don't have time for it."

Allen started loading what was already packed for the boys and the things that he had left behind. After two and a half hours of packing, they were all done. Shantae agreed to pick the boys up from school. She knew that in the heat of the moment neither Taylor or Allen would properly explain to the boys that they would be moving with her and Allen for good. And that it probably would be a long time before they saw their mom again. When the boys got in the car, they were so happy to see Shantae. She took them for ice cream and explained to them that they were about to be moving to Florida, but their mom wouldn't be coming. They were overly excited. At their age, a move like this wasn't a big deal. As long as they would be able to keep in touch with their mom, they would be fine.

When Shantae pulled back up, the boys jumped out and ran to Allen. He had missed him so much. He looked forward to raising his kids. They were his pride and joy. He and Taylor had talked without arguing. They couldn't turn back the hands of time; what was done was done. There was still love between them, but not enough to stay in an unhappy marriage. He understood that she needed time to find herself. She went from being a call girl to his girl. And in his eyes, she was not just a lost girl.

After Taylor said her goodbyes to the boys, they loaded up and prepared to leave. Before Shantae walked away, she told Taylor, "You don't ever have to worry about your boys. I'm going to love them the same way you do. I would never treat them the way you treated Allani." She then jumped in the truck with Allen, and they pulled off.

Never in a million years did she or Allen think that the story would end with the two of them together raising his kids. Love had conquered all. After the pain, lies, obsession, the ups, and downs...Love will always win!

EPILOGUE

~3 years later~

Passion walked the stage while nine months pregnant. She was due any day now. She graduated Valedictorian of her class with a 4.0 GPA She also had perfect attendance. She had doubled up on most of her classes and stayed up so many nights studying hard. Dre had stood by her side, studying with her. He had quizzed her over and over again for her final exam. He rubbed her feet, cooked, and paid all the bills. As he had promised, All Passion had to do was finish school. Dre felt like he owed that to her and her family. He was so proud of her. Throughout it all, she made it to the finish line. Two days later, her water broke, and he rushed her to the hospital. Before he could call anyone, Passion was in the delivery room pushing out a 6lb 12 oz baby girl. They named her Andrea Chosen McCray. Dre and Passion both cried tears of joy. She was so cute, tiny and precious—a perfect reflection of the two of them.

Pain and Candice sat on their porch watching PJ try to keep up with Treasure. She was now six years old, and he was only two. She just found out that she was 2 1\2 months pregnant again. This was it for Candice, but Pain wasn't trying to hear that. Overall, they were doing great. Candice had become Head Nurse at the doctor's office. She was making good money, and she loved her job. Pain had stood on everything he said. He was faithful and happy. He did not miss one thing when it came down to PJ. He loved being a father. Nothing fascinated him more than watching Treasure grow up and start looking more and more like her mother. She loved dressing up and going with her mom to get her nails done. PJ was a splitting image of him. He followed him everywhere. Most days, he went to work with Pain. The two were inseparable.

On the weekends, Pain and Pressure would meet up and take PJ and P2 to the barbershop. Yep, you heard it right...P2. Pressure and Zoey now has a two year old, and he is a mirror image of Pressure. Pressure loved being a father too. It had changed his entire concept of love. Although he loved Zoey dearly, he never really understood the real meaning of the word love until he had P2. This lil' man was his world. He and Zoey were happy. She loved the life that they had built together. She was now a mother, had a legal job, and the finest nigga in the world. Plus, he was good to her. She was grateful, humble and happy.

Four Brother's was doing big numbers. They had expanded and moved to a bigger office. Victoria now was the secretary and answered the phones and set appointments. Business had picked up so much, Zoey needed the help because she was out of the office more than she was in. She was looking at new properties and overseeing that her vision for each house was done the way she had ordered it to be done. She was a beast in that field.

Allen and Shantae had a two-month-old son, and they named him Shanod. Jahrod and Jahnod had gotten so big and Allani was now three years old, and she was spoiled rotten. Shantae had been promoted from Head supervisor to Operation Manager. Allen loved working everyday with the fellas and then going home to his family. He had decided to follow Vincent's lead and bought an 18-wheeler. He had gotten his CDL's and his broker license and was now contracted with a big moving company. He had two drivers that rotated jobs, sometimes they even went out together. It was a great investment. He had made most of the money he invested back, and now it was time to reap the benefits. Shantae and Allen had been through hell and back, but they overcame the obstacles and came out on top. They were deeply in love with each other and often talked about getting married. It was not a major priority to either of them. They had already proven that their love would stand the test of time.

Taylor was also doing great. She worked as a massage therapist . She and Janae had gone to a Meek Mills concert where she met one of the producers of the show. He adored Taylor and asked her about being in a video that he was working on. Taylor was blown away by his persistence and finally accepted. They went out on a few dates and had gotten really close. He wanted more out of the friendship than Taylor was willing to give, so she became distant. Taylor had had enough of love and commitment, so she had no plans on doing any of that any time soon.

She and Janae were inseparable. She would sometimes have threesomes with her and her husband. She enjoyed being the prize in the middle of them and all the extra attention. She had a really nice one-bedroom loft in downtown Detroit and was living life to the fullest. She visited the kids on holidays, and she never missed a birthday. She sent all kinds of really nice expensive gifts for all the kids. The kids called her every night before bed and she answered every time. Taylor, Allen, and Shantae had a very respectful relationship. Everyone knew their position and played it accordingly. Shantae was the better woman for Allen, and Taylor knew that. That did not make her feel any less of a woman. She was the shit and a great mother. Her decision was what was best for her, and she slept well at night.

Chloe and Rein were two peas in a pod. They hustled niggas and both danced at 'King of Diamond.' They had moved back to Florida to be closer to family. They had given up human trafficking after making enough to buy them a condo on south beach, and brand new cars. They partied like rock stars, but they were getting that bag. Neither of them wanted for anything. They played Niggas like dominoes. By the time they realized they was not getting no pooty cat, they were already out of thousands in cash, and their credit cards were maxed out. With or without permission. Their feelings for one another had gotten deep. They were no longer intimate with men. Sex between the two of them was amazing, and the chemistry they had was a force that was not to be reckoned with.

Tank and Dominque took over Marquise's sex trafficking ring, essentially becoming the Madam and the Kingpin of the organization. They turned it into a high-class escorting business, giving the girls that wanted to stay the option to stay and granting the girls that wanted to leave their freedom. They kept in constant contact with Dre and Passion and visited them in Miami frequently.

Mrs. Paulette opened a laundromat, just like she always wanted to do. It was right in the heart of the hood that she grew up in, connected to a busy corner store and was open 24/7. Customers flowed in and out all day and night. It was everything she visioned it would be, and money was great, it never stops flowing in. Chloe had ordered most of the washers and dryers at a great price. They were all stainless-steel heavy-duty appliances that 'til this day had not given her not one problem. She hired two laundry attendants. The young lady worked from 7 a.m. 'til 7 p.m. while the gentleman worked from 7 p.m. 'til 7 a.m. They both were immigrants and needed the money badly. They both agreed to work seven days a week. She tried to give them a day off here and there, but they both refused. She paid them well twelve dollars an hour and they got all kinds of bonuses and gifts. They had become more like family to her. She helped them in any way she could. They ran her business well and took their job very seriously. For that, Mrs. Paulette had even helped them to become legal citizens in the United States. It turned out to be a great investment.

Mr. Vincent ran his trucking business basically by phone. He loved being hands on at Four Brothers with his boys. He was so proud of them, besides they kept him feeling young and alive.

He and Mrs. Paulette were both workaholics and always taking on projects with their kids.

However, at least once a month, they took time for just the two of them. They always put their relationship first, something that they had failed to do the first time around. They would sometimes just get on the road and drive, and wherever that landed at, they made the best of it, but Sundays were always reserved for family. The family was getting bigger and bigger. They now had four grandkids and one more on the way. The family tree was beginning to sprout. It started with just dirt, but with lots of love, nurturing, and attention: it became rich soil with strong roots. With a little sun and rain the roots spread, and now branches were forming, and beautiful leaves were beginning to grow.

Mrs. Paulette and Mr. Vincent had built a solid foundation for their family, and they could now enjoy watching it grow and become stronger and stronger each and every day. Love really does have the power to conquer all things. There is no road map or directions when it comes to finding true love. Anything worth having is worth working for and waiting for.... No Pain, No Gain.

Marcus was sentenced to ten years in Florida State Prison, followed by ten years of probation. He was barred from ever practicing law in the state of Florida again. He promised that he would repay Shantae for everything she did to him, if it was the last thing he ever did. Little did he know, Allen had major connections on the inside, and the hit had already been ordered. He would not be making it out alive.

The End

ABOUT THE AUTHOR:

I was born in Georgia and raised in Florida. I have four kids that have made me a proud grandmother of eight precious grandchildren. I grew up in a loving family, but even still, like a lot of us do, I chose the street-life. However, all good things come to an end. After being sentenced to 36 months in Florida State Prison, I began to really reflect on my life and all the bad choices I had made. After that much-needed self-evaluation, I decided to turn all the negative energy into something positive. Locked in a cell for 21 hours a day, I discovered my love for reading and writing Urban Novels.

Pain and Pressure is the first of many books to come. As I continue my road to success, I pray that you enjoy every novel I have written for your entertainment. There is always a light at the end of the tunnel, and every dark cloud has a silver lining. It's never too late to turn your life around and follow your dreams, and I am a living testimony of that. At age 45, my life has just begun. I am finally happy, healthy, and living a life that is more pleasing to the Man upstairs who has saved me and mercifully given me yet another chance to step into my destiny and show the world that we do not have to be a product of our environment or upbringing. I am that "Rose that grew from the concrete." And my best is yet to come.

Made in the USA
Middletown, DE
05 September 2023

37599983R00194